Praise for 7.

"*The Dryline* is a riveting story with believable characters in an intricate plot. From the beginning, this book grabs your attention as Grubbs combines engineering, oil recovery, greed, and murder in a fascinating South Texas tale. Seeing Grubbs's name as the author is evidence that the book is a great read."
–John W. Raymond, Esquire, BS, MS, JD, MLT

"Grubbs uses cutting-edge forensics to masterfully expose the dark side of ego, competition, and greed in modern day society."
–Foster L. Wade, PhD
Retired Deputy Assistant Secretary, US Department of the Interior
Oil and Gas Industry Executive

To Pete & Claire,
May good always
triumph over
evil!
Best to you both
Jack

The
Dryline

A Seiler Murder Mystery

JACK GRUBBS

The Dryline
A Seiler Murder Mystery

The Small Press
16250 Knoll Trail Drive, Suite 205
Dallas, Texas 75248
www.BBSmallPress.com
(972) 381-0009

www.GrubbsBooks.com
www.GrubbsStuff.com

A New Era in Publishing™

ISBN 978-1-612547-74-9
Library of Congress Control Number 2011939704

Printing in the United States
10 9 8 7 6 5 4 3 2 1

To the men and women of the
United States Armed Forces. They understand
and suffer the consequences of the fight
between good and evil.

STAGE 3: Under pressure, the slug of oil is forced up the outflow line and into the receiving tank.

OIL SLUG OUTFLOW (3)

STAGE 2: Once reservoir is filled, pressurized gas is entered into the chamber. The pressure seats the ball valve.

FULL CHAMBER (2)

Ball Valve

OIL INFLOW (1)

STAGE 1: Oil, under pressure, seeps through screen and into fluid chamber. Ball valve raises to allow chamber to fill.

Jet Extraction Technology System – JETS (Conceptual Schematic)
Donelam Oil Systems, LLC

Acknowledgments

Thanks to Daniel Millwee, editor, and Cynthia Stillar-Wang, director of The Small Press—a division of Brown Books Publishing Group—both of whom smoothed out many of the bumps in my version of the written word and took the novel from my mind and into production.

Thanks to my brother and sister-in-law, Tom and Susie Grubbs, for their taking the time to dig deeply into the story and provide insight into the plot and those technical details that needed to be clear to every reader. Thanks to John and Gracie Raymond, whose attention to detail led to many improvements. Thanks also to Tony Russillo, who was able to cast off the shackles of former military ranks and tell me straight up where I needed to make changes.

My memory is not what it used to be, so I give my absolute thanks to those of you I have not mentioned but who provided solid feedback—and support.

Finally, to my wife, Judy, I can only thank you for getting me back on my feet following a tough injury, patting me on the back, and—lovingly—telling me to get back "on track." I love you, hon.

Prologue

Saturday Night, December 26

Monte's Bar, Luling, Texas

Crack. Pop. The orange five ball rolled swiftly across the smooth, green surface to the far corner, gently kissed the brown leather padding, and dropped into the pocket.

Juan Delgado, a short, wiry Mexican, openly exuded satisfaction with his poolroom prowess. He smiled at the three men circling the pool table and thumped his chest. "*Soy el mejor*–I'm the best." The men's conversations mixed Spanish with English.

Carlos Aguirre gave his new teammate a solid backslap as Juan moved around the table. Juan drew deeply on a cigarette, exhaling slate-gray smoke toward the oblong Budweiser lamp hanging over the table. Adjacent to the poolroom, throngs of beer-drinking, chain-smoking, working-class Texans crowded tables and the bar as music from a 1950s jukebox invited all, young and old, to the dime-sized, sawdust-covered dance floor.

"Two off the six." Juan, a slight buzz in his head, walked around the table, chalked his cue, placed it comfortably into position, and took aim. A stub of Chesterfield Classic Red hung from his lips. *Crack. Pop. Click.* The two ball angled steeply off the six ball, hit two banks, and slowed to a stop in the middle of the table.

"*Mierda*–Shit." Juan grabbed his bottle of Lone Star and took a large swig.

Manuel Rodriguez's turn. He handed his bottle to Emilio Cepeda and moved slowly around the table, eyeing each ball in relation to the others. He was good–so good that Luling no longer fed his voracious appetite for hustling. Manuel could make several hundred dollars on a good weekend in Austin or San Antonio. He especially enjoyed taking money from the rich University of Texas kids. He dried his hands on his Levi's and powdered them with talc. He nodded toward Juan and Carlos and, mimicking Juan, thumped his chest while announcing, "*El rey de la colina*–the king of the hill."

Sure enough, the king was there. Manuel tilted a dirty cowboy hat to the back of his head and carefully lined up his shot. A second later, what seemed a white streak of light hit the nine ball, driving it into a side pocket. The eleven ball quickly followed suit.

Manuel attacked the high balls as Carlos sidled up to Juan and continued an ongoing discussion. With piercing black eyes deeply set into a stone-cut face, Carlos towered over his teammate. He asked, "So you're telling me the people you working for can get oil out of a dry hole?"

"Hell yes, man. We pumping more oil out of that hole than they done for years. We done four other holes in five weeks. Got two machines working damn good. The other two got messed up with the down-hole tubes." Juan drew in one last time on the dying cigarette butt, slowly blew the smoke into the air, and emptied more beer into his gut. He tossed the butt onto the concrete floor and crushed it with his boot.

Manuel continued running the table while Carlos and Juan talked.

Carlos asked, "How're the people you work for? Treat you OK?"

"Got no complaints. I signed on in Odessa and stayed with them when they moved to Luling. I been working with them since last January. Man, it's a cold winter in Odessa. But they pay fair and treat us fair. Told us we'll be working with them for the rest of our lives. They got big plans for everybody."

Ga-thump. The sound of the eight ball hitting the bottom of the opposite side pocket signaled the game's end.

Manuel stood up, resting his hand on top of the vertical cue stick. He claimed victory. "Five beers and I still run the fucking table. Anyone want to challenge El Rey?"

"Hell no," Carlos answered. "Everyone drink your beer and let's go." Carlos polished off his Lone Star and grabbed his denim jacket from the coat hook. He patted Juan on the back. "Juan, want to go with us? We're going to Maria's near Mendoza for food, dancing, and good times with the señoritas."

Juan liked these guys. "Never been out there, but yeah. Let's go. Could be one hell of a night."

No one responded.

The men walked out of the poolroom, moving around dancing couples and crowded tables, toward the battered wooden door opening to the street. Terry Keane, the no-nonsense owner of Monte's, glanced at the men from behind the bar. The former marine, still muscular with a close-cropped haircut, had a concrete rule that no one was to walk out of Monte's sloppy drunk. Have some beer, laugh, dance, and play darts, but don't overdo the drinking, and for damn sure don't be a smartass. Whether you're Terry's friend or not, succumbing to either vice puts you on the outside of Monte's. His wife and co-owner Debbie was a knockout—and maybe tougher than Terry. She'd knock you out herself if you disobeyed the standing orders. Carlos and Terry made eye contact, and Carlos quickly lowered his eyes as he continued toward the door. Terry returned to his customers.

Outside, a vanilla moon beamed down on Monte's and on the long line of flat-faced nineteenth-century Texas storefronts along Davis Street. Oblivious to the stars in the clear sky above their heads, the men trudged into the cold Luling night, hunching their shoulders against the chill.

Carlos asked Juan, "You got a car? I'll ride with you."

Juan pointed to the deep red 1989 Civic parked halfway down the block from Monte's. It looked black in the moonlight. "That's her. She don't look like much, but she never give me a problem. She's the most faithful woman I ever knew."

Emilio and Manuel walked another hundred feet, stopping at a black Ford F-250 truck with extended cab and off-road capability, ideal for working Texas oil country.

Emilio called to Juan and Carlos. "I'll lead the way. Come up close and follow me down the back end of town. I know a shortcut off eighty-six. That's if your little piece of shit can keep up with me." He laughed and climbed into the sleek truck. Manuel jumped into the front passenger side.

Juan laughed as well and looked over at Carlos with a huge grin. "He don't know this baby. I'll be on his ass the whole way." Carlos nodded in agreement.

Five miles out of town, Emilio turned right onto a dirt road. "This is it," he said. A frog jumped in Manuel's stomach. Emilio tapped the brakes a couple of times, drifted to the side of the road, and stopped at a dirt turnaround area.

"Oh shit, man." Juan slammed on the brakes, turning the steering wheel hard left. He slowed the Civic, turned back to the right, and drove forward to the shoulder, parking behind the truck. "What's the problem?"

"*No sé*–Don't know. Let's check it out." Carlos opened the door and walked toward the other two men standing in front of the truck. Juan fell in step behind him.

Carlos arrived just as Emilio raised the hood. "What's wrong?"

"It's the fucking fan belt again. Maybe I trade my truck for your car." Emilio nodded his head toward the Civic.

"No way, man. Who has shit now?" Juan smiled with a hint of superiority.

With Manuel's body halfway into the engine compartment, Emilio spoke. "Carlos, would you and Juan check my tool chest? Need the flashlight, wrenches, and fan belt."

"*No problema.* Juan, give me a hand." He walked to the rear of the pickup. Carlos lowered the tailgate before Juan reached the back of the truck. "Help me pull the tool chest out."

Juan grabbed the left side handle and prepared to pull. "*Estoy listo*–I'm ready."

Carlos reached to the side of the chest, taking a claw hammer from the truck bed. He took a quick look at Juan and followed with a smooth, fierce blow. The hammer rotated slightly as it surged forward, hitting Juan in his temple and puncturing the side of his skull with a near-perfect hole. Juan staggered to his left, weathering the initial effects of the blow. He turned and looked Carlos in the eye. A sad frown formed on his face in the moonlight.

"Por qué . . ." He collapsed onto the road, clipping the tailgate with the left side of his head as he fell.

One

Seven Weeks Earlier,
Friday, October 30

Port Hueneme, California

Port Hueneme lies eight miles southeast of Ventura, California. Seiler Engineering occupied a four-room parcel of a multi-store building on Port Hueneme Road. Owned by Donald Seiler, the company staff consisted of two draftsmen.

Vince Bolduc—at least, that was his name while in California—parked directly in front of the office. He squeezed his way out of the car, his exit impeded by a fast-food waistline and an inconsiderate driver who parked over the stripe. The sun's reflection bounced off the office window, slicing through his eyes and into his brain. *Can't believe I left my sunglasses in New York,* he thought. Vince walked in the door.

"Hey, Vince, come on in," said a voice from a card table in the middle of the room. Don Seiler stuck his hand in Vince's direction without getting up. Vince walked over and gave Don a firm handshake. Elam Duquette, Don's business partner, ignored the new visitor and ended another tale of tales.

1

"And then I threw his sorry ass into the pool, suit and all." The lack of raucous laughter caused Elam to look at the source of disruption. *Who the hell are you?* he thought. Elam didn't take well to someone killing his punch line.

Don spotted Elam's irritation immediately and interceded. "Elam, say hello to an actual paying customer. This is Vince Bolduc. Vince, meet Elam Duquette." Pointing to the two draftsmen, he added, "I think you already know Jay and Mark."

Vince nodded and apologized. "Didn't mean to interrupt. I just thought I'd say hello and see how the design is coming."

"All systems go. Mark's putting the final drawings together now. We'll have them ready by Tuesday." Don changed the subject. "Better than that, you've come across some serious serendipity. We're having a pre-Halloween party. Got Jack Daniels to Coke and everything in between." He pointed back to the wall behind him.

Vince looked in the direction of Don's hand. On a desk littered with assorted paper, books, and manila folders sat a cache of Coke cans, two six-packs of beer, a bottle of Dewar's, and two bottles of Jack Daniels. A small column of stacked plastic glasses and a bowl full of ice rounded out the bar. Two opened bags of chips and a large jar of salsa sat next to the ice bowl.

Elam had driven up from LAX earlier in the day and was four drinks into storytelling. He blew off the interruption. "Hey, Vince, wanna see a humongous fucking fortune? Look over there." He pointed to some engineering drawings on the table to Don's front.

Elam's major vice was his inability to stop talking, but unlike those of bullshitters, his stories were real. Elam got up with a smile, sauntered over to the blueprint, and stuck his finger in the middle of the drawing. "This sucker is straight from the mind of my esteemed colleague, Mr. Don Hudson Seiler. With me doing the marketing and Don doing the engineering, we have a separate little joint venture known as Donelam Oil Systems—that's for 'Don' and 'Elam.' Pretty damn soon Don can forget pissant Seiler Engineering; we're going for the big-time. On the low side, we're going to make us a few hundred million dollars."

Elam laughed, partly from conviction of success, partly from Jack and Coke. He slugged down his current round and walked to the improvised bar for a refill. Elam's blue, flowered rayon shirt hung over baggy, floor-dragging chinos like silk over cow turds. Elam was a paradox: one part commoner and one part F. Scott Fitzgerald character.

Vince glanced at the drawing. Other than its obvious long and narrow outline, there was little that he could discern. His polite smile belied an intense study of the object.

Breaking Vince's interest in the strange mechanical system, Don grabbed his camera and announced, "Everyone get ass to elbow. I'm under orders to take pictures of the party and my unwelcome guests."

The gaggle of testosterone muddled its way behind a drafting table and hammed it up. Don rose slowly and walked to the front of the room. He braced himself against the front door and clicked away several times.

"I did my duty." He paused briefly, then added, "Aw, shit." He offered the camera to Mark. "Cindy wants one of me too." Mark took two more shots and the formal duty, at Don's wife's command, was finished.

For another two hours the five men engaged in a myriad of topics. Women, politics, women, sports, women, and engineering were the subjects of choice. They sang hearty rounds of outrageously bawdy songs, and by party's end, Vince had been fully accepted as a "friend of the company." He also knew a fair amount about a device named JETS, the acronym for Jet Extraction Technology System.

Jay and Mark left around six o'clock. Don suffered from multiple sclerosis and could not drive at night; Elam was less competent to drive than Don. The obvious choice, Vince gave both a ride to Don's home on Millwood Circle in Ventura, where Elam was the guest for the night. Vince and Don poured Elam out of the car and guided him to the house. Vince returned for Elam's bag and turned it over to Don's wife, Cindy. Radiant red hair, a sincere smile, and genuine thanks convinced Vince that Don had hit the jackpot in selecting a mate.

"Join us for dinner. Elam will be fine in an hour, and I have a ton of chicken and beef fajitas," said Cindy as a sincere invitation to Vince.

The hunger gnawing at Vince's stomach said "yes," but his need to put memory onto paper mandated "no." He apologized for his quick departure, climbed into his car, and headed out of the small subdivision and west on Telegraph Road. Oblivious to the heavy traffic, Vince mulled over his impression that Don, Cindy, and Elam were good-natured, hard-working, and naive; a moral nerve tugged at him ever so slightly. He had no idea where his investigation into the whole Seiler family would take him, but he did suspect that the ultimate intentions of his employer were not good. Vince stopped at a chain Italian restaurant and, over lobster ravioli, wrote down everything he could remember about the JETS. Two glasses of wine stunted his appetite for dessert. He had a long drive back to the Marriott LAX.

The shrill ringing rattled in her head, waking her from a fitful sleep. She fumbled at the nightstand before finally grabbing the phone.

"Hello?" Her voice was slurred.

"It's me–Vince."

At first she couldn't put it all together. *Vince? Who?* Her mind, drugged in sleep, struggled for function. Vince? The PI? She started to focus. "Do you have any idea what time it is?"

Vince had forgotten the three-hour time difference. "Damn. I'm sorry, I just forgot. This can wait until tomorrow."

"I'm already awake. What do you want?"

Vince's pleasant thoughts about Don, Cindy, and Elam slammed shut.

"I might have stumbled onto something of significance related to this guy Seiler's brother. Are you familiar with the term 'stripper well'?"

Elizabeth Harker, still groggy but beginning to grasp her surroundings, focused not on stripper wells, but on the possibility that she would be able to bring incalculable grief to the person of Thomas Mannan Seiler. He had ruined her life and she would repay the favor tenfold.

"What do you think?" she said. "I've lived in Texas."

Two

Monday, December 28

Houston, Texas

"Don! Don Seiler. Over here," yelled Delana Lally above the din of the traffic and the hurried travelers heading in all directions. Bush Intercontinental Airport was built with airplane traffic in mind. Vehicular traffic was an afterthought.

Don lifted his cane, smiling beneath a straw hat, and pointed back at Delana. She closed the door with *Delana's Taxi Service* written on it and hurried toward him, leaving the small van easy prey for roving police. Delana and Don hugged briefly.

"Welcome back, stranger. Where's your navy hat?"

"Good to see you, Delana. My navy hat's hiding from me somewhere in my house. How've you been?"

"Good. Business is better than expected this week. Next week will be strong, what with everyone headed home." Delana grabbed Don's single traveling bag and turned toward the van. She looked back at Don. "Need a hand?"

"Nope. Got my cane and put my troubles on the doorstep." He lifted the cane so that she could see that it also doubled as a stubby fishing rod, including a small reel attached at the handle. He had to remove the hook for the flight from California.

Delana hotfooted it back to the van, placing Don's bag in the rear. Don slowly made his way across two lanes of traffic, his right leg barely able to move. The pedestrian crossing was too far away to bother with, so he just counted on the good will of Houston drivers. A pedestrian in traffic could get away with multiple sclerosis in Texas—not so much in New York City. Don took off his hat and leather jacket, tossed them and the cane in the back, and joined Delana in the front seat. They were off to a small ranch deep in the heart of Texas. Delana drove west on Beltway 8 and north on I-45. Tom and Delana were originally introduced by Don's brother Tom, and they had some catching up to do. The friendship began when Delana picked Tom up at Houston Hobby Airport. He found her both polite and a good driver, so he took her phone number. From that day on Delana was the brothers' driver of choice.

"Where you been, baby? Must be six months since I last saw you." Delana looked over at Don, then back to the snarled traffic. Don smiled at the ad hoc accent. A transplant to Texas courtesy of Hurricane Katrina, Delana arrived with seven generations worth of New Orleans dialect. Houston was OK, but she couldn't wait to return to the end of the Mississippi River.

"Really been busy," Don replied. "In spite of the economy, interest in offshore engineering has picked up lately in California. At least my part, the little nuts and bolts, has picked up. Also, I've been moonlighting on an oil field device with a friend. It's got great potential. I called Tom about it last week and we're going to discuss modifications that might make it work better. He understands mechanical things better than I do. I'll be here two, maybe three days. Give you a call for a ride back."

Delana smiled. "Just call me, baby."

Don, the endless mixing of billboards with strip malls negating his visual fondness for Texas countryside, found it easy to forge into Delana's family life. "How's Pete doing? Still on the rigs?"

Delana answered, eyes on the thick traffic, "Yeah, pretty much the same routine. Three weeks on, two weeks off. He's doin' good. He hopes he'll get moved back to the rigs off of Cocodrie. If he does, I'll be headed back home."

Don thought back to the time he spent in the Gulf of Mexico with Poole Offshore. Until his MS had taken its toll, most of Don's life had been a strange elixir of hard work, serious hell-raising, and bit-by-bit maturing.

"When's he get home next?"

"Friday. We're going back to N'awlins to see my Mama on Saturday."

"For some lagniappe, huh?" The idea of lagniappe—a little something extra—permeated life in Louisiana.

"You bet, baby. Those shrimp po'boys and that andoullie sausage are calling us home."

Both could almost smell the aroma. Don added, "Did you know that when I got my first job in the Gulf, I lived in Gretna?"

She did know. Filled with nostalgic tales, they focused their conversation on life in bayou country.

Entering Conroe, they headed west on State Highway 105 beneath a sky shellacked in light blue, not a single cloud in sight. They drove through Montgomery and on to Dobbin. From Dobbin, the van carried them north on FM 1486. The table-flat, monotonous landscape surrounding Houston gave way to gentle rolls of land heavily covered with oak and pine trees. Don's visual nostalgia finally kicked in. The only need to ease off the gas pedal was at a meat market–poolroom combination occupying the only turn in the road. A few homes, hidden in the trees and most needing upkeep, were just enough to give the setting an actual name: Dacus, Texas. Bluebonnets and Indian blankets were more than two months from full bloom, yet harbingers of an early spring permeated the air. They continued another couple of miles.

"Here we go. That's it up ahead, with the stone columns." Don pointed to the entrance to Tom and Susie's home, a small ranch hidden in the trees.

Delana slowed the van, turning right on a gravel and sand road. Two black dogs, both mongrels, ran up the road toward the van. Their ferocious barks were betrayed by wagging tails. The van passed between the stone columns supporting a wrought iron arch with *Broken Wing Ranch* written in black metal letters. The road wound two hundred yards, through oaks and tall pines, in a lazy S-curve to the main house. As they broke into open space, an alabaster home emerged to their front; an open field and a long stand of trees loomed in the distance.

It was Delana's first trip to the ranch. "Oh my, it's beautiful. Beautiful."

"Yeah, it's a great place. Tom flew me out here when they moved in. Big difference from their place in Clear Lake, isn't it?"

"It sure is."

Don pointed to a garage that was connected to the main house by a covered walkway. "Let's stop over there. We can scout the place out. Tom and Susie won't be here for a while."

Delana parked in front of the garage door, lifted Don's thirty-pound bag with incredible ease, and opened his door before he could reach his cane and hat. Delana was small of stature, but strong as a bull.

Don took Delana on a brief tour of the outside of the house. The two dogs, Bear and Catfish, joined them. Tom's office consumed the back half of the garage building. A small sign was affixed next to the door—*Thomas M. Seiler, Accident Analysis, Inc.* The main house was impressive without being overbearing. The sandstone exterior reached up to a metal roof. Two huge picture windows faced south to the open field, into which Tom had carved a small airstrip. The Broken Wing Ranch only covered forty acres, but the thin east-west rectangular shape provided the needed length for the Piper J-3 Cub to take off and land. Tom's second plane, a Grumman Tiger, needed more runway length and was kept at the airport in Conroe. The Tiger was for business and the Cub was for play.

"It is so nice out here," Delana sighed. She pointed to trees just off the north side of the house. "Wish I could just sit under that pine over there and let the world roll by." Unfortunately for Delana, reality quickly set in. She sighed again and remarked, "But I'm the one who needs to roll on down the road. Will you be all right here?" She flicked her neck-length hair behind her ear.

"No problem. I think I'll take your suggestion and sit under the pine. Tom and Susie will be here pretty soon. If I need anything, I'll give you a call."

"Make sure you do."

Don reached into his wallet, took out four twenties, and handed them to Delana. She counted them and gave one back to Don. "Fifty bucks with a ten-dollar tip is more than enough. It's important to me."

Don felt a tinge of guilt. "Understood."

Delana smiled. "But the hug is free."

They hugged and Delana left. He heard the horn beep as she accelerated south on FM 1486. For a minute he stood in the roadway, bathed in gentle solitude of his adopted home state. He loved Texas. Catfish licked at his hand, waking him from his revelry. Don turned and looked across the airstrip to a spot where another little piece of heaven waited: the catfish pond.

He walked to his travel bag, reached in, and grabbed a small paper sack. With his fishing rod–cane, his hat, and one hell of a limp, Don made his way two hundred yards to a bench on a wooden deck at the pond's edge. Nailed to a deck plank at the end of the bench was a small wooden box containing several fishhooks. Each hook had the barb snipped off. He took one and, with limited eyesight and coordination, tied it to the end of the line on his combined fishing rod–walking cane. A large plastic jar filled with fish pellets sat beneath the bench. Don grabbed a handful of the pellets and tossed them in the pond. The crappie hit them en masse, the catfish hugging the bottom of the pond. They would be there soon enough.

"OK kiddos, come to Poppa." While the pellets excited the fish, Don prepared his cane for action. He reached in the paper sack and pulled out the remains of an airport meal–two halves of a roll. He tore off a small piece of bread, added a touch of saliva, and rolled it into a small ball of dough. It held onto the hook just right. His first cast, attacked by the small, aggressive crappie, ended with an empty hook. So did the second. On his third cast, a twenty-inch catfish swallowed everything. Don snagged into him hard, the catfish answering with a surge of twisting power and a dive toward the bottom of the pond. After five seconds the line went limp; the barbless hooks gave the fish an advantage. Still, Don won his share of the battles. It wasn't fishing for tarpon at Port Aransas, but the struggle between man and beast was food for Don's soul. He loved fishing anywhere, anytime. Don, engrossed with landing his third catfish–the crappie didn't count–failed to notice two figures crossing the airstrip.

"Hey, leave my damn fish alone," Tom yelled from the far side of the pond.

Don looked up and smiled. "First time these guys ran up against an expert. How you doing? And who's that good-looking woman with you?" He reeled in the line and stood up to greet his brother and sister-in-law.

Don shook Tom's hand, kissed Susie on the cheek, and reached back into the sack. Tom reached into his jacket pocket and pulled out a Miller Lite for his younger brother.

Susie grabbed a fishing rod from one of two deck-mounted rod holders. While kneading a small bit of Don's bread, she asked him, "Why didn't you take the golf cart? It's yours anytime you want it."

Don glanced off into the distance as if he could see that far. Then he shrugged his shoulders high in the air and answered, "To be honest, I didn't even notice. Needed the exercise anyway."

"So how do you like the fishing cane?" Tom said, referring to his birthday gift to Don.

Don pointed to the far side of the small pond. "Finish your beer and toss the can over there."

Tom did as ordered. Don slowly pulled back his forearm, flexed his wrist, and quickly cast the hook and sinker toward the can. *Ping.* The sinker hit the can at the waterline. Don smiled and thought, *I am one lucky shit.*

"Well I'll be damned," said Tom. He shook his head. "I won't even ask for a repeat performance."

Don laughed. "I've done it ten thousand times, and I'm as good as they come. My legs suck and the can looks like a blur in the water, but my wrist action is the best in the world. I should be on the Ed Sullivan show."

They fished for another hour, until the sun slipped behind the pine trees to the west and allowed the chill to take over.

Don's temperature-sensitive body ached in the waning sunlight. "Well, gang, that's it for me." An uncontrollable shiver shook his body.

"Me too. Getting a little nippy," said Susie, who was

already shivering. "Tomorrow should be warmer. Be a better day for fishing."

Tom stood and added, "Almost time for the steaks anyway." He grabbed Don's empty beer can from the deck and returned it to his pocket. Don reached down to the ground and found a small twig. He stuck it in a small crevice between two lower teeth and rotated it a couple of times. He pushed off the bench and stood up. The threesome, Don wedged between the other two, walked back to the house.

Tom and Don were as close as any two brothers on the face of the planet. Their facial features were different enough to make sibling identification difficult; Don had a slightly thinner nose and darker complexion, while Tom had slightly thinner lips. At five feet eleven, Tom was taller by an inch and a half. Don had movie star eyelashes and sparkling slate-green eyes. Tom's eyes were coffee bean brown. Don, once an outstanding athlete, limped from the ravages of his disease. Tom still ran the Chevron Houston Marathon. They were identifiably brothers in three areas: their personalities, drinking Miller Lite beer, and male pattern balding. Once back at the house, Tom brought Don's bag in and took it to the guest bedroom.

Don surveyed the inside of the house for the second time. "Unbelievable place."

He was more impressed than on his first trip. The foyer opened to a large living room fronting a modern kitchen. Plate glass windows faced the small airstrip, with pine and oak straddling the far side of the runway. The stone fireplace rose starkly between the windows, ending at the cathedral ceiling. The dining room, a small game room, and the master bedroom and bath occupied the west end of the house. Two guest bedrooms sandwiching a shared bath formed the east end. Upstairs, another guestroom and small bath joined a bonus room.

Tom grilled steaks on the concrete patio while Susie finished making salad and potatoes in the kitchen. Don limped to a cushioned wrought-iron chair, affording him a ringside seat to sunset. The sun fell beneath the horizon, a glowing ember marking the waning breath of another day.

"Damn pretty out here." He popped the tops on two beer cans, kept one, and set the other on the serving tray next to Tom.

Tom looked up from his duties and nodded affirmatively. "Yeah, sure is," he added while turning the steaks, "and the taxes in Grimes County are half of what you'd pay in Montgomery County."

Don asked, "Have things settled down since Alvin?" referring to the incident in which Tom killed a man, accused a prominent lawyer of murder, and caused general mayhem in Houston a couple of years before.

Tom answered somewhat reflectively. "Yeah, pretty much. I'll still get a look or two when I'm in Houston or Conroe, but most people don't know me from Adam." He sliced a small piece of sirloin and offered it to Don.

Don took a bite; the hot steak almost seared off the roof of his mouth. He blew several short breaths of hot air, trying to cool the sirloin. Still, it was delicious. "Mmm . . . thith ith ath good ath it geth."

As Don savored the taste of the beef, Tom added, "The good news is that my business has exploded since then. I was prepared to slowly fade into the woodwork; for the first time since I hung my shingle out, I've had to turn cases down."

Don finished his western hors d'oeuvres. He asked, "Whatever happened to the bitch?"

More curiosity than contempt defined Don's question. Tom's confrontation with Elizabeth Harker, former Houston district attorney, and his revealing–at least to his family and to her—her immoral actions in the most sensational murder case in years forced her out of Texas, the practice of law, and the quest for political power. The trial served as the catalyst for Tom's rise to being the most sought-after expert witness in Texas.

The question fed uncomfortably into Tom's mind. He reflected on past history before answering. An unshakable mix of hatred and fear laced his brain. "Harker? Don't really know. She returned to the East as soon as she could. I hope she just slithered off the face of the planet." Tom visualized his last encounter with her. "One sorry person. She's gone from Houston and that's all that matters." He turned the steaks one last time. "These puppies are done."

Three

Monday Evening, December 28

Broken Wing Ranch

After dinner, Tom put a college basketball game on television and took two beers from the refrigerator. The men used the time between the commentary and the slam dunks for Don to describe the extraction system to Tom. Tom's more than three decades as an on-the-board mechanical engineer for NASA's Johnson Space Center rendered him quite capable of handling a little design improvement problem for his brother.

"OK, Don. I get the narrative. Let's see your oil doodad on paper."

"It's our Jet Extraction Technology System. We call it JETS."

Don unrolled a rough drawing onto the coffee table, holding the top down with his beer and the bottom with a ceramic coaster. The drawing depicted a neat, not-to-scale outline of a long, slender device, inside which two pipes were placed extending the entire length of the drawing. At the bottom was a sketch of the critical oil-gathering section. The section consisted of a cylindrical portion with perforations and a bottom chamber with some sort of ball valve attached to it. Tom immediately understood the basics of how the system was to work, but he wanted to hear the specifics from his brother.

"Here's what we're working with." Don pointed to the top of the paper. "We've got an upper system and a lower system. We use the existing well casing and place two smaller steel tubes down the well." He then pointed to the bottom of the page. "At the bottom we have the chamber area, which connects to both pipes. Actually, the tubes are attached to the chamber before we put it down the hole. I'll explain the specifics in a minute. We're using J55 steel pipe for the tubing."

Tom already knew the specifics.

Don took his beer, holding the edge of paper with his left hand. He took a healthy swallow and replaced the can before continuing. "The two pipes—one's the gas line where we send compressed air down, and the other's the product line that handles slugs of oil that are captured. They get pushed out of the top of the well." He gazed up at his brother. "You with me so far?"

"So far."

"I thought so." With growing enthusiasm and a need for approval, Don continued. "Now for the down-hole chamber."

Susie sat down in a plush leather chair. She took the remote and switched away from the basketball game.

"Each tube is attached to the chamber. Once it's in place, oil seeps through the perforations at the bottom of the JETS and into the pump chamber through the hole with the ball valve." Don grinned and asked, "Still with me?"

"Still with you."

"OK. What happens next is that we have a sensor that can tell when the chamber is full. At that point the compressor is turned on, and air pressure forces the oil back out of the bottom of the chamber. But, under pressure, the ball valve seats into the opening. The oil can't escape, and since the pressure continues to build from the air compressor, it has no place to go but up the product line and out the top of the well to a holding tank." Don, similar to the immortal Charlie Chan, solved another mystery.

Don grabbed his beer again, this time allowing the moisture on the paper to keep it attached to the table, and sat back. He swallowed and asked, "Is this sweet or what?"

Tom sat back as well. Resting against the couch cushions, he rolled his head toward Don. "It's sweet. Real sweet."

Don knew Tom too well. Tom had seen some things.

"OK, what's wrong with it?"

Tom smiled and finished off his beer. "No, really, I think it's solid in concept. I do have some questions." He pointed to a specific portion of the drawing and asked, "What do you do for structural integrity of the two lines, the metal tubes?"

Don smiled again, but it was more a smile of guilt than of victory. "You got me on that one. Our biggest problem has been lowering both of the steel tubes down with the chamber without them getting all wrapped around each other. We get caught trying to push a rope. It's a bitch."

"No problem. I've got some ideas." Tom stretched his legs out on the afghan rug. "Now let's talk about the sensor."

The phone rang. Susie got up and walked to the kitchen. The men continued talking.

"It seems to me that if you're trying to keep the number of complex parts to a minimum, we ought to be looking at the sensor as well." Tom was very impressed that the only major moving part within the chamber portion of the JETS was the simple ball valve used to close off oil from escaping out of the bottom. But to Tom's way of thinking, a sensor inside the system was not good. "Let me come up with–"

Susie called to the men. "Don, it's Elam."

Susie gave the phone to Don and walked to the kitchen island.

"Hey, Elam," Don said. "How's it going?" A short wait. "Sorry, I flew into Houston and went fishing. The fish hate cell phones so I turned it off." Another short wait. A grimace on Don's face followed a period of silence. Don stood up, his face looking down at the stone slab floor. He leaned against the back of the couch for balance. "Damn. How'd it happen?"

Tom looked up from the couch and Susie leaned against the granite countertop, both aware that a serious conversation was in progress. Don looked at Tom and Susie, and then pointed his thumb toward the floor.

"Yeah, I'll be there by noon. Let's meet at City Market for lunch so we can talk. We ought to go out to the site before seeing the police. Yeah, I agree. OK. See you tomorrow." Don hit the end button on the phone, stared at it for a moment, then looked back and forth at his hosts. He shook his head and answered their unspoken questions. "One of our workers was killed Saturday night. A great kid. I need to get back to Luling in the morning."

Four

Tuesday, December 29

Broken Wing Ranch

An early morning chill melted beneath the growing sun, allowing the threesome a fine breakfast on the patio. Piled all over the table were hot biscuits, sausage links, crisp bacon, and a large mound of scrambled eggs. The conversation, interrupted only by voracious appetites, focused on the business for the day. Tom's J-3 sat half a football field's distance to their front.

"It's no big deal. I knew you were coming, so I saved the day on my calendar. Even got a five-mile run in while you racked out." Tom hesitated only long enough to finish off a biscuit and stab another sausage link. "Got the Piper gassed and ready to go. Planned to take you up sometime today anyway." He nodded toward the plane. "I'll take you there. You find out what happened and make some decisions with Elam. We'll be back here before dark."

Don acquiesced. "All right. It's a deal. But it's my treat at the Montgomery Steakhouse tomorrow for breakfast." He reached for his cell phone. "I'll tell Elam to pick us up at the airport."

"Good," said Susie as she pushed her chair back and stood up. "But it's warming up fast, so you've got fifteen minutes to finish breakfast, grab your gear, and get airborne. I'll handle the dishes." Her "timed event" comment came from simple physics: the hotter the temperature, the more runway needed. With two men weighing over one hundred and seventy pounds each, cool conditions were critical on a short runway. The only baggage was Don's briefcase and cane.

While Don called Elam, Tom dove into the remaining eggs and sausages.

Fifteen minutes later, Susie hugged Don warmly, kissed Tom affectionately, and stepped away from the Cub.

Tom sided up next to the plane and turned to Don. "Here, let me give you a hand."

"Outta my way."

The doors on Piper Cubs operate opposite to conventional doors, swinging about a horizontal rod and attaching to the wing above the pilot's seat. Don moved to the back end of the cockpit and aligned himself with the tandem passenger's seat. He placed his cane on the floor and, with his hand, lifted his right leg to the foot rung attached to the wing strut. Next he put his right hand on the back of the pilot's seat and his left hand on the passenger seat. He gathered his strength, grimaced slightly, and hopped off his left foot while simultaneously trying to push off with his right leg. The right leg did not respond. It slipped off the rung, catching the bottom of the strut. Don fell butt-first into the grass.

"Fuck!"

Tom bit into his lower lip while reaching a hand toward Don. He was rebuffed.

"I can get myself up. Fuck," he repeated. He struggled to

get up, almost falling a second time.

Susie tightened her jaws and blinked her eyes rapidly to keep away the tears. She looked away.

Don faced the opening once again. He turned around, back to the plane, and tilted his back to the inside of the plane while pushing up from the steel tubing with the palms of his hands. He made it to the floor and, using every bit of his arm strength, lifted himself into the seat.

Don looked at Tom, sweat trickling into his eyes. "I don't want help and I don't want sympathy. Let's hit the road."

Tom said nothing. He prepared the plane for takeoff.

Magneto on. Throttle near idle. Pull the prop. Engine start. Tom pulled the wheel chocks while Don held the heel brakes. Once onboard, Tom guided the plane slowly to the east while Susie walked to the west end of the runway. Tom eyed the windsock and relaxed, knowing he had a light west wind. At the end of the runway, the 1940 Piper J-3 Cub circled and stopped.

Full throttle. The propellers bit into the air, driving the plane forward. The extra weight of the new passenger multiplied the effects of an uneven grass runway. Still, as always, the small yellow plane gathered speed and headed toward freedom.

C'mon. C'mon. Tom willed his way down the runway.

Don enjoyed it all.

Tail wheel up. More speed. More lift. The small yellow plane unchained itself from the runway, rising gently into the sky. A pretty woman waved at the brothers as they flew by. Pine trees, grabbing at the wheels, passed thirty feet below them.

Don spoke through the intercom. "Nice takeoff."

Tom turned around and winked at his brother. They both smiled as the sky opened to their front.

Majestic patterns of dark green pines and beautiful oaks passed beneath them, giving life to the unborn grasses of East Texas. They only needed ten minutes to cover the eighteen miles to Conroe. Tom and Don changed planes at Conroe and flew the Grumman Tiger west to Luling. The coral-blue sky, devoid of even a popcorn cloud, held for the entire trip. Thick stands of pines eventually withered into sparse, open rangeland dotted with mesquite, oak, and pecan trees. Their flight path took them along I-10, a gentle sweep to the northwest, and then generally south-southwest to Luling's Runway 22. Tom eased the Tiger into a smooth glide while yawing into a 10-knot west wind. The landing, smoother than an escalator ride at the mall, impressed both passenger and pilot.

"Smooth as silk, Tom."

"Just another perfect piloting job. Like all my others."

Don smiled, remembering a few other landings. "Yeah, right."

Don tapped Tom on the shoulder and pointed to a man sitting on the left fender of a '91 Cadillac DeVille. "There's Elam, over by the hangar."

Elam Duquette, his graying, unkempt hair blowing in the wind, slid forward and walked toward the parking apron and approaching plane. He looked older than his years. A noticeable limp, the result of a fall from an oil derrick, was one of Elam's personal signatures. More memorable was a broad, kid-like smile stretching beneath a nose that tilted slightly toward his right cheek. He'd won most of his fights, but his proboscis had taken a sizeable number of good shots in the process. God-awful brown chinos hung from his butt. New clothes, a shave, and a haircut would cut at least twenty years from his appearance.

The Tiger rolled to a stop. Tom cut the engine and slid the canopy back. He stepped out onto the wing, grabbing Don's briefcase and cane.

"Hey, Tom, how the hell you doin'? Give me that briefcase."

Elam reached upward.

"Good, Elam. Got some bad cargo though." Tom pointed at Don.

Tom jumped to the ground, shook Elam's hand, and then walked around to Don's side of the plane.

With the canopy completely behind him, Don found it relatively easy to stand up. He lifted his right leg over the side, took his cane from Tom, and stepped onto the wing. It only took the support of Tom's hand to help him to the ground.

Don, buoyed by his triumph over the plane, shook Elam's hand and grinned. "Whew. Pretty damn hot for December."

"Sure is." Elam slapped the fender of his Cadillac. "But Betsy'll cool you off real quick."

Elam, briefcase in hand, led the two brothers toward the waiting Betsy. He spoke out loud to himself. "Got both the Seiler boys with me. What an honor." He transitioned right into the events for the day. "We'll grab some coffee at Buchanan's. I'll bring you up to date on what I know about Juan. I talked to the Luling police, and they'll let us see the preliminary investigation around noon. They called me because my cell phone number was in his wallet. We'll head to City Market for lunch."

Buchanan's coffee was piping hot and only five minutes old. Delicious. Wooden tables and chairs sat on top of wide, 1890-vintage pine floorboards. The walls were painted in vertical stripes of red, white, and blue, and the long counter parallel to the east wall of the café easily handled ten round, swivel-top stools. Buchanan's still offered fountain Cokes and black cows for a quarter; milkshakes were a buck.

"He died from a fall off that transmission tower north of town just off of 128," said Elam as he swallowed hot coffee. "Been drinking and tried to climb the damn thing and fell."

Don said, "I've done stupid shit like that many times, but I never did it alone." He took a quick breath, his face showing an unsure thought. "Who was with him?"

"Can't say anybody. At least, nobody's reported anything. All I know is a rancher saw Juan's car and thought it strange. Checked it out and found him sprawled out on the concrete."

Unpleasant images formed in Tom's mind. "What kind of injuries did he have?"

Elam thought it an unnecessary question, but let it go. "Don't know that either. I did hear one of the cops mention his skull was broken. Like I said, they'll let us see the report around noon."

Tom asked, "Can we take a look at his body?"

"Shit, I guess so, if you want to. Who wants to see a dead body?"

"It's something I do if I get involved before a body has been disposed of. Doesn't happen often, but when it does, it helps me sort things out."

Tom looked at his watch. He wanted the morning coffee social ended and sorting out Juan's death started. He thought, *five more minutes and we need to go.*

Elam changed subjects mid-stream. He leaned forward, both hands squeezing the sans-handle coffee mug, and smiled at Don. "Got a new girlfriend. Early forties and the prettiest one I've ever dated. Very nice woman."

Don shook his head. "Elam, how does someone your age stay so preoccupied with women? You're one beat up SOB, but your dick is always raring to go."

All three laughed.

"Well, yeah, could be. But this one, she'd be a keeper if I weren't such a vagabond. Still, I might be bad merchandise, but I do know class from the feminine side. She's got it."

Don swallowed and leaned forward, looking Elam in the eye. "Elam, compared to you, a water buffalo has class. I hope she didn't see you in that crap." He sat up and finished his coffee.

Before Elam could rebut Don's accusation, Tom interrupted. "Coffee's gone and I've got a trial on Thursday. We need to wrap this up today. Before going to the police station, let's check out where Juan died. I've got the bill."

Tom placed seven dollars on the table and led his partners into the street.

They drove out on County Road 128. Small homes and businesses comingled with the pumpjacks dotting the countryside. The sweet smell of crude oil, reaching back to the glory days of the 1920s, filled their nostrils.

"That's it." Elam pointed toward their right front.

Elam turned right on the dirt road and drove toward the tower. Fine dust billowed behind them. He pulled up some twenty feet from the tower base, stretching and cocking his neck to gaze up the length of the thin steel pyramid.

Once out of the car, each man studied the tower, with both Don and Elam juxtaposing personal thoughts of climbing oil rigs against Juan's death.

"I fell off some scaffolding on an ocean rig in Alaska. Fixing me up was when the docs ran into my MS." Don returned in his mind some twenty years.

"Crazy son of a bitch. At least when I got tore up on the derrick I was doing what I had to do." Just as Don did, Elam retreated into memories. "Never did I go up on a rig for fun."

Tom ignored the conversation and walked toward the nearest concrete footing. Don and Elam followed.

Tom stopped at the edge of the concrete and looked upward. Rising nine hundred feet above the men, the tower, marked by triangular patterns of steel trusses, stretched into the bluish-white haze of the late morning sky. Slowly tracing the near leg from its pinnacle to the ground, Tom visualized from where someone might have jumped or fallen. At the terminus of his gaze, directly at his feet, was a small, circular spot on the concrete. Tom bent over, hands on his knees, and studied the spot.

"Looks like blood." Tom lowered himself to his right knee. He leaned closer to the dark spot, his face no more than twelve inches away. "Not much, though. Strange. It's dry but pretty fresh." He turned his head toward Don. "This must be where your worker hit the ground."

Tom pulled a camera from his stuffed shirt pocket and started taking photographs.

"Damn shame. He was a good kid," Don sighed dejectedly.

Tom stood up and took a mechanical pencil and small spiral notepad from his shirt pocket. He sketched a rough site plan of the tower footprint, including the dirt road terminating at the base. He added the location of the blood found on the concrete footer and made a note concerning the amount of blood found. On a second page he made a two-dimensional sketch of the tower.

Elam was confused at Tom's attention to detail. *This isn't a fucking murder case,* he thought. It was simple to Elam. A worker gets killed playing around—get a new worker.

The Luling police station was on East Pierce Street. On the way, Don and Elam discussed the status of their invention and the interminable delays in obtaining a patent. Tom studied his notes in the back seat.

"You don't look much like next of kin, but what the hell, he'd be glad somebody cared about him." Sergeant Archie Hamblen stapled the copied three-page incident report and handed it to Elam. "The medical examiner said no to releasing a post-mortem to you. If you want, you can see the body at Breuner's

Funeral Home on South Laurel."

Tom asked, "Have you got the yellow pages? I'd like to call them first."

Archie, notwithstanding the look of a junkyard dog, was one friendly cop. "I'll do you better. I've got the number right here. Only had to call it a few times, but you remember funeral home numbers the first time around. Hang on, I'll give them a call for you."

"Let's eat first," said Elam with a twinge of urgency. "I won't be hungry after seeing the kid."

Tom and Don agreed. They left the police station shortly before noon and headed for Davis Street and City Market. Elam caught a lucky break just as he turned onto Davis Street. A car pulled out of a parking space in front of City Market. He quickly turned in to the vacant space, a slight smile of conquest on his face. They got out of the car and walked through the front door toward one of the most succulent aromas known to mankind.

City Market is a Texas culinary gemstone. Long lines are the norm and reach to a back dining room, sometimes out the door to the sidewalk along Davis Street. The front half of the counter area offers souvenir knickknacks, and the back serves as the watering hole for customers. Wooden booths fill opposite walls and numerous benches occupy the center of City Market. Entrance and exit doors protect the cooking grills in the kitchen where Frankie, Ray, and Alex banter with customers ordering sausage, brisket of beef, pork, onions, and half loaves of bread. Iced tea or a good Texas beer from the watering hole closes out the main menu; pecan patties make for a great dessert.

The men joined the queue and slowly edged their way to a square counter area in the main dining room. After they sat down with their food, Tom swallowed some brisket, sliced onion, and bread, chased them with his iced tea, and then focused the other two on the project. "OK, last night we didn't get much into the operational details of the JETS. How about starting with the macro implication of this thing? We'll get into more nuts and bolts later."

Elam started first. "What do you know about stripper wells, Tom?"

"Not much. They're wells that don't have a lot of oil. Most aren't worth the cost of pumping. That's about it."

Elam continued. "That's right. And cost is the big factor. If the price of oil is low and pumping it from stripper wells is expensive, then forget 'em. But suppose there's a device that pumps the oil cheaper than anything else out there, and," Elam pointed his index finger into the air, "suppose the cost of oil rises above what the world has been used to over the years."

Don interjected, "Suppose, hell. OPEC has bounced it all over the place. Soon as the price went over a hundred bucks a barrel I knew the United States was in deep kimchi. Assholes like Chavez in Venezuela are trying to strangle us." His eyes closed slightly and a furrowed V formed along his forehead. "If the Mideast becomes destabilized—and it's a powder keg at best—there's no knowing what the price will be. Add to that the fact that we aren't doing shit to develop additional oil sources. It'll go down from time to time, but in the long run, let's say at least another twenty years until alternative energy is achieved, and the curve will go up."

Tom took another bite as Elam threw out some financial tidbits. "Don's dead on. That's where we come in. For starters, it's not just about our consumption of oil in the states, no sir. The Chinese and Indians have jumped in with both feet. Everybody's using it like it's going out of style. I'm telling you, consumption is going to go ballistic. Check out the quarterly profits of our large oil companies. It's un-fucking-believable. With oil prices soaring, our ability to pump cheap oil with

JETS turns every stripper well into a gold mine. From mom and pop to the major oil companies, we can be in the money." Elam began to get excited. "Don and I checked with the Texas Railroad Commission. It's those folks who monitor and regulate the state oil industry. Of the 350,000 oil and gas wells in Texas, some 115,000 stripper wells pump less than ten barrels a day and another 30,000 pump between ten and a hundred. The owners only keep the small ones running because Texas will make them plug the wells if they don't produce at all. That costs money they don't have. We can make money for each one of them—and for us. Not just here in Texas, but the rest of the country and everywhere else. There are seventy million stripper wells around the world."

Tom listened intensely as the full potential of their system took hold. It would be a new experience to join the ranks of people who considered money by putting four to five additional zeroes before the decimal point.

Elam added, "Let's say that we could get access to only 5 percent of those wells. That's 3.5 million wells. We could pump the oil ourselves, lease the system to users, or sell it outright to a large company. Of course, anything we sell to a company would come with a clause for residual compensation in direct correlation with the amount of oil produced."

"So what's your bottom line?" Tom said and swallowed more tea.

"As conservative as we can be, it would come to no less than one thousand dollars a well. Tom, we're looking at 3.5 billion dollars." He grinned that shit-eating grin of his. "At a minimum."

Tom responded, "You could almost live on that amount and the government would make its own fortune." He chuckled slightly as he processed the difference between a pipe dream and the one-in-a-million jackpot.

"No shit," said Elam and Don in unison.

Don declared, "Young troopers, we're in place for a big payoff."

Tom's last bite disappeared. He chewed, swallowed, and answered, "I agree. When we head back home, Don and I can work on improving your design. What I heard last night tells me that your basic concept is good and we just need to brainstorm the shortcomings." Tom smiled as he stood up. "I can help you. But first, lunch is over. It's time to visit your worker."

Five

Tuesday Afternoon,
December 29

Breuner's Funeral Home

Breuner's Funeral Home was a stone's throw from the main government buildings of Luling, just south of the Southern Pacific Railroad tracks. Don, Tom, and Elam walked up wooden steps to a wraparound porch of an 1880s-vintage Victorian home. A middle-aged woman dressed in a dark blue cotton dress greeted them at the front door. She smiled gently.

"Good afternoon. I'm Mary Otter. You must be the gentlemen wanting to pay respects to Mr. Delgado. Come in." She stepped back slightly, holding the door open.

"I'm Tom Seiler. We appreciate your letting us see Mr. Delgado." Tom offered his hand and she accepted. Don and Elam introduced themselves similarly.

Mary Otter closed the door. She spoke quietly. "Please come this way."

On each side of a large pastel blue foyer, pocket doors opened to double-roomed suites. A small group of well-dressed people spoke quietly in the nearest room to their left.

Mary escorted the men around a circular stairway and down a fairly long hallway; she opened the door to the last room and invited the men inside. Two operating tables occupied the center of the room. Elam shivered, partly from a sudden drop in the temperature and partly from his realization of where they were. *What the hell are we doing here?* he thought. *We can't help Delgado.* Lights above the tables gave evidence to the tables' purpose. Semi-surgical instruments lay near each table in clean trays. Cabinets and drawers covered one wall; what appeared to be three refrigerator doors faced them from the back of the room. Mary Otter moved to the middle door.

Respecting the deceased, Mary whispered, "This is not normal procedure for us, but we understand your situation."

During Tom's phone call to Breuner's he told them of their relationship with Juan. That his call was sanctioned by the Luling Police Department made the unusual visit possible.

Tom spoke for all. "Again, thank you. He was a good man."

Mary nodded and opened the door. The three men looked in immediately and could see the black hair of Juan's head. Mary pulled lightly on the stainless steel body tray; it glided smoothly on rollers, exposing the full body of Juan Delgado. A sheet placed by the staff in anticipation of the visit covered Juan's torso.

Elam flinched and inhaled a large breath. "Damn." He exhaled, remaining silent.

Mary ignored the slight profanity and stepped back out of the way.

The men stared at the body of Juan Delgado. The expressionless face did not seem happy or sad—or anything. It was void.

Tom turned to Mary and asked, "Is it possible to see if he had any injuries to his torso?"

Mary answered quietly, "There were injuries to his head, but nothing to his torso." She was unsure of why Tom wanted to see Juan's body. Still, she returned to the corpse and pulled the sheet down to the pubic hair.

Don and Elam stepped back in silent unison. Tom studied Juan carefully. After a short look at Juan's trunk and arms, Tom moved alongside Juan's head; he studied the obvious fatal injury. The puncture wound had been worked on by the staff but was clearly visible. He noticed the quarter-sized hole at the temple and what appeared to be a rough, three-inch-long bruise extending diagonally down from the puncture. The skin was lacerated over half the length of the bruise. He took out his notepad and started to write. Ten minutes later they thanked Mary Otter for her help and left.

Tom didn't speak until they reached Elam's car. "Let's head back out to the tower."

"Hell, Tom," said Elam, "I'm up to my neck with Juan's death. Why go back out there?"

"Because I need to find an anchor bolt or something else that would puncture Juan's skull like that." He added, "Then we've got to get back to the airfield with two hours of sunlight still left."

They headed toward County Road 128.

Six

Tuesday Afternoon, December 29

Houston, Texas

Concurrent with Tom and Don's approach to Conroe in the Grumman Tiger, a conversation played out in the presidential suite of Wellington Oil and Exploration.

"And you killed him? You fucking killed him?"

"Mr. Miles, you tell me to get rid of him." Carlos, void of bravado, sweated profusely. "I try to do what you want, so I did. I didn't want to kill him, just scare him to quit work. The hammer twisted in my hand."

"But you did, you stupid prick!" Bart Miles stood up and walked around the mahogany desk to where Carlos stood. Bart, his face no more than six inches away from Carlos, spoke viciously to the trembling man. In a fair fight, Carlos could destroy Bart Miles. Bart continued, "Ever heard of a broken leg?" He rammed his finger into Carlos's chest several times. "All we needed was a simple broken leg. Just threaten the guy. Tell him what you'd do to his family if he didn't quit. Is that so hard?"

Carlos whispered, "I'm sorry, Mr. Miles, I . . . I didn't mean to. I thought—"

Bart cut him off. "Shut up. Just shut up."

Bart, short of stature, looked up at the tall Mexican man. He shook his head back and forth while inhaling and exhaling. Small sponges of spittle formed at the corners of his mouth. He started after Carlos again. "What about the other two? How are you going to keep their mouths shut?"

"They always do what I tell them to do. They won't say nothing to nobody."

Bart stepped back and walked to his window overlooking downtown Houston. He scratched at a small scab on the back of his plump neck, playing out problems and plans in his head. Frank Milsap, the chief financial officer, sat placidly in a large burgundy couch, a cup of coffee on the table to his front.

Bart turned back to Carlos and spoke. "You damn well better get hired by those people or your ass is in bigger trouble than you can handle." He walked back to his desk.

Carlos stood motionless in front of the desk. "I will, Mr. Miles. And my men . . ."

Bart ignored Carlos, saying, "Get back out there and get hired. Then let me know. Now, get the hell out of here." He dismissively motioned toward the door.

Carlos nodded without speaking, then turned around and walked toward the door.

Two steps before Carlos got to the door, Bart called to him. "Carlos."

Carlos turned back and looked at Bart.

Bart spoke quietly, but with deafening tone. "If you or your two stupid helpers screw up, your life won't be worth a plug nickel."

They stared at each other. Then Carlos walked out.

"Bart, this is bad shit. We didn't need to hire him in the first place." Frank lifted his feet to the coffee table, a mannerism that had always bothered Bart. He continued. "At some point soon, we are going to have to deal with them. Not very pretty," Frank said and hesitated for a second. "And not very smart."

"I don't need a fucking lecture from you. We needed someone on the inside, and Carlos costs us chicken feed. We'll take care of them when the time comes." He sat down across the coffee table from Frank. "Once we have patent rights to the Donelam oil system, we'll get rid of them."

Frank shifted his feet, hands sliding behind his head. He stared quizzically at the ceiling. "When do we meet with the guy who built it?" Frank could control his emotions far better than Bart. Frank and Bart shared one major similarity: both were amoral.

"Tomorrow afternoon. Actually, we'll be dealing with two of them. The one who appears to be the lead partner will be meeting with us. He talks as though he's the one who makes the decisions. The other guy is an engineer who did most of the design."

Frank squeezed his eyes shut and exhaled loudly. "Where in the hell do you run into these people?" He shook his head.

Bart did not respond.

Frank switched legs, keeping them on Bart's table. Irritating as hell. He proceeded in a new direction. "You never did tell me how you got involved with this company and this extraction system. What's the source?"

"An old friend told me. She said these two had something that might make Wellington a fortune," Bart paused, looking directly into Frank's eyes, "or, if we don't own it, wipe us out."

Bart did not mention any names. But the population of candidates for giving the information had been cut down significantly. The source was a woman.

Later that night, Tom, Don, and Susie ate tacos and drank beer in front of the roaring fire while the television droned on in the background.

"It's just that he died in a strange way," said Tom. "I couldn't find an anchor bolt or other protrusion that explains his wound." Tom, half-buried in plush cushions, stared into the fire. He spoke to no one in particular, saying, "He didn't have any other broken bones and there was very little blood. Strange."

Susie tried, very unsuccessfully, to divide her attention between the TV and the conversation of the two men. As time went on, her attention focused solely on Tom. From deep inside, Susie Seiler recoiled at the Second Coming of the Beast.

"You know me. Got to sort everything out. Again, it's a strange way to die." Tom changed the subject. "So, you want to go over your plans in detail? Or how about tomorrow afternoon? I have a meeting in Houston tomorrow morning."

Tom looked over at this brother sitting in an overstuffed, down-filled club chair. Don's eyes were shut. Tom waved at Susie. Time for bed.

Seven

Wednesday, December 30

Broken Wing Ranch

Tom buzzed the house and then turned south toward Houston and Hobby Airport. Don moaned, sighed while stretching both arms and legs as best he could, and cursed his need for the bathroom. He lifted the covers and maneuvered his body to the side of the bed. Following a twenty-minute shower Don headed toward the kitchen and the aroma of fresh coffee and a hot breakfast.

"Morning, Don." Susie's voice was muffled as she held her hand over the phone. She returned to the phone. "Don's up, I'll call you back in an hour." A short pause allowed the other caller to finish her remarks. "OK. You too. Bye." She returned the phone to its holder and reached for the coffee pot. "How about some scrambled eggs and bacon? They're already made."

Over Don's breakfast and Susie's third cup of coffee, they sat on the porch discussing familial topics first and then the oil extractor project. The early morning sun cast Susie's hair prettier than a reddish Georgia peach.

"Tom's genuinely excited about it." Susie took a quick sip. "He said your ideas and the basic system are good. He wants to see how well it works in the field." With a slight twinkle in her eye, she continued. "Of course, you know Tom. He's already talking about tweaking it here and there. After we went to bed, he got up and went to his office to start on his magic act."

Don pushed his chair back and stretched his legs beneath the table. A wry smiled formed on his lips. "He's one hell of a man."

She answered. "He is. He really is." She turned serious, adding, "But you also ought to know that he may be more impressed with you than you are with him."

Her remark caught him off guard. Bouncing his abject failures in high school, his numerous stints in small town Texas and California jails, and a youth consumed in drinking more than his body could handle, Don felt inadequate in responding to her comment. He swallowed hard and let it go, not even giving himself credit for eventually serving in the US Navy and later graduating from Texas A&M as a civil engineer.

Susie patted him on the arm, breaking the unexpected emotional surge enveloping him. He blinked away forming moisture.

"He'll be back later this afternoon. He can't wait to work some more." She got up and took Don's plate. "He left some notes for you on the drafting table. Said they would be the starting point for your work tonight. How about another cup of coffee?"

Tom crested the pine trees at a steep angle, the J-3 partially hidden by the sinking winter sun. He dropped first, then abruptly lifted the right wing and gunned the engine, flying diagonally across the grassy runway at no more than ten feet. Fifty feet away from Don, Tom gunned the engine again and pulled hard. The Cub responded, arcing up at a forty-five-degree angle directly over Don's head. Don smiled and waved a can of beer toward the sky. Five minutes later Tom returned the plane to the hangar, grabbed a couple of beers, and made his way to the pond. Another warm winter day graced the countryside.

"They still biting?" asked Tom as he popped the top of a can of beer and handed it to Don. He grabbed a pole and sat down on the bench next to his younger brother.

"Caught a couple of eaters but didn't have the heart to do them in. The day's too nice to kill catfish."

The bobber jerked, then disappeared beneath the water. "Hot damn. Here we go." Don yanked the rod up briskly, hooking into another eater. The catfish fought heroically, but couldn't throw the hook.

"Give me your beer." Tom laughed at the sight of Don refusing to give up on either the fish or the beer.

Don relinquished the can, exclaiming out loud, "Sucker's a five-pounder if he's an ounce. Hang on." Good news for the fish; on this day his captor would give him a pardon. Don removed the catfish from the hook, held it up for one last look, and kissed the fish's open mouth before tossing him back in the pond.

Both men leaned back and relaxed.

Tom thought out loud. "I wonder what Jack's life would have turned out to be?"

Over forty years had passed since Jack, the middle brother of the Seiler family, died in a rice paddy near the hamlet of Vo Dat, Vietnam. Over the years Tom and Don kept him alive through story after story. Tom's question had been asked hundreds of times before. Over the years the questions had changed from ones of anger to ones of nostalgia.

"He'd be sitting right here with us. Probably would've caught the biggest fish in the pond." Rapid flashbacks of time spent with Jack danced through Don's mind. A particular scene of Jack at age eleven and Don at age three playing football–with a sock for the football–in the front yard came to mind. Jack was always Princeton and Don would be assigned team names of Georgia, Duke, Army, and Texas. Of course, Don never won. His attention returned to the pond and the time of day. "But since I already got the big one, guess we can call it a day."

Heading back to the office, Tom and Don reminisced over a few more stories.

Tom and Don parked the golf cart at Tom's office. Inside, two work desks, one for Tom and one for Susie, occupied the middle and back of the office. Beige filing cabinets, holding folders for almost three thousand cases, lined an entire wall butting the garage. Two drafting tables stood side by side between built-in bookshelves housing reference books. Aircraft pictures hung from the other walls. A model of train engine #65776 from the famous Missouri–Kansas–Texas railroad, the Katy line, sat on the window ledge. One hundred feet away an actual caboose, renovated for the pure enjoyment of grandchildren, rested quietly in front of some pine trees.

While Tom pulled a second stool to one of the drafting tables, Don spoke. "Tom, what I need from you is good advice. I don't want to eat your lunch as far as time goes. Let's go over this tonight and then I'm headed back tomorrow. Deal?" He pulled a folder full of drawings from his briefcase.

Tom replied. "Not no, but hell no. From what you've told me, you could be on the brink of something big. Not just for you and Elam, but for the entire oil industry." He turned serious. "And I'll tell you what else. It's my American civic duty to eliminate our oil dependency on corrupt, scum-sucking, banana dictatorships. Read that as Hugo Chavez, et al."

Shaking his head, Don laughed out loud. "Tell me how you really feel." Then he turned serious. "But you've got–"

Tom interrupted, "I've got plenty of other work to do and I'll do it. But this is more important than any case I'm working on." He began rolling his sleeves up and turned to the folder. "We'll work on this for the next two hours, then I'll throw your ass out. Tomorrow we'll do the same as today. After that you can head back to California and give me the weekend to tinker with it. That's my final offer." He finished rolling his right sleeve, cocked his head, and leaned toward Don to shake hands.

Tom's argument was rock solid. Don reached back, grasping Tom's hand. "It's a deal."

Eight

Thursday, New Year's Eve

Houston, Texas

Elam pulled into the parking garage at the JP Morgan Chase Tower using the Travis Street entrance. He followed the directions received over the phone and on the third level found a reserved parking space with his name on it. *Not bad,* he thought. *Not bad at all.* He crossed Travis Street, stopping only long enough to take a look at the fifty-five-foot steel and cast-bronze sculpture, "Personage and Birds." The sculpture was not your run-of-the-mill nude; it was a collage of multicolored triangles, cylinders, and rods. Elam thought to himself, *That looks stupid.* He walked in the building.

A security officer noticed Elam staring at the elevators. "Good afternoon, sir. May I help you?" Eyeing the rugged, somewhat disheveled man peering up at him, the officer couldn't help but think of directing him to the shelter on Chenevert Street. But he had seen his share of confused eccentrics walk into the JP Morgan Chase Tower, so he remained courteous and helpful.

"Sure can. Name's Duquette. Elam Duquette. Got a three o'clock meeting with Mr. Miles." Elam glanced at his watch. "He's the CEO."

The guard, amused at what seemed to be a kid's first trip to the zoo, politely answered, "We've got lots of tenants. What is the company you're hunting for?"

"Oh. Mr. Miles at Wellington Oil and Exploration."

The officer replied, "Take the last elevator to the forty-sixth floor." He pointed to the bank of elevators immediately to Elam's left. "Take a left; it will be at the end of the corridor." The officer stepped back, smiled again, and tapped two fingers against his right eyebrow. "Have a nice day."

Elam walked toward the elevator. He was upbeat, enjoying his entrance into the world of the VIP. Elam followed the officer's directions and soon found himself at the entrance to Wellington Oil.

The doors, with *Wellington Oil Exploration, Inc.* cut into neat rows on each frosted glass panel, opened to a magnificent reception area. Once inside, Elam found himself staring at a very pretty receptionist.

Beautiful woman, he couldn't help thinking. *Beautiful.* He eyed the nameplate reading *Macy Buckles.*

"Good afternoon, sir, and welcome to Wellington Oil. May I help you?"

"Sure can. I'm Elam Duquette and I'm supposed to see Mr. Miles right about now."

"Good to have you here, Mr. Duquette. I hope you enjoy your time with us. Mr. Miles will be with you in just a few minutes." She pointed to a leather couch and matching chairs. "Please have a seat. May I get you a cup of coffee or a soft drink?"

An uneasy silence for her. Daydreaming for him.

"Mr. Duquette, may I get you a cup of coffee or soft drink?" Her volume increased just enough to bring him back to reality.

"Huh? Coffee? Yeah, sure." Elam thought the couch looked most comfortable, so he sat down on the middle cushion.

Over his coffee Elam surveyed his surroundings. The dark blue carpet was covered with yellow-gold dashes laid out geometrically like headstones in a national cemetery. Pleasant canary-yellow walls accentuated the carpeting and mahogany furniture. Adorning the walls were pictures of the Texas oil industry up to the 1950s. Wooden derricks, oil-covered wildcatters, and gushing plumes of black gold told stories from the past. The antiseptic cleanliness of the room was too much for Elam; he preferred comfort to clean and beer in a bottle to coffee in a cup.

Bart Miles walked as briskly as possible from his office directly to Elam. He stuck out his hand before Elam could stand up.

"Good to meet you, Mr. Duquette. I'm Bart Miles and we're pleased to have you join us today." His smile was overdone and Elam noticed. Bart continued. "My senior leadership team will be meeting us in the conference room." Bart Miles swept his hands toward double doors at the far end of the complex.

A huge oak conference table dominated the room. Same carpet, same walls, similar pictures. A polarized glass window, comprising the entire outside wall of the room, opened over the Houston skyline. It was magnificent.

Elam offered, "Sure love your place. Pictures remind me of the Wild West."

Bart, not interested in small talk, ignored Elam's comment. "Let me introduce you to my colleagues."

Three men in tailored dress suits rose to greet their visitor. After pleasantries subsided, Bart directed Elam to a seat next to him and nodded to the others to take their seats. In addition to its CEO, the leadership of Wellington Oil and Exploration consisted of Frank Milsap, Morgan Rosewood, the company's senior lawyer, and Jim Bitters, the new executive vice president of oil exploration. The scene before him was surreal; he was sitting somewhere near the top of the world with four of the most influential oilmen in the United States. *Maybe I shouldn't be here,* he thought.

Everyone sat down and Bart Miles started the meeting. "Let me begin with how I came to learn about Elam and his oil extractor."

Nine

Thursday Afternoon,
New Year's Eve

Broken Wing Ranch

Abundant sunlight filled Tom Seiler's office at the ranch. Tom and Don sat at the large drafting table. Tom slid a yellow pad of paper toward Don. The top four pages held a collage of handwritten notes and sketches.

"Let me get down to specifics. What you have right now is a system consisting of two side-by-side cylindrical tubes placed vertically in each stripper well. On average, let's say they go down twenty-five hundred feet. Your prototype is workable in basic theory but not in a mass production application. It fails too often." He looked at Don.

"You mean the constant folding of the small pipes inside the well?"

"Yeah. That and your sensor. Let's start with that since it doesn't take any drawings to explain my thoughts. What you show is a sensing device that measures volume. The problem is that it is installed inside the chamber at the bottom of the well. When it works, great. But every time one of your sensors fails, you have to pull out the entire line and replace it. I say control the cycles using a computer-driven timer at the compressor above ground. Each time you blow out a slug of oil, you can measure its volume using a simple bobber device. If the slug volume is less than the chamber volume, the computer program adjusts the timer to take a little longer. If, on your first cycle, the slug has the same volume as the chamber, then the time is shortened slightly. Eventually, the timing will be virtually exact for removing oil at an optimum rate. It's a simple iterative algorithm. Blow a slug, measure the amount, adjust the timer." Tom looked up at his brother.

Don shook his head and smiled. "This is almost too simple." He added, "So simple that no one else has thought of it." His grin broadened. "OK, now for my major problem. What delicious solution do you have?"

"Look at this." Tom directed his attention back to his sketches.

The rudimentary sketch was a top view of the well casing and JETS. It was a simple rendition of concentric circles.

Tom continued, "The outside cylinder is the existing stripper well steel casing. The sections are joined with sealed connections. Well diameters from bottom to top could range from less than ten to more than twenty-four inches according to the drawings you gave me. Nothing special about it." He moved his finger to a second steel cylinder, drawn inside the first. It had an outside diameter slightly less than five inches. "This represents the steel tubing down through which your system blew air from the compressor. To keep it from folding inside the casing, we'll use structural connectors to center and stabilize the tube within the well casing."

Don responded, "I'm with you. Keep going."

"Finally, this small cylinder is the product line tube." The smallest of the three cylinders had a diameter of approximately two inches. "Again, we'll have a structural connection system to keep the product line set dead in the middle of the system. With both inside tubes unable to move and buckle, the system will be structurally stable."

Tom turned to the second page of sketches while finishing his explanation of the system. "It's no different in concept than what you have. The only difference is in structural stability." He gave a wry smile and continued. "Mine is better. Air goes down the void between the product line cylinder and the gas injection cylinder. In doing so the gas forces the ball valve shut, and the oil slug is forced up the inside of the product line cylinder to the holding tank. Slick as a whistle.

"Now, my concept of the chamber isn't much different from yours—only what I've shown you where my connected concentric cylinders replace your side-by-side lines." Tom sat erect on his drafting stool, appearing satisfied that he had made his case. He leaned forward again and removed the top sketch. "Here's what I've drawn so far on the full system."

From the mule shoe at the bottom, through the ball valve, pump chamber, seating nipple, and steel casing, and finally back to the wellhead assembly, compressor, and timer at the surface of the JETS, Tom described his recommended modifications to improve the efficiency and economics of the system.

Don, his head propped in his right hand, leaned in as close as possible to the drawing sheet. "Yeah. Yeah. Everything makes sense." He paused briefly, lifting his head and rubbing the stubble on his chin. A fleeting grin preceded a pensive, almost sad, frown. "I've got to suck it up and find the money to make the modifications. Elam and I each have more than three hundred thousand into this thing. We need some venture capital."

Just as Tom started to comment, Don cut him off. "I refuse to take anything from you. So forget it before you think it."

"Damn. A little edgy on the finances, aren't you?" Tom respected Don's position and knew that he meant it.

Still, Tom decided to deal himself in. "But OK. You two find some money. Still, if you want, I can buy into all this with services. I can make your design sing on the computer. Not only can I modify your design, I can analyze anything about it. If you make a fortune on this, give me 3 percent of your net profit." Tom rose from the chair, still speaking. "Or, what the hell, give me a flat fee. You name the price. Also, rather than bringing in others to own it, consider going to a bank. They'll jump on it." Tom stood up. "Hang on."

Tom walked to the refrigerator and grabbed two beers. "Here." Tom popped the tops of both cans and gave one to Don. "You and Elam decide how to do it, but I'm in one way or the other. Deal?"

Don's irrepressible grin painted his face. "Deal."

They clicked their cans and swallowed heartily.

"Here's to a Happy New Year."

Ten

Thursday Afternoon,
New Year's Eve

Houston, Texas

I'm telling you, in some cases it'll pump ten times more oil with about 10 percent of the labor." Elam's third announcement of the benefits of his oil extractor bored the Wellington leadership group to distraction. "We call it Jet Extraction Technology System, but a better name would be one sweet baby." He was long on praises and short on specifics.

Bart Miles was on edge but believed the payoff justified putting up with the unnecessary bullshit.

"OK, Elam. We understand what you say it can do, but you need to be more specific about its design and prototype testing. Can I ask you–"

Elam broke in, "Until I get my patent settled I'm not giving out any specs. It'll do exactly what I said it'll do. We've already run some good tests in Luling. Hell, we've even started making improvements in what we got."

Elam's statement piqued Bart's interest. He showed no change of emotion, but asked, "Tell me about the improvements.

Why are we talking about a device that's about to be changed?"

Elam jumped on the question. "We know the potential of what we already have. When you start thinking about how much money our system will make, it's just natural to always be thinking about how to make it even better. It's already big time right now. Only thing I'm going to tell you is that it will be solid as a rock."

Morgan Rosewood tapped a pencil on the table, eyes locked on Elam. "How close are you to getting your patent?"

"Two, three weeks, maybe a month." Elam answered without much conviction.

Morgan dug in. "I don't understand. Mr. Miles mentioned you to us several weeks ago. I would think that if your extractor were really unique, a patent would be pretty simple. Who's your patent lawyer? We might be able to help."

"Herm . . ." Elam stopped short. He squinted his eyes slightly and a quick, untrusting look spread across his face. He changed directions. "You don't need to help. I'll get after my lawyer. As for unique, damn right it's unique." Elam eyed the group of men. An uneasy transformation had begun.

Bart intervened. "No problem, Elam. Tell you what, and I'll be to the point. Your extractor is interesting to us. If it works like you've described, then our interest in it will be significant. In such a case, we would be glad to negotiate purchasing it at a generous price."

Elam replied, "It's going to be worth millions. That's just the opening bid."

Caught between irritation and boredom, Bart brought the meeting to a close. "Fine. Keep us informed on your progress. Any last questions before we adjourn?"

"Just a comment." Morgan turned slightly to his right and, at six feet six, looked down at Elam with a genuine-looking smile. "If your patent lawyer is slowing you down," Morgan raised the palm of his hand as an exclamation point, "and some of them are notoriously bad, just let me know and I'll help you find a better one."

Morgan reached into his shirt pocket and pulled out a business card. He handed it to Elam. "Here's my card. Call me anytime. Have you got a card?"

Elam fumbled with his back pocket, finally pulling out a wallet that bulged like a bullfrog. Searching through various denomination bills, multiple restaurant receipts, and other pieces of debris, he found a couple of business cards stuck together with age and sweat. He peeled them apart, giving one to Morgan. "Here you go. Sometimes I don't answer the phone or email for days, but I'll get back to you soon enough after a call."

Just to lighten his wallet's load, Elam slid the second card to Miles.

Miles stood first. A few less hearty handshakes, a pat on the back, and the meeting ended. Elam disappeared into the elevator and the four executives returned to their offices.

Bart looked at the worn business card in his hand, speaking through an exhale, "Asshole. Dumb asshole." He sat down at his desk, staring blankly over the Houston skyline. He wanted to tear the card up, but thought better of it. He looked again, this time studying the text that gave an address in League City. His thoughts intensified. *League City. A lawyer named Herm or Herman. Possibly has an office in League City.*

Bart reached for the intercom.

"Yes, Mr. Miles."

"Macy, ask Mr. Milsap to stop by my office."

Eleven

Thursday, January 7

Houston, Texas

H is name is Herman Soboda. He's a small-time lawyer in League City." Frank Milsap paused as a young waitress arrived at the table.

"Good afternoon, and welcome to Peregrine. I'm Ginna, with two *N*s." The pretty young lady smiled at her new customers. "May I offer you a cocktail?"

Frank gestured toward his partner. "Bart?"

"Belvedere on the rocks."

Frank added, "And I'll have an Old Parr on the rocks. Thanks, Ginna."

"Thank you. I'll be right back." She turned and walked toward the bar.

Frank continued quietly. He leaned forward, elbows on the table, right arm over left. "He won't be a problem. Either money or duress will take him out of the picture. No problem at all. But, of course, that's your business, not mine."

"You're right. It's not a problem. Once Soboda's gone, we'll have Fred Barrister work his way into the company. Duquette is gullible and won't be a problem. I'll have Fred delay their patent until we have our own. Once we have the plans, he can move it through the system." Bart looked toward the bar. He wanted his drink. "The patent will be ours in three months."

Frank's lips tightened. "Aren't you bringing a lot of people in on this? I'm not sure we should be expanding it." He waited for a benign answer.

Bart was on edge. "Damn it, Frank. Don't you get it? If we're successful, this thing will be worth billions. On the other hand, if this guy pulls it off and Wellington is shut out, we don't get squat. That's not going to happen."

Frank mistrusted Bart, but did not fear him. "Well, here comes an eye opener for you. Why not pay him some decent money? Three, maybe four million will give it to us with no hassles and no legal issues."

"You're dead wrong." Bart tapped his finger on the table. "I've learned that–"

The waitress appeared out of thin air. She placed the drinks in front of each man and a bowl of assorted nuts in the center of the table. "Shall I run a tab?"

Bart answered quickly. "Yeah."

Frank added, "Thank you, Ginna."

Bart swallowed a third of his drink immediately.

They returned to the discussion. Bart said, "This guy has no intention of budging for less than tens of millions. Hell, you heard him yourself."

"Quiet down some. Or invite everyone in here to our table." Frank took a large swallow of his own.

Bart continued. "Since he won't show us the plans, I'll have Aguirre either steal one of the prototypes so we can break it down, or have him spend several nights taking it apart and putting it back together."

Frank signaled Ginna, holding two fingers in the air. She waved and headed back to the bar.

Frank acquiesced with some admonition. "All right, but here's what I don't like. For the first time since we've had, shall I say, projects of our own, you don't seem one bit organized." He bit his lower lip slightly, ala a pensive Bill Clinton. "And, if we go the whole way, I don't feel like giving the profits to Wellington. There damn well better be a mechanism where we pocket the bulk of the profits."

Bart's eyes lifted toward Frank. "I've given it great thought. You and I are about to be pretty good conceptual design wizards. With the help of a mechanical draftsman, our basic concept—which we'll get from their design—will be turned into a fortune, owned by us as individuals, and provided to Wellington for a huge percentage of the profit. You're also the finance wizard. I handle the device and you show us the money. We walk out as billionaires, the company stays solvent, and everyone—except what's-his-name—ends up happy as a pig in shit."

Three more rounds of drinks and two bowls of nuts disappeared as a specific strategy emerged.

Frank left first, headed to a formal dinner party that he did not wish to attend.

Bart called Ginna over. She walked to his table, smiling all the way. "Yes, sir. Are you ready for the check?"

"No. Let me see your menu."

Don was curious. "What's your take on this guy?"

Elam answered quickly. "He'll work out fine. Name's Carlos something. He's eager to work. Sharp, articulate, confident but not too cocky. Said he met Juan several weeks ago playing pool and heard good things about us."

Don, unconvinced, asked, "What's he know about stripper wells?"

"Enough. Has some background as a roustabout and was a car mechanic. I think he's just what we need."

"OK. Let's start him at fourteen bucks an hour and see how he works out."

"Gotcha. You coming out to the site tomorrow?"

"Won't be able to. Tom and I need to finish up the redesign. I'll try to get out there by Monday."

They hung up, satisfied that they were still making progress. Susie walked out onto the patio just as Don pushed the end button to his cell phone.

"How'd you make out?"

Don looked up at his sister-in-law. "Great. Just hired a new kid to replace the one we lost."

Fred called Bart on schedule—right in the middle of Bart's meal. Their conversation played out between bites and completely on a one-way street. Bart Miles did the driving.

"Once Soboda's gone I'll let you know. You immediately call Duquette and take over."

Fred Barrister answered, "No problem. I'll make it happen." He pondered his five-year association with Bart Miles. His first crossing of the line netted him $22,000. All he had to do was provide some purloined bidding documents to Bart. What Fred failed to understand was that he had the talent to make excellent money through sheer competence and initiative. He never needed Bart Miles.

Fred continued the conversation. "Right. Once on board I'll slow down the process."

"Keep me posted on any information he spits out. The guy

talks a lot and will tell you anything you want to know." Bart stabbed a scallop and a few green beans and stuffed them in his mouth. He pointed the fork at an empty seat while toning down his volume. "I know exactly how this is going to turn out. So do you, if you handle it right. When it's done, and you're one big fucking part of it, your payoff goes from thirty thousand to at least a hundred thousand. If it goes really well, I might just quadruple the tab."

Fred sucked in a deep breath and looked up to his gods while thinking of his good fortune. *It can't get any better,* he thought.

Twelve

Monday, January 11

League City, Texas

Herman Soboda clamped the Galveston County Daily News between his arm and side. Small wisps of steam escaped through the air hole of his coffee cup. He entered a modest house on Waco Avenue; chipped white paint signaled a time of better days. His private office was an enigma. Hundreds of legal texts, perfectly arranged alphabetically by topic, lined the front edge of each row of a wall-to-wall bookshelf in military precision. The rest of the office was roughage. Manila folders, all stuffed haphazardly with papers of all sizes and descriptions, lay on his desk, both visitor chairs, and the top of filing cabinets. Two weeks' worth of newspapers lay next to the metallic trashcan. He set his coffee and paper on the desktop and pulled out his worn cotton-weave swivel chair. Looking down, he noticed an envelope on the seat with *Herman Soboda* typed in black ink. Herman's recollection was that he had gone home after his secretary, but since the days passed in a blur, she probably left after him and put it there as a reminder of some sort. He picked it up, sat down in his chair, and opened the letter. He took one sip before unfolding the paper. He started to read . . .

You will do as instructed. If you don't . . .

A consuming chill coursed through his body. That it might be a practical joke didn't enter his mind. He closed the letter but could not put it down; he opened it and read it a second time. The same threatening words spoke to him. He folded the letter and put it in the envelope. He unbuttoned the middle two buttons on his shirt and stuffed the envelope between his undershirt and white dress shirt. His hands trembled.

A small bell rang signaling the arrival of Lucy Mays, his secretary. Following her daily ritual, she stuck her head inside the door.

"And a good day to you, Mister Soboda." She smiled and expected a smile in return. What she saw was ashen. "Mister Soboda, are you all right?"

Herman Soboda looked up at Lucy with a pitiful, lost expression. He continued to shake. "I . . . I . . . I'm not feeling so well." He wanted to reach for his cup but knew he wouldn't be able to keep from spilling it. "I think I'll . . . uh . . . I'll go home." He regrouped slightly. "I'll try to come back later today. Please cancel my morning appointments." As it was, he had no morning appointments.

Herman walked out of the door and straight to his car. He fumbled with his keys. At Main Street he turned left, driving away from his home. He needed to drive and to think.

Outside of Luling some two hundred yards north of County Road 132, a group of men worked on an abandoned stripper well.

"I got it. Hold it for now." Carlos grabbed the lower end of steel tubing. He moved it to within a couple of inches of the previous tube that stood five feet out of the stripper well casing at one end and over twenty feet inside the well, where it was secured to another down-hole section of tubing.

He yelled again. "OK, lower her slowly."

The operator engaged the clutch just enough to lower the new section through the center of a mobile derrick and onto the previous section. Carlos signaled the operator. "Hold it." He instructed the roustabout to join him. "Ready to go, Ricardo. Do it."

The roustabout wrapped cloth around the bottom of the steel tube and carefully secured it with a pipe wrench. Eight turns with the wrench and the new section of product line was in place. A second tube, adjacent to the first, was attached in the same manner. The two tubes were gently lowered into the ground. The process was ready to be repeated.

Elam turned to Don. "The new worker is good. Only been there a couple of days and somehow he's taken charge and getting things done."

Don agreed. "Yeah, I like his attitude, and his time on the learning curve was short. He definitely didn't take long to establish his place in the group. But let's see how he is in July and August."

"Don't even worry about the summer." Elam's eyes twinkled. "By August we'll be so rich it'll make your head spin." He laughed out loud.

Don asked, "What about Tom's modifications? How much longer will that take?"

"Not too long. I use the guys in Odessa; they'll let us fall behind a little in the payments. They'll get a finished product to us in a few weeks. Matter of fact, I'll be telling interested parties that we are already working on generation two and that they will be given rights to the new one without a raise in the price. They already know that you will be calling them to work out the details." Elam smiled.

Don answered, "Good. The sooner, the better. We need to turn the corner before we go broke." He leaned against the side of Elam's car, his energy already sapped.

A very upbeat Elam responded, "Don, I've been down this road before. What we have is the ultimate winner in the oil business. We are going to be very rich sons of bitches.

"By the way, I had a heart-to-heart with Wellington Oil. Arrogant assholes, but I got 'em interested in the JETS to the point they were slobbering all over each other." He brushed dirt from his chin and mouth.

Elam's comment irritated Don. "Damn it, you didn't tell me you were going there. That pisses me off." His eyebrows furrowed, partly covering his eyes. "Shit."

"It was a spur-of-the-moment deal. I was in Houston and just happened to drive by. When I told them who I was, they dropped everything to meet with me. It's a cat and mouse game—and we're the cat." Elam broke into a large grin. "Yeah, we're the hungry cats and they're hungry mice. But, hungry or not, they're just mice."

Elam wiped his forehead with a dirty handkerchief and turned his attention to the work party. He yelled at the workers while giving them a thumbs-up. "Great job. Keep it moving today and you'll earn a twenty-dollar bonus."

Most of the men waved in unison. All but one relished the thought of extra cash. Carlos smiled while thinking to himself, *Twenty bucks? How about twenty thousand for me and jack shit for you?*

Don asked, "Are we going to be ready for next week?"

Elam smiled and patted Don on the back. "You bet. Some Pakistanis. My guess is that they've got money out the gazoo. Don't trust 'em one damn bit. They think they're onto a couple of country bumpkins. And that's good."

Don commented, "I don't trust anybody until we're patented."

Herman Soboda drove aimlessly through the streets of League City and then onto the Gulf Freeway toward Galveston. Over time the trembling subsided, the pounding in his chest abated, and his thoughts became more inquisitive than fearful. *Who did this? What have I done? Who can I go to? When do I call the police?* A touch of bravado entered into his mind. *I'll sue the sorry son of a bitch.* Herman decided to go home and settle down. He needed time to sort through clients to find one with the reason and the balls to threaten him.

Herman's two-story federal house on East Walker Street belied the income of a lower-level attorney. A few very successful cases and the housing market slump of the eighties allowed him such a luxury. A circular driveway flanked by live oaks on both sides led to a small, round portico with stairs ascending to the large, mahogany front door; in turn, the door was centered between four large, black, shuttered windows. Five similar windows spread across the second floor; three dormers protruded from the roof and a chimney sat at each side of the house. The only thing missing from the picture was a pretty, obedient wife. Herman's wife left two years earlier with a real estate developer. Still, he had a black Lab who was loyal to a fault. Herman walked through the unlocked door to a spacious foyer and spiral staircase. He was home.

"Moose," he called to the dog. "Come here, boy. Moose!" The dog did not respond. Herman looked briefly into the spacious living room and the window where Moose normally stood guard. But Moose was absent from duty. The sense of fear re-entered his body. Herman entered the kitchen.

The sight paralyzed him. Moose lay prostrate on the kitchen table, his head hanging over the edge. Moose's tongue pointed listlessly downward and his eyes stared blankly at the floor. Herman recoiled at the sight, barely able to breathe. Panic took over. He looked closer, this time able to see the cause of death. Moose had been disemboweled—not a drop of blood disturbed the table. Four dead tropical fish, arranged in a line between Moose's front and back legs, completed the macabre scene. Herman backed away from the table and half-staggered back to the front door. At the front of his car, he threw up bile and what little remained of bagel and cream cheese. He did not see the envelope resting beneath Moose's head. Inside the envelope were a set of instructions and a stack of fifty crisp hundred-dollar bills.

Thirteen

Tuesday, January 12

Houston, Texas

All rise. The 357th Judicial District Court, South District of Texas, Houston Division, is now in session. The Honorable Lewis L. Pickering presiding." The bailiff began another day of court.

Outside the courtroom, Tom and Don sat on a small wooden deacon's bench. Don decided to go with Tom and watch him testify in a case in which a young woman had been killed and her boyfriend severely disfigured in a service station fire. Don absentmindedly spun his cane like a top, catching it as best he could in response to its unbalanced weight distribution. Tom meticulously sorted through a stack of 3x5 cards. Each card had a title heading and several bullet points that he would study until called to testify. He seldom lost a fact or a linkage between events related to a case.

Just before 10:00 a.m. the courtroom doors opened and people moved in three directions: the women's room, the men's room, and the coffee kiosk in the hallway. Ed Harvey, lawyer for the plaintiff, walked to Tom and Don.

"Tom, you're up as soon as we return from recess." Ed, a smallish man with Alan Ladd's good looks, turned to Don, hand extended. "Hey, Don. Long time. How've you been?"

"Good, Ed. Guess it's been since the Barry Colter ordeal." He shook Ed's hand.

"Yeah. Well, this one won't have the same intrigue. Gruesome, though."

Tom added, "I'm ready."

Ten minutes later Tom was called to the stand; Don followed him into the courtroom and sat down in the back row. Approaching the bailiff, Tom nodded politely to the jury and Judge Pickering. He stopped at the witness stand and was sworn in. Tom sat down, looking quite comfortable. Ed walked directly to his witness. They began.

"Mr. Seiler, I'd like to ask you to introduce yourself to the court. Please begin by giving your complete name and tell them where you live."

"Fine. Thomas Mannan Seiler. I live in Grimes County north of Houston, near Dacus, Texas. No streetlights, just an S-turn in the road." As always, Tom surveyed the jury as he spoke. In addition to wanting to make eyeball-to-eyeball contact, he could sense the mood of the jury. Coming from all walks of life, juries had a natural bias to root for nice people. Tom came across nice. He never could understand why all lawyers and witnesses seemed lost on that fact. Assholes on the stand don't do well.

"And please tell us of your educational background, your career pattern, and what occupation you are engaged in at this time."

"Yes, sir. I grew up in San Antonio. Went to Northeast High School, now known as MacArthur. I went to the University of . . ."

His introduction seldom changed. He was born into a military family, enjoyed a close relationship with his parents and siblings, and suffered personal tragedy at the loss of a son in a boating accident and a brother in Vietnam. A bachelor's degree in mechanical engineering–magna cum laude–from the University of Texas and a master's degree from the University of Houston preceded thirty-two years as an on-the-board mechanical engineer at NASA. He finished by stating that he was a registered professional engineer in the state of Texas.

It didn't take long for Tom to establish himself as a forensic engineering expert.

"What, then, is the function of a whip hose?" Ed asked.

Tom shifted in his chair, looking directly at Ed. He spoke with authority. "If I could, sir, I'd like to explain the full gas-dispensing hose system."

Ed and Tom always orchestrated the ebb and flow of testimony prior to any court proceeding.

"Your honor, a full description would help the jury to understand the significance of Mr. Seiler's findings."

"Go ahead, Mr. Seiler."

Tom began. "Well, if everyone in here were to go to a gas station today, I would ask each of you to look at the fuel hose. You would use the dispensing mechanism which has a nozzle that fits into the gas tank and a handle which, when depressed, initiates gas, under pressure, to flow into the tank. Next would be a relatively long section of rubber hose through which the fuel passes. But . . .," Tom held up his hand as he continued, "slightly over three-quarters of the way up the hose there is a short mechanical device that virtually no one even knows exists."

Don enjoyed Tom's manner of teaching the jury.

Tom opened his right hand comfortably and used his thumb and middle finger to indicate a device four inches long. "It's about this long and it's known as a breakaway device."

Ed Harvey intervened. "Your Honor, I have here the breakaway device that was attached to the hose on the day of the incident. I request that it be entered into evidence as plaintiff exhibit 24." It was entered into evidence. Ed turned back to Tom. "Excuse me for a minute here, Mr. Seiler." He then turned to the jury. "Ladies and gentlemen of the jury, I will be asking Mr. Seiler to explain the breakaway device, but I do ask you to remember that the component that failed in this incident, and that is the key subject of this trial, is this, the whip hose." Ed held a small section of black hose at eye level for all to see, and added, "And not the breakaway device." He lifted the breakaway device to the same level. "We'll get to the whip hose shortly. That being said," he said and turned back to Tom, "Mr. Seiler, please continue by describing the purpose and construction of the breakaway device." He gave it to Tom.

Tom rotated the device in his hand. "It's made of a brass and aluminum alloy, with two sections attached together by an internal locking mechanism." Tom pointed to the interface between the two opposite, yet identical, sections. "In addition to being connected to each other, each section connects back to hose. The end of one section is crimped to the long hose going to the gas tank," Tom paused deliberately, then continued, "and the other section is crimped to that small section of hose Mr. Harvey described as the whip hose."

"Your Honor, I would like to introduce . . ." Ed Harvey entered the actual whip hose in question as exhibit 25. He did not give it to Tom, but asked him to continue with his discussion of the device.

Tom did as asked. "The actual purpose of the breakaway device is simple. On occasion, a customer becomes distracted and inadvertently drives away with the nozzle still stuck in the gas tank. This is known as a drive-away event." Darting eyes and a quick nod identified one of the jurors as a former drive-away culprit. Tom picked him out and gave an almost imperceptible nod of forgiveness. *Good, got one on my side,* he thought.

"When a drive-away event occurs, the breakaway device is designed to separate as the pulling force reaches approximately two hundred and fifty pounds." He pulled on the two ends of the device. "As you can see, I don't have the strength to pull them apart. But your cars do." He gave the device to Ed and sat back in his chair. "When it does separate, valves inside each section close instantaneously to keep gasoline from escaping. The driver . . ." Tom glanced back to his drive-away juror, "has a gasoline hose trailing from his or her car, but everything else is safe. Life remains copasetic."

Ed asked. "And is that how the breakaway device functioned in this case?"

Tom replied, "No, sir. Some three to four months earlier, a drive-away event occurred in which the breakaway device malfunctioned. It just didn't separate, probably because the driver realized he still had the hose in his gas tank and stopped just as the whole system was being stressed. Because it didn't separate, major stresses had occurred at critical locations along the whip hose itself."

"Have you been able to analyze these stresses?"

"Yes, sir." Tom pointed to an easel upon which rested a computer generated model on a poster board.

Ed Harvey looked to Judge Pickering. "Your Honor, I would like to have Mr. Seiler explain his findings at the easel so the jury can understand it."

"Granted. Mr. Seiler, please step down."

Tom walked to the easel. He paused just enough to adjust his tie. Tom began carving out, in layman's terms, purely professional investigation and analysis.

"What we have here, ladies and gentlemen, are the results of a computer program called AutoCAD." Over the years Tom had learned not to get too technical on engineering software. He kept it simple. "In a nutshell, AutoCAD, which stands for Automated Computer Aided Design, takes a model of a physical object, applies appropriate forces in the form of mathematical formulations, and develops a model of where the object would experience areas of stress. What you see here," Tom pointed to the second of three graphic representations, "are color-coded stress concentrations. The colors in orange and red indicate the highest stress concentrations. Those are the areas which need the best structural integrity." Tom waited for about half a minute before continuing the briefing. He pointed to the bottom graphic. "What the computer program can also do is show how the object would deform under these stresses. Take a look at this." Tom showed the elongated whip hose and explained the relationships among stresses, deformation, and sound engineering practice. He directed the jury's attention back to the graphic display. "In this drawing you can see the stress concentrations quite easily. In particular, look at the colors where the whip hose is crimped into the metal annulus of the breakaway device." The entire length of the circular joint between hose and metal was bright orange—a clear indication of high stress. "This would thus be an area where not only the design needs to be correct, but where the actual physical application of the crimping mechanism can have no imperfections."

"Thank you, Mr. Seiler, you can return to the stand."

Tom returned to his seat and sat down. Ed entered the computer graphics into evidence and walked midway between the witness stand and the jury box.

"Ladies and gentlemen, this is the whip hose I just entered into evidence. Had it not failed in the manner in which it did, we would not be here today. Now that he has given an engineering overview of the whip hose, I am going to ask Mr. Seiler to explain exactly what happened—and why it should not have happened."

He walked back to Tom, giving him the whip hose.

"Before I ask you to explain the faults associated with the whip hose in question, please give us your understanding of the events leading up to the incident."

The jury, fully alert, looked forward to Tom's next chapter, gory as it might be.

"Certainly. Mr. Hanson comes to fill up his gas tank. He does absolutely nothing wrong. He puts his credit card in, gets authorized, and then pulls out the hose to begin filling the gas tank. Gasoline enters the hose as soon as he pulls the handle. As he approaches having a full tank, he does what most people do. He engages and disengages the handle numerous times. This constant start–stop of gasoline creates a series of pressure waves that are known as the water hammer effect. A good analogy might be a long train standing still that is hit by another train. Each car is rammed by the car behind it until the front car slams into the engine. In effect, a wave of banging cars moves from the back of the train to the front."

Don leaned back in his chair, musing on his brother's delivery. *How can anyone so damn smart be so clear in explaining these things?*

Tom stopped and turned toward Judge Pickering. "Your Honor, would it be permissible to move closer to the jury in order that they can see the whip hose and the manner in which things unfolded?"

Over the objection of the defense lawyer, Judge Pickering concurred. Tom moved to a place five feet in front of and centered on the jury rail. He continued.

"Unfortunately, the whip hose had already been damaged to the point that the water hammer effect caused the whip hose to separate from the end section of hose that goes back to the dispenser. As I mentioned, there had been a drive-away event three to four months earlier. The reason I know that is because of the damage to the hose." Tom held the hose horizontally in front of the jury. He ran his finger over one end of the hose. "At this end you can see what is known as necking. It's the area that is thinner than the rest of the hose." Tom walked to the left side of the jury and walked slowly in front of each juror. At such a close distance, the jury members could easily see the damaged section of hose. "It happened when the pulling force-stretched the hose beyond its elastic limit. Inside the hose are two helix wires, used for reinforcement and to counter static electricity. They were stretched so much that when the force was released, some permanent deformation remained. Over time spalling occurred, which is nothing more than the flaking off of parts of the damaged whip hose." Tom pulled the whip hose easily out of the connector. "This should not have happened. The hose should have been replaced long before the incident."

Not wishing to be too theatrical, Tom returned to the stand. Without hesitation, he finished his remarks.

"Mr. Hanson's girlfriend, Ms. Marion Culver, had a cigarette. When the whip hose separated from the breakaway device, gasoline spewed all over him and into the car. Tragically, there was a spark, either from the cigarette or from static electricity, which ignited the gas. Mr. Hanson inhaled gasoline and fell to the ground just as the inside was engulfed in flames. The flames traveled underneath and around the car. While people were able to drag him away and smother the flames, Ms. Culver was burned to death." Tom and Ed expected an objection but none was stated.

The more Tom spoke, the more impressed Don became. He had attended Tom's appearance on the stand for the legendary murder case out of Alvin and remembered Tom's skill at relating to the jury. Every answer, to Don's way of thinking, was dead on target.

Don suddenly remembered that Elam had called earlier. He knew it was important, so he quietly, at least as quiet as possible for him, got up and walked out of the back door of the courtroom.

By the time Don returned, Tom was finishing his testimony. Don surveyed the jury and could tell by their attention to Tom's testimony that he had scored well. One company assembled the whip hose incorrectly, and another company did a lousy job of inspecting the equipment. Tom stepped down from the witness stand and disappeared through the double doors of the courtroom. Don joined him on the way out.

"The hell you say." Tom was surprised at the turn of events. "Did he say why?"

"Nothing specific. I just talked to Elam about it. He said a secretary was calling all of the guy's clients, stating that he had medical problems and would not be able to continue with his job." Don reached to the floorboard of Tom's car, grabbed his ugly US Navy Seabee baseball cap, and feverishly molded the bill into an exaggerated semi-circle. Frustration was running roughshod. "I'm beginning to get a little pissed off about all this garbage."

Tom paid the parking toll, smiled at the attendant, and pulled onto San Jacinto Street for the ride home.

Don placed the hat on his head, leaned back, and proclaimed, "I'll be dammed if I'm going to let this slow me down. We've gone too far to kiss it off over some incompetent lawyer."

"Well, hell, let's find ourselves another one. I know lots of lawyers who can help us out."

Don spit out a sliver of fingernail he had just bitten off. "Elam said not to worry because he already has a line on a new lawyer."

"Any idea who the lawyer is?"

"Naw, I don't. But given Elam's last pick, I'm leery as hell about the new one."

"Why don't you just tell him to let me get the next lawyer?"

Don looked back at Tom. "I'll give the guy a few weeks. If he farts around like the last one, I'll can him myself and turn it over to you. I'm headed out to the site tomorrow afternoon and will tell Elam that I'm not putting up with another loser." Don spoke with resignation, changing the subject. "My intent was not to get you all wrapped up into this thing. I've already let you spend too damn much time helping me out. Don't even think about this little roadblock."

"OK, it's your call. Just let me know if and when you want me to make a couple of phone calls."

"I will. I've got to get back to California for a few days to pacify the twenty clients who are screaming their heads off." Don started to turn his attention to the road but remembered something. "By the way, you really snowed that jury with your wit and wisdom." He smiled at Tom.

Tom returned the smile. "Just remember that the graphical displays were the product of Paige's computer analysis of the whip hose. She's as smart an engineer as she is a pretty woman. Yessiree, I sure raised a smart one."

Indeed, his daughter was as smart as they come.

The fact was that Elam knew zilch about good patent lawyers.

Earlier that morning Elam was walking out of his house when his cell phone rang. He didn't recognize the person or the number and thought about ignoring it; he gave in to natural curiosity.

"Duquette," Elam answered brusquely.

"Mister Duquette, hope I didn't get you up." Fred Barrister, sitting in a booth at Skeeter's Eatery, looked absentmindedly out of the diner window. "I'm Fred Barrister. I practice patent law and am a close professional friend of your attorney, Herman Soboda. He mentioned some medical problems have caused him to retire and asked if I would consider working with a few of his more important clients. He said you were his most important."

Elam was not in the mood for second-grade discourse. "Yeah, most important. Whaddya want?"

Elam's acrid response surprised Barrister. He regrouped quickly. "Er, well, based on what he has told me, you have a very interesting product that needs to be patented." He waited for a response. It was a long time in coming.

"Tell you what. You meet me at City Market in Luling tomorrow for lunch at twelve thirty. We'll talk some, and if I think you're any good and won't raise the rates, we'll sign a deal on the spot. If I don't think you're so hot, you'll be the second to know."

Fred took his free hand from his head, switched hands with the phone, and grabbed a pencil. He smiled into the phone. Sort of like landing a fish. He doodled a note about time and location. "Great. I'll see you at noon."

"Twelve thirty."

"Right. See you at twelve thirty."

Fourteen

Wednesday Noon,
January 13

New York City

R aw, sleet-pocked rain sliced into Bart's face from scudding gray clouds into which building facades disappeared along East Twentieth Street. He pulled the collar of his overcoat as tight around his neck as possible, but not tight enough to keep cold droplets of water from seeping down his back. His attention drifted among the unrelenting chill, the squeegee sound of leather shoes in contact with ice water, and the ultimate finish line—the entrance to the Gramercy Tavern, still fifty feet away. City politicians call it the Big Apple, the financial center of the world, and every other title that might be bestowed upon New York City; they forget to call it cold and miserable in the winter. January through March is absolutely awful.

He entered through two sets of double doors, unbuttoned his coat for the waiting check girl, and smoothed back the unkempt hair straddling the sides of his head. He needed a drink. The warmth of the wood-burning oven buoyed his spirits. He glanced around, quite impressed with the arched entrances to individual rooms, gentle-yet-impressive pastel murals, brown draperies, and the soft lighting of candles and copper sconces.

"Well, hello, stranger. Looks like you could use a drink." Elizabeth Harker approached Bart with both hands outstretched. The perfectly symmetrical face. Her soft, dark brown hair fell perfectly onto her shoulders. A stunningly beautiful woman, Liz stood an inch taller than Bart. She leaned forward, turning her head to accept his perfunctory kiss.

Bart Miles kissed her on the cheek and quickly asked, "Liz, my dear, how can you stand this weather? Give me Texas or give me death."

En route to the maître d' Liz flicked her hair playfully. "Weather's bad at times, but what a city. Come with me, I have a favorite spot."

Light music played in the background while Liz and Bart traversed from catch-up pleasantries to the real business at hand. A Catena Zapata Malbec wine for Liz and Belvedere on the rocks for Bart. Liz ordered the portobello tart with goat cheese and Bart decided on the leg of lamb sandwich. By the time the second round of drinks arrived, the pleasantries had ended and Bart and Liz were locked into Don Seiler and an oil extraction device.

"How has it played out so far?" Liz asked as she took a bite of her mushroom and chased it with the wine.

Bart held up a finger and continued chewing. He swallowed, ran his tongue over his teeth, and then answered. "The first thing we did was to get one of our people on the inside. That project turned out to be rough around the edges, but he has their confidence now. He's already running the crew. It was a good choice." He reached for his drink.

"What do you mean 'rough around the edges'?"

Bart set the glass down and looked at Liz matter-of-factly. He needed to protect himself and parsed his words deliberately.

"Someone was taken out. All the way out. Our insider took it upon himself to go to extreme measures. Could have been dicey, but the situation is over. No problem. Let me continue."

Neither Bart nor Liz showed concern for the dead.

Over the next several minutes Bart described what had taken place: they removed a worker and replaced him with the inside contact; they forced the Donelam lawyer to retire and replaced him with a lawyer of Bart's choosing; and preparations to take full ownership of the extraction system were on schedule. All topics were addressed with enough specificity to ease any of Liz's concerns. The service at the Gramercy Tavern was superb to the point of distraction. Bart had to stop talking on several occasions as the well-dressed waitress saw to their every need. The water glasses, barely a sip taken, were removed and replaced with new ones. A second waiter cleared the china and silverware, and then scraped off virtually non-existent breadcrumbs. A new set of dessert silverware was placed in front of each diner with just-in-time perfection. Each round of drinks calmed their souls and whetted their appetites just enough for each to select the pumpkin-spice upside-down cake with cranberries and quince. Bart had a little extra dessert of his own to share with Liz.

He sliced into the cake, plucking a morsel from the plate and plopping it in his mouth. "This is superb. Now, where was I?" He looked down at the plate to find his next bite.

"You were starting to tell me about your return on investment." One should not talk with one's mouth full, but there are important exceptions to every rule.

"Yeah, right." He wiped his mouth, looked around to see who might be listening, then told her, "Liz." A short pause. "This could be billions."

Her eyes opened wide. "Billions? You've got to be kidding. Billions?"

"Billions. We just need the patent. We can lease individual units by the thousands for a flat fee, plus a percentage of revenues from each barrel of crude." He finished off his current drink. "Every time the price of oil is raised, more people will jump at this thing." He leaned forward as far as possible, his eyes twinkling like a kid in love. "We'll let Texaco, Shell, BP, and the others make their fortunes, but their per-capita payoff will pale to ours. The higher speculators and the fuckers in OPEC raise the price, the happier I'll be." He started to lean back, then recovered. "And, as you already know, I don't forget friends. Especially the one who laid this in my lap. We'll go offshore with the money and there will be a bank account for you. Liz, we've seen oil go from thirty dollars a barrel to one hundred and fifty. It's back down some right now, but over the long haul it will keep going up." Bart smiled at the cake. It smiled back.

Liz looked flush. She had no idea what a small touch of revenge could bring her. She pictured Tom Seiler. *Suck it down, you son of a bitch.*

She took a large, controlled breath. "Have you had any contact with either of the Seiler brothers?"

"No, none. I deal with the front guy. He's an overbearing loudmouth who's pretty smart in some ways and dumb as a board in others. His problem is that his bluster clouds his common sense. That's good for us. As for Seiler, he's strictly on the design side of their enterprise."

Bart changed the subject, more out of curiosity than anything else. "That guy Seiler has stuck in your craw since the Barry Colter incident. This is more personal than anything else, isn't it?"

Liz hardened like steel, carefully measuring her words. "You're damn right. He stuck his nose into Barry's lawsuit and drove Barry insane." She swallowed another slug of her wine. "You remember the Vioxx verdict? It was for 253 million dollars for the wife of a guy who already had heart disease. Barry's case was for the same amount. It's also the amount given to some New York Yankee baseball player. Go figure. But, more to the point, Barry actually had grounds for such a suit. He went after the trucking industry. He wanted to make a major statement before tort reform in Texas would screw every trial lawyer in the state. Seiler destroyed him." Liz stared cold daggers into Bart's eyes. "And I was nothing more than fucking collateral damage."

Bart remembered rumors much differently than what was being said. He let it go.

She continued. "I'd like to see the bastard dead." Holding the stem between thumb and forefinger she tipped the bottom of the glass from one side to the other, watching the small amount of remaining liquid slosh back and forth. Her eyes burned holes in the table. "But that would be too simple. This is only the first step. His sister lives in San Antonio; she's next on the list. I've got someone digging into her history right now. Daughter, son, grandkids, they're going to pay for the unadulterated shit Tom Seiler put me through."

Bart realized he had bitten off far more than he cared to chew. He changed the subject back. "Well, all I can say is that you'll end up with an unexpected windfall that will make you very rich and very happy."

A final round of drinks and thoughts of her financial gain to be taken from the Seiler family mellowed Liz's mood. She had cleared her schedule for the remainder of the day. She found Bart Miles very unattractive, particularly compared to Barry Colter. But her emotional state had flip-flopped. As a matter of fact, she was having a wonderful time.

She looked at Bart and thought, *Oh, what the hell?*

"Bart, my hotel's five blocks from here."

Fifteen

Wednesday, January 27

Luling, Texas

Don should not have been driving at all, but Tom was testifying and Don was, well, Don. His physical book read: failing eyesight, barely able to walk, slow reaction time. His mental attitude read: forget the physical book. He drove north out of Luling on State Road 80. A minute later the sweet and sour odor of the oil fields filled his nostrils. He could still smell. He took a right on County Road 132; it was all downhill from there. The asphalt transitioned into a disheveled dirt road along which people had ignored the *No Dumping* sign for years. Without human intervention the cactus and grassland would have been beautiful. But, save a few palm trees planted by the 86 Oil Company, the place was a mess. He passed an old, corrugated metal building on his left; a barbed wire fence, some rusted oil tanks, a hodge-podge of steel framing members, and several pumpjacks cluttered the landscape to his right. Further down the road a ragtag home and a worn-out trailer in the front yard accentuated the abject lack of scenery. The broken windows and the holes in the roof had not shaken a family from the home. A horse, looking as old as the buildings, lifted his head momentarily and then returned to his meal of grass and dust. A second dirt road with rain-filled ruts cut due north into a field of stripper wells–some dead and some barely alive. A single pumpjack was raising and lowering its head, attempting to get at the small pockets of oil remaining in the ground. It groaned like a rusted ship at its final mooring place. Don drove by the pumpjack and a couple of rusted sheds before turning into a fenced area that had been cleared–the JETS testing site. Don glanced at his watch. Four o'clock. To his front he could see Elam in the middle of a small pod of men at the well site; Elam was ranting and raving at something. One look at Elam and the crew signaled a bad day. Don hobbled toward the derrick. Elam looked over toward Don and raised his hands in a "I don't know what the hell is going on" pose. Then Don saw the knotted, crushed metal tubing being pulled from the well hole.

Elam, walking slowly toward Don, growled out, "Same shit as before." He shook his head in dismay, adding, "I just hope you and Tom can get the new design here soon. This just won't fly and I've blown too much smoke at people.

"Old man Pearson is bitching that we're not pumping enough oil and that we're cheating him." Elam lamented about the site owner who bargained for royalties of $10.00 a barrel or $1,000 a month for three years, whichever was higher. The breakdowns were putting Donelam Oil Systems in the hole. "The damn thing breaks every other day. He's pissed and I'm pissed. This is taking too damn long. How soon we gonna get it?"

"I talked to Odessa a couple of hours ago. If I can get the revisions from Tom this week, we'll have it by early to mid-March."

Elam shook his head slowly back and forth. "March? Don, we don't have the time."

Don ignored Elam's comment. He switched his cane temporarily to the left side. "We ought to just hold off until then. I don't know why you keep spending our money on this." He pointed at the failed tubing being lifted from the well casing. "The new design will be easier, stronger, more efficient, and everything else. I'm telling you straight up, it's going to work." He switched the cane back and started walking slowly toward the derrick.

"Because I've got a new group of people coming out tomorrow," Elam shot back. "We don't have enough money not to be showing this around. And besides, there are too damn many other people out there working on this idea. Money's money." Elam cleared his throat and spit on the ground. "When they see this working and I tell them what they will eventually get is much better than this, I'll have 'em in the palm of my hand."

Don's leg bothered him. "Let's go sit down on some chairs."

Elam yelled to the crew. "Keep pulling. We need to have it in place by noon tomorrow."

Carlos gave a wave of the hand and turned to the others. "Let's get after it. We gettin' paid good, let's do it good this time."

Elam walked to the shed and returned with two gray metal chairs. He opened them and placed them on the ground in the sunlight.

Don sat down and rubbed the worst of two bad legs. "You know, I once was the toughest, fastest son of a bitch on a football field you ever saw. I'm still the only player in Texas to run for more than twenty touchdowns and intercept ten passes in a single season." He shook his head in disgust. "And here I can't even walk. Damn."

"Yeah. It sucks. But at least you're not sitting on your ass. You struggle, fight your fucking disease every day, but you're still on the playing field giving it everything you got. I'm not going to patronize you, but you do more than anybody I know. California, Texas, working on this thing when you could be watching television on a couch." Elam leaned forward, hands on his knees. He looked expectantly at Don and added, "I'll tell you what. If I have to carry you around on my back, I'd still rather work with you than anyone else I have ever known. So don't even think about that TV shit."

"Naw. I'm not quitting anything. It's just damn hard not feeling sorry for myself." He sucked in and exhaled deeply. "OK. Thanks for the pep talk. What about the new lawyer? It's been two weeks already."

Elam's nonverbal expression retreated into a clear message of doubt. "I talked to him yesterday. He's had a hard time cranking everything up. He had to take over several of Soboda's clients. Told me the files were a mess but that he has all he needs." Elam blinked his eyes in an attempt to counter dryness from wind and dust. "Said he'll go forward from the point that Soboda was, which wasn't too damn far."

"Well, he sure as hell better get going. I worry about not having a patent." Don added, "By the way, do we have to submit a new patent for our changes? I don't want to get further behind the power curve."

"I actually asked him about that when we talked. It's not a big deal. He's going to make some sort of addendum. You'll need to sign it with me."

"Well, tell him to get his ass in gear. This can't go on forever."

Don changed the subject. "I've got to head back to California in the morning. I'll be back once Odessa has started machining the new system. Is there anything you need from me?"

"Just the new JETS. If Tom's ideas pan out, I am going to turn this into a fortune. I guarantee it." A big toothy grin appeared beneath intense eyes and crooked nose.

"Duquette is putting pressure on me. Still, yesterday's discussion went well." Fred Barrister looked back and forth between Bart Miles and Frank Milsap. The Wellington Oil and Exploration conference table was so large it made him feel small. Nervousness, like small insects, crawled all over him. "He called again this morning and told me he wanted to see the entire file from Soboda, along with all actions I have taken."

"So what are you going to do?" asked Bart. "Because you sure as hell are going to do something."

Fred moved uncomfortably in his very comfortable chair. "Well, I plan to write up a letter that is nothing more than regurgitation of what has already been written, except that it now will have my signature on it." He remembered something that Elam had told him. "One thing that may help is that he told me a new model is being made. I told him that we could write an addendum if the changes are minor. I also told him that if the changes were major, we might have to submit a new patent. He told me that the changes were small but I think he's hedging."

Bart interrupted. "Yeah, he told us about an improved model. That's what we're interested in. How soon do they expect to have it and how long can you hold them off?"

"Based on what he was saying, it should be completed in three to four weeks. I can add several weeks to the timeline by making the argument that their tweaks to the system are considered major changes. Even with minor changes, I can slow the process down while making them think we are moving along." Fred ran his tongue around the outside of his teeth as though cleaning them, a maneuver often made when thinking on his feet. A small grin grew. "One other thing that might make it much easier for us is the concept of being the 'first to invent'."

Fred gave a short class on the significance of being the first to invent a device and its priority over being the first to file a patent. He argued that if the changes being made by Don and Elam could be construed as a new design, and then if Wellington Oil submits plans of basically the same new device, they could claim that Wellington was actually the first to invent the new device. "It all boils down to us being able to obtain either the plans or a prototype of the new design, making a few small modifications, and submitting it first." He grinned wider. "I can get it done easily."

Bart broke in, "I don't want others getting involved. Understood?"

"No problem. I can get the help without anyone knowing what is going on." Fred felt confident. Cocky was more like it.

Frank asked, "If you're the lawyer, why don't you have the plans of the new device already? I mean, how in the hell can someone work with a patent lawyer on a product and not disclose the specific design?"

"I don't know. But legally, he doesn't have to submit the new design until they are ready to. My guess is that they are still working on it. Duquette said he'd give me some details soon, but not everything. Just enough to keep the patent going." The smile widened again. It was huge. Fred Barrister was rocking and rolling. "If they build the prototype, which is exactly what I think they are doing, and if we can have access to it long enough to make our own set of plans, we'll have a better chance of submitting first while steering clear of legal issues." *I just nailed it,* he thought. *I am one smart SOB.*

Bart wrote a couple of notes on a pad of paper, circled a few words, and then looked back at Fred Barrister. "You need to find out what is going on with the plans and the prototype. I can take care of obtaining any prototype and getting our own plans from it."

"I can do it."

"Fine. Frank, any questions?"

"Nope. Seems everything's going well."

Bart spoke dismissively to Fred. "I don't care about whatever else you have going on. This is where your effort will be. I want to see you here once a week. Schedule it with my secretary. That's all." Bart got up and headed for the executive restroom. No handshake. No acknowledgement. His only comment being, "Frank, hang on for a minute."

Once Fred Barrister departed, Bart and Frank analyzed where they were with obtaining the JETS. Bart sat at the head of the table, Frank occupying a seat two chairs away.

"Once he has this new prototype out in Luling or wherever, we'll have Carlos steal it over a weekend. We analyze it, make and submit our own designs for a patent, and, while Barrister sandbags their efforts, walk off with billions."

Frank played devil's advocate. "I still see a lot of 'ifs' in this whole thing. Don't underestimate Duquette. We need to plan this very carefully. Can you really do it?"

Bart shrugged and rebutted Frank's concerns. "This device belongs to us. Period. If they can, OPEC and all the other greedy bastards will eventually move the price to two hundred dollars a barrel. China and India keep increasing the demand and that's not going to change. Hell, the Americans just don't understand, but their days of buck-fifty gas are gone forever. The big oil companies are raking in money by the billion-dollar basket load. As for the United States, all this crap about alternate energy will get bogged down in governmental incompetence. We'll be dead before oil is no longer at the top of the chain." Bart had a hard time sitting still, the anticipation of untold wealth filling him with glee. "And Frank, my good man, it's our turn. We're going to dip into the pot for personal fortunes that may even be too big for your greedy ass." His eyes lit up like a Christmas tree.

Frank softened at Bart's absolute conviction of success.

Bart started to chuckle. "Yes indeed, Frank. We're going to steal this thing right from under their eyes. Can you imagine what they're going to think when we roll our own version off the assembly line? 'Duh, what the hell happened to us?'" Bart laughed and Frank followed. Bart had to stand up. He went to the window and looked down on the people of Houston, scurrying from place to place in search of lofty, mostly unobtainable dreams. He could not take the grin from his face. He turned around, slamming his right fist into his left hand, and smiled at Frank. "This is so damn much fun. All I have to do now is to make sure my sleazebag ex-wife doesn't get one penny of it."

They laughed again.

Sixteen

Saturday, January 30

Broken Wing Ranch

Ensconced in front of his computer, Tom finished the JETS redesign just before his self-imposed deadline of eleven o'clock on the third night. He summed up his evening fairly accurately—*Not the way to spend a Saturday night.* Redesigning the wellhead section had been easy; the down-hole well chamber had not. He placed the AutoCAD drawings of his work on the large drafting table and studied his work. To save some time, Tom would pass the AutoCAD drawings on to Paige and she would run an analysis of the strength of Tom's system.

The different mechanical parts of the system were detailed in sharp lines of differing colors. Top, side, and offset views would be complicated to the average person. To a machinist the drawings would be a simple recipe. Satisfied, Tom reasoned that his modifications would result in a system that was robust, able to get knocked around in the hole, and capable of moving oil at a rate up to thirty barrels an hour. Realistically, a thirty-barrel-per-hour stripper well would be nearly impossible to find. He played around with some figures. The new system would most likely operate much more than eight hours a day, and the price of oil would never be at forty dollars a barrel again. Finally deciding upon a minimal amount of three barrels an hour for at least sixteen hours a day at a conservative price of eighty dollars a barrel, Tom multiplied the numbers on a pad of paper. They totaled $3840 a day. Deep in the recesses of his mind, the global effect of the JETS became real. He inhaled and blew out a huge breath.

The phone rang. Great timing.

"Tom Seiler."

Don said, "Hey, compadre. I'm just checking out how you're doing. How're you doing?"

Doodling circles on the paper, Tom replied, "Good time to call. I've got a question."

"Fire away."

"Assuming that my changes in your design leave us with a robust system, would a production run last sixteen hours a day?" Tom changed his doodle circles to horizontal lines beneath his mathematical calculations.

Don sensed Tom was looking at the payoff to a solid system. "At a minimum."

Tom concluded the questioning. "How about an average of three barrels an hour and eighty dollars a barrel as the price?"

"You're probably low on all estimates. I predict the 'up' time, the product flow, and the cost will be more once we get the final system in operation." Don gave a thumbs-up to Cindy then asked Tom, "Can you FedEx the plans to me? I'd like to see them and then send them to Permian Machining in Odessa."

"I'll fax the small drawings right away and send the large ones tomorrow. I'll also attach them to an e-mail. If they look good to you, I'll send final hard copies to you and Permian.

If there are any problems we can solve it by tomorrow with little time lost. Paige will have run an analysis of its strength by then." Tom added, "I'm also sending you a marketing drawing for Joe Blow. I won't send that to Permian."

Don, pleased with the progress, replied, "OK, sounds good. Gene Starrett at Permian gave me an estimate of a little more than two weeks to complete the prototype. We should have something by mid-February. I'll come back to Texas for a couple of days so we can oversee what's going on. Send it tonight and I'll get back to you tonight."

Tom added, "With two hours' difference in time, I'm not going to answer any more phone calls. After I fax and e-mail you, I'm going to bed."

"Right. I'll get back to you tomorrow."

They hung up. Tom took fifteen minutes to package the drawings and send out his e-mail message. He attached the drawing files to his e-mail message and inserted actual drawings into the holding rack on his fax machine. The first drawing in the buffer was the conceptual design for marketing purposes; the others had all the technical details. Tom sent everything to Don.

The next morning Tom checked his e-mail before heading into Houston. The subject heading for the third message in the queue read:

Don't open this e-mail—plans are perfect—send them out

Seventeen

Monday Afternoon, February 1

San Antonio, Texas

Vic Bolton—at least, that was his name while in Texas—found the address and phone number via the Yahoo! browser. An hour later he pulled into the parking lot at the Red Tree Plaza in Windcrest on the northeast side of San Antonio. The small strip mall had seen better days. A beauty school had been taken over by Marshall's, and behind blank facades, numerous units were vacant. The Children's Medical Clinic, a Szechuan Chinese restaurant, a branch of the Gibraltar Bank, a check-cashing facility, and an insurance company still managed to scrape by . . . along with a small income tax company: Gardner Tax Consulting. Vic waited about five minutes until a sixtyish woman walked out of the office door with *Taxes Need Not Be Taxing* stenciled in coral-blue letters. Vic quickly exited the car and caught her just as she started to open the car door.

"Excuse me, ma'am." He spoke pleasantly.

The woman turned around, clearly nervous and untrusting. He picked up on her nonverbal cues.

"I don't mean to startle you, but I noticed you just came out of the Gardner Tax Office." Vic smiled in an attempt to allay her fears. "I'm hunting for a tax consultant and I just wanted to know what you think about their services. I've lived in San Antonio a grand total of three weeks and need to find a good accountant."

The woman gave a quick sigh of relief and did a complete turn-around. Not only did she feel secure about answering Vic's question, she wanted to tell him the story of her life.

"Oh, they're the best. We always get back much more than we think we should. My husband and I use her for both our personal and our business taxes."

Vic asked, "You mentioned 'her.' Who is 'her'?"

"Nancy. Nancy Gardner. She owns the business. Actually, I think it's only her and a secretary. We heard about her from a friend and let me tell you . . ."

It took ten minutes for Vic to disengage from Elvina Ackerman and her life history. He finally succeeded and, in the process, ascertained that Nancy Gardner was not your average tax consultant. She was good–really good. So good, in fact, that she might be a little bit of a crook. At least he hoped so.

Vic spoke with four more customers. Their comments were identical. More money saved than they thought possible. *She might be a Robin Hood sort of crook,* thought Vic. *I think we have something here.*

Vic, new name and all, walked into the office just short of five o'clock.

Eighteen

Monday, February 15

En Route to Odessa, Texas

It's a virtual dogfight during high traffic hours at Dallas's DFW airport. Don struggled against a crowd either unaware of or oblivious to his disability; no one gave a shit. A twenty-year-old kid hit Don in the back, knocking him into the Skylink.

"Hey, stupid, use your brains." He lifted the cane quickly, then thought better of smacking the rude jerk. He wasn't sure whether he was glad or not that no one would assist him. He did know that he would have been offered help in days gone by.

The new Skylink monorail was far better than the sadistically designed Airtrans system that tortured passengers for decades. Don held on tightly to the vertical pole support as Skylink carried him from Terminal C to Terminal B, slowly shifting his attention to the misfit who had jostled him so rudely. A red, hooded sweatshirt hung loosely over his torso like a cover on a barbecue grill. The hood had been pulled over a black baseball cap straddling his head at an angle and sporting a white, stitched peace sign. Beneath the sweatshirt billowed puffs of faded blue-and-white boxer shorts. His jeans started far below the crack of his buttocks and ended in lumps on top of sandals. Don guessed the kid hadn't seen a bathtub since the day he was born. The scene became picture-perfect when Don focused his eyes on an olive drab knapsack with Chinese signs and a sketch of Chairman Mao. Don assessed the written words, arriving at the conclusion that it was a Chinese message reading *Screw America.* Don's thoughts ran rampant. *So this is the human condition. This pissant loser will profess, "Peace to the world, America is the great Satan," while giving homage to an asshole who murdered thirty-five million Chinese. The little shit is sucking everyone dry at the expense of the American taxpayer.*

So went another trip through the bowels of the DFW Airport.

American Eagle flight 3479 from Dallas touched down at the Midland International Airport, located between Midland and Odessa, on time at 1:05 p.m., an hour after Tom landed in the Grumman Tiger. Don had been up since one o'clock in the morning California time. Tom greeted Don at the walkway exit. They shook hands and turned toward the main terminal area.

Don solved the logistics. "I didn't bring any suitcases. Just the carry-on."

Tom replied, "You're the man, mi amigo. I rented the car and we're ready to go. We'll grab something at Whataburger on the way."

Some one hundred thousand people live in Odessa. Spread out across a small plot of the west Texas Permian Basin, Odessa is known for oil and the high school football team, the latter being the more significant of the two. The book *Friday Night Lights,* depicting the 1988 football team, was a national bestseller and basis for the popular movie and television show of the same name. To this day, residents lament "what if" concerning its loss to Dallas Carter High School. It was irrelevant that Odessa Permian won the state championship the following year and five other times as well. "What if," they always ask, "the Dallas Carter principal hadn't changed the grade of one of their players?" Enough complaining.

Permian Machining occupied two acres of prime Odessa real estate–almost no grass and flat as a table. What was once a small service station had grown into a mammoth-sized, steel-frame building. In an open-bay fabrication section, huge plates of steel lay on tables and specially fabricated steel structures awaited delivery to all parts of Texas. Adjacent to the steel fabrication section was the office complex, housing administrative functions in one building and the mechanical fabrication facility in a second building. Gene Starrett, owner of Permian Machining, greeted them on the front steps of the mechanical fabrication building. A large, broad-chested native and former high school football star at Odessa Permian, Gene had walked onto the University of Texas football team. A total of two plays in two years signaled that he would not be an All-American; he left college and worked as a roustabout in the Rodessa oil field for eight years before realizing that his future lay in steel forming and mechanical systems fabrication. "Welcome back. How about a Coke or some water?"

"No thanks. We just downed a couple of double-meat Whataburgers and Cokes."

Gene nodded his head in agreement. "Then let's get down to some business. I think you'll like what we've done."

The three made small talk as they slowly walked past numerous numerically controlled machining systems to a bay at the back end of the work area. With a "this machine does this" and "that machine does that," Gene gave a guided tour of some of the newer equipment. There was no question that business was good in spite of some economic hard times.

"Here we go." Gene led the other two into a small bay. "I had the guys pull out the insides so you could see how we're doing with each part."

Components of the JETS chamber section lay on top of a forty-foot steel table. In order came the mud anchor, the seepage screen, two seal rings, a seating nipple, ball seat, the ball valve, and a section of the jet barrel. It was an impressive sight to Tom and Don. To Don it was also going to be expensive.

Don walked slowly up and down the table, inspecting each component of the system. Gene walked along with him. Don turned to Gene. "Have you completely assembled it yet?"

"No, not yet. We fit some sections together and the tolerances are right on target. We still have to polish some of the parts, and the seating nipple needs more work. Also, as you can see, we haven't even started the wellhead assembly yet. Give me another three weeks and we'll have everything ready for shipment. Same site in Luling?"

Don answered, "Right. All I need is one day's notice and we'll be ready for it."

"Good. I'll give you a call when we're ready to ship. Given four hundred miles, the driver should be there late in the afternoon. I'm assuming you can offload it."

"No problem at all. We'll have it in the ground the next morning."

Both Tom and Don inspected each part. They asked questions to which Gene gave candid answers. The brothers were satisfied that the redesign of the JETS was proceeding on time and that the system would work as intended. They accepted a second invitation for Cokes and joined Gene in his office to discuss financing. Don's lack of venture capital trapped him in a never-ending carnival shell game. The continual flow of money from his pockets, the home equity loan he and Cindy had taken to keep the project going, and his frustration at not having a confirmed patent of the JETS were ganging up on him. Both Tom and Gene sensed Don's changing emotions as the discussion continued. But Don was determined to see it through.

"All right. We've agreed on $53,000 for the first one, $34,000 for the second, and $22,000 for the display system. I can cover the first but I'll need you to help finance the rest."

Gene responded softly, "No problem. And forget the banks. I'll finance it through the business." He offered Don a finance charge that was more than fair and the deal was sealed. In effect, Donelam would receive three systems for a little more than one hundred thousand dollars. The display pieces would be painted for free. It was a bargain.

The business meeting concluded and Tom and Don were free to go. They were back at the airport by four in the afternoon and airborne in Tom's Grumman Tiger five minutes later, headed for Conroe. Don spent the night and returned to California the next morning.

Nineteen

Friday, March 19

San Antonio, Texas

Nancy Gardner finished packing and placed her suitcase on the kitchen floor. Her daughter Sally waited patiently in front of the television. Granddaughter Erin roughhoused with the family dog. Ludovic was a strong mixed breed, capable of taking one's hand off if he wasn't happy. So far, he was always happy.

"All right ladies, we're off to downtown Dacus. Sally, help me load the trunk."

Sally leaned forward in her couch cushion, staring at the television. "Mom, come here first. Check this out." Sally, an air controller from San Antonio, was a meteorology buff. She turned the sound up. On the screen, Ian Willingham was a few seconds into a weather update.

"You're right, Beth, we have potential problems brewing for tomorrow across much of the state." On a map of the United States a red, cucumber-shaped outline bisected the country. His effervescent smile was replaced by a slightly serious stare.

He pointed to the northern-most edge of red. Sweeping his arm downward from the top of the map, he spoke of trouble. "We're looking at a large mass of unseasonably cold Canadian air pushing through the Northern Plains. Unfortunately, it has already spawned numerous tornadoes, one causing three fatalities near Langdon, North Dakota." He pointed to a spot near the US–Canada border. Then, looking directly into the camera, he added, "Much of Texas will have problems along this boundary of dry air out of Mexico and the extremely moist air from the Gulf. Our best models are showing a dryline extending south to north across Texas, through Oklahoma and into the lower Midwest. The models show extremely severe weather throughout the eastern half of Texas throughout tomorrow. We don't need to jump to conclusions, but I strongly recommend that everyone know what to do in case of severe weather and possible tornadoes." He smiled for the first time. "I'll be back in a few minutes with specific weather and information for taking proper precautions."

"Sure glad we're going to Tom's today." Sally clicked off the television. Sally's gut tightened at the prospect of violent weather churning their way.

Erin grabbed Ludovic in a game-saving tackle. Cristen Jane, Erin's older sister, watched in amusement as she carried more suitcases through the kitchen.

"I just hope the bad weather doesn't hit the ranch until after the party. Susie's put too much effort in it." She opened the door leading from the kitchen to the garage. "You ladies first."

Erin called Ludovic and ran outside to the car. Ludovic jumped into the back seat, his tail wagging in anticipation of a ride to wherever humans want to go. He licked both of his adopted sisters in canine euphoria. They were off to the Broken Wing Ranch.

"Welcome back, hon. Don't sweat on the carpet," Susie called to Tom at the sound of the door chime announcing his return from a five-mile jog through the dirt road leading from the back end of their property line toward the east. Sure enough, sweat poured from every pore in his body.

"Damn muggy out there. I mean, it's worse than a blanket. Bear and Catfish turned back before I got to the end of the runway. Wimps." He grabbed a towel resting on the clothes dryer and started drying from head to toe.

Susie smiled and added, "TV's talking about some severe weather headed our way. Hope it doesn't mess up the party."

"It won't. Nothing messes with a Seiler party."

Outside Bear and Catfish slurped away at their bowl of water. The bowl had a float device attached to a stiff wire. When the water level lowered to a specific level, the wire activated a switch that opened a valve to allow water to refill the bowl. Tom was, indeed, the best mechanical engineer in the state. His specialty was nuts and bolts.

As for his prediction about the coming weather, he would prove to be a lousy meteorologist.

Twenty

Saturday High Noon,
March 20

Broken Wing Ranch

Three signs were tacked eight, six, and four feet high on a pine tree in the front yard. In succession they read *party's on the back patio, park here,* and *first beer's below.* A large arrow pointed down from the bottom sign to a large ice cooler filled with Miller Lite at the foot of the tree. If you wanted a different brand of beer at Tom and Susie's home, you had to bring your own. Cars were already parked everywhere: on the side of the dirt road, in front of the house, even under the tall pines towering over Tom's new caboose. The gathering of the clan had started, celebrating the end of winter and serving as a pre-family reunion in preparation for the June blowout at Port Aransas. Fifty-plus family members and friends from all over Grimes County joined in the revelry. Kids romped in the open field, a couple of the fathers had their youngsters at the catfish pond, country music blared from large speakers at the far end of the patio, and laughter was heard everywhere.

The Piper Cub glided in over the trees, touched down at

the east end of the runway, and slowed to a stop about a hundred feet in front of the celebrating crowd. Tom cut the engine, unlocked the horizontal door, and let it swing down. He stepped out, moved to the passenger seat, and unbuckled a precious cargo. Like a coiled spring, six-year-old Holly fell into her grandfather's arms. Adopted in Russia along with her older siblings, Grant and Caroline, Holly had more zip than a zipper factory. Remnants of an accent were long gone for the little Texan.

"Let's go again, Grampaw. Let's go again."

"Maybe we can go again tomorrow." Tom had to negotiate. "But for now, how about an ice cream cone?"

End of discussion. Holly darted toward Paige screaming, "Mommy, Grampaw says I can have ice cream." She disappeared into the throng.

Holly was the last rider of the day, giving Tom permission to drink his first beer. Neither Tom nor Susie had to worry about personally entertaining anyone. No one needed any coddling in this gang. Laughter, music, and the aroma of shredded pork barbecue and fried chicken permeated the landscape.

"Got seventeen rolls this time. Mighty good for this early in the year." Cyril Diller, a baseball cap pulled low over his eyes, spoke of their agreement: Tom traded hay for the ability to jog through Cyril's property. The specifics called for Cyril to cut the hay often enough to ensure that the ranch looked well groomed. As for the runway, Tom manicured it after "Serial Killer" gave it the rough cut.

Cyril's eyes, averting Tom's, looked off into the distance. His mannerisms—from the shifting eyes, to the hands in his pockets, to his low whispering voice—gave Susie an eerie feeling about their neighbor. She once dubbed Cyril Diller as "Serial Killer" and it stuck like glue. Family and friends came to call him, with affection, by his nefarious nickname, though not to his face. No matter his eccentricities, everyone liked Serial

Killer. He'd probably helped half the people of Grimes County at one time or another. Shifty eyes; not many teeth; dirty as a mongrel; good friend.

Tom answered Serial Killer. "I thought it would be a good spring. Being this early, you might get seven cuttings this year." He tipped his beer. "Here's to a good crop and some fat cattle."

"Hi, Cyril." Susie, along with Paige, walked up next to Tom. "How've you been?" She looked him in the eyes, to no avail.

"Cyril, I'm Paige. I inherited Tom as my father." She stuck out her hand.

He looked everywhere but directly at either of them. He failed to shake hands with Paige, barely answering Susie's friendly question. "Been good. Lot of heat for this time of the year." He looked down at his can. "Better get me another beer." Serial Killer was much like a Dachshund, comfortable with only a select few. Susie wasn't one of the few. Apparently Paige wasn't either. He put his empty hand to the bill of his cap and walked away.

No sooner did Serial Killer leave than Randy and Jeanie Rouse, neighbors who owned five hundred acres west of Richards, Texas, came up.

Looking at the beer in Tom's hand, Randy said, "I see you're finished flying for the day. Now what's Rachel going to think?" He and Jeanie smiled at their granddaughter heading over to join Holly at the ice cream trough.

Tom watched Rachel, already laughing at something funny Holly said. Tom pointed at Rachel and answered, "I think I'm off the hook. And speaking of hooks," Tom gestured slightly toward Paige, "I meant to tell you that your work on the whip hose paid off. Ed Harvey told me that the computer models sold the jury completely. I don't know what the judgment will be, but our side did its duty and your work was dead-on." Once again Tom and Paige had pulled off a forensic coup.

Paige, strikingly pretty with dark brown eyes and a straight Seiler nose, smiled at her father. Memories of a little girl building balsa wood bridges in Tom's office played in her mind. Grin on her face, Paige started to respond, "Well, let's get ready for–"

A horn honked on the highway. Tom, the Rouses, Susie, and Paige looked over just in time to see Delana's taxi pass behind some trees along FM 1486. Betsy the Cadillac trailed the taxi by two car lengths. Two minutes later Don, Cindy, Elam, and Delana walked between the office building and the main house.

"How you doin', ole man?" Don's youthful smile broke across his face. He crowded the beer and cane in one hand and shook Tom's with the other.

Delana and Cindy each gave Tom a peck on the cheek. Friends and family came over to say hello. Most had not met Delana, but all had heard about her and wanted to see her in the flesh. Her inhibitions evaporated in the smiles and friendliness of these people. Tom and Don told some good stories about her life as a taxi driver and her meeting the likes of Sonny Bono, Brooks Robinson, and Denzel Washington. She was also the only person they knew who had ever been held up with a knife to her throat. Nancy, the oldest sibling in the Seiler family, thoroughly enjoyed meeting the taxi driver who was so close to her brothers. After a while Nancy pirated Delana into joining her on the porch. In the hour before Delana had to leave, Nancy told some interesting tales of Tom, Don, and their deceased brother Jack.

Tom emerged from the edge of the pines with a small gaggle of the partygoers. He circled his arm, enticing the women to join the group.

"Nancy, Delana. Come on with us. I want to show you my latest toy." Tom escorted them to the antique train caboose–not a model, but the real thing. Built in 1971 for the Burlington

Northern Railroad, the caboose was painted a beautiful deep red on the outside. A bright thin yellow stripe ran the entire length of the caboose, and just forward of the cupola was a six-foot yellow circle four inches in thickness. A large yellow cross about the same as the Red Cross logo was inscribed in the circle, and along the horizontal bar of the cross, again in deep red, was the lettering *Santa Fe.* The Burlington Northern logo could not compete with the Santa Fe Railroad. The visitors—particularly Nancy, who had seen it in San Antonio during retrofitting—marveled at the glorious relic.

Hanging from the steps, Tom glowed. "The original inside was god-awful so I made some changes. I decided to mix the mind of an old fart with that of an eight-year-old kid. Come on in and see what I got."

Over the next twenty minutes the guests studied the light-paneled walls, the larger-than-manufactured windows, a double deck bed, a small toilet and shower combination, a small kitchenette with stove, a game table for six, a small flat-screen television, and a refrigerator full of soft drinks for the kids and beer for the adults. He could have spent the whole night in his caboose, but enough was enough. Time to get back to the party.

Elam tapped Tom on the shoulder as they walked back toward the hangar. "Tom, I've got to run. How about you, Don, and I talking a few things out?"

Don agreed. "Good idea. Elam's got to head out pretty quick and we ought to just figure out exactly where we are with the JETS."

Tom called to the others. "I'll catch up with everybody. These two want to ruin the day with business talk."

Tom, Don, and Elam peeled off from the main group and walked to Tom's office.

"Elam, you're a wuss. The party's just getting started.

What's the big deal?"

"The big deal, my friend, is that I have a date with a very fine woman."

"Is this Sarah, the new love of your life?"

Elam grinned. "Sure is. She deserves better 'n me, but I'm not telling."

Don interjected, "I ought to tell her what a sorry SOB she's dating." Don scratched at his ear. "But she'll figure it out soon enough." He shook his head and smiled down at his cane.

Tom said, "Don, have you noticed how this societal derelict is talking differently about her than the other poor women he's dated?" He turned back to Elam. "I think she's got you totally under control. Sort of like a lap dog. Hell, you're even dressing as though you know what looks acceptable."

They entered the office and pulled up stools to the larger drafting table.

Tom asked, "OK, where are you two on the JETS?"

Elam rubbed the palm of his right hand across his forehead and started briefing the other two. "Both JETS prototypes arrived from Odessa on Tuesday. We started putting one down-hole Wednesday morning. The other one and the display model are in the shed." Elam had a twinkle in his eye and a skip in his step. "They're both impressive just sitting there. I'll use the display for my briefings to clients."

"How's the down-hole system holding up?"

"Absolutely rock-solid." Elam's voice picked up. "I mean dead-on rock-solid. We tested it yesterday at twenty-five hundred feet." Elam stood up. He looked at his partners through emblazoned eyes. "It seemed to be a typical stripper well, or so we thought. We pumped twenty-three barrels of oil yesterday. Just for discussion's sake, at a hundred dollars a barrel that would make $2,300. Try multiplying that by some 350 days a year." Then his smile covered his entire face. "This morning we pumped eight barrels by ten o'clock. I told the guys to knock off early and enjoy the weekend."

"Are you going to be ready for Wellington Oil's visit on Tuesday?" Don spoke of the first demonstration of the new version.

"Better than that. We'll be ready for Wellington on Tuesday and two others the following week." Elam continued. "Even Exxon and a Saudi Arabian delegation are looking at their schedules as we speak."

Tom reacted quickly, his speech measured. "This is where we need to talk about ethics."

Don and Elam responded differently. Don's face wrinkled with questioning; Elam's face wrinkled with irritation.

"I've heard you talking about Chinese, Pakistanis, and now the Saudis. Are you interested in strictly money where the highest bidder gets your patent?" Tom's words slowed slightly. "China is eating our lunch with some of the stupid trade agreements we've made, the Saudis are a theocracy hell-bent on hating the United States, and the Pakistanis harbor more militant Muslims than you could imagine. If you're getting solid American interest, and it looks like you are, then I say the hell with the foreigners."

Tom's comment sucked the wind from Elam's mouth. But only for two seconds.

"Look, I didn't work on this device for half my life in order to go bankrupt. One device isn't going to change American fortunes one bit. It doesn't mean a damn thing."

Don didn't know which way to turn. Tom did.

"Look, Elam. It belongs to you and Don and you have every right to do what you want with it. I have every right to tell you that I think it is a mistake to give up a patent to foreign enterprises." He leaned closer to Elam, almost violating Elam's personal space. "And since I mentioned the Saudis, did you stop to think that, at this point in history, they don't even need the device? They're still dealing with almost infinite supplies of oil. Any interest they have in JETS is for some bad-assed purpose. Guaranteed."

Elam's uncomfortable silence signaled agreement with Tom's statement.

Don recovered and steered the discussion. "We don't have to sell the patent. If we deal with foreigners, we can do what you said, keep the patent and just sell or lease individual units."

Tom beat Elam in responding. "That's a damn good idea if you're dealing with honest people. But you're not. Don't think for a minute that these foreign companies, including state-owned, won't screw you in a heartbeat. Whether you sell the patent or lease systems, they'll get you. Are you familiar with what the Chinese have done to the intellectual property of our country?" He moved even closer to Elam, face to face. "They've stolen it like they're in one big candy store. As for you, once they get the first JETS system, they'll mass-produce them out the wazoo. We all know that."

Elam's impenetrable belief that he was the toughest son of a bitch in the valley held tight. "I can handle these people. No, I don't trust them, but I could put together an agreement that is airtight."

It was Don's turn to get into Elam's face. "We're partners on this, Elam. Everyone has a say. Don't make any unilateral decisions."

Tom added, "I've talked this whole thing over with some pretty smart people. The consensus is that you'd both be better off setting it up so that you get residual income. The best contract would be one in which you get a sum of money up front, a small chunk of money for each unit built, and a small percentage of gross revenues associated with each barrel of oil recovered."

The conversation slowly meandered over to the status of the patent.

"We're finally making real progress on the patent. I've got something to show you." Elam pulled a folded paper from his shirt pocket. "It's a letter of patentability from Barrister and Associates."

He opened it up and gave it to Donald. Tom looked over Don's shoulder. The letter read:

March 16, 2010
Barrister and Associates
Intellectual Property Attorneys
5718 Westheimer Road, Suite 1400
Houston, Texas 77057

Invention: Jet Extraction Technology System

Inventors: Elam Duquette & Donald H. Seiler

To Whom It May Concern:
We have concluded a patent search on the Jet Extraction Technology System.

Similar patents include:

7,223,556 B4   Belton   Issued 06 Sep 2008
Liquid displaced chamber lift system with closed loop vents

7,004,744 B3   Belton   Issued 21 May 2005
Chamber lift system with double chamber

2,334,781   Gelbert   Issued 28 April 1999
Multi-phase flow transport system

Based upon our investigation of these patents and similar matters related to the designated invention of Duquette and Seiler, it is our opinion that the Jet Extraction Technology System, a.k.a. JETS, as designed, has merit as an original invention. Although there are other inventions related to this one, none has the specific innovations detailed in the device description.

For further information, please contact us at the address above.

Sincerely yours,
Frederick J. Barrister, IP Attorney

Don gave the letter back to Elam, and said, "It sounds good, but how close in time does that put us to owning the patent?"

Elam replied, "I asked and he said if no one contests the letter then we would have it registered within six weeks."

"Six weeks. Shit, this is going on forever."

"Don't knock it. We're almost there. Besides, this letter is on file and it gives us a specific date of submission. No one can steal it from us now."

The letter meant very little to Tom. "Elam, I've been through the patent routine several times. The letter you received is from Barrister, not the patent and copyright office. What you've got might be good information and, then again, it might not mean anything at all."

Don tightened. He started to respond but a knock on the door interrupted the discussion. In walked James, the next-door neighbor. Next door in these parts of the country was three football fields away. "Hey, what kind of host are you? Everybody's getting revved up and you're in here blowing smoke at each other." He shook hands with Don and introduced himself to Elam.

"Damn. You're right. Let's go party. I think we've solved the problems of the world."

The three men got up and followed James toward the caboose platform.

"Damn, I almost forgot." Don tapped Elam on the head.

Elam, halfway down the metal steps of the caboose, looked up at Don. "Forgot what?"

"Another company called and would like to talk to us. Caprock Industries is the name. Out of Lubbock."

"Never heard of them. Probably some small company that can't compete with the big ones. Forget 'em."

Elam stepped onto the gravel bedding and sauntered off toward his car. "Sorry I can't stay, but I've got to get ready for my date tonight and I've got more 'n a hundred miles to drive."

Don added, "Yeah, and I saw *The March of the Penguins* where they walk seventy miles across the Antarctic just to get laid. Still got those hormones."

They shared a hearty laugh. Then Elam turned back to the group, his smile turning serious. "I want both of you to meet her. She's a beautiful woman. She's special." His boyish smile returned. He took a couple of backward steps and then turned around again.

Both Tom and Don were surprised by Elam's statement. Elam's newly found maturity rendered them speechless.

Finally, Tom yelled, "Watch out for the weather tonight. It's going to get rough."

His back to them, Elam waved his arm in salute. Farewell.

Tom, Don, and James headed back to the party.

As they walked along the parched grass, Tom commented, "Don, that small company. Caprock. You ought to call them back."

"I already have."

Twenty-One

Saturday, March 20

Central, South, and Southeast Texas

A south-to-north line of boiling thunderstorms swept eastward along a dryline extending across the state throughout the day. Greenish-black bottoms of thunderclouds swirled in fanatical fury and wind gusts in excess of seventy miles an hour ripped down trees and lifted shingles from roofs. The first tornado descended from the underbelly of a supercell storm near Uvalde, one hundred miles west of San Antonio, at 6:47 p.m. Moving south of the town at forty-five miles an hour, it destroyed one farmhouse and tore down some power lines on Route 173. It died out after eight minutes. Webs of fire swept across the skylines of San Antonio and Austin; both cities dodged the bullet. Other towns would not be so lucky.

Stagnant air hung over the countryside like a blanket of hot, suffocating bayou mud. Elam enjoyed thunderstorms and the evening's menu called for severe weather. He decided to use an early dinner in Seguin as an appetizer and the certain electric symphony as the main course. Pendle Hill on the outskirts of Luling would make for the perfect front-row seats.

Elam pulled up to the small frame house on the outskirts of Gonzales as the sun fell beneath a line of thunderclouds well off to the southwest. Elam, gentrified with Old Spice, tan Dockers, polished loafers, and a horizontally striped blue-and-green polo shirt, walked up the short sidewalk with boyish knots in his stomach. What a few weeks earlier seemed nothing more than a potential sexual interlude had taken a turn. Something about Sarah caused dormant feelings within him to rise like the Phoenix. He respected her; just as important, he hoped that she respected him.

He knocked on the door and waited, hands in pockets. His peaceful gaze at the sky ended when a young man in Levi's, dirty sneakers, and a t-shirt with a sketch of the human brain and the words *This Is Your Brain* appeared at the door. Without acknowledging Elam, he yelled over his shoulder, "Mom, your date is here."

Elam prepared himself for some smartass comment. Instead, his host turned back to Elam and smiled. "Come on in. I'm Joshua, last one of the kids still at home. My friends call me Josh." He held the door with his left hand and reached toward Elam with his right. A firm handshake spoke well of Josh. He led Elam into the living room. It was spotless.

"Hang on a minute." Josh walked toward the back of the house to make sure his mother had heard his call. The back of his t-shirt revealed the complement to the message on the front. Below the words *And This Is Your Brain on Drugs* rested the longhorn logo for the University of Texas. "Mom, Elam's here."

"Be right there." Her call excited Elam, leaving him a love-struck teenager.

Sarah's husband left the family a couple of days after learning that she was pregnant with their fifth child. He didn't stick around to find out that the baby would be their first son. He just up and left. Josh was less than three months from his high school graduation and had never seen his father. He loved his mother deeply but did harbor resentment at never experiencing playing catch in the backyard, fishing on the Guadalupe River, or hearing cheers from his dad at the football games against Luling, Seguin, Lockhart, and other Texas towns where football was a god. Sarah had been too busy raising her children to bring another man into her life. A chance encounter at Pape's Pecan House in Seguin led to her first real romance in more than thirty years. She tried desperately to make right her bad decision of marrying someone she didn't really love. This night would be their fifth time together. Their fourth date ended with some physical sparks, but fire had not yet consumed them.

Elam had his drawbacks, age and talking too much among the leaders, but he was also very open and honest. Early on she had to pry herself into conversations but she appreciated his strengths more than she disliked his weaknesses. She found him a ruggedly handsome man and though they barely knew each other, Sarah noticed the transition in Elam that changed his focus from himself to her. Most surprising of all was her physical reaction to Elam. She returned from that fourth date giddy and delightedly embarrassed at her sexual arousal. The inevitable would happen soon, and she welcomed it as one would welcome a long lost friend.

Elam felt very comfortable with Josh. "So what are your plans after high school?" Uncharacteristically, he waited for Josh's reply.

Josh slumped back in his chair and put his hands behind his head. He looked up, either at heaven or at the ceiling. "I've decided to join the army first and then go to Texas A&M." If he made it, Josh would be the first college graduate in his family. "My great-grandfather jumped in at Normandy with the

82nd Airborne Division at a place called Sainte-Mère-Église. He lied about his age, but not because he was too young. He was pretty old to be jumping out of airplanes. Name was Speer. Sergeant Bob Speer. My mother said he was nicknamed 'spear tip' because he was out front all the time. He was awarded the Silver Star for stopping a German attack. Then, one day while they weren't doing nothing more than walking down a road, a sniper killed him. He never got to see my Grandma Alana. She was four months old when he died." Josh shrugged his shoulders and shook his head. "They got the sniper. I always wished I could have talked to him. There's a letter back in my room that he wrote to Grandma Alana when she was born. My mom gave it to me so I could be proud of my ancestors. I never knew him personally, but I've always been proud of him and he's had an effect on my life. If you'd like to see the letter, I've got it up–"

"Hi, Elam. I see you and Josh have already become friends." Sarah smiled.

Elam stood up. He looked at her and felt almost inadequate. She was wearing a light green cotton dress. A flashback pictured all women in dresses. Damn shame they almost always wear pants these days. She was a very pretty woman, the prettiest he had ever seen. Compared to him, her wrinkles were inconsequential. Sarah had weathered the tough years with grace. Sandy brown hair sprinkled with wisps of gray, skin soft as down, round, dark blue eyes, a straight nose with just a touch of uplift, and a mouth sensual in its symmetry. She loved her kids and never realized the odds against all of them turning out to be such strong, honest people. Through all those years her youngsters gave her reason to smile, to hope, to believe in the future. On this night, she relished the future, whatever it might hold. Her thoughts radiated from her face. Elam felt them.

Dinner at Craig's Sauté and Grill was superb. Nestled on the north side of Seguin, the century-old bungalow had been converted into a charming, well-appointed restaurant in 1988. Three former bedrooms provided semi-private dining, and the modest bar handled waiting customers on busy nights. Reviews in magazines such as *Texas Monthly* and *Country Lifestyle* generated great interest in Craig's.

Elam recommended the pecan-crusted chicken and poblano corn chowder. Sarah decided to forego the chowder, but did add a small Seguin salad. The meal served as a backdrop to Elam and Sarah continuing to learn about each other. Josh's comments about the family served as a catalyst for Sarah's speaking of her children.

She ran her fingers around the top of her wine glass and spoke more into the vessel than to Elam. "It was pretty tough. Still, had I not married him, I would never had my children. I can't tell you how proud I am of them." Tearing ever so slightly, she dabbed at the corner of her eyes and then continued. "I'll be honest, I don't want Josh to leave. We had no money, but he never complained. Worked hard, has always been polite to people, and kept his studies up. He's going to join the army and take advantage of the benefits to make it to Texas A&M. Josh is determined; if he says he's going to make it to A&M, he'll do it. I'm really proud of him."

Sarah drew in a deep breath and held it. Her lips quivered slightly and a mournful smile forecasted the conversation. "He is so excited about being a paratrooper and I am absolutely terrified." Her hands fidgeted, her eyes darting across the room. "It's what he wants to do. One part of me is so proud of him." She thought of the strange-sounding Hindu Kush Mountains in Afghanistan and of young American soldiers being killed in the fighting. "But another part screams in my head, 'don't let him go–don't go–don't go.'" Sarah was no longer talking to Elam; she was pleading with her son. Her skin turned a pallid gray as blood retreated to the internal caverns of her body. She was scared. "I'm so sorry." She took her napkin from her lap and wiped her eyes again.

"Those tears look pretty happy, proud, and hopeful to me. They're the best kind."

They both smiled. Elam gently patted the back of Sarah's hand. He sat back in his chair and thought of this woman. *Remarkable. Beautiful. I love her.* Then he thought of himself. *For once, I need to be an honorable man.*

Time flew.

"May I offer you coffee and dessert?" The tall, winsome waitress studied the infatuated middle-aged couple with amusement and a touch of envy.

Sarah let out a breath. "I'm pretty full. Think I'll pass."

Elam's sweet tooth dictated his answer. "How about if we split the cherry pie?"

Sarah smiled. "That would be excellent."

"One cherry pie, two forks, and two cups of your hot, fresh coffee. Thanks, Allison."

Allison nodded and added, "I'll put some ice cream on it." She walked toward the kitchen with the plates.

Sarah reached out and placed her hand on the table near Elam's coffee cup. "I've been very happy lately."

Elam responded sheepishly, unable to look up. He stared at the hand that was offered to him. Something about this woman was very different from his previous three wives and countless other rolls in the hay. Awkwardly, he put his hand on top of hers. "I've been unlucky with wives." He paused, clearing his throat while remaining fixed on the tablecloth. "Maybe it's more accurate to say the wives were more unlucky."

Sarah reached out with her other hand and placed it over his. "I don't think I'm asking you to marry me." She patted his hand, and unknowingly added what he had been thinking, "but I am asking you to prove that good men still exist." She withdrew her hands and sat back. "And I hope they have good cherry pie."

They did.

The first fatality was an infant pulled from her mother's arms as the suction vortices played helter-skelter with a farmhouse near Pearsall. From Dilley in the south to Gainesville north of Dallas, funnel after funnel dropped from the grotesque underbelly of churning clouds. A monstrous EF-5 twister, half a mile wide at the ground, flattened the small town of Ogelsby north of Fort Hood. Twelve people died. Homes and businesses vanished from their foundations like dust swept from the floor. Nothing was recognizable. Television and radio stations gave nonstop updates as the killer storms came to earth. Marlin took a direct hit and sixteen died; Prairie Dell lost eight residents; a family of four was killed trying to outrun the storm on I-35. Residents of another small town began to take note of the developing events. They lived in Luling, Texas.

Twenty-Two

Saturday Evening,
March 20

Monte's Bar,
Luling, Texas

Oh Maybellene, why can't you be true? You've started back doing the things you used to do.

The dance floor swayed with couples dancing to Chuck Berry's melodic misery. Two bartenders manned the flow of alcohol for another small town Texas Saturday night. Save the annual Watermelon Thump, Monte's was as raucous as it gets in Luling. Bill Haley and the Comets followed Chuck.

In the poolroom Carlos, Emilio, and Manuel drank heavily and worked on a game of snooker. They had work to do, work to be done at night. The sun had been down almost two hours when Carlos took the final shot.

"OK. That's it. Time to go." He sucked in on his cigarette for a final draw, then stubbed it out in a black plastic ashtray. Terry didn't allow the patrons to leave Monte's with open bottles, so Carlos stuffed his bottle inside his denim shirt, wedging it between skin and Levi's. The other two did likewise. They would get more beer at the Jud's Food Store on East Pierce.

Pendle Hill rose almost 150 feet above the surrounding terrain at a height just above the smell of the sweet crude. A dirt road, not much more than a path, wound halfway around the hill, through some pecan trees, and on to a clearing at the top that could handle at least ten cars. A gentle downward slope extended to the west from the crest of the hill.

Just as Elam reached the trees another car, its headlights bouncing up and down, sped by them. "Young kids," he said. "Probably up here drinking, necking, or smoking pot. Or all three." He shook his head. "They saw us coming and decided to book."

At the top of Pendle Hill Elam sighed at the sight of nothing but open space. They were alone. He pulled forward enough for the car to tilt downward slightly. He turned off the headlights, allowing waves of ground stars from farm porches and windows to spread through the darkness to the horizon. A kaleidoscope of color radiated above an invisible line dividing land and sky. Elam reached to his left and pushed on the button to move the seats backward. Next he closed the console to allow Sarah to move closer to him. As he raised the steering wheel she slid in his direction. He placed his arm over her shoulder; she nestled against his chest.

"Comfortable?"

"Yes, for now. It is beautiful out there."

They looked off into the approaching storm.

"Give it another half an hour and you won't believe how beautiful the lightning will be."

They sat silently for a few minutes.

Elam couldn't get over his school-kid feelings. Sarah simply relished being held. Elam felt strong and protective. He traced circles on Sarah's upper arm. It felt sensual and comforting.

"Mmm." She closed her eyes and relaxed.

In her movements Elam sensed an invitation. As romantically as he could, he kissed her on top of her head. "You're just plain different."

"How so?"

His fingers moved to the strap on her dress. "I can't place it, but I caught myself thinking about what kind of person I would have been had I met you in high school." His forefinger gently traced down between cloth and skin.

"I try my best not to think about those things." She shifted slightly, easing more into his body. It was an invitation.

The F-250 slowed at the chain link fence surrounding the site. Carlos got out, pulling a set of keys from his pocket. He walked to the gate and unlocked it.

"Drive it just inside the fence and turn it around. Back it up but give me enough room to maneuver the Deere. Hurry up." Nervous perspiration billowed from his pores.

Emilio drove the truck in the main gate while Carlos worked the tumblers on the lock to the storage shed. Carlos swung the doors open and walked directly to the bucket loader sitting in the middle of the shed. Manuel guided Emilio as he maneuvered the truck around the test well and toward the shed. Staccato bursts of light reflected off their faces. The JETS derrick, an ominous pyramidal skeleton, rose into the black turbulent sky. Thunder rolled through the trees. Emilio stopped the truck in front of the double doors, leaving just enough room for the Deere. If all went well, the chamber display would be back in the shed in thirty hours with none the wiser. Once Emilio and Manuel were inside the shed and had closed the doors, Carlos turned on the light. The shed was a forty-by-fifty-foot rectangle. On a metal shelf near the entrance, three laptop computers and assorted peripheral equipment sat ready for use. Along the left wall were stacked cans of lubricants, two air compressors, and a hoisting mechanism. Rigging tools, transportation straps, three toolboxes, a large pile of rags, and sections of steel chain cluttered shelves along half of the back wall. Along the other half of the back wall, resting on wooden pallets stacked two high, two deep, and five wide, were two sets of new system components—one being a complete well chamber for the JETS, the other being the display model to be used for marketing purposes. The display model had been cut away so that all individual components and their relationship to other components would be readily apparent. Adjacent parts were painted different colors to accentuate the functioning of the JETS. Carlos wanted only the display components to the system. He thought of the few investor groups visiting the site earlier in the development stage of the project. They collectively labeled the initial system as a Rube Goldberg contraption, a term he interpreted as being pejorative. Functional or not, contraptions don't usually demand millions of dollars at the bargaining table.

Carlos ordered the others, "When I get the bucket in place, roll it on. Use those crowbars over there." Carlos pointed to the back shelves. He grabbed a key hanging by a nail on a wooden post and climbed into the cab of the Deere. He yelled again, "Grab some rags so you don't mess the paint. Get a bunch of tie-down straps."

The men did as told without comment.

The display model of the chamber section, though considerably smaller than the actual prototype, measured almost eight feet in length and weighed, even with significant portions cut away, slightly less than three hundred pounds—not particularly easy to get into the bucket. The men lowered the tailgate of the truck in anticipation of tying down the chamber and wellhead assembly.

Carlos backed and turned the Deere until one of the back tires almost touched an air compressor. He drove forward, turning toward the painted display chamber. He lowered the bucket so the bottom of its mouth rested flush with the top surface of the pallets. He articulated the bucket so that the seat of the bucket was lower than the mouth.

"OK. Roll it."

The thunder, now much louder and more threatening, pulsed in delayed rhythm to bolts of lightning streaking through pitch-black sky. Elam kissed Sarah tenderly, gently pressing his lips to hers. Their sexual instincts rose toward a crescendo. Elam reached beneath her skirt and placed his hand on the outside of her panties, touching her and not touching her. Sarah inhaled deeply and allowed a gasp to slip from her mouth. But a car was not the place. Against every physical desire she had ever experienced, she placed her hand on his and whispered, "Elam, please don't. Not now."

Elam, fully aroused, granted her request, lifting his hand while exhaling. He leaned back in his seat and gripped the steering wheel. He wasn't angry; he was more embarrassed than anything else. He spoke. "Guess I'm just too fast. It's not disrespect." He turned toward her.

In the fiery light Sarah saw his face. He understood and agreed with her request.

He continued. "It's just that you're the best thing that's ever happened to me and, no doubt about it, I want all of you. Can't help that." He turned back, his stare returning to the approaching storm.

A minute later Sarah put her hand on top of his. She spoke softly to him. "I want to make love to you." She smiled into the flashing night. "I think I want to make love to you every day for the rest of my life." Both were silent for a moment before Sarah continued. "But I don't want our first time to be in a car." She smiled again, a very tender, intimate smile.

He returned the smile, quietly saying, "I understand. And I agree."

Then he felt her hand move to his body. It was electrifying.

The chamber rolled back on the pallet, its orange paint gouged by the metal bucket teeth. Carlos tore into the others. "Be careful. I got to put this back without no one knowing it's been gone." He looked back at the shelves. "Get some rags and tie them around it. Hurry up."

It was taking longer than Carlos wanted.

Elam spoke, his voice having to compete with thunder. "The Hyatt in San Antonio is perfect. What about Josh?"

"He's very responsible and won't throw any parties." Sarah smiled again, this time a little more impish, as she playfully shook her head and smoothed wrinkles from her skirt.

Elam put the car in reverse and slowly backed to the top of the hill. "No, I mean what's he going to think?"

"Elam, you really do care for me don't you?" She patted him on the knee.

Elam relished the truth of her statement. "Sarah, I'm guilty." Feeling uncomfortable, Elam changed the subject. "On the way back, I'm going to show you something. It's less than a mile from here and will only take a minute. It's impressive." Out of nowhere he added, "It could change my life."

Groundstroke lightning, now less than three miles away, slammed into the cold black countryside.

At 9:40 p.m. Doppler radar indicated a possible tornado paralleling US 90 northeast of Seguin. Two minutes later, with constant bursts of lightning providing visibility, a Texas Highway Patrol Division patrolman on I-10 picked up the view of a lifetime. With each flash of light a dark, sinister apparition grew larger, a rolling black monster covering the full horizon to his north. The cloud was massive, its circular motion unmistakable and its low, moaning growl drowning out any human calls for help. It swallowed everything in its path. The patrolman was stunned, almost unable to comprehend the sight before him. He pulled over as rain and hail slammed into his car. He spoke into his hand-held microphone. "All stations in the vicinity of Luling, get to safety immediately. An EF-5, possibly a mile wide, is bearing down on Luling." He looked again over his shoulder into the black sky. Each bolt of lightning caught the apocalyptic storm growing in size and ferocity. "Tell those people to get down. Get down now! This storm is a killer."

Radio and television announcements streamed continuously while sirens, their high-pitched sound unmistakable in purpose, wailed into the night.

Two black silhouettes appeared against the raging sky. They jumped in the bed of the truck, one at each end. Carlos lowered the bucket as best he could; he rotated and lowered its mouth numerous times in an attempt to place the chamber gently into the truck. Realizing that the chamber would drop almost two feet from the bucket into the bed of the truck, he instructed Manuel and Emilio to move the rags to where the chamber would fall. They held the ends as Carlos made one final movement of the bucket. As the bucket made its last tilt downward, Manuel slipped.

Thud! The truck shook under the impact of three hundred pounds of steel. Over the roar of the wind, a small popping sound was heard. "Aayh!" Manuel screamed and grabbed at his leg. The chamber had rolled directly into his kneecap. "Damn. Damn." He fell to the bed and coiled into a tight ball, crying out, "Help me. Oh shit, this hurts bad. Oh shit."

Carlos ignored Manuel. He jumped down from the Deere and tossed a nylon rope to Emilio. "Help me tie it down so we can get the hell out of here." He tightened the first rope twice around the chamber, tossed one end to Emilio, and tied the other end with half hitches at the cargo shackle. Emilio mirrored the procedure.

"Grab a pallet. When I tilt the wellhead assembly, you slide the pallet under it so I can get the bucket under it. Then push it onto the bucket."

Emilio did as told. Although bulkier than the chamber, the display wellhead assembly fit easily into the bucket. When dumped into the bed of the truck, it struck the chamber, gouging into the painted metal and bending an edge along a cutaway section of the fluid reservoir. It narrowly missed Manuel.

"Hurry, tie it down."

A cool burst of wind blew across their faces. Lightning and thunder enveloped them. Manuel groaned in the truck bed and swore at his bad fortune.

"Get Manuel in the backseat. Now. Let's go."

Carlos needed to get the Deere back into the shed. He climbed back on and started to put it into gear. Finally, they could get the hell out of there and on the road to Louisiana. As Carlos approached the shed, the interior lights flickered briefly and then went out.

In the blackness Carlos heard Emilio yell up to him.

"Carlos, we got company."

Carlos turned completely around and stared down the slick road. Headlights broke the darkness.

Twenty-Three

Saturday Evening,
March 20

The Eye of the Storm

The first raindrops hit the roof and windshield like popping firecrackers as the car emerged from the trees. Wind started to shake the car. Elam looked at Sarah and saw uncomfortable eyes looking skyward.

"How about a rain date? Next Friday I'll show you our extractor first," Elam spoke in competition with the driving rain, "and San Antonio second."

She returned a faint smile. "I'd like that."

He didn't hear her.

Elam turned around when he saw something in the headlights. "What's that?" He leaned forward, trying to will the raindrops off the windshield. Obscured or not, Elam could see two men in a truck bed and another man on the John Deere. "Who the hell are they?"

The two men in the truck were deer in the headlights. Frozen. Emilio held Manuel around the waist but did not move. Uncaring, Manuel groaned.

Elam maneuvered the car until it was five feet from the truck, facing it front to front.

"Elam, let's just go. Please, let's go now." Sarah pleaded and trembled from head to foot.

Elam was no longer aware of Sarah, only the people next to a truck on his property. He opened the car door and walked toward the truck. The truck lights went on as he moved between the two vehicles. Torrents of rain streaked in the glare of lights and pelted each man relentlessly. A bolt of lightning hit a tree less than a football field away.

"Hey, Mr. Duquette." Carlos yelled into the din of the winds. He tried to smile as he climbed out of the driver's compartment of the Deere. The two men in the truck did not move.

Elam yelled back, "Hey, my ass. What're you doing out here?" He looked at Emilio and Manuel. "And who the hell are they?"

Carlos reacted quickly. "I heard about some bad thunderstorms and decided to take the system to a safe place. My uncle owns a garage in Geronimo." Rain splashed off his face, almost like sparklers. Another bolt of lightning blinded them and an instantaneous clap of thunder almost knocked them off their feet.

Elam yelled angrily at Carlos. "I don't care if he owns fucking Manhattan." It wasn't hard putting two and two together. No one is so altruistic as to take equipment from one unsafe place to another unsafe place. "You're a liar and you sorry bastards are trying to steal from me."

Elam lunged forward, delivering a powerful right hook to the side of Carlos's head. Carlos hit the ground. The deer remained frozen.

"Get out of my way. Get the hell out of here." Elam stormed to the back of the truck on the way to the shed.

Carlos, shaken more by the events than the blow to the face, got up immediately. He grabbed a crowbar from the bed of the truck. In a single fluid motion he pulled the weapon back while rushing toward Elam. The power of the hurtling crowbar was devastating.

"No-oooo!!" The pounding rain on closed windows and the thunder exploding in waves muffled her screams. "No . . . no . . . no."

The angled end of the crowbar caught Elam just below the jaw, slicing through muscle and almost breaking his neck. He slumped to the ground. He tried to protect his head from a second blow.

"No." Sarah ran from the car screaming at the attackers. "Let him alone. Please leave him alone." The skies opened over the scene. Blood poured into the muddy water.

Sarah grabbed Carlos, trying to pull him away from Elam. He swung around, catching her with the back of his closed fist. She dropped to the ground like a rock. "Grab her. Hold her down."

Emilio let go of Manuel and rushed toward Sarah. He dropped on top of her, pinning her to the ground next to Elam. Frenzied, Emilio smashed her face with his fist. Her head sank into the mud. He hit her again. Blood flowed from each body, mixing in shallow pools. Elam tried again to roll away from Carlos, but he was too disoriented to move fast. The second strike of the crowbar caught him in the right shoulder. The third strike hit Elam just behind his thumb on the back of his head. His skull cracked like a pecan. Wind whistled in the trees as the sheets of rain gave way to small pellets of hail.

Elam lay in the pond, his body convulsing in the last spasms of life. Sarah, semi-conscious, moaned through a half-open mouth holding blood, water, mud, and phlegm.

Twenty-Four

Saturday Night, March 20

Luling, Texas

Carlos yelled to the others, "Tie the woman up. Put her in the bed of the truck." He wiped his forearm across his brow. The rain came in sheets. Elam lay at his feet.

Manuel could barely move. Carlos swore at him under his breath. "*Puta.*"

Emilio ran back to the shed and grabbed several transportation straps and a bundle of rags. He returned to Sarah, stuffing part of a rag in her mouth, then holding it in place by tying another rag over it to the back of her neck. He rolled her over on her stomach and tied her hands behind her back. Sarah, coming out of a terrible sleep, groaned incoherently. A gag reflex caused her to heave. She opened her eyes, squinting into nickel-sized raindrops. Though groggy she immediately sensed her situation. Abject horror swept over her as she watched the form of a man tying her legs together. Her arms felt as though they were being ripped from her shoulders. She struggled to free them but was helpless. Sledgehammer pain slammed against the inside of her head.

"Get in the truck," Carlos screamed at Manuel. He ran over to Emilio, yelling, "Grab her legs. We're putting her in the truck bed."

Manuel struggled his way to the back door of the crew cab. He lifted himself inside and lay down on the back seat. He was of no use to anyone. Carlos wedged his arms in the openings between Sarah's arms and each side. While Emilio lifted her legs, Carlos lifted Sarah's body. They carried her to the back of the truck. Carlos dropped her on the tailgate like a sack of potatoes. He thought nothing of the pain he inflicted on her. Both men pulled on her shoulders to move her into the bed of the truck. Twice Carlos had to wedge Sarah between the JETS chamber and the tie-down straps used to secure it. Sarah faded again into semi-consciousness, unable to overcome the waves of suffering.

Unsecured debris flew through the air. Branches started to separate from the trees. The shed bucked violently back and forth. Carlos could only think of escaping.

"Help me put him in the truck," Carlos yelled into the wind.

"OK." Emilio robotically obeyed. He was glad that Carlos had a plan.

Carlos only wanted to leave the site.

Carlos and Emilio struggled to put the two hundred–pound Elam in a sitting position at the tailgate. Each one on an arm, the two men lifted Elam at the shoulders to a near standing position and let his body fall backwards into the truck bed. Carlos again pulled on the body as Emilio pushed at the knees.

"Get the tarps and cover them up."

Emilio returned to the shed, sidestepping the flailing double doors. He returned to the truck where Carlos took one of the tarps. Emilio wedged the tarp haphazardly between the tie-down straps and Elam's body, tucking the ends over his head and feet. Carlos did the same with Sarah. Briefly Carlos and Sarah looked at each other face to face. In her look the fear was gone, replaced by an intensity that reached into his soul. Her message was clear: *You are nothing. Nothing at all.* He covered her face and stepped back. For the first time in his adult life, something akin to remorse gnawed at him. His stomach rolled with bile.

Problems continued to mount. Carlos needed to get out of the area immediately. Still, he knew the car had to be moved.

Carlos turned to Emilio and commanded, "Take his car and follow me."

"I never drive a car like that." Emilio was scared.

Carlos screamed again, "I said get in the fucking car and follow me." He paused a split second. "Now!" Then he pointed to some leftover rags. "Take some of them and don't get your hands on nothing."

Emilio ran to the back of the truck and picked up two of the remaining rags. He got in the car and turned the ignition switch. A terrible grinding sound erupted. It took Emilio a moment to realize that the car was still idling.

As Carlos opened the door to the truck, he heard a low groan in the distance. He had never heard such a noise before, but his body sensed danger. The wind ripped at the trees and pummeled his truck. The sound lowered in pitch but rose in volume. In front of incessant forked bolts of lightning, a black turning mass moved toward them: a tornado.

With Carlos in the lead and Emilio trying to control Elam's battered car, the vehicles raced down the mud filled road. Throughout the constant pounding Sarah endured tortuous pain. Elam slept peacefully at the beginning of a new eternity.

Carlos turned north at Route 86 as incredible winds hammered the truck.

Packing furious winds reaching 200 miles an hour, the tornado crossed Guadalupe County into Caldwell County at exactly ten o'clock. Its first lethal strike was Luling, where small homes and farms along US 90 were splintered under the groaning storm and flung to the heavens. The first home, sitting just inside the city limits of Luling, belonged to the Flores family.

Oracio Flores looked one last time into the constant strikes of lightning and the apparition approaching from the west. Twisting masses of cloud and debris, overpowering sounds of shrieking winds, and terrifying vibrations almost lifting him from his feet were incomprehensible. Escape was impossible.

"Margarita! Jose, Juan, Francisco! Get to the bathroom. Now! Now!" Oracio screamed to his threatened family.

Instantaneously the windows exploded, propelling shattered glass into the terrified family. Margarita, blood gushing from gashes in her head and cheeks, reached the bathroom but wouldn't go in; she turned to go back for the boys. Oracio grabbed her by the wrist.

"The boys. We must get the boys," she pleaded, and tried to break free from his grip.

"No. Get in the bathtub," screamed Oracio, his words laced with fear. "Now!" He pulled Margarita from the hallway and shoved her into the bathroom. Then he ran down the hallway toward the boys.

Jose and Francisco struggled against the winds and managed to make it to their father. To his horror, Oracio watched helplessly as Francisco lost his fight for safety. In the flash of an eye the suction carried him out of the disintegrating home and into the pitch-black sky. He was gone. Oracio held the other two in his arms. Unable to move, he pushed his sons to the floor and covered them with his body. He could not hear their crying in the roar of a thousand trains. The walls began collapsing around them, only to be swept away as the tornado engulfed the house. Falling prey to the storm's demands, one by one Oracio and the two boys followed Francisco into the night. "Margarita" was his last word.

"Mi Dio, Mi Dio, Mi Dio . . ." Margarita, huddled in the home's only bathtub, prayed continuously for her family . . . until the ceiling caved in.

Catastrophic damage engulfed the town. A young couple, married two months before, died in a mobile home just to the west of Mimosa Avenue. Thirty-two other lives were snuffed out over the next four minutes. The storm slammed into the northern half of the town, taking with it virtually every structure north and west of the intersection at Davis Street and Laurel Avenue. The Josey House, a Classical Revival home built in 1881, disappeared from the face of the earth. Like dominoes, store after store fell before the onslaught of vicious winds. Two gabled facades with *Walker Bro's* written along the bottom were sheared off the top of the Luling Visitors Center and Central Texas Oil Patch Museum; next, the arched windows and architecturally impressive tan brick facing exploded into an immense debris field simultaneously with the shredding of the first floor canopy. The building simply vanished. Building after building along Davis Street suffered that same consequence—save one. In a miracle of immense scale, little Monte's Bar remained mostly intact and forty-five terrified people survived. They survived not by the strength of the structure but by the vagaries of a multiple-vortex tornado. Others were not as lucky. Elsie Manor, caretaker of the First Baptist Church for thirty years, died beneath a partial collapse of the roof structure. Six employees, dutifully staying late to clean the entire restaurant, died at City Market in a hail of shattered glass and brick. Their timing could not have been worse. All that remained of City Market was a concrete slab. Along the blocks north of Davis Street, mayhem was the order of the night.

Most residents huddled in small storm cellars. For those who didn't, the consequences were severe. The Eyler family fled their home on Myrtle Street. Harold Eyler, owner of Luling Feed Supply, put his wife and three children in the family car and tried to outrun it. It was fantasy to even try; in the confusion, Harold drove into, rather than away from, the funnel. The vicious vortex swallowed the family. Their bodies, grotesquely sandwiched in the twisted metal casket, lay five hundred yards from the road. Twenty-four others, from a ninety-two-year-old great-grandmother to a six-year-old boy found alone in a field almost a mile from his home, died that night, each one plucked randomly from this life. Most had lived, played, and worked in Luling all their lives, taking the good with the bad and enjoying the benefits of a simple, wholesome life. In the days following the tornado, the haunting question would come to be "Why?" It is always an unanswerable question. One thing was certain: the former "Toughest Town in Texas" was crushed into a whimpering, beaten child.

Tom, Susie, Don, and several members of the family were riveted to the television. They watched and listened real time as KHOU television reported the several tornadoes bearing down on town after town.

Alex Sanz, a veteran of Hurricane Katrina, and Allison Triarsi, who missed being in the middle of the Minneapolis Bridge collapse by only a few seconds, were doing a tag team newscast. Alex pointed to a spot on a map of the eastern half of Texas. "The southern storm has just struck Luling. Early reports are that the town has suffered extreme damage. There are no reports of injuries at this time, but we are trying to establish communications with the local police department." Moving his hand to a spot just east of Luling, he continued, "This appears to be an EF-4 or EF-5 tornado and it is still on the ground. People living anywhere in the vicinity of Waelder and LaGrange should immediately seek shelter." He moved his finger up several inches. "We also have confirmation of a tornado on the ground near Marlin." He turned slightly away from the camera, clearly distracted. He stopped his discussion momentarily as information was relayed through his earplug.

The camera turned to Allison. She added to the grim report, "Another report indicates that Prairie Dell has taken a direct hit."

The phalanx moved relentlessly toward Houston, now less than ninety miles away. It was always a crapshoot, the question being, "Will the storms die out in the cooling of the evening skies?"

"Be back in a few minutes," said Tom as he walked toward the front door.

Steve looked up at his father. "Where you headed?"

"Just want to make sure the J-3 is tied down."

Steve jumped up. "I'll give you a hand."

Don offered a sly smile. "And I'll protect the women and children."

Tom decided against taking the golf cart, so both men walked rapidly toward the hangar. Perspiration soaked their shirts.

"So how bad's it going to be around here?" Steve wanted to show bravado but was clearly concerned.

"The chances of a tornado are remote. Doesn't matter how bad the storm system is. But we could get some bad winds. If the hangar goes down I want to be able to save most of the J-3." Just before entering a stand of trees Tom looked to the west. Nothing in sight, not even a hint of lightning.

It was the calm before the storm.

Twenty-Five

Saturday Night,
March 20

North of Luling, Texas

The truck, caught in nature's fury of wind, rain, and debris, swayed drunkenly back and forth along Highway 86. Stark flashes of lightning and coal-black skies grappled for dominance. What light might have emanated from dwellings in the countryside on other nights vanished with the power grid that died at the onset of the storm. In the truck bed, Sarah suffered immeasurable pain as she could do little to protect her head from unceasing impacts with the truck bed. Elam's lifeless body bounced freely two feet away. She wished for the sweetness of death.

Suddenly the rain stopped. A couple of sweeps of the wipers and the road appeared before them. The timing was fortunate. Directly in front of them lay a line of toppled oaks. Carlos stopped. Emilio braked urgently, almost hitting the back of the truck. An oak tree temporarily blocked them.

Carlos stepped out of the truck and walked to the tree. "Shit."

Emilio joined him at the tree.

"There's a chainsaw in the tool chest. Get it."

Before Emilio could respond his attention shifted. Some two hundred yards beyond the tree a highway patrol car hurtled toward them, siren wailing and lights flashing. Carlos walked around the large branch. The only good fortune going Carlos's way was that leaves had just started sprouting and visibility was terrible.

"Put the tarps on them. Hurry."

Emilio ran back to the truck, grabbed at every piece of cloth and strap possible, and started tucking exposed body parts beneath the tarps.

The patrol car skidded to a stop and the two officers exited in a near run. Carlos acted fast; he walked toward them.

"How bad is the road to Luling? Can we get through?" The officers were clearly interested in moving on.

Carlos relaxed just enough to think clearly. "It's bad but it's passable between here and the edge of Luling. I don't know how bad it is in town."

The larger patrolman brought him up to date. "Luling was hit by a tornado. Reports are that they've got a shitpot full of dead and injured." Pointing at the tree, he added, "We need to get this out of here. You got any tools in the truck?"

Think. Think. Carlos responded quickly on his feet. "Yeah. I got some straps and I can pull that tree out of the way." He pointed to the oak covering the asphalt roadway. "I need you to put your spotlight on the small end of the tree." Looking at several larger oaks, none of which completely blocked the road, Carlos realized his good fortune that this particular tree was relatively small.

"Right. No problem."

The two patrolmen walked back toward their car and Carlos ran to the truck.

Carlos reached over the side of the truck bed near the cab and pulled two unused cargo straps from the pile. Next he reached into the tool chest and pulled out a large industrial flashlight. He instructed Emilio, "Get the car out of the way. Cover them people up with more rags and bring the truck up to about ten feet from the tree. Don't act funny. Keep the headlights on high." He turned and walked back toward the glare of the patrol car headlights. He turned on his flashlight as well, hoping to blind the patrolmen's eyes from the contents in the open truck bed.

The patrolmen stepped over the tree and were no more than five feet from the truck when Emilio started backing Elam's car.

Carlos intercepted them with outstretched hands containing ends of the two straps. "Here. Tie both of these around the top end of the tree." He pointed to the far side of the road. "Do it just past the edge of the road over there. Please use half hitches."

The two cops displayed a natural obedience to authority. Carlos knew what he was doing; therefore, Carlos was in charge. Rainfall began anew and another cell of lightning headed their way. Each person went about his business. The patrolmen tied half hitches while Emilio eased the truck toward the tree. Carlos pulled the straps until he felt the tension. He tied the free ends of the straps to lifting shackles affixed to the frame near the front bumper.

Carlos approached the cab and spoke to Emilio. "Get out. Go over by the cops and smile."

They changed places and Carlos put the truck into reverse and pushed down on the gas pedal. The wheels started spinning on the wet asphalt. "Come on, you son of a bitch." Then he realized that he hadn't put it into four-wheel drive. He engaged the drive and steadily increased the power. Initially held by static friction between the large trunk and branches and the rough road surface, the tree finally broke away and the truck surged backwards. Once in motion, the truck performed exactly as Carlos needed it to.

After pulling the tree to where it was almost aligned with the road, Carlos yelled out of the cab, "Can you get by?"

The larger patrolman could be heard over the rain. "Yeah, it's good."

The smaller one gave a quick shot on the siren. Sarah, slowly regaining her senses, heard the distinct change in frequency from a low baritone to high soprano: "Boo-eeep." She struggled as hard as she could and managed to rotate her body slightly. She tried muffled screams and beating her tied feet against the side of the truck.

"Thanks a lot. And good luck." The larger patrolman, riding shotgun, gave Carlos and Emilio a high sign as the car rolled by.

"What's that?" Patrolman Large had heard something from the side of the truck.

"What's what?" Patrolman Small asked as the car accelerated.

"Aw, forget it."

"Whoo, boy. I sure hope Elam made it to his date before all this hit the fan." Don couldn't sit down.

Tom, still glued to the television, responded, "Check him out. Give him a call."

Don agreed. "Guess I could have thought of that." He took the kitchen phone from the wall and dialed Elam. It rang four times.

A professional feminine voice answered, "Elam Duquette,

president of Donelam Oil Systems, is unavailable. Please leave a message and phone number. Thank you."

Don hung up. It did not feel right.

"He didn't answer."

Nancy added, "He may have turned off his phone. I wouldn't have it on if I'm taking someone out to dinner."

It made sense to Don and relieved him just a bit. He needed some fresh air. "I'm off for a beer and fresh air. Who wants one?"

Two male hands rose into the air.

Don made his way to the back porch. The ice chest, moved from the front yard once the guests departed, had half a case of beer left. Don took one and then pulled a chair off the concrete and into the grass overlooking the runway. Inside, the party had turned sober. Eight adults and three children were to ride out whatever came their way. Don, disregarding his MS and the fact that light structures and tornadoes did not mix well, made a bid to sleep in the caboose. The others would fit easily in the two guest rooms.

"Come on Elam, answer the damn phone," Don half-commanded, half-pleaded.

"Elam Duquette, president . . ."

Don closed the cell phone and placed it in his shirt pocket. He stared into the western night sky. It was eerily calm, quiet except for a coyote baying far off in the pines. He thought about his friend. He felt dread. He wondered about the woman.

Carlos turned off of Highway 86 and onto a muddy road. He gunned the engine, swerving back and forth over slippery ruts and puddles. He just wanted to get away from the site. Emilio followed far enough behind not to be hit by the dark rooster tail spewing from the truck. Eventually Carlos slowed into a controllable ride on the worsening road. He made another right turn to a small trail obviously unused for several months. He pulled to a stop and waved the Cadillac to pull in front of him.

Emilio exited the car and ran to the driver's window. Carlos rolled down the window, his eyes almost blank. He needed to think. "Damn. Go turn the damn lights off."

The Cadillac lights, on high beam, sliced through the almost bare countryside, easily seen by any Tom, Dick, or cop in the whole state of Texas. Emilio ran back to the car and turned off the lights.

When he returned, Carlos issued an order. "Take a look in the bed and check on the woman." Carlos could hardly believe how stupid some people could be. "I'm getting into the car so I don't have to listen to his whimpering shit all night." He gestured toward the hapless Manuel. Carlos continued, "I don't want her going nowhere."

Emilio disappeared into the night and Carlos walked to Elam's car. Three Mexican men, one dead body, and a woman struggling to survive were lost in the blackness of an indiscernible spot on the planet.

Carlos leaned forward, resting his forehead on the steering wheel, his hands next to his temples. Labored breathing made it hard to concentrate. He had to think and he needed help. Carlos reached into his pocket and pulled out his cell phone.

While Carlos unsuccessfully tried to make contact with Bart Miles, Emilio made his way to the truck, stopping on the side where Elam lay. He waited until he had some night vision and then glanced quickly at the lifeless form. Satisfied that Elam was dead, Emilio moved over to the woman. He felt the straps tied around her wrists and legs. They were secure. She made a restless, gurgling sound, moving slightly in an attempt to ease her pain. He stared at her, trying to overcome the darkness. Remnants of more than a six-pack of beer numbed his inhibitions. He reached down and moved his arms up and down her body. He dug into her blouse and inside of her bra. Her breast felt strangely cold, but its softness was arousing. Emilio pulled her dress up to her waist. He wanted to feel her crotch but her legs were tied together. He hurriedly untied the ankle straps and grabbed her panties. It was easy to pull them off. He tossed them to the side of the road and climbed over the side of the truck.

Carlos processed his options; his options were few. *Got no choice. She will tell people. I have to kill her. Mr. Miles would do the same thing. No choice.* Carlos knew the inevitable fate for Sarah, but he struggled to make a plan. He lifted his head and stared blankly into the night. He turned the radio on and picked up a station running rampant with descriptions of the ongoing storm. The steady stream of death and damage reports settled Carlos's emotional state. A plan sprung forth from the recesses of his mind.

"Emilio." Carlos called back to Emilio. No answer. Carlos called again, this time louder than he wished.

When no one answered, Carlos got out of the car and walked back to the truck. At the back of the truck, hidden partially but not completely in the darkness of night, Carlos could make out a strange human form in the truck bed. Walking closer, Carlos saw Emilio unbuttoning his pants and the semi-nude Sarah Bettner. Carlos was disgusted.

From his position at the side of the cargo bed, Carlos reached out and slammed Emilio's body against the JETS chamber section. The would-be rapist fell on top of Sarah, evoking muffled moans of agony from the suffering woman. Carlos reached over the side and grabbed Emilio by the neck. Drawing Emilio's face within six inches of his own, Carlos snarled, "You stupid piece of shit. You know DNA? You go in her and you get the big needle. Did you do her?"

Emilio stammered, "No. No. I didn't do nothing." He backed away from Sarah and slid off the back of the truck, head looking down as he buckled his belt.

Carlos commanded, "Get in the cab. Don't do nothing until I come back."

Emilio got into the driver's seat in the truck while Carlos looked over the side of the truck bed. Lightning flashes in the distance illuminated the face of a ravaged, innocent woman. She deserved a better fate. The wind blew colder against his face and body. *Do it. Do it now.* Two sets of eyes made contact. Hers no longer showed fear, only resignation and pity passed on to Carlos. He looked away. Carlos would kill her but he knew she was a real human being and he was a coward. *Do it. Do it now!* Carlos got in the truck bed, leaning over the defenseless woman. He grabbed the loose strap at her legs and wrapped it around both hands, leaving a section of ten inches. Sarah did not fight him. He placed the section of strap at her neck and slowly applied pressure until the air passage began to close. She didn't move. He looked away again while simultaneously applying more pressure. Still there was no fighting by Sarah. A bolt of lightning split the night sky with a brilliant aura. He looked back at her and saw her eyes piercing into him. The clap of thunder roared. All the travesties of hell could not match the evil at his hands. He turned away once more, then leaned down with full body weight. Unable to defeat the body's desire for life, Sarah convulsed in rapid jerks–then she went still. She never made a sound.

Don limped back and forth like the irascible Dr. House. "OK, I've had it. I've got to track Elam down. At a time like this he wouldn't ignore me. He's got to know that the storm went through Luling."

"There're probably a dozen reasons why Elam has his phone off." Tom wanted to assure Don that there wasn't any real problem. "Especially if he had the date of all dates. He'd sure as hell rather be talking to a woman than to you."

The looks on faces verified that no one was buying Tom's version of the situation.

Don answered, "No. He's too wired for that." Don tapped his cane on the stone floor. The popping sound reverberated throughout the living room.

"Tell you what." Tom walked toward the refrigerator, talking as he went. "If he hasn't called by tomorrow morning we'll fly out to Luling. That is, if they will let us land there."

"Hey, everybody, look at that sky!" Sally, the only one who missed the conversation, walked in from the back porch, her eyes like saucers.

The group moved to the porch. Beyond the pine trees standing guard at the west end of the runway, sheet lightning rolled through the night sky, stretching across the entire horizon. Before the faint mumble of thunder could be heard, gentle but ominous vibrations reached each person from afar.

Tom called out to everyone. "OK, troops. Back inside." It was time for the Broken Wing Ranch to batten down the hatches.

At the same moment, Bart Miles answered his cell phone. It was Carlos.

Twenty-Six

Saturday Night,
March 20

Luling, Texas

People emerged from shelters and shattered homes within minutes of the tornado's departure. The residents were shell-shocked, badly beaten by the wind-driven nightmare. Some stumbled from their homes in stark confusion; others began frenzied searches for survivors. Intermittent rain pelted the people and a cold, raw wind made life, at least what was left of life, miserable.

"Hello. Anybody there? Hello. Hello." The young man, a six-battery flashlight in his hand and a baseball cap covering wavy blond hair, called into the debris of what was once a home on Newton Street. "Anybody there? Give me a holler if you can." No response came from the home.

"Nothing here. Let's get to the next one." Joined by another rescuer, he raced to the house next door. Nothing could be found that resembled a structure. Most of the homes had been reduced to slab foundations.

C. T. Scanlan reached back to shake hands with his fellow

survivor. "C. T. Scanlan. We've got some work to do."

A broad-shouldered black man in his mid-fifties answered on the run, "Bert Hines. Let's get after it."

The two men reached the next home in seconds.

"Hello. Anybody there?" C. T. called again.

"Help me. I'm hurt." Weak but clear, a woman's voice floated from the wreckage.

"Hang on. We're coming."

Bert, short labored breaths straining his speech, offered to seek more help. "C. T., do what you can until I get back with more help."

Bert sprinted away in the blackness, searching for any able-bodied person he could find. C. T. Scanlan began a frantic effort to remove splintered siding, studs, sheetrock, sections of the roof trusses, and other debris trapping the woman in her once-modest home.

"I'm hurt. Don't hurt me. It's going to fall on me. Oh, Lord, please help me."

Bert returned twenty minutes later with two other men and rejoined C. T. in the rescue effort. Almost by instinct, the haphazard grabbing of broken wood settled into an organized, efficient conveyor belt of debris removal.

At short intervals C. T. would talk to the woman to keep her calm. "We're getting there. You're going to be all right."

The lady calmed somewhat, but still whimpered through the ordeal. Thirty minutes later she could see the beam from the flashlight. Shortly thereafter, a hole began to form above her head. She called again, "I can see you. Please be careful. I can't find my husband. Please save my husband." Hers was the only voice in the house.

C. T. turned to Bert and the other two men, fear in his eyes. "There's two of them but I've only heard from the woman. Nothing from her husband. He's got to be in there."

"OK, let's do it."

Another fifteen minutes later they reached the woman. C. T.'s first reaction was to just hold her hand for a moment.

"My husband. Can you find my husband?" Her cries came as part despair and part pain. "He put me in the bathroom and left to get something to put over us. Please find my husband. I think he's in the bedroom."

There was no bedroom.

"I will ma'am, I promise. But we've got to get you out of here first. Can you move?" He squeezed her hand again and searched her body with the flashlight. She had blood all over her, most of it from hundreds of small cuts. Then the beam shone on her right leg to a compound fracture just above the ankle. It sickened him. "I'll be right back."

"I hurt bad. Don't leave me. Please don't leave me."

"I'll be right back. I'm going to get some more help." He climbed out of the man-made hole and met with the other men.

"Badly broken leg. Bone's sticking out. How're we going to do this?" He pulled the cap down to further shield his eyes from the latest rainsquall.

One of the others responded. "I'm a volunteer fireman. Never done this for real, only training. I say we get something for a stretcher and put her on it. It's going to hurt like hell, but we'll have to splint her leg immediately. I can give it a try."

The woman, vacillating between excruciating pain and total oblivion to all around her, was pulled to safety two hours later. They found her husband crushed to death against a backyard tree. C. T. and Bert worked another twenty hours before fatigue overtook them.

The same scene played out over Luling, eight other towns in Texas, numerous towns in other states, and in isolated homesteads dotting the open country.

Carlos drove well within the speed limit; his mind raced out of control. The two vehicles had traveled full circle, pulling back into the test site shortly before midnight. The off-and-on rain had turned to intermittent drizzle, but cold winds continued to buffet the countryside. He stopped the Cadillac, got out, and surveyed the surroundings. The site was a mess. The back end of the shed was open and the roof had partially collapsed. The splintered derrick lay on top of the fence and assorted equipment, some from the shed, was spread over the entire area. Carlos breathed a sigh of relief. He went back to Emilio and Manuel.

Looking at Manuel, Carlos growled, "Can you walk or are you still a pussy?"

"My knee must be broke. It hurts bad. Real bad, man."

Carlos felt like killing Manuel for his stupidity. He wondered how he could be using nitwits to help him.

Wiping his eyes, Carlos spoke. "OK, here's what we're going to do. Emilio, help me with the bodies, we're going . . ."

Emilio was puzzled. "What do you mean? They both dead?"

"Shut up." He continued. "We're going to put them back here on the ground. You roll them in the mud real good while I wreck their car. We'll put his body next to the derrick and she will go on the fence." Carlos pointed to a section of twisted chain-link fence.

They dragged Elam's body out of the back of the truck, letting his upper torso hit the ground like a rock.

"Take the truck over there and put her on the fence," ordered Carlos. "Roll her in the mud first. Don't bring the truck back, just leave it there till we finish."

Emilio drove the truck to the fence line while Carlos

climbed back into the Cadillac. He moved the car just outside of the site entrance. He wiped the steering wheel and door handles with a cloth. Then he half-jogged to the equipment park. Fortunately, the bucket loader had not rolled over in the storm. Carlos climbed on and started it up. He drove it to the Cadillac and, using the bucket as a hammer, slammed it down several times on the body and hood of the car. The final blow shattered the windshield. Once finished with the car damage, Carlos used the bucket as a fulcrum and rolled the car over in two moves. It rolled over one full revolution, landing upright and looking to be a total loss. He inspected his work and was satisfied that the car matched the devastation suffered by the rest of the site.

Emilio finished placing Sarah's body on the fence and returned to watch Carlos smashing the car. He trailed the bucket loader back to the equipment park. Carlos stepped down and walked through the site toward Elam. He picked up a four-by-four wooden post. "You use this and break his bones. Then hit him once in the face."

"Carlos, I can't. I can't do that."

"Shut up." Carlos shoved the post into Emilio's chest. "I don't have time for any shit. Do it."

Emilio stared blankly at Carlos while feebly extending his arms to cradle the post.

"Then do the same with the woman. But only break her arms."

Emilio did as instructed while Manuel, horrified at the carnage, watched from the back of the truck cab. After a few minutes he saw Carlos and Emilio standing over the woman's body talking. Carlos took the post from Emilio and used it to hit her in the throat. Manuel could see Carlos giving more instructions to Emilio. Emilio walked a few steps and found another piece of wood on the ground. Then both men worked their way back to the truck while carving ruts into the surface of the ground, hiding tire tracks, footprints, and any other signs that they had been there.

As slowly as possible, Carlos drove away from the scene. The JETS display components remained nestled in the bed of the truck, covered in places with an elixir of blood and rainwater. He prayed for rain to hide evidence. Finally, he got through to Bart Miles.

The weather improved slowly. The rain eased, and throughout the night the post-storm wind abated somewhat to a steady gale. With brisk breezes, dawn broke cool and clear over the entire state. The line of storms moved across Louisiana, Mississippi, Alabama, Georgia, and the Carolinas. The last tornado of the outbreak struck Mullins, South Carolina late the next day, and with it the two-hundred-and-first fatality, a young boy fishing on the Lumber River, was tallied. Not the financial or human loss of Hurricanes Katrina and Ike, the tri-state tornado of 1925, or the super tornado outbreak of 1974, but where the tornadoes touched down, death and destruction reigned supreme.

Twenty-Seven

Sunday Morning,
March 21

On the Road to Luling, Texas

Tom and Don decided upon the truck. Even if a plane were allowed to land at Luling there would be no means of transportation under the existing conditions. Carpenter tools, rope, a chain saw, a 5.5 kW Generac generator, and assorted other rescue gear were placed in the truck bed. Bottled water, a dozen packages of peanut butter crackers, two flashlights, and batteries rested in the cramped back seat.

They stopped at Kott's in Anderson for egg and sausage sandwiches and hot coffee to go.

The owner, Percy Painter, spit some tobacco into a cup. "You boys heard about the storms? Not so bad here as in other towns."

Tom replied, "Yeah, we did. We're headed to Luling to check some property out. Best we can tell the whole town is a mess."

"Yep, that's what folks've been tellin' me all morning." He placed the sandwiches on the counter. "To-go coffee's over there." He pointed to a small table near the front door.

"Thanks." Tom stopped by no less than once a month for over the past year, and every time he was told "To-go coffee's over there."

In ten minutes they were back on the road.

"What do you think we're going to find?" Don asked as he bit into his sandwich.

"Well, I know that Luling's got to be a hellhole, but I'm hoping that the test site made out all right. Just like summer rains, one spot is destroyed and fifty feet away nothing's happened."

"I hope you're right. We don't need a lot of broken shit and we don't have any insurance on the equipment."

Tom, finishing his first bite, added, "Even if there's damage we'll just go back to square one and crank it up again. Hell, Elam's not about to let a tornado interfere with his fun."

"Yeah, guess you're right." Don stared out of the window, wondering what they would find. Then he remembered something. "By the way, I never did get to tell you about that small company in Lubbock."

"Caprock?"

"Yeah. I like their people. I told them we would be glad to give them a demonstration. I'll be setting up a time with them."

"Good. I still feel you ought to be dealing only with American companies."

"You're right. Elam sometimes thinks too much of his abilities to deal with people. He's ornery, but he's also naïve." Don looked down at his sandwich. "Man, these are good."

Their attention quickly returned to the radio. The customary talk-show hosts were pre-empted by nonstop news coverage of the aftermath of the storms. Given the anticipated degree of damage, Tom decided to approach the site from the north side of Luling. From Anderson Tom drove south to Brenham, west to Paige, west past Bastrop, south to Red Rock, and finally toward Luling on FM 86. Between McMahan and Luling the telltale signs of the storm filled the countryside.

Don spoke up. "Look at that." His head swiveled back and forth on its muscular pedestal. Debris everywhere. Branches were stripped from the trunks of the remaining trees and strewn throughout the countryside. Leaves and assorted trash covered the road. Rooftops had been partially torn from homes and buildings. In many cases, the structures themselves no longer existed.

Don recognized the entrance to the site. "That's it, up on the left." He pointed to the small dirt road one hundred yards to their front.

Tom slowed the truck and turned left onto the muddied road. Puddles of brown water covered much of the roadway.

"Oh shit." Don took a deep breath. "I don't believe it." Nearly everything between the highway and the site had been destroyed. Just past the one operational pumpjack Tom turned into the site. It was unrecognizable. The derrick and holding tanks were in shambles, sections of the fence were down, and the maintenance/storage building had partially collapsed. Tom was the first to notice.

"Don, there's someone down where the derrick used to be."

He pulled forward and stopped the truck a few feet from the remains of the derrick. Both men got out and walked to the lifeless body. It was a man lying face down in mud, both legs broken grotesquely below the knees. His head and torso were matted with dry mud. Don stood motionless for a few seconds. With some difficulty, he knelt down.

"It's Elam." He reached out and touched Elam's shoulder. Nothing. Don took a handkerchief from his back pocket and gently brushed Elam's cheek in an attempt to clean his face, or to wake him up. Don crawled around to Elam's front and sat down. He just studied Elam's face.

Don looked up at Tom, but spoke to himself. "This just isn't happening. I don't believe it." He returned his gaze to the cantankerous but loveable Elam Duquette. Don blinked his eyes and asked quietly, "What about his girlfriend?"

"Probably took her home and came back here."

"Maybe, but it doesn't seem to square with time. The tornado hit sometime around ten o'clock. It's possible they never got together and he just came out here to secure everything he could."

Tom massaged his forehead and then stood up. "We need to look around."

Tom gave a hand and helped Don stand up. They looked around the site. It was an absolute mess; the brisk breeze only added to their chill. Tom caught sight of something in the distance that did not mesh with everything else. Don stood over Elam's body while Tom walked some fifty feet away trying to focus on the object. He stopped.

"There. At the fence." Tom called to his brother and pointed to the northern perimeter of the site.

What otherwise would be mistaken as a large laundry bag lay straddled atop the chain link fence turned on its side. Tom waited for Don to reach him and then they both walked to the body. Her dress had blown partially over her upper torso, revealing her bare buttocks. Tom leaned down and pulled the dress over her legs.

"Maybe they came here to make love. I can't understand another reason for no panties."

"Could've been the wind."

Tom agreed. "Yeah, maybe."

Tom reached for his Blackberry. "Let me get the police or EMS out here."

Don waved his hand. "If you don't mind, I'd rather take them both directly to Breuner's Funeral Home."

Ignoring the pigeons, Bart Miles paced nervously back and forth in front of a statue of the patriot Dick Dowling standing guard above a picturesque section of Houston's Hermann Park. Bart was tense to the point that he was unaware of Frank's presence.

"This privacy shit is a little unnecessary."

Frank's words startled Bart. He spun around, his eyes like saucers. "What the . . ." He changed his words. "Damn it, Frank, don't come up to me like that."

"It's Sunday morning. Why aren't we just sitting down at the office? Don't you think we're being a little childish?" Frank frowned at his obviously excitable colleague. Frank dressed for a cold, windy weekend. He wore jeans, sneakers, a dark green sweatshirt, and a blue ski jacket he normally used only in Colorado.

Bart dressed in business attire, affording him little protection from the wind. Bart was cold. He shot back, "It's not so childish when we're going to talk about murder. Let's take a walk." He turned and headed away from the circular concrete walkway surrounding the monument and toward the Hermann Park Golf Course.

"It's Carlos, isn't it? I told you he was going to screw everything up."

Frank caught up with the shorter Bart. Bart took small steps, but at twice the speed of a normal person.

"Carlos killed them both. Duquette and a woman. At Duquette's work site. It's done, end of story." Bart looked down at the pavement, his voice far from forceful. "He called back later and told me he had taken both of them back to the testing site. The tornado had made a mess of the place. We are very fortunate . . ." Again Bart made use of "we." "They'll be looked at as two of the many people killed by the storm."

Frank asked, "Did Carlos manage to get the extraction device out of there?"

"Yeah, the new display model is already in Louisiana. We've got until sunrise tomorrow to get it back to the test site. Tornado or not, it won't take long for people to realize that it's missing." Bart timed the conversation. He made a short U-turn and walked back toward Dick Dowling.

Frank, breathing rapidly, asked, "Who's going to break it down?"

"A guy in Breaux Bridge, Louisiana. Jason French. Does mechanical drawing; he worked for me when we sued McAllister Oil. Knows his stuff. He said he could have it broken down, studied, and reassembled by midnight. We can get it back in the early morning. He'll make the drawings and send them to us. There's no problem."

"What about the Mexicans?"

"I've got to work on it. Their part has gotten out of hand, so we need to take care of them soon."

"Don't give me this 'we' shit. The whole mess is your baby."

"Is it?" Bart stopped mid-stream and squared face-to-face with Frank. "Every time we talk money, you smile and put your hands out. Every time something gets dicey, you run and hide."

"Horseshit." Frank scowled at Bart, his veins popping vertically along his neck. He grabbed Bart's arm just enough to turn him to his left. "I've done more shit for you than you can shake a stick at. Without me you wouldn't have jack." Frank stuck his finger in Bart's chest. "Tell you what. You do your part and I'll do mine. And right now your part is fucked up. Again, what about the Mexicans?"

Bart turned back and started walking at a slower pace. He waited until a small group of people passed them by.

"You're right, they're a liability. After we get the device back to the test site, I'll take care of them." He added, "You need to get the patent finished." His eyes lifted slightly. "Losing his partner will occupy the guy Seiler for a while anyway. Bottom line, we're still on track."

"OK, good. I need to get back. We need to get this whole damn thing under control."

"It's under control, so don't start running scared on me."

"It better be."

The two men separated and walked to their cars.

From his pigeon-ravaged pedestal, Dick Dowling looked down on Bart and Frank. A community giant of compassion, vision, and outlandish enjoyment of life, Dick was best known as a hero during the Civil War who once led a band of fifty unruly Irishmen and defeated a northern invasion force of twenty-seven ships and six thousand soldiers at Sabine Pass. Just like Bart Miles, he had been an entrepreneur. Just like Bart Miles, he had invested in the oil and gas industry. Just like Bart Miles, he had amassed a fortune. Unlike Bart Miles, before his death in 1867, Dick Dowling had balls and strength of character.

Twenty-Eight

Sunday Afternoon,
March 21

Luling, Texas

Déjà vu. Six hours after Don and Tom brought the bodies to Breuner's Funeral Home, Mary Otter invited them into the same room that held Juan Delgado three months earlier. Don considered the possibility that Juan would pop out of one of the stainless steel doors. He shivered.

Mary pulled cold, stainless steel body trays from two of the refrigeration units. Elam and Sarah lay side by side, only their heads uncovered. Both had been cleaned. Their eyes closed over chalk-gray, expressionless faces.

Tom spoke first. "Mary, could we see the upper half of Mr. Duquette's body?"

Mary Otter pulled Elam's sheet down to his navel.

Tom leaned over Elam's body without touching the tray. His eyes executed search patterns over Don's friend. Grim-faced, he studied Elam's body with intense precision. He took out his pad of paper and started writing notes. Five minutes later Tom requested the sheet be lifted to expose

Elam's broken legs. He studied the body and wrote more notes.

Tom's actions, though done many times in different situations, confused Don. In reverence to their environment, Don whispered, "What are you doing?"

"Same thing I always do, taking notes."

Mary stood by quietly, giving space to the brothers.

"Could we see her body? Just the extremities, would do?"

Mary lifted the sheet to expose her chest above her breasts and her legs from mid-thigh to feet. Then she gently lifted the sides of the sheets, exposing Sarah's symmetrically broken forearms. Don watched as Tom repeated the procedures over Sarah's body. Tom was more sensitive with her than with Elam.

Tom finished writing and turned to Mary.

"How many bodies do you have here?"

Mary Otter was also confused by Tom's actions. Still, she had no reason to be evasive. "We have eight, six from the tornado and two scheduled for burial on Tuesday. The county morgue couldn't handle everything. We've been working straight since the storm."

"I'd like to see any two other storm victims." Tom spoke flatly but with authority.

Without answering, Mary moved to the next two doors. Tom took advantage of the short interlude and took six pictures, three of Elam and three of Sarah. He quickly turned and followed Mary. She pulled out the bodies of an elderly woman and a man probably in his early forties. Circumstances allowed the improper protocol. Tom studied each body for no more than two minutes. After looking at the second body, Tom wrote some final notes, then put his pad back.

"That's enough. Thank you, Mary." Then he remembered something. "Oh, we should have asked sooner, did you ever identify the woman?"

"No, not yet. She had no identification on her."

Don spoke, "Her first name is Sarah. I would think she lived within an hour of Luling. I do remember something being said about dinner in Seguin."

"Thank you. That should help us some."

"How long will the bodies remain here?"

"It's hard to tell. There's so much confusion. If there's no next of kin for Mr. Duquette, the police will allow you to claim the body. That is, if you desire."

Don confirmed her assumption. "Thanks, Mary. We will take Elam." He pulled a business card from his wallet, borrowed Tom's pencil to jot down the phone number at the ranch, and gave it to her. "I'll contact you the day after tomorrow. If you need anything before then, give me a call."

"I will."

Don added, "If you learn anything about Sarah, please let me know. We'd like to talk to her family as well."

"I will. I'm sure they would want to meet you."

Before they hit the bottom step at Breuner's Funeral Home, Tom defined the future.

"Don, something's not right." He stopped and squinted into the sun over Don's shoulder. "And the JETS is the key."

Jason French leaned over the sink, washing with Boraxo hand cleaner. A heavy, dirty, gray beard hid his freckled cheeks and wide jowls. He rinsed and dried his hands, took off his dirty undershirt, and replaced it with a denim long-sleeved shirt. His shop, sitting alone on a bayou just south of Beaux Bridge, was little more than a cinder-block room some twenty feet by forty feet. Fluorescent light panels were spaced at six-foot intervals in both directions. The assembled JETS display model lay on a long wooden table beneath a small gantry. Jason walked back to the table and took his assemblage of notes and drawings. He studied them, took a few final pictures, wrote additional notes, and then smiled. Next he called Bart Miles.

"I studied it and took pictures. I know exactly how it works. You can tell your workers to come and get it."

"What can you tell me about it?" Bart picked at a small scab on his neck. Nervous habit.

"Actually, it's ingenious as hell. Pretty simple mechanism that gets the job done. Very little in the way of moving parts, so they won't have big maintenance problems. I've made some early sketches of it."

"Can you take the basic drawings and make just enough changes to render it a new design?"

"Yeah. No problem. What's your time schedule on this?"

Bart hesitated a couple of seconds, thinking of timing issues. "If you can have them to me by Friday it will be worth six thousand dollars."

Jason quickly did the math. From start to finish he would spend no more than twenty hours. Three hundred dollars an hour is not bad pay. And, of course, a good job will lead to more jobs down the pike.

"They'll be delivered directly to you by Friday morning." He added a caveat. "I won't put my name on any of the drawings. What you do with what I send you is strictly your choice."

Bart thought of something else. "OK. Good. One more thing though, give me the preliminary drawings as well. I'll give them to my draftsman. Don't put your name on them either."

"No problem."

"I'll have my people pick them up in a couple of hours. Just leave the door unlocked."

"Great. It'll be open."

Both men hung up.

Twenty-Nine

Sunday Night,
March 21

Luling, Texas

Fifty-plus years had come and gone since the brothers slept overnight in a vehicle. In those days Tom drove from San Antonio to Port Aransas with Jack and Don for a weekend of fishing. Life on the beach with nothing more than fishing gear, a small World War II pup tent, and the inside of their 1946 Cadillac was the fruit of brotherhood. Don usually slept in the tent; Tom and Jack slept either under the stars or inside the car, the choice dictated by evening weather. The current accommodations felt worlds away from their youth. With permission from the Otter family they parked in the funeral home parking lot. They would need to use the wide-open spaces for late-night nature calls, but the Breuners had offered them use of bathroom facilities early in the morning. Tom insisted that Don use the bed of the truck and he would take the front seat. Tom fashioned pillows out of two rain jackets and a duck-hunting vest. He gave the vest to Don. He next rolled down the cab window and turned up the radio volume. On KTSA in San

Antonio Christian Bove and Elizabeth Ruiz were providing tag-team coverage of the tornado outbreak. Eventually, hours of tornado coverage wore the two men down. Tom turned it off.

Don, his head resting not far from Tom, spoke what was on his mind. As though to himself, he asked, "Can there be any other way they died?" He locked his arms beneath his neck and looked at nothing more than the inky blackness punctured with a million stars. Don wanted any explanation other than what Tom hypothesized.

"You watch *Storm Stories* on the Weather Channel?" Tom called back through the open window.

"Yeah, sometimes. Why?"

"Well, I'd hazard to guess that Jim Cantore tells more hurricane and tornado stories than anything else. In every story I remember, they talk to survivors and, when possible, show them shortly after the storm hit." Tom arched his neck back, trying to feel some softness from the wadded up rain jackets. It wasn't working. "I can't think of one case where they showed a tornado victim or survivor who didn't have hundreds of cuts and bruises. Neither Elam nor Sarah had any signs of small debris injuries. Nothing at all other than major breaks of his legs and her arms. What we have, Don, is some bad shit. Simple as that."

"Maybe they were killed by steel bars in the back of the shed. It might have happened that way."

"You don't believe that any more than I do. They weren't even found in the back of the shed. My question is, why would anyone want to kill them? Hell's bells, he was all bark and no bite and she seemed to be a very loving woman." Tom shifted in the seat. Sleep would come hard this night.

Don asked, "But why? Could she have been stalked by her ex-husband or some jealous psycho?"

Tom ignored Don's rhetorical question. "I noticed something else; there was a symmetrical wound on her neck. My first reaction was that she had been strangled. It almost looked like she was wearing a brown necklace."

"Yeah, that's about the only thing I remember about her. Except that she was a striking woman." He tried to make light of the situation. "Don't know why she was hanging around with Elam."

"In this case, it cost her everything."

Don agreed silently. He tried to roll over on his side but it hurt his leg too much. Nothing doing. He heard Tom trying to get comfortable as well. "I think maybe we should have gone to Nancy's. San Antonio is an hour away." He tightened the collar of his jacket as much as he could and, lying flat on his back, closed his eyes.

"Yeah. Let's give it a few minutes. If we can't sleep, we're off to her place. If so, we need to come back at the crack of dawn. I've still got to get back to Houston in the afternoon."

Don was already asleep.

The F-250 eased down the dirt trail. Emilio looked ahead in silence while Carlos concentrated on staying ahead of the events swirling around them like deer flies. They entered the test site shortly before four thirty in the morning.

"Stop at the loader and let me off. Then follow me in the truck." Carlos pointed to the bucket loader still sitting where it had been left the night before.

Carlos started up the Deere and drove to a small stand of pecan trees just outside of the fence line. Emilio followed with the truck.

"OK, get the chain and tie it around the chamber." He

pointed toward a debris pile. "Use some rags to keep from scratching it."

Emilio did as told. He tied two sections of chain around the chamber and then hooked the two open ends of chain onto the teeth of the bucket loader. Rather than trying to tie the chains, Emilio simply connected each one with an open S-hook. Carlos lifted the JETS chamber and placed it on the ground.

"That's got it." He pointed to the tracks. "We've got to get rid of these tracks. I'll put the loader back where it was and you move the truck. Then sweep all these tracks away." Carlos surveyed the scene and then added to his instructions. "Grab a section of the metal sheeting and place it on top of the chamber."

Carlos drove the loader back to its original location and turned off the ignition. He wiped off some of his fingerprints; since he had driven the Deere many times during work, Carlos wasn't overly concerned about eliminating all prints. Emilio pulled the sheet of corrugated metal to the chamber. He wedged a corner of the sheet under the chamber and partially wrapped it around the lower half. He used a tree branch as a broom and in ten minutes had done a reasonable job of concealing both truck and bucket loader tracks.

Carlos thought of his predicament. Three people had been killed and he was hanging in the breeze.

Thirty

Monday Morning,
March 22

Breuner's Funeral Home Parking Lot

Tom heard the car first. *Thank God!* he thought. His aching bladder woke him from intermittent sleep an hour earlier. Don was still down for the count, his body exhausted from the day before. Tom got out, stretched his arms into the air, and arched his back. Sentinel shadows, peering low through the oaks, stood guard over the parking lot and side of Breuner's Funeral Home.

"Hey, Don, time to get up." Tom reached over the side of the truck and tugged lightly at Don's head.

"Hmm." Don sighed heavily. He looked up and said hello to the world. "Shit."

Tom walked over to the young man emerging from his car. They talked briefly and then Tom returned to Don. "He knows about us and has invited us in to use the bathroom. He'll put some coffee on. We picked the right funeral home."

Tom and Don heard the latest local information over coffee with Myron Fortier.

"As of last night the toll here was over thirty. Several other towns got hit. Hit bad. Yeah, and I'm sure sorry 'bout your friend. Tornadoes aren't selective. They take who they take. My dad was lucky to survive the second Wichita Falls storm. Got wedged into a crevasse of an overpass with a lot of others. Several of them were sucked out and killed." Myron sipped on his coffee.

Don asked questions about a funeral for Elam. And for Sarah. "Suppose they can't find any relatives for her. Can they be buried together?"

"Don't rightly know. You'd better ask Bill or Mary Otter. They know the law better'n I do."

"How about Elam's funeral? I'd like to have him buried in Stafford, southwest of Houston. I'm pretty sure that's where he grew up. I don't think he has any relatives. I'll be calling the cemetery down there today to make arrangements."

Myron nodded his head. "All you have to do is set a date and give them our phone number. We handle everything from there. You can speak to the Otters about financial matters."

They agreed that Tom and Don would stop by shortly before noon to sign all the paperwork and to make some preliminary decisions about Sarah. Myron told them of a restaurant that was open in Fentress, some ten to twelve miles northwest of Luling. Tom and Don thanked him for the hospitality and departed for Fentress.

A tall man in his late thirties, his tanned, sinewy muscles stretching an orange t-shirt, picked up the phone. A call at this early hour meant business. His was a profession affording plenty of free time for relaxation, interrupted with infrequent episodes of riveting human drama. His contracts carried a price tag heavy enough for him to afford eight hundred feet of waterfront property on the tip of a tiny peninsula overlooking Lake Livingston. The cedar log home was splendid in every respect, not the least being a porch wrapping around three-quarters of the home. The phone interrupted an early morning breakfast.

"Bartok."

"Mr. Bartok, this is Mr. Austin. I am very interested in three parcels of property. I can offer twenty thousand for each piece."

Bartok sensed urgency. He also knew what different customers could afford. "I'll have to check the properties out. Prices are still running high in this part of Texas. Once I've seen them I'll give you a reasonable price."

Bart winced. Both men knew he would offer something less than he would have to pay. "Well, for now all I want you to do is to look at the properties. I'll send you some information on each parcel in the next couple of days. Don't make any offers yet."

"Fine. I can meet any time schedule you have." Bartok added, "I'll need 25 percent once we agree on the price, and the remainder as soon as we close." Bartok hung up before Bart could speak.

Bart Miles mailed the information to a PO box in Onalaska.

Tom and Don returned to the site shortly before 10:00 a.m. comfortably full from bacon and eggs in Fentress. The site was as remembered—a total mess. This time, however, they were focusing on the site, not Elam and Sarah.

"Let's start at the fence and walk the perimeter. See what we've got." Tom put on his baseball cap, *BWR* and a Piper Cub logo on it, got out of the truck and walked to Don's side. "Let me have your coffee cup."

Don gave Tom his cup and exited the vehicle. They surveyed the area, still unable to fathom the force of the storm.

They took two trips around the area. The first walkthrough, with neither speaking a word, helped them comprehend the full scope of what had happened. The second tour involved detailed forensic analysis. Utter destruction befell the site. Two-thirds of the fence had been ripped apart, most of the pecan and oak trees were down or stripped bare, only a small part of the derrick was recognizable, and much of the shed was down as they had already noted. Surrounded by large black pools of oil and mud, the day-tank for storing each day's collection of oil looked like a crushed tin can. The trailer-mounted gas compressor and tank assembly had rolled over, snapping the connection to the wellhead assembly. The plus side of the ledger included the good condition of the down-hole components, the remarkable condition of the Deere bucket loader, and the display chamber, partially hidden by tin sheeting. Both men walked to the chamber.

"How the hell did it get over here?" Don turned back and looked at the shed. The chamber had moved at least forty feet. Don tapped on the chamber cylinder lightly with his cane. Then he added, "Help me get this sheeting off of it."

Tom pulled the thin metal sheeting; all of a sudden it ruptured. "Ah! Shit." Tom jumped back, grabbing his hand. A torn metal sliver had sliced his palm. Blood poured from his right hand. "Don, grab my handkerchief from my back pocket."

Don took the handkerchief and wrapped it around Tom's bleeding palm. Eyeing the wound, Don offered a medical opinion. "Damn, that's nasty. You're going to need stitches. Stitches in the palm sucks, trust me." He made a contorted smile in remembrance of a motorcycle accident and subsequent encounter with a barbed-wire fence. "You got any Band-Aids in the car?"

"Yeah. Hang on. I'll get them." Tom returned to the truck

for a couple of minutes, returning with three strips of Band-Aids securing the wound.

"OK, now we can get down to business. This is unbelievable." Tom gingerly pulled out his pad of paper.

Tom asked questions, sometimes silently to himself and sometimes of Don, made notes, took photographs, and sketched the site. Small amounts of his own blood stained his small notebook. He and Don measured off distances to key items. Each remembered exactly where the bodies of Elam and Sarah had been found. The locations were indicated with an *E* and an *S*. The photo count reached fifty. Don answered Tom's questions and offered commentary to the scene.

Tom looked at his watch. "I've got all I need for now. I need to get back to Houston."

They walked side by side toward the truck. Tom was preoccupied with his hand wound and Don was thinking about Elam. Then he saw something out of place. He stopped midlimp. Tom, unaware of his brother's moving in a different direction, kept walking.

As he approached the bucket loader, Don called out, "Hey, Tom, look at this." He stood less than ten feet from the Deere.

Tom walked over to Don and then followed his stare to the ground. He paused for a couple of seconds and then asked, "You talking about the tracks?"

"Yeah. This thing has been driven since the tornado." Don straddled a wide track that appeared to have been partially obscured. "Some of those tracks have been brushed over. There's no way rain wouldn't have washed everything away. You saw all the puddles." Hair bristled at his neck and arms.

"Just a second." Tom grabbed his cell phone and called Susie.

"It's me. Do me a favor and call Tim Whipple. Let him know that I won't make it today. Check to see what my schedule is for tomorrow. I think I've got a meeting with Boyer and Clark tomorrow afternoon. I can meet with Tim late in the morning."

Don felt uneasy taking Tom away from more of his work. But he knew he would have done the same thing for Tom. He waited as Tom listened to Susie's response.

"Things just aren't adding up over here. I can't talk about it now but I'll give you everything when we get back tonight." Another pause. "I know, hon. No, it's not another Alvin case. At least, I don't think so." Another pause. "OK, yeah, it may be. Speaking of getting together, if you have Bill Newton's number, give him a call and see if we can't get into his brain. I need to go. I love you." A final pause. "OK, I will." He closed the cell phone and then knelt down at one of the tracks. A moment later he stood up and pulled the camera out.

Tom spoke as he took pictures. "It's hard to tell what's gone on here. I think we probably drove all around here too much."

"Can you tell if there is a different tire track than on your truck?"

"I just can't tell. We must've driven over here five times and maneuvered the truck all around the area." Tom took more pictures while mumbling to himself all the time. "Shit. Why wasn't I more careful? Shit."

They repeated the process at the site where Sarah was found.

They were ready to leave when Don realized that they hadn't even looked at Elam's Cadillac. Pockmarked dents covered the front, left side, and top of the car. The top of the car and the left side light were smashed. Impact spider webs could be seen over the front, left, and back windshields. That Tom could open the driver's door without problem was no small miracle. The keys were in the ignition. Tom turned the key and Betsy the Cadillac started immediately. She was a survivor.

Don said, "Let's just leave the car here for the time being. We can come back later and have it repaired." The car's condition reflected the same sense of despair that Don felt.

Tom replied, "I think it would be better for you to drive the pickup back and I'll follow you in Elam's car. We need to look it over before we turn it over to anyone. I'll make sure I don't disturb any possible fingerprints. Can you still drive?"

"Yeah, guess you're right. And yes, if it's daylight I can drive. But it'll be a slow trip home 'cause I have to use my left leg on the gas and brake."

Tom and Don met with Mary Otter before heading back to Elam's car for the slow ride back to the ranch. On the way back, and violating all common sense for someone with MS, Don made several phone calls to cancel the scheduled demonstrations. At Wellington Oil and Exploration, Bart Miles did not care to answer the phone so Macy Buckles relayed Don's message. Bart received the news with little emotion. To Bart Miles, Don Seiler was irrelevant.

"And basically that's everything we have at this point. Elam's car is on the other side of the hangar." Tom looked at Susie. "I think it's time to get everyone together again."

"Just like Alvin." Susie was unable to block out Tom's narrow escape from death. She also remembered that the book had not been completely sealed on that case. She wanted to run away. "Not going to the police last time almost cost you your life. What reason do you have now?"

"I'm sorry, honey, it's just that sixth sense. Given the massive storm deaths, I am sure that they will just want to put everything to bed. They're doing the best they can, but the Luling police don't have the resources at this point."

The grandfather clock chimed in the end of another day.

Tom stood up and walked to the recycle bag. He tossed the beer can in it and turned back to Susie.

"Maybe we ought to go to the police. But let's get everyone together first and see what we have."

Susie leaned forward, putting her elbows on her knees and her head in her hands. Don remained mute. Tom waited for Susie.

She looked up at her husband. "I've already called everyone, including Bill Newton. Dinner here at eight and we'll talk around the table."

"Who's coming?"

"Steve, Paige, Ross, Nancy, and Bill Newton." Susie stood up. She walked to her husband and put her arms around him. He hugged her for a moment then kissed her forehead.

Susie ended the discussion. "Time for bed."

Tom fell asleep in five minutes. Susie cried until two o'clock.

Tom was gone by the time Don woke up, having eaten a pre-sunrise breakfast with Susie. In turn, she saved some eggs, sausage, a biscuit, and coffee for Don. The ringing phone interrupted their light conversation. Susie grabbed Don's coffee cup and walked back into the house. "I'll bring you back some coffee."

Don sat on a partially eaten cushioned chair looking over the runway and thought of Elam. He couldn't put the events together neatly, but he made a commitment. *Elam, we're going to get it done. I promise you, JETS will make it.* He needed to take action. He grabbed his cell phone and dialed.

"Carlos, this is Don Seiler. How're you today?"

"Mr. Seiler. I'm good. I'm sorry about the things in Luling.

I was waiting for you to call. Can I help you?" Carlos was eager to please Don.

"You sure can. Here's what's going on." Don described the complete damage done at the site. "I want you to gather the crew and clean the mess up as best you can." He then got very specific with Carlos. "I want the display chamber put some-place safe. Pick up all the fencing and debris. If any of it can be saved, then save it. Take the rest and stack it just outside of the fence line. We'll take it to the dump later on."

Carlos asked, "Are we going to be able to keep working? I know everyone will want to put everything back together."

"Thanks. And yes, we're going to make it work. Once you have it cleaned up I will arrange for a new shed and fencing." He thought of something. "By the way, place any broken parts to the actual JETS in a separate spot and cover them up with something. We need to make sure we can rebuild it."

"I will, Mr. Seiler."

"OK, I'll see you out there tomorrow afternoon. It will be pretty late. Any questions?"

"No. I will call you if we have problems. The crew will clean up tomorrow morning. Felix won't be with us until next week. His wife was injured pretty bad and his home has bad damage."

"I understand. See you tomorrow." Don, charging himself to remember to check up on Felix and his wife, hung up.

———————————————————

Carlos relaxed. He put down the phone as a huge smile spread uncontrollably across his face. He exhaled and whispered, "*Gracias Dios.*" He thought, *I can take care of any evidence. No suspicions—no problems.*

He picked the phone up again and started dialing.

Thirty-One

Tuesday Night,
March 23

Broken Wing Ranch

The dogs had a field day barking at each car coming down the access road. As guard dogs they were pretty far down the totem pole, unless licking a burglar to death counted. Nancy drove the furthest, almost three hours from San Antonio. Ross and Paige came from Clear Lake, picking Steve up on the way. Steve's wife Kelly needed to stay home with their three daughters and brand-new son. Bill Newton was the last to arrive, ceremoniously sniffed and licked by the two dogs. Bear and Catfish turned him over to Susie.

"Welcome back, Bill. It's so good to see you again." Susie met him at the front door.

"It's been too long. Sure wish Renae and I could have made your barn party." Bill smiled and leaned down to give Susie a hug. At six–four with a barn-sized chest, Bill Newton would have been an imposing figure had it not been for his boyish smile. As a Houston Police Department detective Bill struck fear into the hearts of many bad guys. He limped noticeably from a leg wound suffered not in a confrontation with hoodlums, but from an AK-47 round in Vietnam.

Tom walked into the foyer. "Let go of my wife." He stuck out his hand and welcomed Bill. "Grab a beer and let's go make some steaks."

Everyone came over to welcome Bill back to the fold. He had been instrumental in helping Tom out of serious trouble in the Alvin case and had been made part of the family since then.

Tom cooked the steaks; Susie and Paige set the table and prepared the vegetables, rolls, and potatoes. Nancy joined the men on the back porch. The timing and meal were nearly perfect. In a strange manner of understanding, no one mentioned the upcoming discussion. When Tom was ready to change the subject he would let them know. He let them know.

"Hate to change the subject, but we have a major problem. I want to show you something. I'll be back in a minute." He got up and walked toward his bedroom.

Susie spoke. "Everyone sit. Paige and I will get the dessert." She got up and started reaching for the dishes.

"I'm not that old," Nancy said and got up as well.

The dinner dishes were cleared and replaced with coffee and pound cake. Tom returned with an easel on which sat a whiteboard housing horizontally taped strips of butcher paper. He pulled out his chair at the head of the table and replaced it with the easel.

"Again, thanks to everyone for coming over. I apologize for being vague over the phone, but I thought it better to just let you know it is important and to give everyone exactly the same information here at the ranch." He picked up his coffee and took a sip.

"We could be wrong, but Don and I believe," Tom turned to Don, "and Don, you add anything in here at all that I may have forgotten . . ." He turned back to the audience. "Don and I believe that his friend and partner, Elam Duquette, was murdered at the test site in Luling. So was the woman he was with."

Excluding Susie and Don, Tom's statement caught everyone by surprise. All except Bill knew of the oil extraction system; they also knew that Elam Duquette died on the night of the Luling tornado.

Tom continued. "What I want to do is to give you every bit of information I have, to include pieces of a puzzle that fit together and pieces that don't fit at all. Then I need all of us to figure out where we go from here."

Tom surveyed their faces. There were no questions, only anticipation.

He removed the top strip of butcher paper. Beneath it, the first of several small bullets read:

- *Elam dead at test site—taken to local funeral home*

"We found him face down in the middle of the testing site. He was covered with mud. He looked as though he had been rolled in it."

He pulled off the second strip:

- *Woman—Sarah???—dead at site perimeter—funeral home*

"All of you, except you Bill, saw Elam at the barn party on Saturday. He left early because he had a date with the woman named Sarah." Tom wished he could turn the clock backwards.

Without further comment, Tom pulled another strip:

- *Initial conclusion—both killed in Luling tornado*

Just the wording fixated the group. Each one knew something would follow in the next strip. Without speaking a word, Tom peeled off three more strips.

- *Breuner's—injuries were not tornado-inflicted*
- *Virtually no cuts—few abrasions*
- *Sarah—marks on neck consistent with strangulation*

"We've talked it over for hours trying to come up with some reasoning behind it all. Our conclusion is that both were murdered." He pulled off a final strip at the bottom of the whiteboard:

Murdered??
- *Jealous boyfriend tracked them down*
- *Random encounter—killed in a confrontation*
- *Question—why were they there?*
- *Linkage to JETS?*

"Fire away. What are you thinking?"

Paige spoke first. "Dad, why don't you take what you have to the police?"

Ross, Steve, Nancy, and Susie nodded in agreement. Don didn't. Neither did Bill.

Bill pushed back from the table and answered the question. "I think I know why. It's because there probably isn't enough evidence to cause a ruffle to the Luling police."

Don added, "That's what we think also. So far, the Luling police have been good to work with. But they're up to their necks in disaster recovery and filling out reports. Strange things happen in a tornado that might seem plausible in unusual deaths. If I were in the Luling police department my mind would be on other things."

"So that's one side of it," said Nancy. "The other side of it is that by not going to the police, both of you," Nancy looked at her brothers, "might be headed down the same road as you were with the murders in Alvin." She almost pleaded. "And I don't really want to lose the two brothers I have left."

Tom felt uncomfortable, not wanting to disregard Nancy's comments but still in a mindset of solving a senseless murder. "OK, understood. We're taking this all in. What other comments do you have?"

Nancy started the process of sorting out specifics.

"Is there going to be a coroner's report on Elam and the woman, Sarah?"

Don replied, "Mary Otter from the funeral home mentioned that a medical examiner would examine all of the bodies. I can only assume that there will be official reports." He looked around the table. "I'll call to make sure."

Ross pointed at the bottom bullets. "You've got some different possibilities there. Which do you think it is and why?"

"Good question." Tom threw it back at the others. "But we need order to our questions. We can take each one and brainstorm it." He tore a sheet of butcher paper from its pad and taped it over the whiteboard. "Which one do we start with?"

Nancy stood up and offered, "Before we go any further, let me take over as secretary. It'll free you to lead the discussion."

Tom relaxed at Nancy's sage offer and handed the marker to her. He moved to the other side of the whiteboard. "OK, let's get some ideas."

Paige said, "Let's start with the most unlikely. I don't think for a minute that a jealous lover is involved in this."

"But suppose it was? What questions do we need to ask?"

The next few minutes were spent debunking the jealous lover theory. The questions centered on identifying her and whether or not she had boyfriends or an estranged husband. Assuming that someone was jealous of her, how would he have known where the testing site was? In spite of a general consensus that the jealous lover did not exist, the group decided to try to identify her and then find out where Elam may have taken her for dinner. If they could answer those questions, then people from her hometown or the restaurant may be able to provide some information about who else may have followed her that night. The mission fell to Don and Paige.

The second possibility was that they had gone to the site to be alone and ran into vandals or thieves. A similar discussion resulted in another task, this one for Steve. He would check with the Luling police to see if any gangs had caused trouble in the area. Tom got along well with the Luling police and would make initial introductions.

"Our last major possibility seems to be the JETS."

Bill asked, "Before you get into this one, tell me about the JETS. What is it?"

"Good question. Probably only Don and I really know what it is. Hang on." Tom walked to the kitchen and returned with a plastic Dunkin' Donuts coffee mug and two straws. The mug was half-full of water. He was chewing gum.

"What we've got is a device that is ideal for getting oil out of stripper wells. They exist all around the world." He stopped talking long enough to chew rapidly on the piece of gum. When satisfied, Tom punctured the small air escape hole with a kitchen knife making it just large enough to insert a straw. Then he lifted the small drinking tab and inserted the second straw. He used the gum to make airtight seals around both straws. He proudly looked at his work—two straws sticking out of a cup—and turned back to his audience.

"Don's oil extraction device, the Jet Extraction Technology System, which we call JETS, is not much more complicated that what I have here." He held his contraption up and rotated it in the air. "In simple terms, we put a cylinder into the ground with an opening near the bottom. Oil under pressure seeps through pores in layers of rock into a chamber through a ball valve opening at the bottom." Tom halted for a couple of seconds and then pointed to the bottom of the mug. "Obviously I don't have a ball valve here, but use your imagination. In the JETS the ball valve is free to move when there is no pressure in the chamber. That's what I have here, a slug of liquid in a container." Then he pointed to one of the straws. "That is, until we use compressed air to force the valve to seat against the opening at the bottom of the chamber. Once the ball valve has seated, it's really no different than this cup and straws. We continue forcing air into the chamber and the gathered slug has no place to go except up through an outflow pipe to a holding tank on the ground." He pointed to the second straw. "The result is all physics." Tom inhaled, placed his mouth over one of the straws and blew. A geyser of water shot out of the second straw straight into the air almost to the ceiling. It arched slightly and splashed on the tile floor.

Tom's histrionics were impressive and each person had a feel for the JETS.

"Oops. Sorry." With sheepish grin Tom grabbed some towels and wiped the water off the floor. Susie gave him a motherly smile.

He concluded his demonstration with some statistics. "You don't need to know anything more about the mechanics of the JETS. It's important enough to say it has been pushing about 15 percent more oil out of the ground than current pumpjack systems." He rocked his forearm back and forth. "And it does it using about one-tenth the labor. Not a bad system."

Don finished the sales pitch. "Also, it's only got one major moving part below ground, so exchanging parts won't be needed as much as on pumpjacks." He felt his explanation had been good—and he waited for questions.

Bill inquired, "And this device is worth how much?"

The others already knew the answer to Bill's question.

Don beat Tom to the answer, "We don't really know. On

the low side, maybe a couple million. On the high side . . .," he hesitated, "easily in the billions."

Tom added, "And that brings us to the possibility that there may be people who would be willing to kill to have the rights to the JETS." He unconsciously rubbed his head and continued. "I know some of you know more about the JETS than others, but we're open to any thoughts at all about the different possibilities."

Steve spoke. "For starters, let's don't waste time on the lover theory. My money is on some sorry bastard who knows the financial implications of the device."

Like the House of Commons, mumbled agreement ruffled through the group.

"OK then, let's get with it. Nancy, let me borrow the marker for a minute." Tom taped a blank sheet to the whiteboard. He wrote the letters *JETS* in the middle of the sheet and then drew a large ring around the letters. He gave the marker back to Nancy, saying, "List the items around the ring."

Nancy took the marker and nodded.

Tom told the group, "Spit out anything that pops in your mind."

Susie put things into perspective. "If it's murder, then everyone here is in danger to some degree."

Tom wasn't sure if Susie was accusing him of being lax about the safety of other people. He did know she made a valid point. Without any emotional reaction he asked Nancy to place *murder* immediately beneath the letters.

Questions and thoughts came fast and furious. Nancy, unable to keep tabs on attribution, jotted thoughts on the paper as they were fired in her direction.

"Who knows about the device?"

"What companies have been involved in demonstrations?"

"Are foreign companies involved?"

"How trustworthy is the work crew?"

"What do we know about the company that built the prototype?"

"Speaking of the crew, what's the story about the worker who was killed? Is there any connection?"

"Elam talked a lot. Who else knows about the system?"

"How trustworthy was the woman?"

Ross remembered Don's frustration concerning getting a patent. He asked, "Getting a patent has been problematic. What do we know about the patent lawyer?"

His question made Don pause. He turned to Ross. "Damn good question. As a matter of fact, our first patent lawyer dropped us like a hot potato. There was a story about his health."

"Well, we sure as hell ought to be checking up on his health again."

"For that matter, we need to check up on the new lawyer. What're their names?"

Don answered, "The first guy was Herman Soboda. He's from League City. The guy we have now is Fred Barrister. I left dealing with him up to Elam. I don't really know much about either of them." He shrugged.

Steve volunteered. "I'll check into the lawyers. I might know some people who have heard of them."

Bill added, "I can work with you on that. Our home is in Pasadena, and Renae and I are out in the League City area a lot."

Steve signaled a thumbs-up.

The group fell silent for a few seconds.

Tom spoke to the group. "OK, this is what we've got to sort out. Let's discuss each topic one last time and then figure out who's going to do what."

The first cut at solving the mystery was displayed neatly

before them. Randomly spaced around the drawn circle were those topics that might link one to another: "Elam," "Juan D.," "Sarah," "Foreign Oil Companies," "US Oil Companies," "Workers," "Banks," "Coroner's Report," "Patent Lawyers," "Acquaintances," and "Permian Machinery."

Before continuing with any discussion, Tom asked Nancy to print a single word below JETS in the center of the circle: "MURDER?"

Each topic on the circle was discussed thoroughly. At least two people were assigned to work together on each item. Paige and Ross would work as a single entity and would have another member also work on anything to which they were assigned. Tom and Susie were handled in the same manner. A timeline was given for each team to accomplish a task. A final list outlined the tasks and teams:

- Juan–Tom/Susie & Don
- Elam–Don & Tom/Susie
- Foreign oil companies–Ross/Paige & Nancy/Bill
- Domestic oil companies–Ross/Paige & Nancy/Bill
- Work crew–Don & Tom/Susie
- Acquaintances–Bill & Don
- Lawyers–Bill & Steve
- Banks–Ross/Paige & Nancy
- Sarah?–Tom & Don
- Permian Machinery–Don & Tom/Susie

All agreed that anyone could join another group if they saw a reason to do so.

The meeting lasted until shortly past midnight. They ingested enough caffeine to keep Rip Van Winkle awake. Still, work awaited most of the group the next morning. Handshakes and hugs closed the initial meeting. The next meeting would be held a week from Friday. While the others said their goodbyes, Nancy copied everything down on legal paper. Bear and Catfish, tails wagging, escorted everyone to the cars. They followed alongside the caravan as it moved down the gravel road to the highway. Taillights disappeared over a small crest. Satisfied that they had done their duty, the two dogs returned to guard the ranch.

Nancy, Tom, and Don stayed up for another hour. Without comment Susie went to bed.

"Are we doing the right thing?" Tom asked.

No answer.

Tom finished off a beer and headed for the refrigerator. "Who wants a drink?"

Neither sibling replied to the drink order.

Finally, Nancy spoke. "At this point I can understand what we're doing. But the real question is, will you and Don ever turn this over to the police?" She sipped at her wine.

Don answered, "It's a fair question. Who knows?" He squinted his eyes and yawned. He was very tired. Lugging MS around all day, every day, is exhausting work. "I'll tell you what, though. Any son of a bitch comes to take the JETS is on a one-way trip."

"That's the kind of thinking that scares me." Nancy could detach herself from the situation better than her brothers. Maybe it was a female thing, but all three of her brothers had a reputation for short fuses when it came to dirtbags. "I'll tell you what you need. You need to listen to Susie and to me. Your John Wayne mindset can get you killed."

Tom sat down, beer in hand. "Yeah, understood. But we also know you're right in an intellectual sense. Maybe it's unfortunate, but we view the world differently than a lot of people. Don and I don't run from anybody who's an asshole. We just don't do it."

Don nodded his head in agreement.

Nancy retorted. "All the more reason to listen to us."

It was a stalemate. Tom and Don weren't very good at discretion when it came to moral turpitude.

Don yawned again. He slowly stood up and announced his departure. "Lady and gentleman, I'm going to bed. I have a flight to California in the morning. I will see you when the sun is up."

End of the first meeting.

Don and Nancy went to their rooms in the guest wing of the house. Tom turned off the lights and headed for the bedroom. He undressed in the dark, made a quick stop in the bathroom, and slid under the covers next to Susie. She had her back to him. He hoped that she was sleeping. Unexpectedly, she rolled over next to him. He adjusted himself to wrap his left arm behind her head and down her arm. Her warmth comforted him.

"Why do we have to go through this again?" She choked on her feelings, stuffing down the need to scream out loud. "Why don't you trust the police? Don't you realize that you can be killed?"

Tom squeezed her arm. He felt inadequate. He couldn't remember all the events surrounding the Alvin incident, and he tried desperately to remember if he had made a promise never to put himself—and others—in danger. *Is this the only way?* he wondered.

"I'm not sure. We were pulled into the killings in Alvin and I just couldn't get out of it." He knew he had more freedom this time to turn it over to the police. Still, Tom's gut told him that someone was trying to steal from Don and, if successful, would destroy Don's life. But it went beyond Don. He was as much a vigilante as anything else. His never-ending struggle between the concept of justice and vile revenge against morally bankrupt people gnawed away at the fabric of his life. Revenge and justice. Failure to separate the two had placed Tom into a moral prison from which he could not escape. The stress reached out and physically touched him. He moved his right hand to his head and ran his index finger along the outside of his ear. The smooth texture of skin abruptly changed to a discernable indentation. Another time, another place. Another inch and the bullet would have pierced his skull. Was he insane to even consider tracking down a murderer? Luck is as random as the wind, and he had his share of good luck in Alvin.

"Honey, give me until we all meet again. If the police are willing to run with what we have, then I could turn it over to them."

Both of them knew the difference between the words "could" and "will" created a huge chasm of misunderstanding.

Susie rolled over without saying a word. Sleep could not help her.

Thirty-Two

Wednesday Morning, March 24

Broken Wing Ranch

A better way is 105 east to 237 to US 77 south. It's a nice drive and takes you right in to I-10." Tom used a red felt-tipped pen to outline the route on a map of Texas.

Nancy studied the map and nodded. Tom folded it in such a way to make it as small as possible while covering the route from the ranch to San Antonio.

Tom added, "Follow me to 105, then I'm headed south to Bush Intercontinental with Don. Need to make it to Crosby for some on-site analysis and then downtown for a deposition. Busy day."

Nancy and Susie said their good-byes. Susie's eyes were noticeably bloodshot. The day was just starting and the wind had already been taken from her sails.

Don gave Susie a kiss. "Hang in there, Susie. I'll be back in a few days to brighten your life."

She hugged Don. Her hug was tighter than usual and she couldn't look him in the eyes. Her emotions were frayed.

Tom gave Susie a kiss. "I'll be back around six thirty." This time it was Tom who gave a tighter hug than usual.

Her response was void of emotion. She didn't even know whether it was anger or fear that filled her body; either way she felt that she was going to be sick.

Over Don's protestations Tom parked in short-term parking and carried Don's bag to ticketing. They didn't have much time so Don went directly to security.

Don and Tom shook hands.

Don made a final comment. "We're going to figure this mess out. You take care of Susie. She's in trouble."

Tom bit his lip and turned away.

As Tom entered the Sam Houston Parkway his cell phone played a few bars of Beethoven's *Eroica*. He reached into the homemade harness and pushed the receive button. "Tom Seiler."

"Hi Tom. This is Mary Otter. I just wanted to let you know that we have identified the woman."

Macy Buckles escorted Fred Barrister down the hall. She opened the door and preceded Fred into the room.

"Mr. Barrister, sir."

"Thanks, Macy." Bart rose from his desk and walked briskly toward Fred. "Good to see you, Fred. Have a seat."

Macy quietly closed the door and went about her business.

"Now that is one pretty woman." Fred licked his lips.

Bart ignored the comment. He was interested in business and business only.

"Show me what you've got." He directed Fred to one of two oversized leather couches. Beveled glass lay over an ivory inlay teak coffee table, the legs S-curving downward to lion's paws.

Strong and beautiful in its own right, the table was nevertheless out of place in a room dedicated to everything Texas.

Fred sat down and unlocked his briefcase. He took out a folder holding numerous documents. He pulled out the sheet on top and handed it to Bart, saying, "It's the final letter written to obtain the patent for Wellington Oil. The enclosures are the supporting drawings." He leaned back, allowing Bart time to digest the contents.

Bart bit at his lips as he studied the document. "What're the downsides?"

"None at all. The letter I wrote the day you put me on this put everything into motion. We did our homework, the new plans you gave me don't require any real new inquiry, and I've got a couple of friends who are helping it along."

Bart looked deeply at Fred, his eyebrows turning down at the bridge of his nose. "What do you mean, friends?"

Fred held out his hand in mock self-defense. "Just friends. They have no information about peripheral issues. They've helped speed up the process many times before. And I've helped them with free advice from time to time. We just wash each others hands when necessary."

"How long?"

"How long what?"

"Damn, Fred. What the fuck are we talking about? How long until I own the patent?"

Fred felt a little stupid. "Oh, sorry, I just lost my train of thought for a moment. My guess is that it won't be more than a couple of weeks. Maybe three. Remember, this has been in the works for almost three months already."

Bart was losing patience. "I don't want guesses. Give me a firm timeframe for the longest it will take. Without guesswork."

"Six weeks at the longest." Fred began to feel uncomfortable, perspiration popping up on his neck and face. He had undertaken several legal actions for Bart and found him to be a rather negative person. This time the nonverbal was threatening. "I just can't control the pace without bringing undue interest to the patent."

Bart stood up and walked to his desk. He pulled out an envelope. He returned to Fred and handed the envelope to him. Fred opened it and looked inside. The first thing he saw was a cashier's check in the amount of twenty-three hundred dollars. Behind the check was a stack of hundred-dollar bills. Fred didn't count them but rightly assumed that the count would be forty-seven.

Four hours after landing at LAX Don hunched over his drafting desk designing a cantilever support for lifting supplies from a crew boat to a deep-sea oil platform. He couldn't climb the oil platforms anymore but his knowledge of deep-water rigs made him a sought-after structural engineer for the offshore oil industry. From time to time he kept a project for himself. Jay and Mark had enough work to keep them employed and Don wanted to maintain his drafting skills. He had AutoCAD for computer drafting, but time spent on the drawing board was enjoyable. The phone rang.

Don picked up the phone on the second ring. "Seiler Engineering, Don speaking."

"Hey, Don, it's Tom."

"What's goin' on, amigo?"

"I just got out of my deposition. We had a slam dunk and this baby's going to settlement." Tom realized he was getting off track. He continued, "I wanted to call you this morning but couldn't with you in the air. Mary Otter found out who Sarah is."

Don sat straight up, placing his drafting pencil on the desk. "What did they tell you?"

"Her name is Sarah Bettner. She's from Gonzales. It was not easy to find out. Her teenage son had been looking all over the state for her. The kid figured that she was somewhere with Elam when one of the tornadoes hit. Mary Otter told me that when he identified her body he went ballistic."

Don sighed, knowing he couldn't really comprehend the agony her son was going through.

Tom continued. "When he settled down Mary asked if he would want to meet friends of Elam since we had said we wanted to meet the family. At first he said no but just before he left he changed his mind. Mary gave me his phone and address."

"What did he have to say?" Don moved to his office chair and sat down.

"I haven't talked to him. Matter of fact, I thought it would be better if you made the first call."

Don grimaced in resignation. "Yeah, guess you're right. What's his phone number?"

Tom gave Don Sarah's address and phone number along with her son's name. Then they discussed what to do.

"How about if I come back tomorrow or the next day? I'll call her son and see if he wants us to help with the funeral arrangements. I would like to let him know that she was talked about with some reverence from one irreverent SOB, if you know what I mean."

As they talked, Don continued doodling with abstract notes about airlines, times, and independent thoughts of what to say to the young man whose life had been crushed.

"I have to testify in a case on Friday and it might be an all-day affair. How about Saturday?" Tom cleared his throat, a reflex action while he thought of the next subject. "And I have one major question. Should we tell him of our suspicions?"

"I don't know. We can discuss that when I get there. For now I'll try to get him to agree to have her funeral on Monday. If he agrees we can have Elam's on Tuesday. His won't be a big deal."

"Good idea. I'll call Mary right away and let her know of our tentative plans. If the son agrees then just let me know and I'll take care of both funerals."

Except around a single lamp in the living room corner, the house was fading into darkness. Josh didn't want to answer the phone. For that matter, he had no desire to talk to anyone—not family, friends, or the media. His sisters wouldn't start arriving until the next morning. He stared at the phone with grief and anger, gritting his teeth. A discipline instilled into him by his mother always called him to meet life head on. He glanced at the display and saw a number with area code 805. Not knowing where it was coming from, Josh reluctantly picked up the phone.

"This is Josh Bettner."

Don finished a hard swallow, invoking a short void while admitting to himself, *I'm no good at this.* He said, "Josh, I'm Don Seiler. I was a friend of Mr. Elam Duquette." Don grasped for words that might lessen the severity of the conversation. "I, uh, spoke with Mrs. Otter and she mentioned that you agreed to speak with my older brother and me."

Josh bore no ill will toward Don. That someone involved in this utter tragedy with his mother would care to call meant something good. He didn't know exactly what to make of Don, but it was a positive sign that a link had been established. He answered, "Thanks for calling, Mr. Seiler. I appreciate your concern. Is there anything I can do for you?"

"Josh, I understand that I can't feel what you are going through right now, but I did want you to know that I had heard a lot about your mom from Mr. Duquette. Rather than talk about her on the phone, would you mind if I come over to Gonzales with my brother to talk with you? I think you will want to hear what we do know about the two of them."

It was a strange conversation in that almost immediately both men felt some sort of kinship. Neither could describe it, but it did exist.

"That would be fine, Mr. Seiler. All but one of my sisters will be here tomorrow. My other sister will arrive on Saturday. Would Saturday afternoon be a good time? I'm sure my sisters would want to speak with you as well.

Don answered, "That would be perfect. I'm in California right now. My brother will be free on Saturday, so it will work well for both of us." He paused shortly, not really knowing what to say. He ended with, "Josh, is there anything my brother or I can do right now to help you arrange for the funeral?"

Southwest Airlines flight 1172 touched down at Houston Hobby on time at 3:40 p.m. Susie met Don and Cindy at baggage claim and called Tom, illegally parked in the loading zone. Within fifteen minutes they cruised down the Gulf Freeway heading north. Quick overviews of family life and the cost of booking flights a day in advance led into discussing coming events. At least baggage went free on Southwest Airlines.

Tom changed the subject. "So what's our schedule for meeting Josh Bettner?"

"I told him we'd be out to his place Saturday afternoon. His mother's funeral is set for Wednesday morning at eleven. You really don't need to go. I should talk to him before the funeral."

"I'm pretty well caught up on my current workload, so Saturday belongs to me. You going to mention the possibility of murder?" Tom squeezed the steering wheel.

Don had pondered the question many times. If it looks like murder, walks like murder, smells like murder, then it is probably murder. Still, he didn't want to tell Josh until both he and Tom had some concrete evidence as to what happened and exactly who was behind it.

"Not yet. We need to put a few more pieces of the puzzle together."

Tom agreed, "Yeah, I think you're right."

Susie and Cindy stared blankly out of their windows. Susie's insides were being torn apart.

Thirty-Three

Friday, March 26

Downtown Houston, Texas

The phone interrupted the morning monotony.

"Steve Seiler."

"Steve, this is Bill Newton. Got a few minutes?"

Steve pushed a stack of papers to the back of his desk and pulled a pad of yellow paper from his desk drawer. "Sure, Bill, what's goin' on?" He shifted the phone to his right hand and grabbed a pencil in his left.

"I just wanted to bring you up to date on what I've found out about the two lawyers who worked with Don and Elam. I'll hit the highlights and we can get into more depth over a beer in a couple of days."

"I could use one right now. There ought to be a pox on all mothers who want their boys to grow up to be lawyers." Steve surveyed his cluttered desk and the stack of files on his coffee table.

"Tell you what," Bill said. "I'll give you my phone number. Just call when you get a chance."

"Naw. Now's a good time. None of this shit is important to anyone except a bunch of plaintiffs. What've you got so far?"

Bill answered quickly, slight excitement noticeable in his voice. "I originally didn't think there would be anything with these guys. Now I do."

Steve could hear Bill fumbling with some paper.

Bill continued, "The guy Soboda had a modest business in League City. His phone line was disconnected so I checked with a lawyer friend from Webster. He'd known Soboda for a long time. Described him as a decent guy who made it on his own dealing with odds and ends, including patents. They weren't close buddies, but they shot the breeze on occasion at lawyer functions. Probably the same sissy stuff you do."

Steve snorted once and answered, "No defense here. We are a conceited bunch."

Bill continued, "The one thing that is interesting is that he not only quit his business overnight, Soboda has been a total recluse since then. He hasn't been to any legal functions anymore, and no one has seen him since he quit. Like I said, no phone. I tried to contact his former secretary but no luck there. I'll keep trying, and I'll try to follow up on his purported illness. For me, the bottom line is that he did quit under strange circumstances. It's a very long stretch from quitting to being linked up with Elam's death, but a connection is not out of the question. As for the Barrister connection . . ."

Steve interrupted, "I've got some background on him." He caught himself. "But let's go over your stuff first."

"Right. Only thing I know is that Barrister has a successful practice as a patent lawyer. Does other stuff as well. It looks like he has two or three junior lawyers working for him. He has an office on Westheimer Road, lives in a palace in River Oaks, and owns season tickets for the Rockets and Texans, not that the tickets represent anything great. I'll keep nosing around on him. What else do you know?"

Steve answered, "The bad news is that I was going to tell you exactly what you just told me." Both men smiled.

Steve continued, "I haven't been able to determine what associations he has with other attorneys and companies. It strikes me that he might be too well-off for the type of law he's practicing. I do give him the benefit of the doubt in that I haven't found anything suspicious other than his possessions. Oh, and that includes a forty-eight-foot yacht." Steve unconsciously looked at his pinstriped blue suit and, loosened at the collar, his immaculate red and white diagonally striped tie, and then added, "But, as you know, all of us lawyers charge too damn much for our services."

Bill laughed, "I agree. Still, there's at least enough for us to keep looking at possible connections. Unfortunately, I'm in the thick of the multiple homicides out by the Galleria. My time's limited for the next couple of weeks, but I'll do what I can."

"I understand." Steve jotted a couple of quick notes on the paper. "I'll start by checking out connections between either lawyer and any of the corporations that Don has been dealing with. We can compare notes on the JETS later on this week."

"The what?"

"The Jet Extraction Technology System."

"Oh, yeah, right."

Dwarfing the 1973 Kawasaki 350 Mach II, Bartok turned north on Highway 80 heading out of Luling toward Lockhart. The 2008 black Harley-Davidson Road King remained at his home on Lake Livingston. The shotgun pipes would only bring attention to a motorcyclist. When needed, the Kawasaki would be much easier to move into and out of brush. He passed through sparsely treed, gently rolling countryside, musing at why such a lightly traveled road would be built to such magnificent standards. Texas is replete with fine state roads. Highway transportation lobbies do very well in Texas.

Ten miles out of Luling, Bartok slowed and turned west on Route 20. No sooner had he entered the town of Fentress than he left it. The four hundred or so residents were nowhere to be seen. About a mile from town center, Bartok reached the Fentress Bridge. He slowed the motorcycle to a crawl and began surveying the site from east to west. Near the east abutment he noticed a dirt turnaround perched above the San Marcos River. The river ran on the north side of and parallel to the road at the turnaround; another sixty feet west and it turned abruptly to the south, where it passed beneath the bridge. The bridge ran two hundred feet to the west abutment, with piers giving support at forty-foot distances from each end. Low guardrails served as the only protection for vehicles. At the west end of the bridge, Route 20 continued on, turning slightly toward the southwest. Once across the bridge and just before reaching River Grove Road, Bartok eyed a large patch of sawgrass and heavy underbrush. He turned right on River Grove Road and stopped. He looked carefully at his surroundings; hiding the small motorcycle would be simple. He turned around and slowly drove back across the bridge. Back at the east end of the bridge Bartok noticed a flood gage with markings up to six feet. *This will do. Just need a good rain and access to the targets.*

Bartok pulled in to the small turnaround and shut down the engine. He got off and walked to the edge of the embankment and visualized future events. The ledge had been undercut by water scour and the depth of the river appeared to be about ten feet. Rising water from rain could take the depth up to well over twenty feet. He spent a few minutes surveying both sides of the bridge, taking pictures, and mentally rehearsing actions to be taken. Satisfied that the location was ideal, he departed.

Bartok left Fentress, continuing west on FM 20. Having insurance and in possession of his helmet exemption, Bartok was bareheaded. The helmet always took away from the freedom of the road; however, on this day the lowering sun pierced his eyes and his head pounded. Seventeen miles later he turned south on State Highway 123 at the outskirts of Seguin and quickly took another left on US 90 East. Twenty miles and twenty-five minutes later, Bartok entered the center of Luling. He drove the streets from Willow Avenue in the east to Mesquite in the west and from Houston Street in the south to Goliad in the north. He decided against stopping for a meal at Luling Bar-B-Q, prudence guiding his actions. Bartok did stop briefly across the street from Monte's Bar. He pulled out a picture of Carlos Aguirre and a slip of paper. On it were notes cryptically describing Carlos's habits, including his Friday and Saturday nights at Monte's. Bartok studied the bar and the street pattern. He committed everything to memory. Then he rotated the throttle and gently accelerated down Davis Street.

Thirty-Four

Saturday, March 27

Gonzales, Texas

High noon. Tom and Don drove by Apache Stadium along Tate Street.

Tom slowed the car and pointed to the stadium. "I can't tell if this is the stadium I played in or not. We came here undefeated and ready to kick some butt. By game time the whole stadium was packed. It was unreal. More people in the stands than lived in the whole county." He stopped the car and just stared at the stands. "They beat us something like thirty-six to zip. Enough for our undefeated season. They were really good."

Don added, "Yeah, I remember a couple of those kinds of games myself. By the time I got to high school we were 4A and played mostly San Antonio teams. Good days."

Tom accelerated the car and continued on to Cavett Street. A modest and immaculate frame house now belonging to the children of Sarah Bettner rested near the northern end of the street. Small bushes sprouted beautiful multicolored flowers that bloomed the week following the storms. A pecan tree stood strong in front of a porch extending the entire front of the house. Tom parked the car and they got out.

Tom rang the doorbell and the two men waited. After a few seconds a young man appeared at the door.

He looked first at Tom and asked, "Mr. Seiler?" His eyes were bloodshot and his cheeks red. He made no attempt to hide the fact that he had been crying.

Don answered. "I'm Don Seiler. And my brother, Tom." Tom nodded. "We know this is a terrible time, but we felt it was important to meet you."

Josh opened the door wide and stepped toward the men. He shook their hands and asked them in.

Sitting on the couch was a young woman. She had nice features, save her eyes. Her eyes were as red as Josh's.

Josh walked to his sister and introduced her. "This is my sister Glenda. From Buena Vista, Colorado."

Tom and Don nodded uncomfortably.

"We're so sorry." Don looked back and forth trying to address brother and sister. "We apologize for coming at a time like this, but we have something important to share about your mother."

Glenda patted the couch. "Please have a seat. We're glad you stopped by."

The doorbell rang. Josh opened the door and welcomed an elderly couple. Over the next three hours a steady stream of people came to offer condolences. The uncomfortable feelings they had when they arrived faded with each ring of the doorbell. Tom made a quick run to the Corner Stop on Texas 146 for drinks and chips. Finally, in the kitchen, Tom and Don were alone with Josh.

"Josh, we mentioned that we wanted to talk to you about your mother. Would you mind if we just went out back?"

Josh didn't hesitate. "Sure. Let's go."

They walked out of the back door into the yard. A few pecan trees and a single oak provided ample shade from the sun. The three men sat down on a picnic bench.

Don began, "Josh, the reason we had to see you was to tell you what Elam told us about her. But first let me tell you a little about Elam."

Don described all the basic strengths and weaknesses of his friend Elam—irreverent, outspoken, confident to the point of cockiness, and above all, loyal to a fault. Then he switched to speaking of Sarah.

"Over the last few weeks Elam seemed to change. He changed a lot. I don't think I've ever seen someone's personality take on a different character like his did." Don leaned closer to Josh. "He started telling us about a woman he had met and what a wonderful person she was. Elam could be very irreverent at times, but even his language took on a higher level than normal. I don't know how often they dated, but I do know that the last two months were probably the best he ever had."

Josh looked intently at Don and spoke quietly, "My mother seemed to be reacting the same way. She never complained about her life, but I could tell how happy she was over the last few weeks. The night . . ." Josh had to hold fast, his lips quivering. He looked down for a few seconds. He looked up and continued, "The night they died she was happier than I think I had ever seen her." He smiled for the first time. "I even joked with her and teased her about having a boyfriend. She was a happy girl." His big smile held for a moment before disintegrating into giant sobs. Josh held his head in his hands and wailed before two strange men. He took a handkerchief from his back pocket and blew his nose. He wiped his eyes on his forearms and straightened up.

"Takes a hell of a man to cry. You don't need to say another word to let us know about you and your mom." Tom was standing and grasped Josh's shoulder.

Don added, "The way you described your mother is exactly the same way Elam was last Saturday." Don leaned forward on the bench. "Tom, Elam, and I had an important meeting concerning an oil drilling device we were developing. I mean, it was very important. Still," Don grinned, "he couldn't go five minutes without referring to his upcoming date with her." He turned serious. "The last words I heard him say were about your mother." He wanted us to meet her. His exact words were something like, 'She's a beautiful woman. She's special.'"

Don's lips quivered and his eyes watered. "Josh, your mother was changing Elam for the better. He would have been a good man for her. She was the best thing that ever happened to him."

"Josh." Glenda called from the back door. "Evelyn is here."

Josh stood up. "I need to get back with all the friends. And another of my sisters just showed up. Come on back in and join us."

"We really have to head back now."

"Are you coming to the funeral? It's on Wednesday at eleven o'clock. We'd all be honored and my mom would be honored. It will be at the Henson Chapel Methodist Church. And, if you would, I'd like to ask you to tell my sisters someday exactly what you just told me."

Don answered immediately, "I'll be there."

Tom replied, "I need to change my schedule, but I hope to make it as well."

Josh answered, "Thank you. I appreciate it." He started toward the house as the two brothers made their way to the side of the house.

Josh stopped and turned around. He asked, "If you find out anything else about my mother, please let me know."

Tom responded, "Absolutely. It's a promise."

Josh gave them a wave and headed into the house.

At curbside, Tom hesitated before walking around to the driver's side. "Wherever it leads us, we're going to figure this out."

Bart's cell phone rang.

"Hello."

"I've checked into the three parcels for you. Very good properties and they're in mint condition."

"I appreciate the information. I will forward the paperwork immediately." Bart studied his fingernails. "But hold off on buying the properties until I've made up my mind."

"Right."

The caller hung up. Bart leaned back in his chair. Perspiration stained his shirt at the collar and armpits. Twice before he had used Bartok's services and all had turned out well. It appeared that this time would be no exception. So why did he feel so ill at ease? He stood up and walked to the window. Thoughts of three men dying were snuffed out quickly with visions of the payoff. He knew the oil industry and he understood the potential of the JETS. It was well worth the uneasiness one has when forced to kill three human beings.

Thirty-Five

Wednesday, March 31

Gonzales, Texas

The town's people were packed like cordwood inside the Henson Chapel Methodist Church. Metallic chairs were brought from the community hall to minimize the number of standing mourners. Others stood along the walls of the church.

Josh gave the final of three eulogies.

"And I speak for my sisters as well as me. There was not one day that we didn't feel loved by our mother. I want so much to hold her." He stopped momentarily, unable to speak.

Muffled guttural sobs interrupted the silence.

Josh gathered himself and then looked out over the despairing congregation. "My mother often listened to a song from one of those Broadway plays. We would sit on the front porch just talking and listening to the music. Always at the end of the song she would stop talking and say 'feel these words.' The words were so simple. 'To love another person is to see the face of God.' In the love she has given to us . . .," he sucked in his breath, "we have all seen the face of God."

Josh descended from the small pulpit and sat down. The preacher gave his final benediction and asked all to stand.

As the casket was being prepared for its slow trip down the aisle, two members of the choir, a man and a woman, sang a portion of the finale from *Les Miserables*.

Hold my hand, where chains will never bind you . . . to love another person is to see the face of God.

The choir then broke into "Amazing Grace." A resounding sound of hope filled the church as the pallbearers, Josh at the front, carried Sarah to the waiting hearse. Sarah's four daughters followed behind with their husbands and children.

Against their personal desires, Tom and Don followed the funeral caravan to Gonzales Memorial Cemetery. They stood beneath cypress trees at the back of the mourning crowd, unable to hear the final prayers or the sobs of Josh and his sisters. Don looked around at some of the tombstones. Some citizens had rested there since 1838. He tried to read the inscriptions without distracting others. Clyde G. Reed, born in 1893, was described in an unusual manner: *He loved cats.* His wife, Lillie Grace Reed, born on April 6, 1900 and died March 1, 1970, had an inscription more appropriate: *Safe in the arms of Jesus.* Don formed mental pictures of the couple and wondered what people would picture upon seeing his tombstone with something like *One cantankerous old bastard* written on it. He smiled briefly and then turned his attention to the closing prayer for Sarah Bettner.

Bill Newton pushed the doorbell button for the third time. Steve surveyed a landscape far removed from days of manicured shrubs and a freshly cut lawn. The grass had not been touched in a long time. Clumps grew between the expansion joints of the concrete driveway.

Steve commented on their surroundings. "Place could use some help."

"I'd say nobody lives here but the car out there says otherwise. We'll have to come back and check him out later." Bill leaned forward, cupping his hands around his eyes, and peered through the side window. Open pocket doors at the end of the foyer allowed him to see through to the back of the house. The only sign of life was a television set turned on to an unintelligible program. Beyond the television were windows opening to a dense, tree-filled backyard.

"The guy's home but obviously doesn't want visitors."

"Screw him. My uncle's best friend is dead and I want to know why. Let's check out the back."

"Suits me."

They walked down the front steps and around the side of the house. A large brick patio, pockmarked with assorted debris and out-of-control grass, swept up to a large covered porch and floor-to-ceiling glass windows spanning the back of the house.

Once on the back porch they both saw Herman Soboda standing near the pocket doors looking toward the front door. His posture indicated that he was hiding in his own house.

Satisfied that the unwelcome visitors had gone, Herman Soboda turned back toward his chair. At first it didn't register much as his eyes were trained on the floor. Something out of place caught his attention. He first saw their legs and then his eyes lifted to see two large men peering in at him.

"Mr. Soboda. We need to–"

Herman Soboda ran from the room in terror, his untied bathrobe flapping behind him. He disappeared up the staircase.

"Shit. He's paranoid about something." Steve shook his head in near disbelief.

"Should we break in and try to settle him down?"

"Why not leave a note? We can tell him we aren't a threat and that we will be back in two hours. I could use some lunch anyway."

"Good idea. I've got it." Bill took his small pocket notebook from his jacket and scrawled a note:

> *Mr. Soboda,*
> *We are not a threat. We are trying to gather information concerning a friend. We'll be back at 2:00 p.m. and we need to speak with you. We also may be able to help you.*
> *Thanks,*
> *Bill Newton and Steve Seiler*

Bill set a patio chair up facing the window and placed the note on it. He weighed it down with two small stones.

"How about Mexican? There's a place on Main Street called Esteban's Café and Cantina."

"*Bien, mi amigo.*"

Tom and Don drove around town before stopping by the reception. The main square, accentuated and dominated by the multi-story Gonzales County Courthouse with its red brick exterior, sandstone-colored arches over the windows, typical small town clock, and steep roofs, reflected Gonzales's early-nineteenth century birth. On top of the courthouse rested a widow's watch. Around the square, restaurants, antiques shops, and assorted small businesses flourished. A quick forage through neighborhoods provided an almost surreal look at small-town Texas. Homes ranged from the tiniest, yet well-kept, bungalows to the Belle Oaks Inn, a beautiful, two-story plantation home on St. Peters Street. Whether it is the Belle Oaks Inn of Gonzales or any of the other thousands of bed-and-breakfast homes throughout the state, the ambiance is always accentuated by the friendly countenance of the owners. From Booker on the Oklahoma border to Donna near the Mexican border, these small towns can be charming, desolate, or both. A highway sign in Booker proclaims *Booker— Next 9 Exits,* signaling that small towns also have a sense of humor.

An hour was enough time. They parked a full block away, relegated to the location by the large number of cars clogging both sides of the street. People surrounded the house in small clusters. In the backyard children played on hastily built rope swings beneath the oak tree and a Jungle Jim climbing set. Laughter sprang out in bits and pieces.

Tom mused, "Doesn't take long to get on with life. A bunch of them don't remember why they came."

Don surveyed the crowd and answered, "Maybe that's good. When I kick the bucket I want you to set up a big party at your hangar. Have an open casket with me and my shit-eating grin. At the end of it all, take a backhoe and bury me by the catfish pond."

Tom chuckled and answered, "Who the hell do I bring other than our family?"

"Just the same people you invite to every party you give. You know half of East Texas. Tell 'em that since we're like clones you just want to see how they'll act at your funeral." Don picked up his step.

"If they knew we're so much alike they'd all be singing good riddance and pissing on your grave. That would kill the catfish."

Don stopped and turned to Tom. "You know, I'm serious. You damn well better bring me back to Texas. I don't want to be buried in pissant California. Yeah, you bury me here."

Tom had never given it any thought and this was not the time for death wishes. "Let's drink a couple of beers and figure it out later."

They eased their way through the crowd and made it into the house unscathed. The living room was packed. A lot of townsfolk were friends of the family.

Tom spoke quietly into Don's ear. "You head for the kitchen and the beer and I'll get some food. Meet you on the back porch."

The table in the dining room was packed with food. Roast beef, ham, sausage, fried chicken, potato salad, cold slaw, pickles, succotash, cornbread, rolls, and a myriad of condiments spread out like a mammoth jigsaw puzzle. Tom piled food on the two plates, juggling them as he went, and then retreated to the back porch.

They exchanged a beer for a plate of food. Tom sat down next to Don on the edge of the porch floor. The roast beef on a roll, covered in horseradish, couldn't be beat.

"I'm glad you could make it."

The brothers looked up to see Josh and two of his sisters. "Meet my sisters Ella and Evelyn."

Tom put his plate and beer on the porch, grabbed Don's plate and beer, then helped Don stand up.

Ella spoke first. "Thank you for coming. Josh told us about your friend and what you had said about our mother. It means a lot to us."

They were very pretty young women and it was hard to tell who might have been the older. It didn't matter.

Neither Bill nor Steve was accustomed to long lunches, but League City didn't offer much in the way of sightseeing. With Mexican cantina music playing in the background, they passed the time over a couple of beers and combination plates of chicken enchiladas, tacos, and flautas.

"Guess we can head back now. I'm not getting my hopes up that he will see us. He's one strange cowboy." Steve added, "This one's on me." Having learned his tipping habits from his father, Steve placed two twenty-dollar bills on the table, enough for the food and a very healthy tip.

Ten minutes later they were back at the house ringing on the doorbell. After four attempts Bill admitted defeat. "He's not going to answer. We need to catch him outside. Have you ever done any surveillance?"

"Naw, but I'm game. Too bad the Astros aren't playing today."

They turned and started down the steps. Both heard a slight metallic click and turned around. The door opened partway.

"What do you need?" Herman Soboda peered through the opening, uncertainty on his face.

Steve answered, "Mr. Soboda, I'm Steve Seiler and this is my partner Bill Newton. You were doing some legal work for my uncle. We need to discuss it with you."

"Yeah, OK, come on in." He backed away and opened the door.

Bill and Steve walked into the house. It hadn't been cleaned in a long time, and it smelled of dirty clothes and mildew. In the midday sunlight dust could be seen on every piece of furniture. Herman noticed their stares and unconsciously rubbed his hand over a week's growth of stubble. "I haven't been doing well lately. I know it needs a cleaning."

"Naw, it's fine." Bill continued looking around at the disgrace.

Herman took them into what had once been a sitting room. He turned off the television and asked the two men to have a seat. He repeated his original question: "What do you need?"

"Whew, I can't handle this stuff. She must have been everything Elam said she was."

Don looked out at the homes heading out of Gonzales. "Yeah, they thought the world of her. Does make you think about the wrath of God, doesn't it?"

Tom didn't respond. He was thinking about who might have killed Sarah and Elam.

I-10 carried them east. Bear and Catfish welcomed them home. Susie met them at the door, as did the scent of beef brisket.

Thirty-Six

Friday Night,
April 2

Broken Wing Ranch

Beams of light quickly diffused onto an opaque curtain of fog. The car slowed to a crawl, just passing the mailbox of the Broken Wing Ranch. It stopped on the asphalt pavement and then slowly moved to the side of the road.

"Terrible night. Just terrible." Steve spoke more to himself than to Bill. He squinted tightly as though his actions would allow him to see more than three feet in front of the hood. It didn't.

Bill answered, "Glad you volunteered to drive. You're clear from behind. I think we're at the driveway."

Steve backed up a few more feet and turned into the driveway. Bear and Catfish knew by the sound of car wheels rolling over crushed stone that visitors had arrived. They bolted through the dark pines to the approaching car, the sounds of their barking breaking the silence of the night before fading into the softness of the mist.

Susie heard the dogs; ten seconds later she saw the

headlights flickering through the maze of trees and underbrush. "They're here, Tom."

Tom got up and walked to the kitchen entrance just as Bill and Steve got to the door. Don started to rise, still capturing the end of a storyline on ESPN.

"First ones here deserve the porte-cochère. The others get the rain." Tom shook hands with Bill and Steve. "Got beer or coffee to go with the cake."

Bill and Steve pulled off their coats and placed them on top of the clothes dryer. Steve rubbed his hands together before grabbing a beer out of the refrigerator. Bill walked straight to Susie and gave her a gentle hug before siding up to the coffee pot. Don shook hands as well.

Five minutes later Bear and Catfish welcomed Ross and Paige to the ranch. Casual bantering was underway inside.

The phone rang. Nancy had called earlier to say that she had to join the conversation by phone because of the weather. Susie answered and switched the phone to speaker mode.

"Hi, Nancy. Everyone's here. I've got you on the speaker."

Tom used Nancy's call to start the meeting. "OK, troops, get what you need and let's get started."

Refills of beer or coffee, coasters, small serving trays with pound cake and cookies, notepads and pencils, and seven people crowded the dining room table. Each person save Tom settled in a chair and prepared for the meeting.

Tom, standing next to the easel at the end of the table, spoke. "I'd like to cover our topics as shown here." He lifted the blank front sheet over the back of the easel. On the underlying paper was written:

AGENDA
Elam & Sarah—Tom
Soboda/Barrister—Steve/Bill

Oil Companies—Ross/Paige/Nancy
Other

Tom stated the agenda out loud so that Nancy could follow the discussion, and then added, "Given that Steve and Bill have done a lot of work on the lawyers, I've taken Bill off of the oil company list so that he and Steve can concentrate on the legal end of our investigation. Nancy, how's that sit with you?"

Nancy answered, her voice coming from the phone in the middle of the table, "No problem. Being so far away, I've been looking at oil companies independently of everyone else anyway."

"Good. I'll start with what Don and I found out about Elam and his girlfriend, Sarah." He lifted another sheet, exposing a blank sheet. He wrote Elam and Sarah very neatly across the top of the sheet.

"First, you already know we are convinced that Elam and Sarah were not killed by the tornado. What I didn't show you at our first meeting were these photos." He stopped to let his words sink into the minds of the others. "Nancy, I'm passing the pictures to everyone here. It'll take a couple of minutes."

"OK."

Six sets of eyes stared intently at Tom. Nancy sensed the silence.

Tom reached down and opened his briefcase. He pulled out a set of pictures and stared at the top one as though for the first time. Since taking the pictures at the site and at Breuner's Funeral Home, Tom had been unable to keep from studying them constantly. He was not a forensic pathologist, but his layman's grasp of physical injury was acute. He gave the stack to Don, sitting next to him. The pictures traveled one by one down the human conveyor belt. Susie did not look down, choosing instead to pass them on to Paige.

Tom began, "Don, anything you want to mention about the photos?"

Don leaned to his left, cocked his head, and answered, "The only thing I'd say right now is that, unlike Tom, I haven't seen many dead people. But what I do know is that I looked at the injuries on Elam and Sarah and then at injuries of victims of the storm. There were unmistakable differences."

Satisfied that the others understood the difference in the injuries suffered by Sarah and Elam from those of the storm victims, Tom gave the group some bad news. "We did have one big setback and I don't know what can be done about it. I called Luling this week and found out that full internal autopsies had not been performed. The cause of death has been listed for both of them as the result of blunt trauma subsequent to the tornado."

A few sighs were followed by Tom's adding, "I know— it's a bitch. But depending on how things turn out in our investigation, we may have to revisit the topic of autopsies. I'll keep everyone posted."

Tom moved to the second agenda item. "Bill, Steve, what do you know about the lawyers?"

Bill turned it over to Steve. "Since you're the lawyer, the floor belongs to you."

Steve nodded to Bill, cleared his throat, and dove into the topic.

"Well, to begin with, we don't know much about Fred Barrister. Unlike Soboda, Barrister lives pretty high on the hog."

Don wanted to speak, but decided to wait. His lips tightened and legs jerked in small spasms in an unconscious reaction toward Fred Barrister.

Steve continued, "As for Soboda, things are very strange. Even though he trusted us, Soboda was reluctant to open up.

He's a basket case. He stuttered through our conversation and constantly looked around the room and out the back patio door." Steve leaned forward, speaking into the receiver connecting the group with Nancy. "He was terrified that he was being watched. Still, he eventually gave us some important information."

Piece by piece, Steve unraveled the puzzle of Herman Soboda. The note that was left on his chair, his gutted dog, virtually drawn and quartered with goldfish laid side by side next to the canine corpse, and the stack of hundred-dollar bills.

"Here." Steve pulled a piece of paper from his shirt pocket and unfolded it. He passed it to his left. "This is a copy of the note that he found at his office."

Nancy said via the speaker, "I need someone to read it out loud."

Paige, note in hand, replied, "I've got it, Nancy. It reads, 'You will do as instructed. If you don't . . .'" Paige read the note word for word.

No one spoke, each person caught up in the words and their clear meaning.

Steve broke the silence. "The down side to what we've learned is that Soboda has no idea why he was targeted. When all of this happened, he was working on a slew of cases. Most of them were related to patents, but he had a few ad hoc projects as well." He gestured toward Bill, "Anything else, Bill?"

Bill sat up, his large torso dwarfing his chair. "I'll be checking out Barrister in the next few days. But from what Steve and I have put together so far, there doesn't appear to be any direct linkage between Barrister and Soboda. As Steve mentioned, Soboda knows Barrister in name only. Soboda's absolutely terrified that he'll be killed if it gets out that he gave us any information. Bottom line, this is classified stuff."

Tom asked, "Any other thoughts?"

Ross answered, "From my perspective, we either have a coincidence of immense proportion or something's just not right. I'll bet dollars to donuts that Soboda's situation is linked to the JETS."

Bill said, "I've interviewed hundreds of witnesses over my time with HPD. Some were straight up and some were pathological liars. Soboda told us the truth." Bill looked over to Ross. "I think your concerns are valid. There's got to be some sort of conspiracy. If so, then it's possible that Barrister is linked to it." Bill shook his head with a touch of disdain. "Bottom line is that we're in a very serious situation. My task is Barrister and I'll check him out closely over the next couple of weeks."

A light bulb went off in Don's head. He stood up, placing his hands on the table. "Here's a final tidbit to chew on. Somewhere I remember talking to Elam out at the site. I think Elam said that Barrister told him that he, Barrister, had been offered several cases from Soboda. Sounds like he knows Soboda, but what you're saying is that Soboda doesn't know Barrister. We may have ourselves a liar of the first order. Unfortunately, even if he is a liar, it may not stand up in court."

Don's remark ignited another thirty minutes of discussion before Tom brought all to a close. Everyone helped put dishes and glasses back in the kitchen. One by one each bade farewell to Tom, Don and Susie, and walked into the night.

Inside, Don, exhausted, called it a night. Tom straightened out the couch, placing the pillows neatly in order, as Susie rinsed and placed glasses, silverware, and plates into the dishwasher. Tom tied the garbage bag together and took it outside. Susie wiped off the dining room table, the granite kitchen tops, and the inside of the sink. Both were quiet as they went about their tasks. They finished the nightly ritual of brushing teeth, using the bathroom, and turning out the lights.

They turned toward each other and kissed gently. Susie rolled over on her right side and Tom turned toward her.

Susie broke the silence. "We've been here before. I'm scared again and I don't know what to do."

Tom squeezed her left shoulder and placed his right hand on her head. He ran his fingers through her hair as he spoke. "I don't know what to do either. I think we need to take a long walk tomorrow and sort things out. You with me?" They both knew that Tom was trying to end the discussion.

The personification of teammate, Susie agreed. "It's a date. Now get some sleep." Tears, birthed by melancholy and fear, rolled down her cheeks.

Tom looked up into the darkness at the churning fan blades. It was shortly after three o'clock. He hadn't been able to separate himself from the events closing in on him and the family. Impressions of human beings who would stop at nothing to satisfy greed forged their way into his mind. Some he recognized from the past; others surged into his imagination as he contemplated what was happening at this time in his life. He sensed his body tightening as visions of physical confrontation played out in his mind. A mysterious, very dangerous tide was coming in. Tom gently lifted the covers and edged his way out of bed. He stepped into moccasin slippers, grabbed his Levi's and shirt, and quietly made his way to the patio.

The evening felt neither warm nor cold. Tom leaned back in his chair, feeling slightly boxed in by the fog. Distant barking momentarily detracted the demons in his head.

But they came back.

In his mind's eye Tom replayed times when he had confronted evil, always in the form of human beings. He hated them and reviled at what they do to others—not only his friends, but also to other warm-hearted, good people. The scum of the earth continually spitting upon the salt of the earth. They were about to do it again. The question was no different than from earlier times: *What are you going to do about it?* Tom looked into the dark. *What should I do?*

Tom heard the sound of the doorknob. He turned around.

"I'd like to be your friend tonight. Are you game for company?" Susie, clad in robe and cotton pajamas, stepped through the door.

"Actually, I need the perfect friend right now. And she just arrived." He managed a slight smile as he pulled her chair closer to him.

Susie sat down and touched hands with Tom.

Susie crossed her legs and looked toward the flagpole. "I wish the fog would go away. The stars have always given me hope."

Tom looked down toward the concrete slab. "I've killed another human being. There should have been another way. But it happened." Tom bit the inside corner of his lip. He looked at his wife and squeezed her hand. Looking back down, he continued. "I still can't reconcile it all. I wanted to kill him. It wasn't about justice; it was about rage and killing. I want to say I'm sorry and confess to whoever God is, but I know that deep down there is a small portion of satisfaction about killing him. Doesn't matter that he was a sociopath. I struggle with it all the time and can feel it eating me from the inside." He repeated, "I wanted to kill him." He shook his head dejectedly. "I have the same emotions right now about those who are involved with this whole sordid mess."

Susie squeezed his hand, saying nothing for a moment. Then she said, "Tom, you are a good man. A remarkable man. You live your life with uncompromising integrity. Your only weakness that I see is not being able to rise above your anger at other people's failings. You are a protector. From talking to Don and Nancy, I know that you have always been a protector. I also know that, in spite of your raw emotions, you would never kill anyone out of stark rage. You had no choice–either you killed him or he would have killed you."

Tom sat mute as Susie's word took root. *You had no choice.*

Susie scooted her chair back and stood up. "Please take me for a walk."

Thirty-Seven

Monday Early Evening, April 5

First Presbyterian Church, Luling, Texas

In 1874 the Galveston, Harrisburg, and San Antonio Railroad linked to the main north–south wagon road between Austin and South Texas at a small junction forty miles east of San Antonio. Bit by bit a few stores and homes were built, giving birth to the little town of Luling, Texas. Beyond the cargo of supplies, the railroad also delivered a sizeable number of unsavory characters. Cattle and some of the most undesirable cowboys alive stamped the seal of "tough and unkempt" to the town. Its citizens can't be sure, but talk has it that the railroad may have been suffering guilt pangs when it deeded land for building churches. Guns and God were the order of the day. In 1877 the Reverend Philip H. Hensley and fourteen followers established the First Presbyterian Church of Luling. The building, located on South Pecan, was completed in 1882. A block away, the Catholic Church of St. John was established in 1879. Both churches had dual missions: to save Luling from the ravages of sin and, in doing so, to give life to the town for centuries to come. Those first preachers and priests must have been proud, although pride may not be allowed in heaven, to look down from on high and see these churches, two of some twenty-five in a town of less than six thousand, selected for the salvation of Luling, Texas.

The initial planning meeting of the town's leadership was held at the First Presbyterian Church less than a week after the tornado. The Catholic Church of St. John was chosen for a larger town meeting concerning the future of Luling. The beige brick portion of the church facing South Pecan Street was adorned with brown, glass-filled doors having stained glass sections on the sides. Above that entrance was a large, brown cross. A bell tower stood sentinel over Travis Street and a beautiful palm tree. The choice of St. John was based on logistics; it could accommodate slightly more than three hundred people as long as they didn't mind standing along the walls, and there was a large parking lot and parish hall across South Pecan Street where families could gather for a post-meeting potluck supper. The corrugated metal building had a meeting hall and religious education classrooms.

Raw winds enveloped the people of Luling with bone-chilling, soul-starving rain. Twelve of the seventeen days following the tornado had seen inclement weather. Electricity still did not exist north of Davis Street, the San Marcos River flooded lowlands on the south side of town, construction materials had been slow to arrive, and the pale of funeral after funeral had assaulted families without mercy. Still, people came to St. John's. By the carload they kept coming. Cars and pickup trucks were bumper to bumper along Crockett and Bowie Streets, and along Pecan from Milam Street to the tracks of the Southern Pacific Railroad. Because of the huge crowd, only one member represented families unless the primary member had a disability. Families separated in the parking lot, with most going to the parish hall and others to the church. Inside the church people squeezed against each other in the pews and lined up body to body along the side and back walls. Those in pews or with chairs sat down. The others shifted their weight to reach a sense of comfort.

At 6:15 p.m. Father Jose, admired and loved by the town's Catholics and non-Catholics alike, walked to the pulpit. Quiet spread in a soft wave over the ecumenical gathering. It was the first of several moments during the evening that would later be described as solitude. He looked over the church and then gently asked all to stand and join him in a moment of silence and prayer. They rose from chairs and pews; those already standing became slightly more erect. The silence became more deafening, only the lightest of sounds emanating from the parish hall breaking the silence. Then Father Jose gave a prayer.

He ended simply. "And that we, with all our grief and all our hopes, do believe that you will be with us on our separate and collective journeys. In the name of the father, the son, and the holy spirit. Amen."

Catholics made the sign of the cross and others offered "amen" in their own way.

Father Jose asked all to be seated and introduced Luling's mayor, Jose Murratti.

Mayor Murratti walked to the podium. Obviously nervous, he tapped on the microphone while volunteers passed through the crowd giving out 3x5 cards and pencils. The mayor continued tapping while gathering his thoughts. A couple of light coughs preceded his first words.

"Ladies and gentlemen, may I have your attention?" The crowd responded slowly, the people abuzz with the purpose of the cards.

"We have much to accomplish tonight, so let's get started." He smiled meekly before turning serious. His eyes closed slightly, parallel lines slicing across his brow. "We are here tonight for the sole purpose of deciding what the future of Luling will be. The history of this town is all about grit. It's about strong men who drove cattle, farmed the land, and worked the oil rigs. Some of the early settlers served the Confederacy. Their descendants have fought in two world wars, Korea, Vietnam, Afghanistan, and Iraq. On the day of the tornado, four of our kids were serving in Iraq, six in Afghanistan. Our women have kept our families together, nurtured our young, and have been the bonding agent in making us who we are. Even in Iraq, two of our daughters are fighting side by side with men. There is not another town, in Texas or the whole of our country, where Mexicans and other Hispanics, blacks, and whites get along as we do. We are not Mexican American, African American, or Italian American. We are American. Just as we have shared the great surges of the good times for Luling, we are now forced to share in its tragedy."

Jose paused long enough to survey the gathering. He saw the full character of Luling to his front; they were imperfect yet value-laden people for whom the best adjective might indeed be the word "grit." For every kid who failed, twenty succeeded. Yes, they were people he freely chose for his life's journey. They were family.

He continued. "Our tragedy is forcing us to look at the future of this town. Over half of Luling does not exist anymore. I look at the destruction and wonder if we have any chance at all. We know what Hurricane Katrina did to entire towns in Louisiana and the Gulf Coast. Some of those people failed to make it; others fought together to overcome the devastation and rebuild a new future. Our situation asks of us this question: Should we move to San Antonio, Austin, or any of our sister towns on the Texas Independence Trail?"

Jose paused again as the sound of whispered thoughts responded to his words.

"Answering that question is our task for tonight. Of course, saying yes or no is only part of our task, as other issues are associated with our collective answer.

"Please give me your full attention." He waited momentarily. "Hold the noise down."

The cavernous room went silent.

"On one side of your card I need three items." Jose leaned forward, arms resting against the pulpit. "First, write down the number one and a yes-or-no answer to the question, 'Do you plan to stay and live in Luling?'"

Jose had to repeat himself twice for a crowd that intently wanted to follow the rules. Then he moved on.

"Next, write down the number two and state whether or not you want to speak to the people here tonight. Just answer yes or no."

He waited one minute.

"Finally, on the bottom of the card, and only if you want to, put down your name and some way that we can contact you. An address, phone number, or email address would be fine. If you answered yes to question number two, we must have your name."

Heads bowed down prayerfully as each person wrote the information on the card.

"Now, turn the card over. At the top, please write down the damages your home may have suffered. Using the exact words, put down 'none,' 'moderate,' or 'total' for indicating the degree of damage." He paused briefly. He wanted to ask each person if he or she had lost family members but decided against it in deference to exposed raw emotions.

"At the bottom of the back side of the card I ask you to write down a single question. Make it a question that affects the whole town, and make it the single most important question you can think of."

Jose glanced down to a woman in the front pew. Karen McDougal, a middle-aged woman with small dark curls dotted with touches of salt, a serious-yet-motherly expression emanating from her oval face, looked up and nodded to the mayor. Karen McDougal was the editor of the Luling Newsboy and Signal.

Jose continued, "I have formed a committee to discern answers to your questions. Ada Pittinger, our executive director at the Chamber of Commerce, Trey Butler, executive director of the Luling Economic Development Corporation, Reverend Colin Keller of the Episcopal Church of the Annunciation, and Karen McDougal, our editor, have agreed to work with me to answer every question coming from this community. Karen will print our answers to your questions in the Newsboy. Please write your questions." After a short pause, Jose interrupted the crowd, "Sorry. I have two other items. First, if you have more questions, send them to Karen. Also, we will have future meetings if you want them. It's up to the community. OK, write your questions."

After the townspeople wrote their questions, Jose outlined the procedure for the rest of the meeting while volunteers collected the cards. "It is now six thirty-eight. I will end the meeting promptly at eight fifteen. Your cards are being sorted into two groups: those wanting to speak and those who don't. For those of you who do want to speak, I will select cards randomly." He leaned into the microphone for added emphasis. "Please be respectful of everyone and keep your remarks to no more than three minutes. You must abide by this rule. I will let you know when you're down to fifteen seconds. I will call as many speakers as I can prior to eight o'clock. At that point I will try to put some perspective on what appears to be the most prevalent questions written on the cards. Do not ask questions of the speakers because of the time schedule. Now, hang on for a couple of minutes while we sort the cards.

The crowd morphed into a kaleidoscope of turning heads enveloped in a muffled buzz of intense discussions.

Finally, Jose turned to a young woman holding a sizeable stack of cards. He leaned over and she whispered in his ear. He shook his head and patted the woman on the shoulder. He walked to the podium and the buzz of the crowd melted into the air.

"Before we turn to speakers I do have the first results of the question 'Do you plan to stay and live in Luling?'" A slight smile crossed his lips and his furrowed brow smoothed. "We have 312 cards. Of those, 226 plan to stay, 61 intend to leave, and 25 are undecided. With that, we'll begin."

The first two speakers provided little substance to the gathering. Both were so emotional that what they said was impossible to understand. Jose Murratti began to doubt the significance of the meeting. The third speaker spoke eloquently as to why he was compelled to leave.

Wayne Anston grabbed the remote microphone from the volunteer and started speaking.

"We came here eight years ago from Borger to work for Salt Flat Pipe and Supply. Our neighbors all along Newton Street welcomed us with open arms. Maye fell in love with everything about Luling. Everybody's nice, willing to help with any problem. We'd have cookouts for the neighborhood and all kids could play together in safety." Wayne wiped his eyes and blinked hard, trying to hide the red and the tears. "We was happy and never had no intention of ever leavin'. Audrey saw every day as a time to play to her hearts con . . ." Wayne's lips started quivering uncontrollably. He reached up and placed his hand over his mouth. Sorrow blanketed the church like molten lava. People cried with him, men as much as women. Most wanted someone to hold close. Many, both friends and total strangers, grabbed and squeezed each other's hands.

"Audrey . . . my Audrey. Oh my God, my Maye and my Audrey."

Wayne suddenly lifted up and looked toward either heaven, in resigned faith, or just to the ceiling of a meaningless church. He calmed down, inhaling deeply, and spoke again.

"My family is dead, my home destroyed, my job lost. I will never understand it. I love the people and the town. I wish I could stay, but I can't. I can handle everything except the memories of what happened to my wife and daughter. If I stay I will never escape the pain. I'm sorry, I just have to go."

Wayne gave the microphone back to the volunteer, turned, and with head down, walked slowly back into the crowd.

"Next is Terry Keane."

Terry Keane stood among people lined against the left side of the church. His denim shirt and Levi's were covered with grime and dust, a natural consequence of working dawn to late evening day after day to repair his building on Davis Street. He took the microphone and stepped forward a couple of steps.

"Most of you know I came here a couple of years ago and bought Monte's from Craig Ballen." He glanced quickly around the room to assess any hostility. He found none. "I reckon some of you don't approve of a bar in Luling. I can understand that, but maybe everyone should know something else about Monte's." He cleared his throat. "Patrons'll tell you that I make 'em leave before they've had too much to drink. I made changes to the place since buying it from Craig, but I didn't change the sign reading 'Absolutely no beer in or out of these doors.' But, like most people have been saying about their friends here, my customers are good people too. There's not many places in this whole part of Texas where you can go have a drink, laugh, dance, shoot some pool, play darts, and relax, but not be allowed to get sloppy drunk."

The more he spoke, the more connected he became with the crowd.

"I'm not a church-goin' man but I do believe in God. Since the storm I asked him a million times, 'Why did you save Debbie, Annabeth, Leroy, me, and forty-one customers at Monte's that night?' and the only sense of an answer I get is that the survival of my bar might be a sign to us. Luling is like my bar in many ways. It's not perfect, but it's always full of good people and, until the storm, a place where people enjoy living. I want Monte's to survive, but more important is that I want Luling to survive."

Terry moved against a pew and looked at Jose Murratti. "Mister mayor, I know the Roughneck Cookoff and Oil City Car Show had to be cancelled over the weekend. But I also want to be the first to vote for having the Thump this year. It's about who we are, and I reckon if the Thump survives, then we'll make it as well. I'm staying."

Terry gave the microphone back and moved against the wall. On both sides, a couple of men patted him on the shoulder.

For another hour some people spoke of staying while others spoke of going. For the last speaker Jose shuffled the cards one last time. He removed one from the center of the stack.

"Margarita Flores."

Margarita Flores sucked in several short breaths. She couldn't stop trembling at the thought that her card had been picked. But she knew she had to go through with it. Margarita had been born in her parents' home on North Hackberry, met her husband Oracio in high school, worked for the Luling Visitors Center, and was quite possibly the best ambassador the town ever had. She was the poster child of the pretty, petite

Latina woman. Coal-black hair cut at the neck matched her almond-shaped dark eyes. Possessed of a small, straight nose, gentle, soft lips, dimples like gentle folds in a down blanket, and even though forced on this occasion, a smile to warm all hearts, Margarita's features defined physical beauty. Her actions throughout her life defined beauty of the soul.

The microphone bounced back and forth in rhythm with her trembling hands. She prayed a silent request that God would speak through her. Margarita began talking while sensing she was watching herself from a distant place.

"I am so nervous, but I know I need to talk to my friends. Please help me through this." Her voice was low and her first words came in quivering streams. "Because I have lived my life in Luling and because I worked at the Visitors Center, I think I know almost everybody here tonight." She paused to gather strength for the next word to be spoken. "Oracio . . . Oracio also knew many of you. Our boys were good boys. They were like their father: honest, happy, helpful, and full of dreams for the future. I have . . ." She stopped speaking, lowered her head, and prayed again. Removing her right hand from the microphone, Margarita wiped her eyes. She spoke again, this time with more strength in each word, saying, "I have lost almost everything. The four people in my life I love the most. They made me so happy. They are gone. They are gone with all of the others and with so many homes and businesses. Many of us seem to have no future." She hesitated but for a moment. "But we do."

Muffled whispers moved through the people. Cries, overpowering attempts to choke them off, came from sporadic locations throughout the church. Margarita's words were almost too much for the people to take.

She continued speaking. "But we do. We do have a future." She smiled, her dimples serving as centurions at the gates of hope. "I cannot explain why God did not divert the tornado, from Luling or the other towns that suffer as we do. I do know that he will help us to move forward. The only explanation for my grief is that my suffering, mirrored in your suffering, is a measure of how much I have been able to love. I love Oracio, Jose, Juan, and Francisco so much. I see them in the daylight and I see them in my dreams. Our first kiss, our wedding, the births of our boys . . . so many memories. And my memories of Luling are so much the same. I must now live for the rebirth of our town."

Her allotted time was coming to a close.

"For those of you who cannot stay, I can only say I understand. We wish you the very best in life. My home, and I will have a home some day, will always be a sign of welcome to you."

She looked up at the mayor. He nodded his head for her to go on.

"I will stay. Tomorrow I will be stronger than I am today. And each day will get better. The day will come when I smile more than I cry. Then I will know I am home again. Our Visitors Center will open tomorrow in a tent next to Luling Bar-B-Q. I will be there telling visitors to come back to Luling time and time again, eat our barbecue, join us each year for the Watermelon Thump and other events, and possibly share but a small part of our grief and a large part of our future. I will send an invitation for them to enjoy our people and, for some, to come and live among us." Margarita opened her arms to the audience, slowly turned in a full circle, and then drew the microphone to her breast with one hand, leaving the other arm outstretched to her friends. She smiled broadly. "I love my people, my Luling people. I will stay."

As Margarita returned to her pew, clapping began at sporadic locations in the church. Then it began to build. A crescendo cascaded upon the people. They stood, tears flowing like rain, and cheered for their town. Margarita sat with her face down in her hands, overwhelmed by the outpouring of spirit. Those around her called to her.

"Margarita, stand up. Stand up. See what you have done."

She looked up, and then stood up. She couldn't believe it.

"Luling, Luling, Luling!"

Across the street inside the parish hall, families stood in awe as the sounds from the church reverberated through the building.

Thirty-Eight

Wednesday, April 7

Office of Wellington Oil,
Houston, Texas

Don pulled into the parking garage and found his designated reserved parking space. Ironically, it was the same space Elam had been offered in December. He forged his way to the JP Morgan Chase Tower, stopping once to rest and consider "Personage and Birds." He thought, *Slick sculpture.*

Don's eyes swept upward from the sculpture and along the immense façade of the tower. He couldn't put his finger on it, but uncomfortable thoughts bounced around in his mind. Don remembered Elam making comments about the senior executives at Wellington. *What did he say about them?* The sun that a few minutes earlier had been a warm release from the unseasonably cold and damp spring now bore down on Don with a vengeance. He hadn't been in the sunlight more than five minutes, but he was sweating like a mid-July cotton picker. His back, armpits, and head grew damp, then wet. Time to move on. He wiped the sweat from his face with an old Hardee's napkin. The sun exacerbated the damage to Don's nervous system, cutting off the command from the brain to raise his right leg. Like a drunken sailor, which he had been too often during his time in the navy, Don plodded toward the entrance and the air-conditioned cavern of the JP Morgan Chase Tower.

Ada Pittinger opened the front door.

"Welcome to Luling, Texas, and the Francis-Ainsworth House. I'm delighted to have you here."

The husky husband, a wide grin across his face, reached toward Ada. "We're Johnny and Roseanne DeNardo, and we are honored to be your first guests since the storm. We owe you thanks for not canceling our reservation since it's the first time we've ever been to Texas."

Ada invited them in. "Please, come in. For sure, the best thing we can do to get back on our feet is to welcome people to our home. The comeback for Luling is officially underway and you're part of it."

The couple walked in and registered. Ada helped move their luggage to Sarah's Suite. They chatted back and forth while Ada described the amenities of the room, protocol for meals, and the delight of the sun porch.

"And where are you from again?"

Roseanne answered, "Pen Argyl, Pennsylvania. Lived there all our lives." She looked around the room, quite satisfied that they would enjoy their one-day stay in Luling. "We're officially among the retired and are on our first trip ever around the whole United States."

"Well, I am absolutely partisan about it, but I expect you'll find Texans to be friendly, helpful, and, well, pretty boisterous."

Johnny laughed at her comment. "We've already found that out. We haven't met a rotten person in the whole state."

Johnny just hadn't looked hard enough.

The pain in Don's leg took away from his ability to focus fully on the discussion.

"So, Mr. Seiler, what I understand is that you really are not any closer to a patent than when we met with Mr. Duquette." Morgan Rosewood's words frustrated Don. The words were acrid, demeaning, and accurate. The assault continued. "That being the case, we don't have much confidence at this point in your ability to come through on your end of the project. It's one thing to sell something to us that is working, yet all we've seen were a few pictures of a bunch of junk at a stripper well site."

Don had blown it. He forgot to bring pictures of the new prototype. It didn't really matter to Bart Miles and Frank Milsap since, courtesy of Jason French, they had plenty of pictures of the JETS display model.

Don replied, "I've got more than pictures. Since we had to cancel our initial demonstration, I'm offering a second one. I'll show you the operation in full swing with our new system."

Bart was tired and irritated. He had little use for Don Seiler and viewed him as nothing more than cannon fodder. He just wanted the JETS, lock, stock, and barrel. He raised his arm, his palm outward and his fingers spread out like spider's legs. The message was clear: Bart Miles was taking control of the discussion. He leaned forward from the other side of the conference table and slowly reformed his hand into a pointer. It pointed at Don.

"You and your former partner have jacked us around for months. Either you're ready to do business or you're not. I'm tired of all this shit. Here's the deal." He continued pointing, his hand moving back and forth like a strutting rooster's head. "We'll go to Luling and watch your dog and pony show. If we like it and you have a patent, we'll offer you a fair price for rights to the system and the patent. If we like it and you don't have a patent, we'll offer you $400,000 for ownership of what you have done to date. If we don't like it, the deal comes to a close." Bart sat back into his chair and folded his arms in Buddha fashion, his portly body accentuating the pose.

The room went stone silent. Don processed the conversation through the pain in his leg. One thing about Don Seiler, with good people he was as gentle as a lamb. With abusive people he had a very short fuse and a very volatile persona.

Before Don could respond Bart unfolded his arms and joined his hands, doing horizontal pushups with his fingertips. His lips pursed and eyes slowly closed. He wasn't quite finished. "You know, we have other people working on a similar device—and they may be closer to a patent than you are."

Bart's statement hit Don hard—too hard. Beyond its arrogance, the statement was sinister. It was a subtle statement that Wellington Oil might be dealing from a stacked deck. A poker player in his own right, Don showed no reaction. He thought for a moment to capture the essence of his reply.

"Well, Mr. Miles . . . and everyone here, let me tell you what I think." His voice resonated in a steady tenor, belying the intense desire on his part to wrap his hands around the throat of Bart Miles and choke the living shit out of him. "I think if you were so close you wouldn't be making any offer at all. And the other side of the coin is the fact that people besides Wellington Oil are interested in the JETS as well. And they act with dignity that totally escapes you. This is a hostile environment and, being blunt about it, I'm not sure I want to deal with you at all. I just have a strong aversion to arrogant assholes."

Don moved his chair back and started to rise. Jim Bitters glanced quickly at Bart, expecting a strong reaction. There was none. He spoke up. "Hang on a minute, everyone. Somehow we've taken a potentially great situation for everyone and turned it into a dogfight."

Bart growled at Jim. "Your dog's not in this fight, so back the fuck off." Bart's outstretched hand almost covered Jim's face, blocking his view of Don. Stunned at his relegation to plebian status, Jim sank back in his seat trying to comprehend what was going on.

Bart, his tone more deliberate than abrasive, addressed Don. "When is the demonstration?"

Don stood erect and stared at Bart, half-placidly and half-contemptuously. He stared just long enough to make Bart uncomfortable. "A week from tomorrow. Ten o'clock in the morning on the north side of Luling. I'll give directions to your secretary." Without waiting for a reply and, through sheer willpower, Don walked out of the room without using his cane.

As the door shut, Jim Bitters and Bart Miles simultaneously went after each other.

"Just what the—"

"Shut the fuck up! You handle the field business and stay the fuck out of mine." Bart's beet red face almost exploded.

Jim had had it. He rose and walked to the door, then turned around. "That device is my business, and you're about to lose it for us." He turned the handle, opened the door, and walked halfway through it before adding, "And by the way, a vocabulary in which the mode word is 'fuck' isn't very impressive."

He shut the door, muffling the words "fuck you" coming from inside the room.

"Thank you, Mr. Seiler. I'll make sure they make it next week. Have a nice day." Macy Buckles smiled at him, aware that Don had encountered the dark side of Bart's personality.

Jim caught up with Don at the secretary's desk. "Don, hang on, I'm heading out as well."

Just before they stepped in the elevator, Jim whispered, "Let me take the lead on talking until we get outside of the building."

Both cameras and the microphone were on, capturing a very benign conversation.

"I'll have a couple of my engineers with me for the demonstration. If you don't mind, they'll be there early for the set up."

Don replied, "Not a problem. My crew will be on site by seven in the morning."

A few more inconsequential words filled the remaining time to the lobby. Stepping directly into a western sun, the two men squinted simultaneously at each other.

Jim spoke. "Your perception of Bart Miles is probably correct. He can be a real son of a bitch at times. But the company has good rank-and-file people. If your system works as it's been described, then Wellington Oil needs it."

Don considered Jim a decent man. He did not feel the same of the company's senior leadership. "Jim, you hit the nail on the head. The only reason I didn't tell your dickhead CEO that everything was off the table is because of the little people I met in your company. Right now Wellington Oil is last on my list. Miles is an asshole."

Don's limp having returned, they slowly crossed into the parking structure. Jim's car was parked in space four.

As he reached for his keys, Jim asked, "Can I give you a lift to your car?"

Don raised his cane. "No thanks. My friend here," he

smiled at his metallic companion, "she'll take me."

Jim answered, "Great," and started toward his car. He stopped and called back to Don. "Don, let me give you one piece of advice to chew on." Jim cleared his throat with a soft, insecure cough. "If it does work out well and your patent is clear, don't take a penny less than ten million. You deserve a fair price, even if you have to put up with some overbearing behavior."

Bart Miles looked down forty-five floors to the street. He processed what he just saw–Jim Bitters and Don Seiler talking on the way to their cars. Frank and Morgan waited for Bart to say something. Bart knew the patent would soon be theirs, one way or another. He preferred buying the JETS patent for pennies on the dollar, since there would be no legal issues at all. But procedures for the Wellington patent were well underway. He certainly held the stronger hand at this point.

It was a short wait. Bart didn't say a word. He walked out of the room.

Thirty-Nine

Wednesday, April 14

The Francis-Ainsworth House,
Luling, Texas

Petroleum engineer Ed Bishop stacked suitcases in the back of the rented Ford Expedition while the other two Caprock representatives exchanged morning greetings with Don and Tom outside the bed and breakfast on Pecan Street. Ed, raised a Nebraskan, and Heather Brace, a top-notch acquisitions lawyer from Corsicana, looked the part. They were dressed in faded jeans and used work boots. Bostonian Ken Farmer, senior vice president for technology acquisitions, looked as though he had just walked out of the western clothes department at Shepler's Western Wear in San Antonio. The location was idyllic, notwithstanding the fact that less than two hundred yards to the north devastation could be seen everywhere.

"We owe you for the recommendation. Phenomenal place." Ken, large in every dimension, glanced back at the Francis-Ainsworth House, grabbed his stomach, and added, "I slept like a baby and the Crème Brûlée French Toast was absolutely unbelievable. Ed couldn't stop talking about the

Mexican Frittata. Ada added tortillas, fruit, bacon, juice, coffee, and everything else you can think of for all of us." Ken sighed pleasantly. "Why don't we sleep all day and check your site out tomorrow?" Light chuckles all around.

Built in 1896, the Francis-Ainsworth House reflected a comfortable, simply designed treasure. The white exterior gracefully hid behind a porch on the lower level; a spindled balcony above stretched across the entire second floor. A railed staircase overlooked the grand foyer, and antiques, including an elegant Steinway piano, adorned a small formal living room. Many great novels were read in the General's Library. Immaculate grounds, shaded with pecan trees and a single palm tree, served many a joyous wedding reception. Sam and Ada Pittinger bought it three years earlier with full realization that it represented both hope for an enjoyable livelihood and a possible albatross of never-ending maintenance and empty rooms. Their gracious hospitality had not quite killed the albatross.

Don's eyes brightened. "Next time you ought to check out the whole town. Luling took a huge hit from the storm, but it's coming back." Next he asked Heather, "How did you sleep?"

Heather thought of the previous night. "I haven't had as pleasant a night in ten years." She continued as Ed joined the group. "Wish you two had joined us. We sat on the balcony for two hours sipping wine, talking of life, and enjoying the stars and that warm touch of a breeze."

Tom, ever a gentleman but addicted to punctuality, checked his watch and announced, "Don't mean to be rude, but we probably ought to head out now. The crew's been on site for a pretty good while."

All agreed with mumbled, unnecessary apologies.

"Go it is." Don turned toward Tom's car and pointed the thumb of his free hand into the air.

Tom and Don waited as the Caprock party climbed into the Expedition. Ed Bishop tapped on the horn and they were off. Ada walked onto the front porch and waved "so long," not "good-bye," to the departing vehicles. The tiny caravan turned onto Bowie Street, passed the town library and made a left at Magnolia Street, heading north on US 183 toward Lockhart. Tom looked into the rear view mirror and could see the silhouettes of turning heads as Ed, Ken, and Heather surveyed the total destruction from the storm. Conversation among the Caprock contingent bounced back and forth between the charm of Luling, the good old days of the oil boom, and the sheer determination needed to survive a blow such as that delivered to the town.

Tom and Don spent the ride assessing their chances of success and the caliber of the Caprock delegation.

"Don't guess I'll ever get it." Don looked into the passenger side rear view mirror at the entourage following them. "These people strike me as the kind we ought to be dealing with. They're competent, friendly, and forthright. At least, they sure seem that way at first glance."

"Yeah, they strike me pretty much the same way. But it is only a first glance." Tom reached for a bottle of water, took a swallow, and asked, "And you're seeing the opposite side of the coin in a company like Wellington?"

"I wasn't making any comparisons, but that's a pretty fair statement." Don tapped his cane back and forth between his hands. "Decent people on one side and mostly assholes on the other." He shook his head forlornly as he spoke. "It's about tone. Tone set by leaders of companies. It you've got schmucks at the top passing out greed and abusiveness, then schmuckness rolls down the company walls. It's the endless battle between a culture of integrity and blatant mob rule." He kept shaking his head. "It's not fair to those who give all they have to an organization. Nope, I just don't get it."

Tom looked over quickly at Don and then returned his gaze to the highway. His eyebrows lowered slightly. "So what're you going to do?" He turned right on Texas 86.

Don stopped the rhythmic movement of the cane. "About what?"

Tom slowed the car. "About the possibility that everybody who sees it will be impressed with the JETS. The Chinese, Pakistanis, Wellington, Caprock, Exxon, Shell, and whoever else checks it out." Tom turned right again at County Road 132 and then left onto the dirt access road leading to the demonstration site.

"You mean, suppose it works and everyone bids on it, except that Caprock can't bid as much as the others?"

"That's exactly what I mean."

Don chewed on the question. "I'm not sure." He chewed some more before continuing, "You know me and my righteousness. I've got to watch it." Don eyed the one working pumpjack on the dirt road while he measured his words. "I'm in shitty health and I need to think about Cindy and Jayme. I also need to think about the people who have gotten us this far, including those guys up there." Don pointed toward a group of men milling around to their front.

Tom lowered the window as he slowed the car. He drove to the left of the entrance gate and waved his arm to signal Ed to park next to them. Don reached around to the back seat and grabbed a rolled section of butcher paper.

Ed, Heather, and Ken each gazed at the surroundings. Trees ringed the demonstration site. Inside they could see the repaired maintenance shed, a storage tank of some sort, and assorted items in the yard.

Carlos emerged from the crew as most of the other men took deep, sweet inhalations from their cigarettes and tossed the butts on the ground. Carlos, confident in his step, walked up to Don and extended his hand. "Hello, Mr. Seiler. We are ready for your friends."

Don tucked the butcher paper under his armpits, switched hands holding his cane, and reached out to shake hands with Carlos. He turned to the visitors. He semi-patted Carlos on the shoulder and directed him toward their guests.

"Heather, Ken, Ed, this is our foreman, Carlos Aguirre. I'm counting on him to impress you this morning."

Carlos reached out first to Heather and then to Ed and Ken. He gave all a firm handshake. "I'm glad to meet you. We'll have some water for you right away." He turned back to Tom, "Welcome back, Mr. Seiler." He returned his attention to Don. "I can take the paper and get everything ready." He grasped the butcher paper just as Don released his arm pressure.

Don responded, "Thanks, Carlos. I'm going to take them to the back first, and then you can run the demonstration. Have them come over here first to meet everyone."

"OK, Mr. Seiler." Carlos walked to the crew and gave the paper to one of the men to place on an easel in the back of the yard.

Don turned back to the group. "Don't need to keep you out here too long. Sun's going to get after us. Before starting, let me introduce the crew." He introduced the rank and file by name. Don, even when he had a sufficient stack of money from his engineering business, never measured the worth of a man or woman on anything other than character and competence. He was more than loyal to the crew, and with the exception of a Judas named Carlos, they were absolutely loyal to him. The Caprock members took note of Don's respect for the crew. They had already met Carlos. The other five, Felix, Eduardo, Hugo, Alejandro, and Wendell, shook hands and smiled with respect and anticipation. With the exception of Wendell Akers, the crew looked like typical, strong, dusty oil field workers. Wendell caught the attention of everyone he ever met. A bull-chested man of average height, bedecked with black curly hair and sporting sideburns from the seventies, he was a very different breed of cat. But beyond his physical features, it was his attire that set him apart from the rest of the planet. He wore sneakers, Wrangler jeans, a baseball cap resting backwards on top of the curls, and, of all things, a black Hawaiian shirt with printed colored flowers and coconuts. No one had ever commented on the way he dressed—and nothing would change on this day.

Don addressed the group. "I'll start with another overview of the JETS and then show you what it does." He switched the cane back to his right hand and slowly moved toward the back of the site. Don walked a short distance toward the northeast quadrant of the site and the maintenance building. "That's our maintenance and supply building." He pointed toward the inside of the repaired metal shell structure. "It has enough room for us to break down the JETS to its basic components and analyze how we might improve on our basic design. We use it to store hand tools and other accessories, and in bad weather, we keep our bucket loader inside."

All eyes tried focusing on the interior of the building. It was too dark to see much of anything inside.

Don, pointing to the west, continued. The group shifted its attention from the maintenance building to what was obviously the JETS system for the demonstration. An air compressor, the wellhead assembly, and a storage tank were the main components visible to the visitors. "Over there is the system that we'll be demonstrating for you. Unfortunately, the most important part of our invention is twenty-five hundred feet beneath us. We'll get to that after I give you a feel for how it operates and go over the actual components. Now, let's get down to the nuts and bolts."

As Don led the group toward the back end of the site, the work crew took up positions for what they hoped would be an impressive and financially productive demonstration of the JETS. Intense solar radiation, his efforts to walk without a limp, and pure anticipation withered Don's body; sweat rose into the sweltering air. The group followed Don to a long improvised table consisting of sheets of plywood placed on top of wooden pallets. On top of the plywood rested the cutaway display model of the chamber section of the JETS. An easel from which hung the sheets of paper brought by Don stood to their immediate front.

Don moved to the easel. The cover page read:

> *Donelam Oil Systems, LLC*
> *Pump on Demand*
> *Computerized*
> *Jet Extraction Technology System*
> *(JETS)*

He waited just a moment while a crewmember passed out water bottles to the Caprock visitors. They gladly accepted. It was time to make the sale.

"Welcome to Donelam Oil Systems." He wiped his brow. "It's getting hot, so I'll be wise and make this as short as possible. Just fire away with any questions when they pop into your mind."

Without wasting time, Don lifted the front page up and over the back of the easel. On the second page were Tom's original four freehand sketches of a rudimentary pumping system. The first sketch was an illustration of the chamber configuration; the following three sketches depicted the three-stage cycle for extracting oil from the site. Ken and Ed felt comfortable with the sketches. Heather might just as well try deciphering Sanskrit.

Don understood the possibility of confusion and viewed Heather to be just as important as the other two. He was well prepared to give a demonstration similar to that which Tom had given back in the family dining room. He took a live bait aerator from a small table next to the easel. It was nothing more than a small battery-operated air compressor with a tube running into a plastic jar. A second tube exited out of the top of the jar. With the exception of the opening at the end of the exit tube, the jar was completely sealed. It was filled with water.

"Our oil extraction device, the Jet Extraction Technology System, is not much more complicated that what I have here."

He turned on a switch to the system. The small compressor whirred into action, forcing air into the jar. Water, obeying the natural laws of physics, immediately began spewing out of the exit tube and into the air.

From that point on Don gave a near-perfect replay of Tom's simplified version of the JETS. "Oil, similar to the water in this jar, seeps through an open valve and fills the chamber; air pressure is applied; under pressure, the valve is closed and the oil can only go up and out of the system."

Don let the machine run until most of the water puddled on the ground.

"Next I'd like to show you a full scale display of the down-hole chamber section. It's over here."

With the group huddled at the edge of the display, Don began the detailed description of the functioning of the JETS. "Let me begin over here at the mud anchor." Piece by piece, Don described each component. From the mud anchor, Don covered the screen through which oil seeped into the system, the ball valve apparatus which, when not under pressure from the compressor, allowed oil to move into the chamber reservoir, the concentric gas inflow tube through which the compressed air would move and force the ball valve closed, and the smaller concentric outflow product tube through which slugs of oil would be transferred to the holding tank. Don emphasized that the length and diameter of the chamber, and thus the volume of an oil slug, would vary from well to well. Then he asked for questions. No questions. He finished with emphasis on the ball valve. "Please remember that, unlike any other system in existence today, the ball valve is the only moving part in the entire down-hole section. It's sturdy, reliable, and," his toothy grin advertised his growing ego, "it will last almost forever."

Don looked at the visitors in anticipation of questions. None were asked. Either all had gone very well or they were too tired and hot to speak. "Please join me over here." Don moved toward the full JETS system.

"OK, Carlos, bring up some oil."

Immediately Carlos barked out some commands, first in Spanish and then in English. The crew started a set sequence of actions. One man moved to the compressor and turned it on; another sat down at a small computer console less than ten feet from the compressor. Wendell Akers, the eccentric cowboy, grasped the hose leading from the down-hole system into the holding tank. A handyman, his down-hole work complete, joined Wendell at the holding tank.

Satisfied that the process was underway, Don spoke confidently. "I wish I could make it more spectacular, but the system is so simple that its full capability may seem lost in the mundane process that you are about to see." He added, "In order to give you a feel for the entire operation, we'll bring up the amount of oil that has already seeped into the chamber reservoir. For the next cycle, we'll be starting from scratch. For that cycle there will be a period of time during which it appears that nothing is happening. Actually, the chamber is filling with oil."

Soon thereafter a small vibration, accompanied by a slight gurgling sound, could be felt. *Whoosh.* A slug of oil emptied into the holding tank and the system shut off.

Wendell Akers placed a measuring stick into the holding tank. He pulled it out and read it: "Eleven gallons."

Don spoke to the group enthusiastically. "That slug of oil was about eleven gallons. The system has already started the next cycle. It's on a timing system."

The group stood in relative silence for several minutes. In between idle chitchat Don directed their attention to the crewmember at the computer. Finally, they watched the man nod his head at Don and tap at the keyboard. The compressor turned on.

Above the noise of the compressor, Don spoke to the gathering. "Let's move over to the holding tank. Don't get too close."

He hobbled to within a few feet of the tank and stopped. Once again the vibration and gurgling sound returned. Then a spray of dark, rich oil spewed from the hose into the tank. A smattering of oil showered beyond the confines of the tank, barely missing the Caprock representatives. In an involuntary reflex, all three stepped back quickly. The slug of oil came out of the hose for some fifteen seconds.

"Come on over and take a look." Don moved to the tank.

Each of the Caprock people looked at the pool of oil resting at the bottom.

Wendell Akers measured the amount of oil. "Almost twenty-two gallons."

Don verified what everyone knew. "That means each cycle produced ten-plus gallons of oil." He took out his handkerchief and wiped off his face. "Now for your mathematics refresher.

The circular area of inflow is approximately 13.75 square inches and the chamber length is 15 feet, or 180 inches. Thus, the total volume of the chamber comes to 2,475 cubic inches. Using 231 cubic inches per gallon, each slug of oil comes to about 10.7 gallons. Since there are 42 US gallons in a barrel, each slug produces slightly more than a quarter barrel." He surveyed the gathering. Ed and Ken followed the math; Heather took Don's explanation as an act of faith. Don continued, "The full cycle time at this well is about thirty minutes, giving us two cycles per hour, or forty-eight cycles per day. The total oil produced daily comes to twelve barrels. At a conservative estimate of $80 a barrel, this well can bring in $960 a day without anyone touching it." He made a small exclamation point. "And this is a small well.

"Unless you have any questions or want to see another cycle, why don't we have a seat back in those chairs?" Don gestured toward the maintenance building and several folding metal chairs.

A second round of drinks was provided. It was getting hotter by the minute. Don asked for questions.

Ken just wanted to make sure he understood everything. "Based on my understanding, each slug of oil will be somewhere over ten gallons. Am I correct in assuming that the only variable is time to fill the chamber reservoir?"

"For this system, yes. In other wells, the actual amount of each slug will be a function of the volume of the reservoir chamber. We can tailor the length and diameter of the chamber as needed. Chamber lengths can be manufactured according to the strata of oil deposits."

Ed followed with another question. "I'll be honest, I'm impressed with what I saw. But what do you know about this hole? Is there a lot of oil around or is this a typical stripper well?"

"This is a random stripper well. We picked the site based on our stretched financial situation, not an in-depth investigation. The well," Don pointed to the down-hole component, "had a pumpjack operation until about ten years ago. They took the pumpjack down because not enough oil could be produced to make it profitable. Although they are supposed to be plugged if no longer used, small owners don't have the money to plug them. Hundreds of thousands of unplugged wells exist in the United States. As for the world, we're talking about tens of millions."

It was Heather's turn. "This may sound strange, but for as long as the oil industry has been around, why hasn't this been thought of before?"

Don placed his cane between his knees and rested both hands on it. He shrugged his shoulders. "People have been working on oil extraction devices for years. The problem I think they encountered is that, prior to the JETS, there was a mindset that the device had to be complicated." He smiled broadly, saying, "My initial design was simple, but it had real-world problems, so I turned it over to the former best design engineer at NASA." Don looked to his right. "That engineer, who has tools sitting on the moon today from the Apollo missions, just happens to be my brother. Tom took my design and turned it into the ultimate oil extractor. While there may be some devices out there that can get more oil in the same amount of time, the maintenance costs have always been much more than we've experienced with the JETS. Overall, I do believe we designed the near-perfect widget."

"What financial analyses have you conducted to compare with other systems out there?" Ken Farmer wiped his forehead.

Before Don could answer, the compressor turned on, making it difficult to hear. Don raised his voice. "Sorry about the noise, the compressor is working on the next cycle. But let me get to your question.

"I don't know if you got it or not, but we sent a booklet to your corporate headquarters when we first made contact with you. I have updated copies of our economic analysis of the system. The downside is that we are a very small operation and don't have financial analysts all over the place. We did give our initial results to an economist, and he came back with a figure that says a system of this type producing fifteen barrels a day and amortized over eight years has a break-even point of thirty-seven dollars a barrel in current dollars. Even if the numbers are off by 20 percent, the system is far," Don emphasized the point, "*far* better than the conventional pumpjack."

Tom felt good about turning the entire briefing over to Don. Tom was the mechanical engineer, but Don knew his stuff.

Ken responded with apparent satisfaction, "OK, we'll take a look at your economic work and bounce it off of some of our folks."

Another slug of oil was delivered to the holding tank, the compressor turned off, and quiet reigned supreme.

Tom commented to Don. "Don, you might want to . . ." He suddenly realized that he was almost yelling at everyone. He lowered his voice. "Sorry about that. I just thought you might want to mention the computer."

"Oh, yeah, you're right. The computer console you see," Don pointed to the now unmanned laptop, "doesn't really exist in our final product. Each system will have a small timing and volume device. It's very simple. First, the system is set to deliver oil based on an approximate time to fill the chamber. Then it measures the volume of oil that is delivered to the storage tank. If the amount of delivered oil is smaller than the volumetric size of the chamber reservoir, then the time between deliveries is lengthened until the volume of oil entering the holding tank is equal to the size of the chamber reservoir. It's a simple iterative process. Once every twenty-four hours the system is automatically recalibrated so that system efficiency is maximized." He smiled. "I've got to admit that the whole timing device was the product of Tom's brain, not mine. As a failsafe operation we have a manual override just in case the timing system goes down. And remember, this part of the process occurs above ground. Not having a down-hole sensor alleviates major maintenance problems."

The Caprock representatives nodded their heads in unison. Looking like the Cheshire cat, Don smiled.

A few more questions were asked, and Don gave Ken a packet of photos of the new JETS.

Ken wiped his forehead and asked, "Don and Tom, while things are still fresh in our minds, do you mind if we have a small 'sort things out' session?"

"No, not at all. Take as long as you like."

Tom and Don moved inside the shed and spent the next several minutes congratulating the crew on a job well done. Concurrently, Ed, Ken, and Heather sat in their chairs and went over the pros and cons of the JETS. Don glanced over and noticed a jovial mood from the Caprock bench. Clearly a good sign.

The threesome got up and walked toward Tom and Don. Don asked the crew to give them some privacy. Carlos stayed as close as he could without irritating Don. Ken spoke as he put his right hand forward.

"Don, Tom, we want to say thanks for the demonstration of your JETS and for your hospitality last night and today." He got right to the point. "We won't beat around the bush. Your JETS is impressive; it does exactly what you promised. We'll brief our CEO and he'll most likely take it to our board of directors in early May. Assuming that they agree, we'll probably be asking you to come up to Lubbock to discuss where we go from here.

I know there will be a lot of questions. I'll let you know of any issues that may need to be addressed when you do come up."

Tom answered first. "If you can, let us know as early as possible. I've got a tough schedule coming up, and I need to be there to keep Don out of trouble."

Don smirked. "That would help me too. I'm headed back to California on Friday to catch up on some business. Unless something big comes up, I'll be back in Texas on the fifth or sixth of May."

Ken answered. "Sounds good. Our target ought to be the second week in May." He deferred to the other two. "Anything else?"

Heather didn't really have a question, only a statement. "One thing we will need is documentation for your patent. I know that will be a major item at the board meeting."

Ed had no questions, only thanks for a very enjoyable and worthwhile trip to Luling.

Given that all had gone very well and without interruption, the Caprock party looked good for making a mid-afternoon flight out of San Antonio. Don gave them better instructions to I-10 West than their GPS would have. They shook hands with Tom and Don; they also thanked the crew before climbing into the Expedition. The dust trail looked like a ribbon of good fortune.

"Well, pardner, what do you think?" Don smirked at his older brother.

"Best I can tell, we just landed our first fish." Clearly referring to the types of companies that they might be dealing with, Tom added, "May not be the biggest fish, but it sure smells better than the others."

The weight of the world jumped right off of Don's shoulder. His optimism called for a huge payoff for his multi-year effort; his pessimism reminded him that he shouldn't be counting any chickens at this point. Still, he was very relieved, and very satisfied.

Tom rained on his parade. "We've got to get the patent right away. It's the only sticking point for Caprock. It'll be the same with the others."

Don replied, a little wind taken from his sails, "That's priority number one. I'm going to get all over Barrister." He perked up. "Still, chalk this up as a good day. The difference between our first prototype and this just tickles the hell out of me."

Don turned around and called to Carlos.

"Yes, Mr. Seiler."

"Carlos, everyone did a superb job today. The people appreciated your efforts." Don patted Carlos on the shoulder. "Tell you what. Get everything set up again for tomorrow and then have the crew take the rest of the day off." He turned serious. "Just remind them that tomorrow's visit probably won't be as friendly. We can't afford today's success to turn into tomorrow's disaster."

"I understand, Mr. Seiler. We will be ready."

The crew, with Carlos working as hard as the others, put each piece of display equipment back in the shed. They emptied the holding tank and cleaned it out as best they could. Finally, the computer was taken to the shed. Satisfied that the cleanup was finished, Carlos announced that they were finished for the day but to be ready for an early morning: "*Stamos listos para la demostracion. Pero recuerden que tenemos que estar aqui mañana. Muy temprano.*"

The men filtered out, jumped in their trucks and headed out to a half-day break. The demonstration could not have gone better, and hopes for each man's future soared. High-fives and solid laughter dominated the scene. Shortly, contrails of dust floated along the road. Only Carlos remained. He looked around at the site and studied the exposed top of the demonstration JETS.

Carlos locked the doors to the maintenance shed, closed the swinging gate sections to the fence, snapped the lock shut, and spun the combination wheels. He walked to his truck contemplating what might be in store for him. He was shrewd enough to know that someone was going to make a fortune off of the system, and his mind worked to place him at the money trough. *But how?*

At the truck, Carlos pulled out his cell phone and dialed.

Bart answered his secretary's page regarding a Mr. Aguirre. "Thanks, Macy." He waited a second and spoke. "What've you got?"

Carlos answered quickly. "We did the demonstration for Caprock. It worked very good this time. Got plenty of oil out of the ground." He wiped sweat from his brow with his hand. "The people who came like it. It's much better than the other one."

"What were they saying to each other? Did you pick up anything specific?"

"They told Mr. Seiler that they liked it . . . one man said 'it is impressive' . . . and wanted to discuss it at a big meeting. They want to have a meeting in Lubbock next month."

Bart leaned forward into his desk. "What else did they discuss?"

"They talk only a few minutes." Then he remembered one more piece of discussion. "The woman, I think she is a lawyer, said something about a patent." Carlos swallowed, his mouth dry and thirsty. "Mr. Seiler said he understood. He didn't say nothing more. I listened but they didn't talk about money."

Bart's face tightened slightly. That the demonstration had gone so well was upsetting. Still, he knew that he held an ace in the hole.

"OK. Make sure you listen very carefully to what they talk about before we come out tomorrow morning. Give me a call tomorrow night on my cell phone."

"I will call you tomor–"

Bart hung the phone up before Carlos finished speaking. He called Fred Barrister.

"Where do we stand on the patent?"

Fred Barrister felt proud. Bart's call came only minutes before Fred had intended to call Bart.

"The patent should be yours very soon." Fred smiled into the phone. "There are two components to all this. First, your submission has been dated prior to the Donelam Oil Systems submission. That's critical in case of a lawsuit. Secondly, I was told by my contact that your system," Fred spoke as though there was an actual difference in the two submissions, "has been approved at the examiner level and is already working its way through the system. As for–"

Bart interrupted Fred. "Speed it up. I want the patent this week."

Fred answered, his voice somewhat tight. "Er, there's really nothing I can do. It's out of the hands of my contacts and it would be unwise to raise any red flags on this."

"You keep on top of this every day. I don't want it screwed up."

"It won't be. I give it three weeks at the most." Fred remembered his second point. "I almost forgot. I did manage to slow down the other patent application in the bureaucracy. Still, it would be wise to continue with the demonstration tomorrow."

"Yeah, yeah. Just get this shit done."

Bart hung up and punched a button on the intercom. "Jim Bitters."

"Jim, something important came up for tomorrow. Take whomever you need for the extraction demonstration. You can brief me when you get back."

Jim was perplexed, his mind asking, *You've been catatonic over this, so why the change?* "Sure, Bart, I'll be headed down early in the morning. Troy Easton will go with me. I'll give you a complete rundown."

Forty

Wednesday, May 5

Broken Wing Ranch

"Oh When the Saints" played lustily in Don's ear, waking him from an afternoon nap. He rolled over and slapped his hand over the nightstand until hitting his cell phone. He put it up to his ear.

"Don Seiler." He sounded more awake than he was.

"Don, this is Ken Farmer from Caprock. Did I get you at a bad time?"

Depends on what you're about to say, he thought. "No, not at all. Got back to Texas yesterday and I'm just sorting things out. What can I do for you?"

Ken's upbeat nature answered Don's earlier question. *This is going to be good!* Don thought.

"Senior leadership accepted our assessment. We'd like to meet with you and any of your leadership team to discuss preliminary agreements for a contract for the JETS."

Don almost dropped the phone. He drew in a large breath and spoke through the exhale. He failed at not appearing eager. "That's fine with me. I can round up my gang in pretty short order. Can you give me any specifics of what Caprock is considering?"

"Absolutely. For background, I'm sure you were aware that we were enthusiastic about the JETS at your demonstration. Bob Ames, our CEO, had to discuss acquisition and new technology matters with our board of directors before going any further. Heather and I spent most of yesterday afternoon discussing workable strategies for both parties. To be honest, we're not even locked into a final proposition. We are considering everything from purchasing the JETS outright to some sort of leasing agreement, or a combination of both. We'll come up with specific options and bounce them off of your team. You can do the same."

Don was euphoric. It went beyond blood, sweat, and tears. His money, health, hopes of a secure future for Cindy and Jayme, and a huge chunk of self-esteem were all invested in the JETS.

"Sounds good to me. Do you have a couple of dates so that I can schedule it with Tom and his son Steve? Steve's a young but very solid lawyer."

Don thought about the seven years since the idea behind the JETS was born. His quest to succeed with the JETS had drained his bankroll, and the MS had sapped physical strength from his body.

Ken interrupted Don's thoughts. "How does ten o'clock on either Monday or Tuesday morning at our Lubbock office sound? Both days are blocked out on our calendar. We're looking forward to a successful venture for everyone involved."

Don looked at one of the multitude of American flags adorning the guest room walls. "We'll go for Monday. I'll let you know if anyone has a problem. I can sort it out today and let you know no later than tomorrow."

"Great." Ken cleared his throat. "Oh, there is one item to mention. Before we go final, you do need clear title to the JETS."

The patent, thought Don, *the never-ending saga with the patent. The big fucking elephant in the room.* Don replied without hesitation, "I'm expecting the patent this week, hopefully today." Don's response sounded convincing and caused no concern on Ken Farmer's part. But for Don, his stomach churned.

Don remembered one other factor. He did not really want to mention it, but integrity demanded disclosure. "Ken, I do need to discuss one other factor with you."

Ken answered immediately with no sense of surprise or betrayal, "Are you going to mention other companies that are involved?"

"Yes. How'd you know?"

"You'd be crazy not to. We understand that. It's our belief that the proposal we'll make to you will make up for our relatively small size. We fully understand that if you don't come out a winner with us, we come out losers in the long run."

Don was almost without words. "Uh, I appreciate it and look forward to the meeting."

"Great. We'll see you on Monday at 10:00 a.m. unless you need to reschedule."

They hung up. Don just stood there looking at his cell phone. "Well, I'll be damned." But Don's euphoria died quickly. *The patent. I need the patent.*

Other than the delay with the patent, all had gone well. Even the demonstration for Jim Bitters at Wellington went every bit as well as that for Caprock. A call from Exxon was at least neutral. The only fly in the ointment was the patent. The damn patent.

Forty-One

Thursday, May 6

Houston, Texas

Fred Barrister took a close look at the facsimile. The ballooning smile said it all.

Written from top to bottom along the left side of the cover page were the words "The United States of America." At the bottom was the seal of the United States Patent and Trademark Office, Department of Commerce. On the right side of the page was the introduction:

> The Director of the United States Patent and Trademark Office has received an application for a patent for a new and useful invention. The title and description of the invention are enclosed. The requirements of law have been complied with, and it has been determined that a patent on the invention shall be granted under the law. Therefore . . . .

David Kappos, Director of the United States Patent and

Trademark Office, auto-signed the patent approval.

Fred had seen literally thousands of patent approvals. Yet he studied this document as though it were his first. Everything was in place: the name of the device, the patent number, date of patent, an abstract of the device, appropriate drawings, and a complete discussion of the invention, including a summary, background information, objectives of the invention, and descriptions of the drawings and embodiments of the invention. Everything looked to be in perfect order, so much so that the document almost guaranteed a payoff in the hundreds of thousands of dollars. The only entries causing emotional conflict were at the top of the first page:

> *Pressurized Deep Well Oil Lift System*
> *Inventor: Bartholomew M. Miles, Houston, TX (US)*
> *Assignee: Wellington Oil and Exploration, Inc.,*
> *Houston, TX (US)*

He finished his third reading of the approval letter. Bart Miles and Wellington Oil had been awarded the patent. Bart Miles knew nothing of the system, yet he was the inventor of the patent. It no longer mattered what Don Seiler had done. The money it would take to overturn the patent award was far beyond the resources of a small-time engineer. He knew that he had to handle Don Seiler with finesse, but all in all, it was not a problem. Seiler and his failed patent attempt would soon be forgotten.

Fred called Bart Miles with the good news.

"I've got a friend in the US Patent and Trademark Office who forwarded a copy of the patent award. Wellington Oil is the owner of its own patent for the Pressurized Deep Well Oil Lift System." Fred Barrister was the cock of the walk. In short order he would be a well-compensated cock of the walk.

"Great job, Fred. You've just helped move Wellington Oil from the back of the bus." Bart laughed out loud and added, "Hell's bells, we own the bus."

Fred laughed out loud as well.

Miles stopped laughing and continued, "What about Seiler? Any problems?"

Fred knew the question was coming. "No. None at all. There's nothing he can do. It's just a simple matter of one company being faster than another one. He'll be pissed and rant and rave, but he's not a concern at all. The device belongs to you."

Don limped into the kitchen just as Susie finished pouring him a cup of coffee.

"You must have heard me dragging my beat-up body in here. Thanks." He reached for the hot cup.

Susie, releasing the cup into Don's hand, answered, "I heard you in your room talking and I thought you'd need something to get you energized for a little fishing. Anything important with the phone call?"

Don grinned broadly. "One of the best calls of my life. Caprock wants to meet with us to discuss an agreement of some sort. Tom will be tickled when he hears. Let's give him a call."

She wiped her hands with a Texas logo dishtowel and answered, "We'll have to wait until he's finished testifying this morning. He said he would call once he got off the stand."

Susie's phone interrupted. It was Nancy.

"Hi, Nancy, how are you?"

Unheard by Don, Nancy answered. "Great. I just heard on the news that Luling is going to have the Watermelon Thump again this year. There's going to be a big push by San Antonio to help them out. All the stations are giving free advertising for the Thump. The mayor is trying to get the entire city to support all the towns that were hit by the tornadoes. I thought Tom would be glad to know. I'll call Don just as soon as I hang up."

"No need to. He's here. Let me put you on the speaker."

Susie hit the speaker button on the phone and extended her hand toward Don, indicating that the phone was his.

"Hey, Nancy. What's up?"

Nancy told Don the news just relayed to Susie. He was pleased. For all of its pre-tornado idiosyncrasies, Luling was almost a second home to Don. Whether it involved talking to the other customers standing in line at City Market, drinking an occasional beer with the dancing patrons at Monte's, or busting his butt with his crew out at the site, Don had grown to love the town. There were nights when he wished he had never left Texas. *Who knows? Maybe I'll come back to this neck of the woods.* He thought of what they might do once Cindy retired from the California school system. A cozy home on the outskirts of Luling or some place on Texas water took center stage.

"Count me in for the Thump." His lips puckered up unconsciously as he continued. "I'm going to give the seed-spitting contest another shot this year. Third time will be a charm. Tell you what else . . ."

Don and Nancy talked of the Caprock phone call and the news of Luling for another twenty minutes; Susie chimed in here and there.

Nancy brought closure to the conversation. "OK, brother Don, time for me to find something to eat tonight. Of course that means going to the deli."

"And Susie and I have some catfish to attend to." He pointed his finger first at Susie and then at his chest.

They exchanged goodbyes and hung up.

Don turned to Susie. "Got one more phone call to make and then we can motor to the pond."

"Make your call and I'll meet you at the back patio."

"Mr. Barrister, Mr. Seiler is on the phone."

Fred Barrister looked at the phone momentarily and then answered, "Melanie, tell him I am out of the office through the weekend. Send him to voicemail."

"Yes, Mr. Barrister." She pushed the intercom button and returned to the phone. "I'm sorry, Mr. Seiler. Mr. Barrister is out of the office until Monday. Would you care to leave a voicemail message?"

The secretary's message did not sit well. Given the interplay, Don knew that Fred Barrister was in his office but reluctant to talk. *He damn well better have the patent ready to go.*

"No. Just let him know I need to speak with him before the weekend. He has my number."

Tom called just as Don and Susie reached the pond. A few comments concerning Tom's testimony quickly transitioned into the Caprock situation.

"So what we have here is a legitimate possibility to seal the deal with someone we want to have the JETS. Caprock may not be the biggest player but they play fair. On the down side, Barrister has me worried. I know the sorry fucker was in his office. It smells." Don turned to Susie, "Oops, excuse the language."

Susie never swore, but on this occasion she managed a genuine smile.

Tom answered, "My testimony will last no longer than tomorrow, so count me in for Monday in Lubbock. Give Steve a call. It's not his kind of law, but we need someone who does know patent legalese. I'd call him myself but I've got to head back to the courtroom."

"Steve was already on my list, after some catfish of course. If Steve can't make it on Monday, Caprock has agreed to Tuesday. We're on for 10:00 a.m. either day. I'll sort out the details. In the meantime, go kick some courtroom butt."

"Butt-kicking to commence. *Adios.*"

Susie hooked into a fair-sized catfish. The fish tried to dive and shake the hook, but even with the barb removed, Susie was the better contender. She brought in the three-pound catfish and gently removed the hook. Holding the fish firmly in her free hand, she asked, "Are you hungry for fried catfish tonight?"

Don loved to fish but he never liked killing them. "Actually, I'm more in the mood for a hand-picked steak at Papa's on the Lake."

Susie tossed the catfish back in the pond and turned to Don. "You know, all I've heard about is your demonstration with the Caprock company. What ever happened to the Wellington people and Exxon?"

Don pulled his baitless line from the water. He reached into the cooler and grabbed two beers, handing one to Susie. "To be honest, I was hacked a little that Exxon barely noticed us at all. I received a call from a mid-level minion telling me that Exxon is still looking at our system but that, given the volatility of oil prices today, they're still emphasizing offshore research. Normally I'd be surprised if I ever hear from them again, but with all the constraints on offshore drilling, oil prices might drive them in our direction. We'll see how it goes."

"What about Wellington?"

"They're strange as well. We gave them a demonstration the day after Caprock. All went well." He shifted on the bench, placing his fishing rod on the ground. "The lead guy at the demo is straight-up. I met him when I went to speak with the company and he was the only one worth a damn. The people around and above him are arrogant jerks. I don't think he has much clout. I tried to discuss financial matters, but he couldn't speak to them at all. I'm surprised that he hasn't kissed Wellington good-bye."

Susie nodded her head and suggested, "Enough of them. Let's get some more catfish."

Bart Miles, Frank Milsap, and Morgan Rosewood sat at the conference table. Bart ended the meeting.

"Bitters is history. We don't need him around here. Morgan, you figure it out legally, but get rid of him with as little severance as possible. He's gone."

Forty-Two

Monday, May 10

Lubbock, Texas

Hampton Inn's complimentary breakfast was a far cry from the western omelets at the Montgomery Steakhouse. Tom drove the rental car; Steve relaxed in the back seat, finishing up a banana and cup of coffee; Don stared blankly across the endless expanse of flat land. This was the chance he had worked years to reach. Don had rehearsed this final briefing many times, yet uneasy snippets of what might take place, good and bad, still streamed through his head. During most of his trips to the pond Don briefed the catfish out loud as to what he planned to share with his potential buyers. Not a single catfish ever voiced disapproval. Don's final remarks before entering negotiations would be clear, yet succinct. A few PowerPoint slides would trigger the flow of his comments. Simple enough. Still, Don continued to rehearse in his mind as the flat asphalt ribbon passed beneath the car, his head unconsciously nodding up and down.

Tom broke the silence. "Are you ready for some history?"

Don, preoccupied with the upcoming meeting, sat mute, staring out of the window. Steve answered, "Fire away."

Tom pointed toward the center of downtown Lubbock and to a building looming over the prairie. "See the tall building downtown? That's where we're headed. It's the NTS Tower. Exactly thirty-nine years ago tomorrow Lubbock was hit by an EF-5 tornado. Killed twenty-eight people and crushed the downtown area. At times it was a mile wide. The NTS Tower, known as the Great Plains Life Building back then, was actually twisted by the winds. Still, they were able to repair it. As for Lubbock, on that day the city looked just like Luling looks today. Just thought you'd like to know."

Steve made a minor comment; Don stared out at nothing, his thoughts focused on upcoming events, the most important of which was ownership of the patent.

Twenty minutes later they reached the NTS Tower. Caprock had a suite of offices on the sixteenth floor.

Heather Brace met them at ground level.

"Good to see you. How was your night?" Her words were light, friendly, and sincere. She reached forward, first to Don.

Don grinned and squinted into the sun. "It wasn't the Ainsworth House, but it was your typically clean and friendly Hampton Inn." He released his grip and turned toward Steve. "Heather, meet Steve. He's my nephew and, less significantly, Tom's son."

"Good to meet you, Heather," Steve said. "Uncle Don mentioned that your visit to Luling was more fun than work."

She laughed. "It sure was. All we need to do now is to make it to the Watermelon Thump one of these days."

Tom interjected. "Speaking of the Thump, they're going to have it this year, even with half the town destroyed. That's a tough town."

Heather and Tom shook hands. The group chatted as they moved inside the NTS Building and up to the Caprock office suite.

More austere than the offices of Wellington Oil, Caprock nevertheless had enough trappings to suggest it had been successful over the years. The conference room overlooked downtown Lubbock and out to the horizon almost an infinite distance away. Confirming that oil company offices are clones of each other, pictures of oil derricks and plumes of "black gold" spewing from the belly of the earth were spaced evenly along the walls. Cordial greetings and introductions were made, and the group moved to a large serving table. None of the Seilers had met the CEO, Bob Ames, or Sam Shelton, the CFO of Caprock. First impressions were good on both sides of the aisle. Steve readied Don's laptop for the presentation as the others gathered for coffee and Danish. Tom made a second plate for Steve. Tom and Steve were offered seats on each side of Don's. A screen descended from the ceiling and everyone was ready to go.

Don began. "I appreciate your hospitality and the opportunity to consider entering into an agreement for our Jet Extraction Technology System, better known as JETS." The rehearsals paid immediate dividends. Don moved swiftly and comfortably into the functioning and capabilities of the JETS.

Don's early remarks caught Ken, Ed, and Heather off guard; numerous pictures captured the contingent from Caprock having a very good time before and during the on-site demonstration. Comingled with slides of the visitors were slides of the JETS. Of particular note was the output of the demonstration—a significant volume of oil in the holding tank. The display model with the cutaway sections and the disassembled system were shown on the screen so that Don could describe what purpose was served by each component.

Finishing out the presentation were three slides showing the capacities of the system. His presentation was fluid, short, and sweet.

"And that is pretty much the entire JETS. The bad news is that the system appears too simple. The good news is that the system *is* simple." Don turned off the computer and took his seat.

Bob looked around the table, first at his own people and then at Don. "Thanks, Don. I don't think you could have been clearer in describing the JETS. From here I'd like to open it up for questions from our side, and then we can get into the nitty-gritty over some of the legal issues." He looked at Sam. "Questions?"

Each of the Capstone people had minor questions. How long have you been working on this? How much money has been spent to date? What do you know of competitive designs? Don fielded them with solid nuts-and-bolts answers. Tom came into the discussion to help answer a question involving the ability to swap out parts without much delay in the oil extraction process.

Bob Ames allowed the discussion to progress to a point where he was satisfied that not only did the JETS have great potential, but that they were dealing with honest, smart people. He looked down at his writing pad and reached into his shirt pocket for his pen. He circled two notes he had scribbled down during the questioning period.

"Don't anyone forget your next questions, but I'd like to jump in here on a couple of items." The room went silent. Bob saw the immediate stiffness in the room and decided to lighten the mood. He shook his head sideways and chuckled. "Hey, wait a minute. I'm only going to ask questions, not execute someone. Matter of fact, let's have another round of coffee or drinks." He got up and grabbed his coffee cup.

Ten minutes later the group reassembled. Bob sat down and rubbed his hands back and forth as though washing them with a bar of soap. He looked across the table to the three Seilers and spoke. "From everything I have heard firsthand from my people and from what I have gained in reading your materials and seeing your presentation, I am satisfied that the product is as stated and that we're dealing with honest people. In effect, I see the potential for a very strong relationship with you." He paused, taking a sip of coffee. He put down his cup and continued. "But I am also a pragmatist. We are not as large a company as many others, yet I know we have attributes that, to me, could assure you great success with this venture. I also know that there are companies capable of tripling your compensation in the short run. My concept is that we could have a very long-term, win-win relationship. That being the case, my questions to you are first, what kind of company do you want to deal with, and second, who else are you dealing with at this point?"

Before allowing them much time to ponder his questions, Bob added, "Let me clarify my second question. You don't have to give me specific names, but I would like an idea of the nature of the companies you are interacting with at this time."

Tom was elated at the question. *Finally have the moment of truth for Don. Now we'll know where we're headed. Money versus honor.*

"Mr. Ames, I'd first like—"

Bob Ames cut Don off. "Please call me Bob."

"Right." Don coughed, an unconscious reflex when restarting his train of thought. "Bob, I want you to know that everyone we have met at Caprock has come across as forthright and honest." The eye contact between Don and the others was obvious. There was a desire to base an agreement on trust and friendship. But compensation was also a major factor. "In terms of people, you and your company win hands down. Not even close. In a nutshell, I've just answered your first question. We'd like to work with you."

Steve edged his foot to the right and tapped Tom gently. Tom nodded his head.

But Don was also a pragmatist. He continued, "At the same time, I do have to ensure that our interests are protected. To be honest, I doubt that you will end up as the highest bidder. Which brings me to the answer to your second question. So far we have given the demonstration to you and to Wellington Oil and Exploration out of Houston, Star Oil, a Pakistani company, and Mumbai Geo-Energy, from India. We have met with two other companies and given them briefings. Recently we received letters of continued interest from Exxon and Shell." Don had no problem naming specific companies.

The face on each Caprock member revealed a concern at having to deal with the very top of the food chain. The JETS might have more potential than the analysts on the floor below believed.

"I appreciate your candor." Bob looked at his colleagues. "All right, I asked some questions and I received some straight answers. It's now your turn to finish up any other questions."

There were but a few more questions and all were minor— except one.

To this point in time, Heather had not asked a single question. But it had to come.

"Don." Heather's demeanor revealed that she hated even asking the question. It was her job. "From our side we have been in solid agreement about the JETS. I know that we discussed it briefly when I last spoke with you, but we need to know about the patent. Do you have it yet?"

He knew it was coming, but the question hit Don in the stomach like shrapnel. He thought back to his phone call to Barrister before they left the Lubbock Preston Smith International Airport terminal.

"Barrister Legal. How may I direct your call?"

"This is Don Seiler. I need to speak with Mr. Barrister. The matter is urgent." He held a cell phone to his ear, left hand kneading a sand-filled stress balloon.

The secretary repeated the line she had been instructed to say on countless occasions. *"I'm sorry, sir, Mr. Barrister is in court all day. Would you like to leave a message in his voicemail?"*

Tom and Steve huddled around Don. They could see the frustration building up in his face.

As politely, under the circumstances, as possible, Don accepted the voicemail.

"This is Fred Barrister. I'm sorry I can't take your call. Please leave a message and I will get back with you as soon as possible. Thank you."

Don spoke in a monotone—a deadly serious monotone. *"This is Don Seiler. Get this straight. You have been stonewalling me for months on our patent. Either you call me or I will occupy your office until you walk in the door. I have a potential offer waiting and the only roadblock is a simple patent that a simple, competent lawyer would have received long before now. Call me immediately or get ready for some serious trouble.*

"That sorry son of a bitch!" Don closed his cell phone and turned to Tom and Steve. His face was sorrowful. He sensed that he was being had by the likes of a Bernie Madoff.

The remaining half hour of discussion lasted forever. Caprock could not speak to specific compensation. Sam Shelton and

Ken Farmer spoke in generalities about the basic options that Don and Tom had already heard. The conference room was cool, yet small beads of sweat popped up on Don's head. A touch of nausea swept over him. The question almost slipped by without his knowing.

"Once we receive your patent, can you come back then?"

Don tried to put together the first part of the question: *The patent is the only obstacle.* He blinked his eyes tightly, knowing that everyone was looking at him. He answered, "What I will do is call you immediately upon receiving it. I'm confident that it's ours, but I understand your concern." A timid smile broke across his face. "Who should I call to set up the next meeting?"

Ken replied, "I'm a good contact. Just give me a call."

"Great."

Bob Ames brought the meeting to a close. "I know it seems more muddled right now than any of us wants, but we can wait a few days to do everything right. Let's call it a day. Ken, you and Don can set up the next meeting."

The parties shook hands and spoke lighthearted pleasantries before breaking into small departing groups. Tom, Don, and Steve caught the elevator by themselves. A blanket of defeat covered them.

They ate a mid-afternoon lunch at a Whataburger on the way out of town. Don barely picked at his burger. Tom's appetite wasn't much better. Steve finished off his burger and fries, along with a few of Don's fries. Their first serious business meeting gained little.

"Why don't you give him a call back right now? That sorry shithead is blowing you off and we don't know why. Hell, I'll be glad to do it," offered Tom as he swallowed from his large cup of iced-tea.

"It won't help. His secretary will stonewall me. I'm going

to his office once we get back. The son of a bitch will play hell getting away from me." Redness spread across Don's normally tan face. "Let's hit the road."

The men walked into the hot Lubbock sunlight. Tom, the infamously slow driver, had given them plenty of time to make it to the airport. Countless cars passed Tom on the highway; Tom passed no one. Their conversation concerning what they were going to do next had just started when Don's cell phone vibrated. He took it from the holder and viewed the incoming number. Barrister.

Don signaled to Tom and Steve to keep quiet. He put the phone on speaker. Tom slowed the car even more so all could hear. Steve stretched his lanky body over the back seat while Tom leaned to his right. Don pushed the talk button.

"Don Seiler."

"Mr. Seiler, this is Fred Barrister. Sorry I didn't get back to you sooner, but I've been traveling a great deal over the last six weeks. I just got out of court and I'm headed straight to Bush Intercontinental for a flight to Minneapolis. I won't get back until next week."

Don went straight to the point. "All I want is verification of our patent. I want it immediately."

Barrister's turn. A pregnant pause ensued. Steve took a small recorder from his inside coat pocket, clicked it on, and held it next to the phone.

Fred Barrister finally broke the silence. "Mr. Seiler, I'm very upset and will do all possible to turn things around, but I was informed this afternoon that your patent has been denied. I was called by my secretary and I don't have much in the way of details."

Everyone at both ends of the conversation waited for Don's response. Don sat mute, partly stunned and partly making plans.

The silence forced Barrister to continue with babble. "I want you to know that I will find out what the rationale was for the decision and see if there is anything we can do."

After another prolonged silence Don asked, "Did Mr. Duquette approach you or did you approach him to work on our patent?" Don's question was a bolt out of the blue.

This time the silence told a story. Fred Barrister was searching his mind for a reasonable answer, not necessarily a truthful answer.

"Virtually all of my work comes from word of mouth. Yes, I'm pretty sure he called me because he had ended his relationship with his previous attorney."

"Seems to me Texas has a large ration of shitty patent attorneys." Don did not allow Barrister to reply. "You well know that my partner died in March. What do you know about his death?"

Fred Barrister almost choked on the question. *What's he asking? Duquette died in the storm. Or did he die differently?*

Steve held the recorder as close to the cell phone as possible. He looked into Tom's eyes. Tom slowed the car again and pulled over to the shoulder. They waited for a response.

Barrister realized that the blocking of the JETS patent might spin out of control; he also knew that he certainly did not have a complete picture of all that had taken place. He addressed Don's question.

"What the hell does that mean? You're the one who told me about his death. That's all I know." He didn't like the insinuation and showed his anger. "I'd recommend you be careful with what you're saying."

The timing could not have been worse. A highway patrol car pulled in behind the car. Tom saw him first and pointed over his shoulder. Don looked in the side mirror and decided to end the conversation.

"You get some answers and get them damn quick. You'll hear from me tomorrow and you damn well better be ready." Don hung up.

The highway patrolman walked up to the lowering window. He bent down slightly, eyeing the three men. "You having a problem?"

It didn't matter whether there was a body in the trunk or the driver was coming home from choir practice, an uncertain twinge of guilt takes over when a cop arrives on the scene. Tom answered meekly, "No, officer, none at all. My brother had an important phone call and I pulled over so he could hear better." He looked at the officer with a guilty grin.

The patrolman chuckled slightly. "Well, you're about the only car in Texas to pull off the road for a phone call. I'll keep my lights on and you can leave first. Have a good day." He gave a two-fingered salute and walked back to his car.

Tom eased back into traffic and slowly accelerated. Within a minute the black and gray patrol car passed them.

They returned the rental car and walked directly to security. They were in the first boarding group, and Don's medical condition dictated a quick move to the bulkhead. Soon Southwest flight 1117 backed away from the gate.

"Don, keep it down." Tom, sitting in the middle seat of the Boeing 737, tried to limit the conversation to only his brother and son. Don didn't care who heard them.

"The sons of bitches are stealing it from us. I bust my ass and my wallet for years, screw up Cindy and Jayme's lives, and some bastards are laughing it up while ripping me off." Don looked blankly at the bulkhead, his mind focused on an unknown group of people laughing at him. He tried to picture faceless villains who would do something like this.

Tom broke in, "We've all got to settle down. Other than it's been denied, we don't know anything. We don't need to be careless about this. Tomorrow we'll find out what the hell happened."

Steve listened, wisely refraining any comment lest he set Don off again.

The pilot applied full throttle and the plane began accelerating down the runway.

"Barrister won't get a plug nickel from me. I'm dragging his ass into court."

The jet flew directly southeast for just over an hour. Don ranted and raved. Tom tried pouring water on the fire. Steve slept.

The ranting and raving continued from Houston Hobby to Bellaire. Tom stopped at Steve's two-story brick home on Mimosa. Steve put his hand on the door handle and turned it. He started to open the door, but then he paused. "Have you talked to Bill Newton? He was going to dig into what Barrister is all about. It might be wise to get all the information possible before talking to Barrister tomorrow."

Tom answered, "Good idea. Bill's a bulldog in these situations. If it weren't for Bill, things in Alvin and Indianola would have come out far different." Tom spoke again of the murder case that brought him a brief stint in the national limelight. What Tom did not know was that the events swirling around them were born in the aftermath of Alvin.

Tom reached for his phone and started to dial. "I'll get him."

After two rings Bill answered his phone. "Bill Newton."

"Bill, it's Tom. Our meeting with Caprock went well, with one huge exception."

Bill answered, "You're going to tell me it's the patent. Right?"

"Unfortunately. Barrister called us from court three hours ago and told us the patent had been denied. He said he didn't have all the details but he will call us tomorrow from up north. He's out at Bush right now."

Bill sat up and surveyed his surroundings. He put his cell phone on speaker and placed it on the middle console. "Tom, we have ourselves quite the situation. Barrister must be one brilliant guy if he's been in court today and if he's flying out shortly. I'm in the parking lot next to his office. Except for an hour-plus lunch, he's been in his office all day. So we've just now caught him in a lie. I don't know whether it's a little white lie or a criminal lie. But it is a lie. I've taken a few days off and it's going to be just like the days when I played basketball; he's not going anywhere without me in his shorts."

Forty-Three

Tuesday, May 11

Broken Wing Ranch

Don and Susie sat on the patio beneath a coral-blue sky and a warm, westerly breeze. Don's irritation from the day before had not abated; no sky, no breeze, and no Mockingbird songs could settle him down. He and Susie talked while both nibbled at toast, drank too much coffee, and discussed nothing of significance until mid-morning. It was a little before ten when Susie couldn't handle it any longer.

"Don, you're counting the minutes until calling your lawyer. You go ahead and I'll clean up a little. Bring you back a last cup of coffee in a few minutes."

Susie gathered the two small plates and both cups. Don grabbed his phone.

Barrister looked at the ringing cell phone. He read the caller ID and was ready. "Hello, Mr. Seiler, I was expecting your call."

"What have you found out?" No greetings, just get to the point.

Fred decided upon a diplomatic offensive. Be direct, be firm, and be respectful. "Unfortunately, I've had little opportunity to talk to people in the patent office. I did manage to contact a mid-level manager who accessed the file and discussed the letter they mailed to me. It basically says that your patent was not filed prior to the submission of the accepted patent."

Don was furious. "This is horseshit and you know it. We received a letter a long time ago saying that the patent looked clear. Who received the accepted patent? When was it filed? How in the hell do we go about contesting their patent?"

Fred Barrister answered with just enough specificity to make sense. "Here's the problem." He looked down at notes written on legal-sized yellow lined pages. "We're faced with the concept of 'priority.' In the US, even if someone has filed an earlier patent, if you can prove that you were the first to invent the product, in your case the Jet Extraction Technology System, then you would have priority over someone who may have filed the patent before you."

Don perked up, sensing that they might be able to overturn events. Barrister's next comments crushed everything.

"But in this case, what happened is that when you changed your design you rendered the device not only newer but, at least in the eyes of the patent examiners, also as a different device than was in your original submission." Barrister tapped the point of his pencil on a pad of paper. "The unfortunate consequence is that the timing was such that the accepted patent application was classified as essentially in the same category as your new version of the JETS. It was filed first."

As kids, Tom was the most serious, Jack the most gregarious, and Don the biggest hell-raiser. Nancy was the big sister and had to put up with the antics of her younger brothers. Not an easy task for any girl. Like his brothers, Don had a very high boiling point, but, exactly like Tom, once he reached it there would be hell to pay. He knew that Barrister was lying about more than not being in court and certainly not being in Minneapolis. Had they both been teenagers, Don would have beaten the shit out of Fred Barrister.

Susie opened the patio door and walked over to Don with a hot cup of coffee. He pointed at her indicating he wanted her to sit down next to him. She complied. He opened the cell phone, automatically turning on the speaker.

With a resigned tone, Don replied, "Like I said, it doesn't matter how it's packaged, horseshit is horseshit. This is my invention and I expect you to be professional and find a way for our patent to be approved."

"I'll give it everything I have. I haven't had time to respond to this, but, if there is a chance that we can contest the patent, I'll do it." Barrister swallowed from the hot cup of coffee given to him by his secretary. "But I must tell you straight up that contested patent actions are rarely successful."

While the latter comment was valid, both men knew that Barrister had no intention of making a difference in the outcome as it stood at that point.

Don ended the conversation, knowing he needed to think things through. "OK. Let me know what's going on." He hung up.

Barrister thought to himself, *easier than I expected.*

Don flipped his cell phone shut and looked at it as though Barrister was living inside. He raised his cup in the direction of Susie and offered a toast. "Here's to justice." They clinked cups and drank. Then he added, "I need your help."

Susie left a message on Tom's cell phone giving a quick replay of the bombshell from Fred Barrister. She and Don were driving to Luling and would get back around seven o'clock. Hamburgers would be in the refrigerator ready to grill. He needed to pick up buns and onions at Walmart in Montgomery. Don called Carlos.

"This is Carlos, Mr. Seiler. How are you doing?"

"Listen, Carlos, get the whole crew together. I need to talk to everyone later today. I'm over near Houston and will be at the site by mid-afternoon. Set it up for three o'clock."

"We will be ready." He wasn't sure of the exact nature of the meeting, but Carlos knew it was probably the tip of the spear for the fight that was to follow between Don and Wellington Oil.

Susie drove while Don's mind vacillated between the building war to be fought over the JETS patent and his sincere desire to return to Texas.

"This is a great state." Don focused on Texas with medicinal purpose. "I'm sorry I ever left it. No income tax. Government isn't in your face. They believe in states' rights. People know how to enjoy themselves. Perry's done a pretty good job as governor. Everybody's proud to be from Texas." He smiled. "Nothing against cotton, but being born in Alabama has been a pox on my life. I'm Texan through and through." Don surveyed the brush, trees, gently rolling knolls, and cattle grazing on prairie grass. He visualized his current home and continued talking. "Hell, California is the biggest handout state in the US. The official pastime in government there is to be able to top the last stupid law with a newer, stupider law. We're bankrupt and the entitlements just keep building. It's beautiful out there, but boy does it suck."

Susie, born and bred in Dickinson, Texas, understood completely. Other than an occasional trip to Colorado and one spectacular visit to the Big Apple, Susie had barely stepped over the state line. She loved Texas, came from small-town stock, and always knew that she had been blessed by her surroundings. Her Texas twang, and it was a major twang for sure, had not kept her from a successful career at the Johnson Space Center in Clear Lake.

"God, it was fun." A kaleidoscope of events blazed through Don's mind. "We did some stupid things in those days. But I'll tell you, Susie, there wasn't a single day that I didn't laugh about something."

Susie had heard most of the tales from Don's past, but didn't mind mingling some of her own experiences with Don's escapades. It made the trip go faster and protected Don from his troubles.

Susie turned off the asphalt pavement and onto the gravel road. Don's mind reacted in a binary fashion, switching automatically from halcyon thoughts of his youth to the dreaded meeting with the crew that had served Elam and him so well. Don felt obligated to let them know exactly what was going on because major consequences were in store for their lives. Susie took the last left turn and drove up the dusty road to the perimeter fence.

The crewmembers milled at the edge of the maintenance shed, the lengthening shade giving them refuge from the sun.

Susie shut down the engine and said, "I'll wait here. You go ahead."

Don paused before opening his door. "Susie, if you don't mind, I'd really like to have you go with me. I know you'll feel uncomfortable, but I need you to pay attention to what I say. You can recall my message and I'll know what needs to be said in the future."

Susie did feel uncomfortable. But Don was family. "OK, I'll listen, but please don't ask me to contribute."

Don smiled and gave Susie a pat on her shoulder. He got out. She got out.

Don left his cane in the car and walked awkwardly toward the gathering group. Possibly the most weather-beaten piece of apparel in the western hemisphere, his four-decade-old Seabee hat laid cocked forward on his head. Aesthetically, it looked like hell; functionally, it was a trusted companion. The sun's brightness forced him into a tight squint. Susie, protected with a long-sleeved white shirt, long cotton pants, and a baseball cap with the Broken Wing Ranch logo, walked beside Don. Her smile was concocted. Susie never liked being center of attention; she felt completely claustrophobic and semi-nude.

Carlos formed the crew, still in the shade, into a tight semi-circle. Two with well-worn straw cowboy hats, two with baseball caps, one with a dark green bandana, and Carlos, bareheaded, watched as Don struggled with his malady. On occasion his upbeat nature and his absolute aversion to complain about his MS had been topics of praise among the men. He was the owner and the designer of the system and, by world standards, had the right to lord some power over them; he always treated them as equals. He knew their first and last names as well as those of spouses and children. Each one had received some assistance for personal matters while working for Don. Not only Don, but Elam as well. There was a lot of trust and respect for Don among the men. Of course, Judas still walked among them.

"Grab a seat against the shed and relax."

The men sat down in the dust, their backs against the side of the maintenance building. Don waited until satisfied that they were comfortable and then turned toward Susie. "Before I get started—and don't get up—I just want to introduce Tom's wife, Susie. She's as good as they come, and she's protecting all the drivers in the state by driving today." Each crewmember smiled at Susie and three of them gave friendly waves. Susie, very uncomfortable, nodded but did not speak.

Then Don got down to business. "Let me get right to what I need to say." He cleared his throat. "I was informed earlier today by our attorney that we . . ." Holding up both hands, palms facing the crew and fingers open and extended, Don stopped in mid-sentence. "Let me back up. How many of you do not know what a patent is?"

There were no illegal immigrants in the crew. All were American citizens; three of the six had gone through high school in Luling, one in Cuero, and one in Oklahoma. Only one of the crew did not have a high school diploma. After a couple of seconds of deliberation, one man raised his hand.

Don acknowledged the smallest, and youngest, of the men. "Thanks, Felix." Don knew that there had to be a couple of others who didn't understand. "To be honest, patents are much misunderstood. What a patent does is protect the work of people who have designed something of value. In the United States, it gives exclusive rights to a designer, or designers, of products that make life better for society. For a certain period of time, several years in fact, no one can produce or use the product without the permission of the person holding the patent." Don, surprised at his personal grasp of the subject, began to settle into a clear description of a patent, the patent process, and pitfalls associated with patents.

He continued. "In our case, all of you know that Elam Duquette and I came up with a basic design for the JETS. All except Carlos and Hugo were here when we had our first successful run." Heads nodded and smiles broke out. Don remembered it as though it happened the day before. Euphoria. "What we did at that time was take our design and submit it to the United States Patent Office for a patent. If approved, it would have meant that we had exclusive rights to manufacture, use, sell, or lease the JETS." Don wobbled just a little, fighting the effects of prolonged standing. He shifted his weight to his left side. "My game plan all along has been to keep this crew intact so that you could install JETS units all over the country. With the price of oil as high as $150 and bouncing all over the place, my prediction was that each of you would have very well-paying work for at least as long as I was around. At first, everything looked good to us. But, as all of you know, we did have some problems with the folding of the inflow and outflow sections. My brother, Tom, an expert in mechanical design, figured out a new design that we're using now.

"Now let me know if you don't understand what I'm saying." Don paused, his brow furrowing deeply. He put the thumb of his left hand and pressed it back and forth into the palm of his right. "Although our initial design appeared to be satisfactory, when we submitted the improved version of the JETS, our clock was changed to a new date. Unfortunately, some other company submitted a design very similar to what we have now and a ruling was made that gave all of the patent rights to this other company." He interjected, "I don't know who the other company is, but I am very concerned that we may have lost everything."

Carlos knew who the other company was. He shifted uncomfortably in the dust. *Did I pick the wrong people?* He began to sweat.

Don called to the crewmember closest to the shed door. "Felix, could you get Susie and me a chair and a bottle of water?" Felix jumped up and headed into the shed. In fifteen seconds he returned with two folding chairs and two bottles of water. He gave the bottles to Don and Susie and then unfolded both chairs. Don and Susie sat down.

Don unscrewed the bottle cap and took a large swallow. "Thanks. Now, where was I?" He returned to his original train of thought. "Oh, OK. So what I'm trying to tell you is that we have a major problem in that all of our work might have to be stopped because we don't own the patent to our version of the JETS. If we can't get relief then all of us are affected. All of my work and what I have invested in this project will be lost." He leaned forward. "Much more important is that if we close down each of you will be out of work. I want you to know that I could have held off for a few weeks, but I didn't want you to be blindsided and wind up without a job at all. For now, I'm going to continue as long as I can, but you probably need to start looking for other opportunities. If you find a job then take it. I already appreciate the allegiance you have given to me and also to Elam. As for the company having rights to the patent, I'm going to fight like hell." Don's lips quivered ever so lightly. Susie couldn't swallow at all. He went silent for a few seconds before continuing. "If you do find other employment and then it turns out that we end up with a patent, your job will be waiting for you if you so choose. As for tomorrow, keep on pumping." He looked at Carlos. "As a matter of fact, I'd like you to inspect that stripper well off of Highway 80 that we discussed."

Don ended his remarks. "I'm sorry all this happened. Have you got any questions?"

The silence lasted some ten seconds. Time seemed infinite to Susie. Finally, Alejandro spoke up. "Mr. Seiler, what will you do if we have to stop?"

Don looked back at Alejandro and then searched each of the faces. "Don't really know." He stuck his right leg out and shook it as best he could. "Given my physical condition, I'll probably go fishing. It's for certain that if we lose everything here, I'm going to retire. I won't be running around in limousines, but my Ford truck, my fishing rods, and my beautiful wife are all that I need."

Eduardo Sena, the only chunky member of the crew, but one of the hardest-working, spoke up. "Mr. Seiler, I will be here tomorrow. And for as long as I can." Heads nodded in agreement.

Don knew it was a sincere gesture. "Thanks, Eduardo. I appreciate your loyalty." He also knew that, without compensation to care for one's family, the crew's time with Don was very limited.

Don brought the meeting to a close with an early invitation. "Regardless of how things turn out—and I'm not through fighting for the company—I'm inviting anyone who can come to meet my brother and me at Monte's on Saturday night of the Watermelon Thump. All the beer is on me. Make it between ten and eleven."

"I'll get there early to save a table," Felix spoke up first, also offering a service to the crew, "and to make sure the beer is cold."

Everyone laughed. But it was stilted laughter.

Don shook hands with everyone and walked back to the car with Susie. He gave a thumbs-up as they drove down the dusty road. He was tired and the bottles of water did little for his thirst.

"Can you handle a quick beer at Monte's?" he asked.

Susie smiled. "Sure. You drink a beer and talk. I'll drink a Sprite and take copious notes about today's meeting."

Carlos instructed the crew to shut down the day's operation and secure all equipment. Twenty minutes later, the others headed back to their homes. Carlos looked around the site. It was stone quiet. His uneasy feeling clamped on to him like a steel trap.

He dialed Houston.

The vibrator announced an incoming call. Bart Miles had no desire to speak to Carlos but thought better of ignoring him. Heightened senses had taken over since the Wellington Oil patent had been approved. Negotiations were underway with Brighton Manufacturing to produce an initial order of forty units of Wellington's Pressurized Deep Well Oil Lift System. Bart pushed the send button and answered.

"Yeah."

"Mr. Miles, this is Carlos."

I know who you are, dumb shit. "What do you want?"

Carlos knew he was falling into a bottomless canyon. Since the night Juan Delgado died, Miles had been distancing himself from Carlos. Miles still wanted Carlos's services, but he did not want anything to wipe off of Carlos and onto him.

Carlos tried to be as cryptic as possible. "We had a meeting with the owner today. He told us that he was going to maybe lose the business and that we should look for new jobs."

Bart Miles sat up, air filling his lungs. An immediate surge of power coursed through his body. Sweet music.

"Did he say anything specific?"

Much of the meeting lay scrambled in Carlos's mind. He did remember a few morsels. "He said that he was going to keep us going as long as he could. He invited us to be his guests at the Watermelon Thump next month in Luling."

Bart's answer and instructions showed no emotion whatsoever. "Keep me posted." He hung up.

Carlos looked down at his phone. He was unsure of the future. Very unsure.

Bart called Macy and instructed her, "Get me some information on the Watermelon Thump held in Luling each year."

Macy immediately set about her task.

Bart Miles dialed Bartok.

After three rings voicemail took over. "The party you are

trying to reach is not available. At the tone, please leave a message."

Bart Miles left a short message. "Please purchase the three properties that we discussed. If possible, make the closing in the next couple of weeks." He hung up.

At the other end, Bartok listened one additional time. Then he transferred the taped message to a second digital recorder.

Forty-Four

Tuesday Afternoon, May 11

Houston, Texas

While Don and Susie endured the long trip back to the Broken Wing Ranch, Bill Newton spent much of the afternoon in a parking lot fighting off boredom. He picked at his fingernails, ate some potato chips, drank coffee, and listened to Rush Limbaugh. He switched satellite radio between Sean Hannity on the far right and Randi Rhodes on the far left. A conservative by nature, Bill's only link to Randi was that she started her radio career in the same town he was born: Seminole, Texas. He finished off his coffee and turned to the CD player. Multiple episodes of "Chicken Man," the 1960s audio spoof of superheroes, provided respite from a long day staking out Don's lawyer. Bill sat in one of more than forty cars in the parking lot. From eighty yards away he was indiscernible from any other driver using the strip-mall facilities.

"Wellllll! Does Chicken Man's mama know he was catching Choo Choo doing the Cha Cha at Chi Chi's?" The narrator excitedly summed up the episode with questions of the future concerning the fantastic winged crusader, the weekend warrior who struck fear and terror into the hearts of evildoers, and, in his real life, the mild-mannered Benton Harbor, ordinary shoe salesman in Midland City. Bill laughed out loud. As nonsensical as it might be, Bill's bizarre camaraderie with Chicken Man had a real foundation. Neither liked scumbags; both were willing to go out on a limb, so to speak, to see that justice was served; and both had met their fair share of defeats to go along with the victories. One other thing tied them together: many years before, Chicken Man provided a small escape for a recuperating marine rifleman badly wounded in the jungles of Vietnam. During his first six weeks at Walter Reed Army Medical Center, Bill savored Chicken Man's ability to help him laugh in the face of unrelenting pain. The only thing better than Chicken Man was a young army nurse—Bill married her. On this day Bill Newton played Chicken Man.

Fred Barrister came around from the far side of the building and went straight to his car. He was out of the parking lot and onto Westheimer Road in seconds. Heavy traffic slowed Bill's exit from the lot. "Come on, get out of the way." By the time he wedged into the traffic, for which he heard the horn of an irate driver, Bill trailed Barrister by at least ten cars. He lost him in the traffic. Bill accelerated, passing a few cars by weaving in and out of the lanes. No luck. *Shit,* he thought. Bill had no choice but to anticipate Barrister's destination. He turned south on Shepherd Drive, caught US 59 heading east, and headed downtown.

Fred Barrister sat in a dark leather armchair in front of the expansive walnut desk. The window behind Bart opened to another magnificent view to the southwest. The Wells Fargo Plaza and the Williams Tower stood tall and erect over downtown Houston. In spite of the intense conversation, Fred could not help but to sneak glimpses through the windows to the world beyond.

Bart looked down at the multi-page document, rubbed his hands together, and swallowed from his bottle of Evian. He grabbed the top page; it was a facsimile copy of the patent approval from the United States Patent and Copyright Office. Bart held it up, allowing the front to face Fred Barrister.

Bart made a statement and asked a question. "OK. So the upside is that official notification is on the way. We do have the patent. Is that correct?"

"Yes. The official hardcopy will arrive tomorrow or Thursday. It's a done deal." Fred answered with confidence. He paused for a second and then added, "You will have an official letter from me by tomorrow evening. At that point, you can do whatever you want."

Bart was thrilled with the news, yet his facial expression showed a hint of concern. "Do we even have a downside?"

Fred placed both hands on the arms of the chair and pushed himself up and back. *What a great chair,* he couldn't help but think. He answered, "The only possible problem would be if the patent is challenged in a court of law. If Seiler does challenge, I don't think he has the financial resources to mount a long-term case. Beyond that, what we have is completely legal. He changed from his original design and we beat him to the punch with the new design. It's business and it happens every day."

Both Miles and Barrister scratched at their faces as if mirroring each other. They looked silly. Neither commented about the fact that the new patent was physically stolen from the site in Luling and that the new plans were nothing more than a near-duplicate redrawing of the components of the prototype JETS. Bart sat back and relaxed.

"All right, let's wrap this up tighter'n a drum. Send me your normal billing and we'll take care of it. I'll handle your bonus once I'm satisfied that we are in total control of the device and that no legal issues are pending. It will go through your external bank account."

Satisfaction could be seen on Fred Barrister's face. He tried not to show any expression at all but, remembering back to Bart's first discussion of compensation, the thought of possibly receiving $400,000 left him light-headed. *Maybe half a million!*

Bart bluntly interrupted Barrister's daydreaming. "Hey, are you even listening to me?"

Fred reconnected with reality. He jerked his head away from the Houston skyline and answered, "Oh, I'm, uh, sorry. I apologize. Could you repeat that?"

"Stop counting your money and listen to me."

Bart did not ever want anyone, especially a two-bit patent lawyer, blowing him off. His irritation showed. Fred Barrister had a healthy fear of Bart Miles. He knew that if it ever came to a serious problem Bart Miles would not hesitate to throw him under the bus—even a real bus.

"Sorry, I—"

Bart cut him off with a sweep of his hand. Then he pushed a pad of lined paper to the edge of the desk. "I want you to write down exactly what documents I will receive. On a separate piece of paper, list any possible challenges or problems that we may have." Bart stood up and shrugged his shoulders. "I'll be back in ten minutes."

"Where's the reserved parking area for Wellington Oil and Exploration?"

The security officer looked up at Bill Newton. Even with his slumped shoulders, Bill towered over the officer. The man looked down at his clipboard.

"It's on the third level."

"Thanks." Bill got back into his car and left.

The JP Morgan Chase Tower parking garage is a major structure in its own right, and it is always crowded during business hours. Bill found the Wellington parking area and slowed to a crawl. One by one he inspected each car. It didn't take long. He checked the Texas license plate to verify that he had reconnected with Fred Barrister. It was Barrister's car. Bill had two basic choices. First, he could sit where he was and wait for Barrister to return. Secondly, since option one only gave a high probability but not a certainty of where Barrister was headed, Bill could try finding the offices of Wellington Oil and, possibly, Fred Barrister. He chose option two. He had to park on the next-higher level, caught the stairs to street level, and walked across to the entrance without even acknowledging "Personage and Birds."

Bart studied the pages upon which Fred had printed the required information. He tapped his right index finger on the desktop and chewed on the inside of his cheek. Then he spoke. "All right. This does it for now. I want those documents tomorrow."

"I'll have them hand-delivered to you." Fred tried some bravado. "Bart, you are the owner of the patent."

"You better hope so. Now, sign these papers."

Barrister looked at Bart in disbelief. *What the hell is he doing?*

Fred answered, a noticeable quiver in his voice, "Why do you need a signature on these? I'll bring you a signed letter tomorrow."

Bart Miles had snookered the lawyer. "Sign it or there will

be no bonus. You're in this up to your neck. Sign them." He placed an expensive presidential pen on top of the two pages.

Fred Barrister weighed his options. If he wanted the huge payoff he had few, if any, options. Some of the information concerning possible legal issues could be problematic. On the other hand, he had been somewhat vague in how he wrote each item. He hated risk but decided that what he had written would not convict him in court. He also surmised that he had enough on Bart Miles to make it a two-way street.

"I'll sign, but this is not part of our contract." Barrister took the pen and wrote his signature on each page. He attempted to make the two new signatures look somewhat different from his official signature. A handwriting expert would have a field day. Fred gave the pen to Bart. *What an asshole.* There was no handshake. Barrister just walked out of the office. Without reacting to Macy Buckles's friendly farewell, he exited the double doors and headed toward the elevator. He was preoccupied and did not notice the large, slightly disheveled man waiting for an up elevator.

Late afternoon traffic is a never-ending nightmare in Houston. For Bill Newton, it was nice; he followed Barrister to his home in River Oaks without problem. Coming out of downtown, Bill trailed Barrister by a few cars along Allen Parkway and on to the point at which it turns into Kirby Drive. Traffic subsided considerably along Inwood Drive; only one car separated Bill from Fred Barrister. Barrister made his last turn at Pinehill Lane. Bill slowed at the corner and watched Barrister drive into his driveway. With Chicken Man defeating evildoers on the CD, Bill Newton was solving a few problems of his own.

Tom arrived at the ranch half an hour before Don and Susie. Bear and Catfish, unconditional lovers, ran alongside Susie's car barking and wagging their tails in happy unison. This night was particularly exciting because they could smell hamburgers on the grill. Whenever Tom grilled hamburgers or sausage, Bear and Catfish were certain to have their fair share.

The sun dropped below the horizon, but its brightness still reflected off the wisps of cirrus clouds approaching from the southwest at forty thousand feet. A harbinger of rain. One by one, stars started popping up all over the darkening sky. The threesome took turns casting appreciative glances at the evening tapestry. In the midst of such a beautiful evening, the mood remained somber.

"You're getting screwed, no question about it." Tom stood up. "Who wants another hamburger?"

Bear, Catfish, and Don answered in the affirmative. Tom placed a hamburger on a bun for Don. He followed suit with one for himself. He cut two other hamburgers into pieces and dropped them into the dogs' bowls. By the time Don grabbed onions for his hamburger, the dogs had finished dinner, with the possible hope that maybe, just maybe, Tom would give them more. Tom returned with two Miller Lites and a Diet Coke.

Tom continued as he prepared his second hamburger, "I don't know how everything ties together, but we're going to solve this puzzle. Some heads will roll."

Don's cell phone vibrated. "Hang on a minute." He answered the call.

"Hey, Bill. Good to hear from you. What's up?"

About five seconds later Don's eyes lit up. He replied to Bill. "Damn. Now I'm beginning to understand things. Wait a minute, I want to put Tom and Susie on the speaker." Don flipped the lid open on the phone. "Go ahead and tell Tom and Susie."

Bill, his voice clear in the quiet evening, repeated his comment. "Hey, Tom and Susie. I just told Don that I followed the lawyer Barrister from his office to downtown Houston. He went to Wellington Oil at the JP Morgan Tower. I had lost him in traffic so I went to whatever floor Wellington is on and waited. I was there about ten minutes when Barrister walked out. That means he was there for no more than half an hour. I don't know exactly what it means except that Barrister and Wellington Oil are working together on something."

Don replied, "Yeah, and I can tell you what it is. He and Wellington are screwing me. Barrister told me I lost the patent to some other company but he didn't tell me who." He paused, his mouth forming a tight thin line. "But they better be ready for a ram because I'm not going to sit around while they shovel me shit."

Bill offered a suggestion. "I can stop over at the ranch tomorrow night or any day this week if you want."

Tom nodded his head up and down.

"You're on. We'll call and see who else can make it and when the best time will be. Thanks, Bill."

Don and Bill exchanged final cordialities and hung up. Tom swallowed the remainder of his beer, crushed the can, picked up Don's empty can, and headed back for another round.

Susie changed her drink of choice. "Get me one as well."

Over the beer Tom outlined what they knew. "Elam starts it all because he talked too much to Wellington Oil. Herman Soboda quits unexpectedly as their lawyer. His departure was under duress. Then Elam, not knowing jack shit, suddenly hires a lawyer unknown to any of us. Elam gets killed. Elam's girlfriend, Sarah, is killed. The patent is handed to another company. Barrister meets with Wellington Oil and

Exploration.

"We are in the thick of a criminal enterprise, and at this point we're in last place. I don't know how everything ties in, but I'm afraid that we're dealing with a few greedy assholes. The good news is that we're not dealing with organized crime. Instead, our problem is probably at the top of Wellington Oil." Tom stood up and walked to the column at the patio's edge. A gentle breeze ruffled the flags to his front. Tom looked off toward the west. The predicted clouds of the upcoming rain front would not arrive until early morning, but darkness had settled in over the Broken Wing Ranch. A different storm, well beyond meteorology, brewed in their minds.

They targeted the meeting for Saturday afternoon. Tom suggested a new member. "We should invite Josh Bettner."

Forty-Five

Saturday, May 15

Fentress, Texas

Bartok crossed to the far side of the Fentress Bridge with the parking lights piercing the blackness. He cut the lights just as he turned right at River Grove Road. BMNT, Begin Morning Nautical Twilight, was still an hour away. He cupped his hands over his opened eyes for a full minute, acclimating them to the darkness. A starlight scope would have been ideal, but Bartok was still good at navigating in blackout conditions. He lifted his hands away from his eyes and looked around. They were adjusted enough to allow him to make out the silhouetted forms of trees and brush. He grabbed a camouflaged poncho from the seat and stuffed it into his jacket. Once out of the truck, he moved to the back and lowered the tailgate. He pulled out the ramp and rolled the small Kawasaki down to the road. Bartok pushed the motorcycle into the brush, laid it on its side, and covered it with the poncho. He covered everything with leaves and broken branches. Unless a person blindly stumbled over the motorcycle it would be impossible to notice its being there. Even if it were discovered, the license plate was stolen and the motorcycle VIN had been filed off. Bartok returned to his truck and headed toward a Motel 6 in San Marcos where he had booked a room for two nights.

Wet weather arrived at the Broken Wing Ranch earlier than predicted. Tom wanted to take Josh Bettner up in the J-3 before enduring what might be a very stressful meeting, but the weather prevailed. Earlier discussions revealed that Josh's flying experience was zero. Not one flight. The winds were light but the clouds came in low, with light rain and patches of fog blanketing the area. Josh would have to wait one more day.

Other than the dogs, Susie saw Josh first and met him at the front door.

"So you're Josh. Tom and Don have said a lot of good things about you. Come on in and get warm." Susie backed into the entranceway and motioned Josh to follow.

The other attendees were already gathered. Tom and Don shook hands with Josh and then introduced him to the others. Nancy was not able to make it. The weather in San Antonio was foggy and heavy rain was predicted for the weekend.

Ross spoke to Josh. "Don tells me you're going to be an Aggie. Good choice, Josh. In addition to some great academics, you'll get to watch them kick UT's butt." Ross smiled broadly at Josh.

Josh, Coke in hand, answered, "I do plan to go to A&M, but I'll be joining the army right out of high school. My goal is to get assigned to the 82nd Airborne Division and eventually do what I can in Afghanistan."

Tom felt attached to Josh. "You can't make a better choice. This country needs people like you. And as for being in the

82nd, it's a proud division. My younger brother Jack served in the 82nd and in the 173rd Airborne Brigade. Both were tough, elite units." Tom leaned forward, tweaked his right eyebrow, and added, "He was an Army Ranger, and they didn't take any trash from anyone."

Josh smiled, already hoping to learn something of airborne units from Tom's brother. "Did he make a career of it? If I like it, I could envision spending twenty years jumping out of airplanes and playing in the woods."

Tom's voice softened just a touch. "He probably would have been a general," Tom shook his head and continued, "but he was killed in Vietnam." Tom realized that what he said was not too bright so he clarified his intent. "If he were to talk to you today, he would tell you to go in a heartbeat. We talked a lot the week before he left for Okinawa to join the 173rd. And yes, he loved jumping out of airplanes and playing in the woods. But the one thing he said that has stayed with me was something like, 'It may not ever be appreciated by those who don't care or don't understand what the United States is all about, but I am honored to serve my country.' He also talked about the young soldiers and how energetic and loyal they were. No doubt about it, he would have stayed."

Tom patted Josh on the shoulder. "I guess you'll have to finish up some of his business." He brightened up and smiled. "As a matter of fact, the 82nd and 173rd have both fought in Afghanistan. Just take your pick. How about another Coke?" Tom's last comment allowed the conversation to change.

Macy Buckles tapped on the door and turned the doorknob. She timidly looked in at Bart Miles as he lifted his head up from a small stack of papers. He smiled.

"Come in, Macy." Bart spoke more gently to her than to anyone else on the face of the planet. Only once had he made an advance toward her. She rebuffed him immediately and had threatened to quit. A swift apology and a serious pay raise kept her with the company. They both treaded lightly around each other. Bart's thoughts centered on a sexual relationship sometime in the future; Macy's thoughts centered on employment elsewhere.

"Mr. Miles, it's the package from Mr. Barrister. I've dried it off as best I could."

Bart smiled again. "Thanks, Macy. The packet should have kept the letter dry." He took the packet from Macy, eyeing it carefully. He looked back up at Macy with puppy dog eyes. "And thanks for coming in on a Saturday. I appreciate it."

Macy smiled and left the room.

Bart pulled at the fastening band and opened the packet. He peered inside and then pulled out two documents. The first was a transmittal letter from Mr. Frederick Barrister. He quickly switched it to the back. The second document, several pages in length, bore a circular logo with an eagle posed over the emblem of the United States. It was the approval of the patent. A broad grin swept across his face.

The weather might have cancelled the flying and eating outside, but it didn't stop the gang from socializing prior to the meeting. The steaks came from the Olde World Farms in Montgomery. From well done to blood-rare, Tom masterfully prepared each one as ordered. Green beans and baked potatoes rounded out the main course. Friendly bantering and jokes veiled the serious nature of the upcoming meeting. That was just the way things went in the extended family. There was a time to be serious and a time to relax. Tom and Susie decided earlier in the day that they would wait until after dinner to get into the specifics of the meeting. Avoiding politics the entire evening, each participant thoroughly enjoyed the calm before the storm. Josh felt very comfortable and had no problem speaking his mind throughout dinner. What he didn't know, and what nagged at both Tom and Don, was that there were things that he needed to know that would affect him for the rest of his life.

The marble cake and ice cream, either chocolate or vanilla, were delicious. Some fun was made of the portion gulped down by Bill Newton. Seeing that dessert was on its last legs, Tom eyed Don and signaled him with raised eyebrows.

Don nodded and slowly stood up. He addressed the table. "It's about time we got started on the meeting." He then spoke to Josh with a noticeable degree of tenderness, "Josh, would you join Tom and me on the patio for a minute?"

Susie knew what was going to happen. She stood up and announced, "OK everyone, bring your dishes to the kitchen. Paige and I will do the dishes while Steve, Bill, and Ross set everything up for the meeting."

People, including Josh, took their cues and proceeded to accomplish each small mission.

"Have a seat, Josh." Don pointed to a chair looking directly at the flagpole. "Too dark for much of a view, but you get the seat of honor."

Josh did as requested. He did not feel threatened, but he knew that something important would be discussed. It would be about his mom. Tom and Don took seats next to Josh, Don sitting in the middle.

Don looked Josh in the eye and placed his hand on top of Josh's arm. Then he spoke.

"Josh, we've thought about meeting with you on several occasions to talk about the night of the tornado. But it wasn't until this week that we've become convinced that we know what events took place and why. It's important to us that we speak with you face to face."

Josh was a very smart young man. He looked back at both men and shook his head. "You're going to tell me something about my mother that will make things worse, aren't you?"

Don replied without hesitation, "Yes. We believe that she and Elam Duquette were murdered."

Josh sat up erect, his body tighter than a guy wire. Part of him accepted what was being told to him while another part was in denial. He remained motionless for half a minute. Tom and Don gave him space.

Josh took in a deep breath, a breath caught between a need to express rage and a need to cry. "What happened?"

"Tom has a better hand on putting pieces of puzzles together, so he'll let you know everything."

For the next half hour Tom went over the details of what he and Don had learned in the wake of the tornado. Tom further explained that the others, cleaning up the dishes and setting up for the meeting, knew what conclusions were reached concerning Sarah Bettner. He also explained that he had instructed them not to say anything to Josh until the formal meeting started. The duty to inform Josh fell squarely on the shoulders of Don and Tom. A steady rain fell over the ranch.

Once Tom finished going over all he knew, Josh sat stoically, absorbing what he had been told. His reaction was not theatrical cursing at being the last to know. He understood. "My only question is, how much did she suffer?"

Tom, his eyes bloodshot, answered solemnly, "Josh, I have thought about your question since we were at the funeral home in Luling. I will not lie to you." He swallowed hard, never taking his eyes off of Josh. "Your mother did suffer. If there is anything good, it's that she was not sexually assaulted. My personal belief is that she died because she was a witness to Elam's death. In that case, she was probably killed as quickly as possible." Enough said.

Josh studied the two men who brought him such terrible news. He wished they never entered his life; at the same time, he wanted their friendship—and their help. He spoke quietly. "I don't know how else you could have told me. I appreciate it. I think it's time to have your meeting."

When they walked back into the dining room everyone was standing. No one knew what to do. Each person ached inside, yet it took Josh to put perspective on everything.

"I know it's tough on everyone here. Both Mr. Seilers told me everything they know about my mother." He looked down at the floor while gathering his thoughts. He looked up at made eye contact with each person in the room. Then he spoke again. "My mother was a great woman. I mean, a really great woman. Her death intersects with everyone here, and I guess that puts us all in the same situation. Please help me to dignify her life not only in bringing the guilty to justice, but also in remembering a woman who lived a tough life with never a complaint, only love." A gentle smile broke the hardness of what he had just been told. "Each one of you would have loved her." He smiled again. "Not as much as I do, but you'd love her nevertheless." Josh ended his comments: "We've got business to do." He sat down.

The blank whiteboard was in position at the end of the table. Tom left the room for a minute and returned with stapled sets of paper, one for each member at the table. On them were notes, some neatly written by both Nancy and Tom at the end of the previous meetings and some written earlier in the day. Each person studied the notes. Although not completely clear to Josh, the notes allowed the others to recall previous discussions and link the information to new discoveries. As for

Josh, he studied each sheet and pieced together the general train of thought as everyone sorted through all of the events. Tom did not show the photographs of Elam and Sarah because of Josh. If Josh wanted them at a later date, Tom would give them to him. Tom called Nancy and put her on the speaker. Quick pleasantries, including her expression of sympathy for Josh, were made and the meeting started.

Tom began. "All right, let's get right to the point. Don and I are convinced that Elam and Josh's mom died at the hands of someone who wanted possession of the JETS. We believe the leadership at Wellington Oil is the focal point of everything." He surveyed his audience and added, "To discuss all of this I thought the following order makes the most sense. Don first, to discuss what happened with the patent. Then Bill will address the lawyer, Barrister. Steve will follow up with a strategy to contest the loss of the JETS patent. Ross and Paige can discuss what they know about oil companies other than Wellington. I'll finish up and try to wrap everything together. Then we can begin the process for tying all the loose ends together."

Paige volunteered to put the notes on the whiteboard. She wrote *Don* on the board.

"Don, the floor is yours."

Don pushed back on his chair and looked up at Paige. "I called Barrister over several days and all I got was a stone wall from his secretary. Finally he called me back and bluntly told me that we had lost the patent. He said that when Tom made improvements to what we had, his work constituted a new design of the JETS. What we did submit as our final design was almost identical to a design submitted prior to ours. Barrister didn't tell me what company got the patent but Bill has found a link to Wellington Oil. I'll let him give you the details. Standard patent disclosure will verify our suspicions shortly." Don's voice grew in volume as he spoke. "I told Barrister that I wanted him to contest the patent or I would sue him. On the face of it all, I don't have a chance of suing him unless a conspiracy can be shown. I'll let that be a starting point for Bill to tell you what he has found out."

Don answered several questions before Paige placed *lost patent–Wellington?–new design* to the right of Don's name on the board.

Bill took over next. He explained his waiting outside of Barrister's office and following him downtown to the JP Morgan Chase Tower. "So what we have is either an almost unfathomable coincidence or the *conspiracy* we are looking for. And remember that Barrister lied to Don about where he was and what he was doing. The whole thing stinks."

Each person remained busy writing notes on legal paper. Paige waited until the question had been asked before adding bullets:

- *Barrister to Wellington*
- *Meeting*
- *Conspiracy*

Next up were Ross and Paige. Paige, standing at the whiteboard, assumed the speaking duties.

"After talking to Dad and Don, I did a Google search and checked Angie's List for any legal issues affecting Wellington Oil. While certainly having its fair share of legal issues, the company hasn't been brought up on any charges. There were some minor articles concerning possible bribery, including both money and sex, by Wellington to get some offshore drilling leases. I think they lucked out because of all the furor recently about alleged reports of Chevron's bribing the Mineral Management Service of the Department of Interior." Paige underlined the word conspiracy. "But there was enough smoke there to convince me that Wellington Oil has major ethical issues. Making the leap from bribery to a murder conspiracy is a stretch, but it's not impossible."

Nancy asked via the speaker. "Paige, did you find any information pointing to a named individual at Wellington Oil?"

"I did. One of the articles on Google mentioned a lawyer named Milsap who was described as 'ruthless.' I also saw a couple of comments knocking the CEO and the lawyer. My opinion is that the comments came from inside the company. Sounded like disgruntled employees. I can't verify illegal activities but I'm convinced that they are not of the 'white-driven snow' variety." Paige concluded her remarks. "That's it for the company at this point." She looked around the room and, seeing no questions on the faces around her, turned the meeting back to Tom.

Tom, in turn, gave Steve the floor.

Steve, at the back end of the table, leaned forward on his elbows. As lawyers often do, Steve made his disclaimer. "Patent law is not my area of expertise." He wasted no time in going on offense. "But I did some checking and we have problems. But we have both problems and options. If Wellington Oil is granted a patent for some sort of oil extraction device, and if it's in lieu of ours, we can contest the patent. If we do, it will be a hassle. What we would need to show is that a patent granted to Wellington Oil was either not valid or represents an infringement on our design. In other words, we need to show that they basically stole the JETS." Steve placed his large hands on the arms of the captain's chair and slid back. "In order to succeed, we need to do some first-rate detective work. Like I said, it's not my law. On the other hand, I know the best contract and patent lawyer in Texas, and that's the guy I think we ought to engage. He's good, he's honest, and he's funny as hell."

Tom grunted toward Don. "Should have done that when the whole thing blew up."

A couple of procedural questions were chewed on and Steve was asked to approach his nomination of a patent lawyer. The attorney had a successful practice in Sugar Land.

Prior to Tom's summation of the meeting, the floor was opened to all. Josh remained quiet while the others bantered back and forth with insight, out-of-the-box thoughts, and commitments to future courses of action. From San Antonio, Nancy stayed in the thick of the meeting via the speaker. Drinks in the form of beer, coffee, and Cokes were served nonstop. While Catfish slept, Bear kept his nose glued to the glass door next to the dining room. Ever the optimist, he longed to be part of the gathering. Tom stood at one end of the whiteboard and Paige, marker in hand, stood at the other end. Father and daughter taking notes and creating order out of chaos. Still a great team. Time passed rapidly. Finally the ideas and insights started to take on some redundancy.

Tom took charge. "I think we've done all we can do at this point."

His proclamation resonated with everyone and a collective sigh rose from the group.

Tom motioned to the whiteboard. It was covered with bulleted phrases, arrows, names, and themes. "We've covered a lot of ground tonight." He looked across the table at Josh. "Josh, I'm glad you came. I noticed you haven't spoken at all during the meeting. I imagine that you probably do have many questions. All I can say is that we're going to get a lot of them answered. Once the questions have been addressed, we are going to take some very decisive action."

Josh just nodded his approval. Tom then addressed everyone.

"As background to my remarks, just remember that Don and I have been in constant contact with each of you." Tom placed his hands in the back pockets of his Levi's, palms out. "I might be right and I might be wrong, but what I plan to do is give you a picture of exactly what I think has happened. There are some holes in it and it will be up to us to fill them in.

"For starters, the JETS is unique and I agree with Don that it could be worth billions. As in billions of dollars. Unfortunately, a design of this nature is always an invitation for SOB competitors to come to the trough. And that's what's happening to us." Tom stopped midstream, puckered his mouth to the side, and inhaled an anger-abating breath. "I went online today and did a Google search of Wellington. Under the 'news' link on their website I found a reference to work they're doing on stripper well research operations." Tom's tone and inflection turned hard. "But here's the kicker: Discussions of their research only go back three weeks. It took Don and Elam some seven years to design the JETS, but Wellington pulls it off in three weeks. Absolute horseshit."

Tom talked and Paige placed appropriate bullets on the whiteboard.

Tom rolled on with his analysis. "In effect, if Wellington is the company receiving a patent for something very similar to the JETS, it will have been stolen from Don. It makes no sense for them to come to us for a system and then, poof, have their own. As a matter of fact," Tom directed his comments to Don, "something has stuck in my mind since we first visited the site following the tornado. Don, you and I were so caught up in finding Elam that we didn't notice if the display version of the JETS was on site or not. And when we did find Elam and Mrs. Bettner . . ." Tom hesitated slightly and glanced over to Josh.

Josh quickly interrupted Tom's comments, "Please call her Sarah. She'd want that."

"Thanks, Josh. I do believe I know her." He licked his lower lip and continued. "When we found them we were so absorbed in their recovery that neither of us even thought of the display model of the JETS. I've gone back in my mind a hundred times and I can't remember seeing it that night. When we came back later to the site we noticed some strange tracks and evidence that the Deere might have been moved. At that time the display stuck out like a sore thumb. I think someone stole it, copied it, and submitted our basic design." He looked directly at Josh. "And Elam and Sarah were murdered in the process."

The room went silent as Tom paused again. "I haven't pieced it all together but somehow all these things are tied together. Wellington Oil, the lawyer Soboda quitting and turning it over to Barrister, whom none of us knew. The sudden emergence of a new patent by Wellington while our patent was being held up. It's an inside job and it may have all started with the killing of one of Don's roughnecks." Tom's demeanor began to change. His brow furrowed as intense anger moved across his face.

Susie saw the look on Tom's face. It made her sick. Her mind returned to the murders in Alvin and Tom's narrow escape. She was terrified and felt air being sucked from her lungs. Susie just wanted to run away. Tom's disease of not being able to choose justice over revenge had returned.

Tom looked at Susie and instinctively knew what she was thinking. He tried to put her at ease. "What we need to do is continue gathering all the evidence we can. Once we have enough we will be able to turn everything over to either the Luling police or the Houston police, whoever has the jurisdiction over all of this. Unlike Alvin, we're not dealing with a corrupt judicial system. We're going to get it done."

Tom glanced at the wall clock and realized that the meeting had gone on longer than he had anticipated. "It's almost ten o'clock, and everyone has a long drive tonight and work tomorrow. Let's call it for now. I'll make copies of all that Paige has taken down and mail it to you. Let's continue marching. As a final point, I recommend that Steve contact his patent lawyer friend."

Everyone agreed to bring another lawyer into the mix. The meeting ended and each member got up quietly, still contemplating all that had been discussed. Cordial farewells, which included Nancy, were made, and one by one each person departed. Tired to the bone, Josh savored Susie's invitation to spend the night at the ranch. Bear and Catfish, satisfied that the last guest was safely on the way home, walked back to the porch.

The foursome continued talking in the living room until Susie noticed the weights hanging from Josh's eyelids.

"Josh, why don't you call it a night? We're night owls and you've had more than a long day."

Josh had been too polite to leave before the others but he jumped at the opportunity. He appreciated that Susie understood how tired he was. *She's just like Mom,* he thought.

"Thank you, Mrs. Seiler." His smile was cut off by a large, uncontrollable yawn that made everyone laugh. He sheepishly got up and bade all a good night.

Tom, Susie, and Don talked for another thirty minutes before the long day caught up with everyone but Tom.

"I'll be in shortly. Just want to see the Military Channel for a few minutes. *World War II Commanders* is coming on now."

Susie leaned down and kissed Tom on the forehead. Following Susie's female affection, Don provided the male version by going to the refrigerator and grabbing one last beer for Tom.

Tom looked up at Don and reached for the beer. "Thanks." He added one last comment. "Something's going to pop on this. I feel it."

Don looked down and responded, "Yeah, I feel it too." He patted Tom on the shoulder as he limped toward his room. He was pulling his shirt out when all of a sudden he stopped at the door and turned around. His eyes were bright and alert as he stared deeply into his brother's eyes.

"Tom. I just remembered something. Soboda told Steve and Bill that he did not know Barrister in person. I wasn't quite sure, but now I remember clearly. I'm certain that Elam flat-out stated that Barrister told him over the phone that Soboda was a friend and asked him to take over on the JETS patent." He pounded a fist into an open palm, the clear popping sound echoing off the walls. "Damn, I remember for sure. That's the link between them."

Tom lowered the volume on the TV and replied, "That's a start." A small frown traced across his face. "The only problem is that we have nothing to verify that. In court it will go down as hearsay. But at least we know that, for us, the link is solid. We're going to checkmate Barrister on this."

"Yeah, the son of a bitch will pay. Now I can sleep easy tonight." Don disappeared into the bedroom.

Tom put the volume back up and leaned back in the soft leather chair. The documentary on Marshal Georgi Zhukov, who claimed more victories against Hitler than any other commander, was in progress.

Tom looked down at his watch—11:13 p.m.

Forty-Six

Saturday Night,
May 15

Monte's Bar,
Luling, Texas

Happy women bellowed "Hell yeah!" on cue to Gretchen Wilson's "Redneck Woman." Laughter floated on smoke wings above the throng of Saturday night revelers. The weekend was in full bloom and with it a semblance of normal life in Luling. Terry and Debbie shared bartender duties with a pixie named Annabeth. The larger-than-expected crowd made it difficult to ignore the anticipated profits. From Shiner Bock to Abita Amber and all of the standards in between, a constant exchange of cold bottles of beer for money was taking place. At 11:13 p.m. Annabeth smiled as she felt the small fortune stuffed into both front pockets of her work apron. The happier the crowd, the larger the tips.

In the poolroom Carlos and Emilio watched Manuel struggle against the stranger. Manuel was more intense than usual, clearly rattled by an opponent with talent greater than his own. He lined up a rather simple one-bank shot . . . and missed.

"Fuck! Fuck, fuck, fuck." He slammed the base of his cue onto the concrete floor in disgust. "Fuck. My leg is screwing with me." Manuel grabbed his beer and took a large swallow. He hobbled back against the wall, placing his non-beer-holding hand on top of his cue stick.

Manuel's opponent, tall and sinewy, said nothing. His large hand moved slowly across his face from moustache and stubble beard to his chin. He moved to the end of the table nearest the cue ball and surveyed the arrangement of balls. He bridged the cue gently between his thumb and index finger. His palm and all four fingers rested firmly, comfortably, on the green surface. Three deliberate strokes preceded a firm thrust of the cue into the ball. *Crack! Pop!* It caught the eight ball at a slight angle and sent it three-quarters of the length of the table, where it dropped into its intended pocket.

"Sure kicked your ass." Carlos thought it funny that someone had finally beaten Manuel at his own game. "Yeah, he stuck you good."

"A hundred bucks, friend." The stranger showed little emotion as he put the cue in the rack.

"Fuck. My knee fucked me up."

"Not your knee. It was your brain." Emilio laughed at the flustered loser.

Manuel pulled five twenties out of his wallet and reluctantly turned them over. Never hustle a hustler.

"I'm a good winner," the stranger said, "so the next round's on me. What's your beer?"

Easy to please, they all ordered Lone Star.

The three Mexicans turned their attention back to the table. Two of them continued laughing at the third.

Bartok removed his eyeglasses from his shirt pocket, put them on, and eased his way through the crowd to the bar. He waited patiently until Annabeth worked her way down to him.

"What'll you have, sweetheart?" She smiled quickly at him, wanting to be friendly almost as much as she wanted to be fast.

"Three Lone Stars and a Bud."

"Gotcha."

Annabeth moved to the beer cooler and started grabbing beer bottles. Bartok pulled three pills from his pants pocket and waited until she returned.

He gave her a ten-dollar bill to cover the beers and a two-dollar tip. If desired, he could afford to tip her ten thousand dollars. Bartok, surrounded by the lively crowd, had no problem placing a single pill in each of the Lone Stars. He took his time, ensuring the pills dissolved by the time he reentered the poolroom.

The final pool game folded under the effects from a variant strain of flunitrazepam, commonly called Rohypnol—the date rape drug of choice.

"Jeez," Manuel said as he wiped his forehead and sat down on one of two chairs in the room, "I feel so damn tired."

"I know. I feel it too." Bartok leaned on the table and shook his head. "I could use some fresh air. Want to join me?"

Carlos replied, "One minute. Let me finish the game." He lined up his shot and fired away. He scratched, missing the three ball completely. He shook his head as much to clear it as to signify disgust. "Shit. Let's go."

By the time the men walked out of Monte's, Manuel was staggering. Terry watched them closely. He wanted everyone to have a good time and to spend lots of money, but he didn't want to be held responsible for an accident caused by his drunken patrons.

"Hey," Terry called over the bar. "Hey!" he called, louder.

Bartok turned around but said nothing.

"You guys all right?"

Bartok answered, "We're fine. Need some air. Thanks." He turned back, grabbing Manuel by the arm.

Neither the steady pellets of cold rain nor the buffeting wind could revive the three men.

"Where's your car?" Bartok asked Emilio as he pulled a pair of leather gloves from his coat pocket and put them on.

"No car. It's truck. Forrr two-fiffy." Emilio slurred his answer. He stumbled as he started across North Cypress Avenue.

Carlos struggled to regain his senses. He knew something wasn't right but could not clear his mind enough to make independent decisions. He followed the others to the truck.

Emilio tried climbing into the driver's seat as Bartok helped Manuel into the back. Carlos made it to the front passenger seat but couldn't find the button to lower the window. Bartok walked around to the driver's side; Emilio stood facing the seat but doing nothing. Bartok reached into Emilio's pocket and pulled the keys out. Emilio offered no resistance as he was put into the back with Manuel. The three passengers were unconscious before Bartok started the engine.

Bartok was in no hurry. Late night traffic was always sporadic. His mind was alert and his body relaxed. Business is business—no more, no less. Flashing red lights from a highway patrol car on South Magnolia Avenue caused only a slight rise in blood pressure. Driving with three drunks was innocent enough.

He turned left and headed north on Highway 80. Sparse clusters of lights signaled small farms and simple homes. In the eleven miles from Monte's to the Fentress Bridge two cars passed going in the opposite direction. He looked into his rear view mirror and saw only inky blackness. He surveyed his cargo again and was satisfied they were helpless. *It's time,* he thought.

Bartok pulled into a small overlook at the east end of the bridge facing the river. The precipice of the turnaround area stood a little more than ten feet above the churning, pregnant San Marcos River. Having carried out two previous contracts in a similar manner provided him all the expertise he needed. He lowered the windows, turned off the ignition, and got out.

"Hmm, ga . . ." Carlos mumbled unintelligible sounds.

Bartok moved to the rear seat and grabbed Emilio. Dead weight. Bartok, hands beneath Emilio's arms, pulled him out of the back, dragged him to the driver's seat, and jimmied him in as best he could. Bartok struggled with the seatbelt but finally snapped the safety lock. Up to this point in time his actions appeared legal.

Just as Bartok closed the door he saw a stream of light coming from the opposite side of the bridge. "Shit."

He moved quickly to the passenger side near the front fender. He was in defilade from the car as it passed by. The approaching driver slowed to a crawl, either from curiosity or to make sure that water had not started to cover the roadway. The driver seemed to look in Bartok's direction as it passed by the truck, but once he cleared some ponding water he accelerated and disappeared. The night's blackness smothered the bridge again. The winds pushed hard against trees and brush. Sheets of rain enveloped the truck and its contents.

Bartok reached across Carlos's torso and started the engine. He got out and closed the door. He wiped water from his face and reached in with Manuel's cane, fitting its rubber cap to the gas pedal. He pushed down gently. The truck moved forward slowly, the wheels grabbing at the crushed stone just enough for traction. At the lip of the overhang Bartok tossed the cane toward Manuel and simultaneously hopped off of the running board. The truck body glided effortlessly over the edge. The only sound was a thud from the undercarriage hitting the edge of the overhang. Obeying the laws of nature, the truck began to flip. It hit the water nose-down. The river's turbulence was hungry and unrelenting. Water poured in the open windows, belching out air as the raging current sucked the vehicle and its passengers under. The fomenting water groaned as it took its meal. Bartok stepped back from the precipice and the sounds of the furious river quieted. He reached the roadway, aware of his deep rhythmic breathing and the percussion of rain tapping at his shoulders above the surging water.

Bartok turned toward the bridge. The struggle for survival playing out beneath the water was of no concern.

Ice-cold water shocked Carlos's senses. His mind was jumbled, unable to comprehend the environment. Carlos unknowingly fought for his life, trying to escape the full force of the water roaring in against his face and body. The drug still held him prisoner. The truck rolled over in the water. Carlos could see nothing, but instinctively reached for the seat belt. He grabbed at it and pulled. He had no strength. The belt was locked tight. Air seeped from his lungs but he fought the impulse to inhale. The blackness surrounding him made it impossible to know whether or not he was upright in the water. The need for air began to overtake him. Again he assaulted the belt snap. His mouth involuntarily opened in search of air; water was sucked into his throat. He gagged again. His actions slowed. His final thrust at the release mechanism preceded his drift into a deep sleep. His head bounced against the truck roof. Carlos felt soothed by the warm, gentle water.

Bartok walked neither slow nor fast across the bridge. The San Marcos breached the bridge substructure, forcing him to walk ankle-deep through the water. Another fifteen minutes and the surge of water would render the bridge impassable. Beyond the far end of the bridge Bartok reached River Grove Road. From the road he circled far around the brush to the back of the sawgrass to avoid signs of disruption. The darkness confused him somewhat and it took an extra minute to find the motorcycle. The rain, growing colder by the minute, increased in intensity. Bartok sank ankle deep into the muck. He was in full control but still irritated that he had not accounted for the changing soil conditions. He removed the brush, rolled up the camouflage poncho tightly, and stuffed it into his jacket; then he lifted the motorcycle, struggling to get it to the hardtop. Once on the roadway he turned the ignition. It started immediately. Leaving the motorcycle in neutral, Bartok returned to the brush and swept away his tracks with stalks of sawgrass. He tossed the stalks back to where he had pulled them, removed his gloves, rung them out, and put them back as he returned to his motorcycle. He eased onto FM 20 toward Seguin.

The wind and rain pelted Bartok relentlessly. He endured far worse conditions in years past, but this night clearly passed muster for being plain lousy. Twenty-five minutes later he arrived in Luling. His hands ached and, upon arriving next to his truck, needed to be pried off of the handlebars. He rubbed them together vigorously, gloves included, before pulling the ramp out of the bed of the truck. He loaded the motorcycle onto the bed and reached into the toolbox. He replaced the work boots he wore with a pair that were the correct size and then placed the old boots, gloves, poncho, and eyeglasses into a heavy-duty construction bag. Finally, he tossed the bag onto the passenger's seat; all of it would be discarded before evening's end. Bartok climbed into the driver's seat, started the ignition, and drove away. At Davis and North Cypress Street he glanced over to see a happy couple walking out of Monte's Bar.

Forty-Seven

Monday, May 17

Houston, Texas

D on, cane in hand, entered the law office of Fred Barrister shortly after 9:00 a.m. He patted down his disheveled, windblown hair and walked to the chest-high receptionist's counter. The office was of average size, having a reception area, conference room, and three private offices. Leather chairs were the stuff of lawyers.

Same old shit at the reception counter as on the phone.

"I'm sorry. He doesn't seem to have an appointment scheduled with you today. Would you like me to set up an appointment for another day?"

Don answered with syrupy sweetness. "No thanks. I'm not in a hurry. I'll just wait."

"I'm afraid that he will be gone most of the day." Now she sounded slightly dismissive.

Don had played these events in his head the night before. He remained pleasant. "No problem. I'll wait." He grabbed a 2007 *Sports Illustrated* and sat down on a leather chair directly facing down the hall to Fred Barrister's office. His position also afforded him an angled view of the side door. Barrister could not leave without Don seeing him. Raising his head just enough to be able to notice the door to Barrister's office, Don's attention faintly turned to the article covering Appalachian State's incredible victory over Michigan on a blocked field goal. Sweet stuff. Don breathed deeply, caught in a memory of his eighty-seven-yard run against San Antonio Lee. He squeezed his shriveled right leg. *Such is life.* Then his thoughts turned to Mike, his son, who back in the eighties led the nation in scoring while playing for Chillicothe High School near Wichita Falls. The way they ran the ball, they looked like twin brothers: *We both had it.*

By noon Don had read virtually every page of the magazine. There was no other *Sports Illustrated* and he had no desire to read the political rhetoric of *Time* magazine. He knew he was the proverbial cog in the wheel and did not mind that he had not been offered a drink all morning. The receptionist remained a captive behind the counter.

Don broke out of his reverie when a figure appeared down the hall. He eyed the person only to see one of the young lawyers walking toward the front door on the way to lunch. Don shook off the enjoyable thoughts of days gone by and began thinking of all that had taken place over the last several months. Something was wrong with the whole picture, and Barrister was dead center in the tangled events.

Don's cell phone vibrated. He grabbed the phone and pushed the talk button. "Don Seiler."

"Mr. Seiler. This is Felix Calderon."

Don answered. "Hey, Felix. Hang on just a minute." He got up and limped out of the front door.

The receptionist did not look up.

Outside, Don felt the warmth of the clearing skies. The

blowing wind did another job on his hair. He leaned on his cane and squinted into the bright sun. "OK, yeah, what's up, Felix?"

"Mr. Seiler, Carlos told us to meet at the shed this morning but he's not here. He said we got lots of work today. But he's not here. Do you know what we are supposed to be doing?"

Slightly confused and concerned, Don answered, "Other than making sure everything is in working order, I don't know what he had planned. Have you tried his cell phone?"

"I called him many times but he didn't answer."

Since joining Donelam, Carlos had never missed a day of work; for that matter, Carlos had never been late to work.

Just then Barrister walked around the opposite side of the office. Don quickly ended the conversation. "Felix, I have to go. Have everything secured and then tell everyone to take the rest of the day off. I'll meet you at," Don paused, trying to process everything, then changed his message, "no, I'll give you a call tonight to let you know what to do. If you hear from Carlos, tell him to call me immediately. I have to go. Thanks."

Don looked at Barrister walking toward his car from the opposite side of the building. He did a double take, first looking back to the front door and then to the side of the building. There weren't any other doors. *Well I'll be damned. He snuck out of his office window.*

"Hey! Barrister. Hold it right there." Don called to Fred Barrister and started his walk toward Barrister's car.

Barrister called back. "I'm sorry, I have a critical meeting in twenty minutes. See my secretary for a meeting." Fred Barrister continued walking rapidly to his car.

Don was slow and unsteady, but he picked up his gait as best he could. Fortunately, at least for Don, the car was parked in a way that had the passenger side closest to Don. Before

Barrister could start the car, Don opened the passenger door and slid in.

"I have to leave immediately. Get out of my car." He started to turn the ignition key.

"Turn off the engine or I'll break your sorry-ass nose. My legs are gone but my arms aren't." He leaned to his left and, with quickness and strength belying his medical condition, bore downward hard on Barrister's right hand. The swift, strong impulse broke Barrister's grip on the keys. Don grabbed the full bundle of keys and removed them.

In defeat, Fred angled back against the seat and looked up in frustration.

Don leaned back in his seat, holding the keys tightly in his hand. MS or not, Don was as strong as a bull–a very large bull. Akin to the Caine Mutiny's Captain Queeg, he rotated the keys in his right hand. Seconds passed agonizingly slow. Then Don spoke, quietly, evenly.

"Here's what I think is going on. Either you're the worst lawyer in the country or you're involved with my losing the patent. And, to state the obvious, I don't believe for a minute that you are incompetent. That, Mr. Barrister, leaves us with a dilemma. Either you get our patent back or I'll sue you. Beyond that, I am going to do everything possible to find criminal intent in what you have done." Don leaned toward Barrister, their faces not six inches apart. "I'm not the dumb hick you think I am. I don't know right now, but I will find out who you're working with." Don did not share the fact that Bill Newton had followed Barrister to Wellington Oil. "It won't take long."

Don leaned back again and stared straight through the car window. The rough, brittle branches of mesquite trees swayed ever so slightly in the brisk wind. The only noise in the warming car was the metal-on-metal sound of the keys being rubbed together.

Sweat poured from Fred Barrister's forehead and onto his lips. For once, he did not know how to react to the circumstances. The sound of the keys rattled him. Finally, he responded. "Mr. Seiler,"–Barrister had not used Don's first name in weeks–"I told you before that I will work to sort this out. I assure you that I have worked completely on your behalf and will continue to do so. There is nothing else I can say."

Don looked straight ahead. Like the mesquite, Don Seiler was as hard as they come. Without looking at Barrister or saying a word, Don dropped the keys between his legs to the floorboard and opened the door. Cane in right hand, he closed the door gently with his left hand. It was quiet inside the car– but all hell was breaking loose. As though he had not a care in the world, Don limped to his own car.

Just as Don turned the ignition, his cell phone rang. It was Tom.

"I won't be on the stand until late-afternoon, if at all. If you're downtown, let's meet at Market Square for lunch."

Don answered, "Works for me. I'm pulling out of Barrister's parking lot now and can meet you there in thirty minutes."

Shortly after 1:00 p.m. Don walked beneath the faded striped awning and through the double doors to the Market Square Bar & Grill. The crowd was typically busy, but the normal, uncontrolled noise and chaos were beginning to die out. In the back Tom sat at a small, round table beneath pictures hanging from the red-brown brick wall. He waved at Don and pulled a chair back for his brother. An ice-cold Miller Lite and a large glass of ice water sat at Don's place. Tom was only drinking water.

Don sat down and grabbed the water glass. "Mmm, aah. Nectar from the gods." Don gulped down half the glass. "I spent the whole morning at Barrister's law office and haven't had anything to drink. My head's pounding and I'm hungry as hell." He took another third of the glass before putting it down and grabbing his beer.

"Enjoy that beer and get set for a great burger. The motto of this place is 'It's every Texan's right to hold a burger in one hand and a beer in the other!'"

"Sure sounds justified to me. What's good here?"

Tom smiled and then looked down at the menu. "Take what you want, but their jalapeño burger is as good as it gets."

Don accepted the recommendation and ordered his burger well done. Tom decided on the beef fajita salad. Tom's testimony for the afternoon involved a woman who was injured at a supermarket by a fall. In defending the HEB grocery store chain, he would explain that the poor, unfortunate woman had four other incidents where she was the unfortunate victim of negligence on the part of a commercial enterprise.

"It should be fun. I'll be addressing coefficients of friction, the warning signs in both Spanish and English, and the surveillance camera." Tom shook his head and added, "But there is a problem with the case. It's an out-and-out scam and we'll be able to prove it's a scam. Still, there's a high probability that she'll win. She's the small, motherly type who comes across as Mary Poppins. But in reality, she's a common crook. Just like her lawyer. I've seen good juries, bad juries, and just plain stupid juries."

"I've seen too much of that crap in my dealings as well." Don envied the variety of Tom's cases and always found them interesting. He reached for his beer and added, "Tell you what. You identify the dirtbags and, if they get off scot-free, I'll ride vigilante and clean their clocks." He took a large swallow.

Tom answered, "Good idea." He then changed the subject, asking, "So what's your plan from here?" He poked his straw into the ice cubes.

"Well, it's been almost a week since he told me the patent has been lost, but the SOB hasn't sent me the letter yet."

Tom frowned, trying to switch gears from his upcoming testimony to the situation with the JETS.

Don continued, "We need to do this wisely. Before confronting him anymore, I think we ought to continue gathering as much information as possible."

"Do you have official verification that Wellington is the one who will receive the patent?"

"Not yet. Like I said, he hasn't given me a damn thing. I think he's stalling and at the same time trying to come up with a plan to make me happily go away. It doesn't make sense because it will be public knowledge in a matter of days anyway."

The jalapeño burger was as good as advertised and the fries weren't far behind. The conversation continued between bites and over the diminishing noise.

Tom asked, "Has Steve been in touch with that patent lawyer that he says is squared away?"

"He said he would call the guy today. We can set up a meeting this week. Unfortunately, if he is as good as Steve says, why in the hell didn't we get him to begin with?"

Tom forced a sad grin of lost opportunity and replied, "At the time, Steve wasn't even aware of anything. Remember, it was Elam who was our mastermind."

Don sat up, hands out. "No, no. I wasn't knocking Steve. He's been phenomenal. I was just bitching to whoever is supposed to be running the universe."

"Yeah, you're right. This world is definitely screwed up. I may be old school, but greed and corruption have run amuck and the United States is sucking wind like never before." Tom took his last bite of the fajita. "But you know what?" His eyes brightened. "I've thought about our country, the shit you're going through, and the mess I had in Alvin. Spent a lot of time thinking about all the crap people put on to other people. And I've come to a decision."

Don grinned and wiped a bit of mayonnaise from the corner of his mouth. "OK, I'll bite. What's the verdict?"

"I'm not going to take shit from any dirtbag again. Matter of fact, the plaintiff's lawyer for my case today is a poster boy for assholes. Care to sit in?"

"Sure. I need some humor in my life."

Fred Barrister sat in his car in the parking lot, the engine idling quietly. He had barely touched his lunch and had no desire to work. He wanted to get the hell away from Don Seiler and his brother, and from the likes of Bart Miles. For that matter, he didn't want to be in Texas. He spoke into the cell phone.

"What I'm telling you is that Seiler is not dumb. The guy's a solid engineer and behind the twang and bad health is a smart guy. His brother, and you know him from the Colter case, is the best forensic expert witness in Southeast Texas." Fred Barrister's voice was urgent. "They are going to dig and dig into this. I'm worried. They are about to come after us."

Bart Miles was irritated that his pissant patent attorney was withering under the pressure. He looked up at the pictures of oil wells and paused. The silence was deafening. He finally said, "Coming after us? They can't come after us. They don't have shit. Stop being a fucking crybaby." He backed off slightly. "Look, as long as there is no indication that our design was anything but good engineering, we don't have any legal problems. The only problems we can have are if you start running scared. Just close the damn door on them. Rather than acting like a child, start weighing your concerns against what you will make once everything is complete."

Bart's last comment made complete sense, but nagging fear didn't come to a halt over a hefty price tag. Fred Barrister was scared. He wished he had never heard of Bart Miles. But the money was reason enough to see everything through.

Bart's next comment made things very clear. "And remember, if things fall apart on this, you will be penniless and headed for prison." The translation was easy—Fred Barrister was in Bart Mile's back pocket.

Bart hung up before Barrister could reply. He called Frank Milsap. Five minutes later the two men sat in Bart's office contemplating the latest turn of events.

"Nobody knows anything about how we designed the oil extractor. Nothing, absolutely nothing, ties it to the Seiler design except for physical similarity, and that doesn't mean squat in a courtroom." Bart spoke more to himself than to Frank.

Frank answered. "For the most part, I agree with you. The one stickler is that the older Seiler, the NASA guy, has a propensity to solve puzzles. From what I know and have heard, he digs deeply into strange situations. He likes solving puzzles and that's how he views this whole thing with the oil extractor. He went far beyond physical analysis with the case in Alvin and he could do it here." His fingers tapped the arms of his chair to the rhythm of a simple drum line. He continued. "Tell you what. Why not get Elizabeth Harker on the line and find out what she can tell you about the Seilers?" He grinned sourly. "After all, she lost her ass to them."

Bart answered quickly. "Good idea. Yeah, good idea." Then he added, "Can't you stop pounding on the chair?"

"I'm not at all surprised. If you get tied up with Seiler, the older one, be careful. Very careful." Liz Harker's entire body tightened. The name Seiler caused seething hate to overtake her body. Contrary to popular opinion, time does not heal all wounds; in some cases time serves as fertile soil. It had been a good while, but she hated Tom Seiler no less, possibly even more, than when he beat her to a pulp in a courtroom. He cost her everything. She wanted payback. But it had to be a careful payback.

Bart answered, "I'm headed up to New Jersey tomorrow. Can we get together for lunch on Wednesday to compare notes? I'd rather do it face to face."

"Actually, I'm going to be in Tuxedo Park on Wednesday. I'm wrapped up in the morning but have the afternoon off. Do you know a place?"

Bart suggested, "Let's meet at the Park Steakhouse in Park Ridge. It's on Kinderkamack Road. I don't remember the exact address. It's got excellent food and it will keep you out of the city. I recommend one thirty. We won't have to worry about the lunch crowd."

"One thirty it is. I'll meet you there."

Bart smiled into thin air. He had no desire to go to New York City, except if Liz Harker wanted to play house. Playing house was the furthest thing from her mind.

Bart began thinking of solutions to Fred Barrister's concerns. He thought of Bartok.

Don, legs aching the whole time, sat on the hard wooden bench for the entire afternoon. Tom was not called to the stand. *Damn.* If he knew that Tom would not be called to the stand until Wednesday morning, Don would have considered slitting his wrists. At least he could enjoy another lunch at Market Square.

Forty-Eight

Wednesday, May 26

Angleton, Texas

Tom and Don parked themselves on the same wooden bench outside of the courtroom while Tom waited to testify. Tom had spent hundreds of hours in courtrooms and enjoyed almost every moment–especially when his testimony delivered the guilty into the hands of federal and state law enforcement; Don had spent several hours in courtrooms and did not enjoy any of it. Even on this morning he felt uncomfortable just being there. Shortly before 11:00 a.m. Tom was called to testify. Don followed Tom into the courtroom and found a seat.

Don stretched out as best he could in the fourth row of the half-empty courtroom. It was only mid-morning and both legs hurt; he rubbed the muscle just above each knee with little success. Don looked down at his right leg. It was wasting away, but at least he had a leg. He remembered his last personal visit to the 412th District Court; it wasn't an enjoyable experience. While a student at San Jacinto College he appeared along with two friends before an irascible judge by the name of Lindsey Harris. Don's crime was that of youth—throwing beer bottles at mailboxes in a drunken stupor. To his very good fortune, Don and Judge Harris both had served in the United States Navy: Don on the aircraft carrier USS John Hancock, CVA-19, and later at Cam Ranh Bay, South Vietnam, and the judge on the aircraft carrier USS Benjamin Franklin, CV-13, during World War II. Don's appearance before the judge was a life-changing event. Even after four years in the navy, Don was too cocky for his own good. Don never forgot the moment Judge Harris moved from his chair and sat down in a vacant chair near the bench. To the astonishment of the entire court, the judge removed a prosthesis from his right leg. From just below the knee down, nothing remained. He tossed the prosthesis on the floor only to instruct Don to pick it up, study it, and give it back. A pin dropping in the room would sound like an explosion. Don, scared and embarrassed, did exactly as requested. He picked it up and looked at it from top to bottom. Without a word he handed the prosthesis back to Judge Harris. The small gathering of people in the courtroom evenly divided their attention—50 percent stared at Don and 50 percent stared at Judge Harris. It didn't take long before all attention was on the judge.

Taking his time, Judge Harris attached the prosthesis to the stump of his leg. He returned to his chair. Don remembered his admonishment:

> *Young man, I am going to give you probation under one condition. You will go to the library and read up on what happened to the aircraft carrier Benjamin Franklin on March 19, 1945. In particular, read of Lieutenant Don*

Gary. He saved my life and the lives of many other men.
Over the years he and countless other sailors, some heroic
in battle and others in the conduct of their daily lives, have
made me proud to have served in the United States Navy.
You, at this time of your life, are doing nothing to honor
those who served and died for this country. You are taking
away from the fabric of American life and I have little
respect for you. You will write a report concerning what
took place on the Franklin, the actions of Lieutenant Gary,
and most of all, what you are going to do with the rest of
your life. You will hand deliver it to me no later than a
week from today or you will go to jail for three months.

In many ways, just as Lieutenant Gary saved his life, Judge Harris saved Don's life. The judge's dressing down was the most significant emotional event in Don's life; he never forgot it.

This judge, Judge Harry Landon, did not look at all like Judge Harris. Judge Harris was a short, stocky man whose discourse was curt and to the point, while Judge Landon was tall, thin, and quiet in demeanor. The difference in the two men allowed Don to focus on Tom's testimony and not his own past transgressions.

Tom walked down the center aisle toward the bailiff, slightly tipping his head to the jury.

Since the sensational trial concerning the Alvin murders, the law firm of Duffy, Guyer and White called upon Tom's services at every opportunity. Once again, Tom was teamed with Ed Harvey.

Tom was sworn in and Ed asked him the same background questions he always did.

As simple as the case appeared at face value, it was replete with strange and interesting characters. The sights and sounds of an active courtroom brought back memories of the absolute chaos from Tom's confrontation with the second-most powerful lawyer in Houston. Midway through Tom's testimony Don remembered an urgent voicemail he had received from Wendell Akers. Don glanced at his watch and then back to his brother. No question about it, Tom was applying the predicted ass-whooping to the opponent's case. *It'll have to wait,* he thought.

"It is true then, Mr. Seiler, that you are not an expert in biomedical engineering?" The plaintiff's attorney's attempt to discredit Tom was obvious to all. It wasn't even a case of biomedical engineering; it was about mechanical engineering.

Tom couldn't conceal a grin as he replied, "Not really, but I did stay at a Holiday Inn Express last night."

The entire courtroom erupted in laughter. Virtually everyone remembered the television commercial; it was completely lost on the attorney. He was exasperated and objected.

Judge Landon interrupted quickly, "Mr. Seiler's words will be stricken from the record." He scowled insincerely at Tom and instructed him, "Mr. Seiler, we can do without the comedy. You will answer all questions without levity." But Judge Landon couldn't help himself and belched out a guffaw of his own, only to entice the courtroom, including the jury, to follow his lead in laughing out loud. He apologized to the court but spent the next hour stuffing laughter inside.

Tom handled each adversarial question with sound engineering principles and a touch of homegrown philosophy that put the jury in the palm of his hand. The surveillance tapes seemed to lock in a case of faked falling. The manner in which Mrs. Little Old Lady fell did not follow the laws of gravity. Still, juries are unpredictable. In a strange turn of events, the hour went faster than anyone wanted. But the judge was aware of time. He looked at his watch.

"Given the time, we'll recess for lunch. Proceedings will begin at two o'clock. Jury out at 11:45 a.m."

Don stood up and stretched while waiting for Tom. Ed Harvey was joining them for lunch to plan for the cross-examination. They had two hours allowed for solid strategic planning. Sixteen hundred miles away another two-hour lunch would take place.

Forty-Nine

Wednesday Afternoon,
May 26

Park Ridge, New Jersey

Kinderkamack Road twists and turns through suburban northern New Jersey. Some of the road is commercial, covered with Dunkin' Donuts, banks, diners, traffic lights, service stations, and other eyesores of modern society. Other sections of the road are beautiful. By late May the white oaks, black walnuts, sycamores, paper birches, and hickory trees are in full bloom, mottled patterns of dark green stretch from tree to tree, matched by emerald carpeting over an endless stretch of manicured lawns, and on occasion, fair weather clouds dance beneath the deep blue sky while spikes of brilliant sunlight pierce the foliage along the winding road. Homes along Kinderkamack range from modest to upper-middle class, with many of the split-level variety showing signs of renovation and new paint.

Spring was everywhere. Shrubs sprouted in front of small bay windows and flowers of all sorts bloomed in planting beds at mailboxes and along sidewalks. It was the perfect day for taking a drive, holding hands during a stroll through the woods, or as on this day, talking criminal activities over a fine meal. The Park Steakhouse sat at 151 Kinderkamack Road in Park Ridge.

Liz arrived fifteen minutes late. The hostess greeted her and directed Liz to Bart's table. He rose and gave her a perfunctory kiss on the cheek.

"Nice place once you get inside," Liz said as she sat down. Then she smiled and added, "What's that building across the street all about? It looks like we're on Route 66. And the Gulf station down the street tells me I'm in the middle of urban sprawl."

Bart nodded in agreement. "Yes, you're right. But you're in here and just wait until we eat."

The Park Steakhouse seemed to be a quaint anomaly in the middle of chaos. Liz surveyed the restaurant and was quickly taken by its quiet charm. It had very nice décor, not overly done, with rust-colored walls and nondescript paintings hanging at various locations. The tables were comfortable, with white linen and formal dinnerware. Acoustical tile ceiling, not very aesthetic, with chandeliers hanging at strategic locations, allowed for pleasant conversation. Looking through a large see-through glass panel with an undefined inscription crafted in the glass, she could see a V-shaped mahogany bar with mirrors and wine racks along the back wall.

Bart nursed a Johnny Walker Blue Label. Liz ordered a half carafe of Ferrari-Carano 2001. They chitchatted for a couple of minutes before addressing the reason for their meeting.

"So, you're pleased with the little business present I found for you?" Her eyes twinkled above the rim of her wine glass.

Bart twisted his glass, took a swallow. He held the scotch blend for a few seconds before sending it pleasantly down his throat. He answered, "I would say so. We've received the patent and are wrapping up the legalities. I don't see much of a problem, save one."

She eyed him sharply. "And that one is?"

"Seiler. Both of the Seilers. What should I anticipate from them?" Bart finished his first drink and signaled to the waitress.

Liz Harker shook her head slowly left and right, the right side of her mouth lifting and tightening. She said, "In the long run you might want to make that all three Seilers. They have a sister who is smart and tough. She's not a big player right now, but if things go bad, she'll be one hell of an asset to her brothers. She could challenge any lawyer in a courtroom. You would be very wise to include her in your little list of obstacles." Liz leaned toward Bart, her voice very quiet. "Before I give you any advice, you need to tell me why you are so concerned. I started the ball rolling on this and it can't get screwed up."

Bart looked over, wanting to know where in the hell his drink was. He made eye contact with the waitress and raised his hand. The young lady fidgeted a few seconds waiting on the bartender and then hurried over with his drink. Noticing that Liz's wine glass was almost empty, the waitress refilled the glass. Liz and Bart both went light; they ordered Bibb salads and appetizers, with littleneck clams for Liz and jumbo lump crabmeat for Bart.

Once alone again, Bart gave an overview of where things stood at the moment. They put a mole in the crew, managed to study the JETS enough to develop their own plans, used a patent lawyer to delay the Seiler patent while speeding theirs up. For his own protection, Bart left some of the gory details out of the discussion. He was more interested in gathering information than in true confessions.

He continued, "When Barrister gave him the news about losing the patent the one with MS, Don Seiler, became belligerent and threatened to haul him into court." Bart stared deeply into Liz Harker's eyes. "When he came to Wellington to talk about the device we got into a pissing contest." His eyebrows furrowed just a bit, enough that conveyed a message of concern. "As you well know, I have been known to intimidate people to my advantage. He didn't back off one bit. In fact, he's the only man ever to call me an asshole to my face." Bart stopped talking, instead pondering the fact that yes, indeed, someone saw him for who he really was. He noticed a contorted smile on Liz's face.

"So what? Many people have big mouths. My only concern is whether or not he can cause trouble, not whether or not he likes you." Still smiling, Liz ran a finger around the top of her wine glass.

Bart returned a less genuine smile and acknowledged that Liz was right. The only thing that should matter to either of them was neutralizing the Seilers.

Bart changed to the subject of Tom Seiler. "Tell me more about Tom Seiler. I know he has stuck in your craw for a long time."

Both picked at their meals, Liz barely taking a bite at all. Instead, she focused solely on the one person in the world who cost her everything. Rage, restrained only on her exterior, seethed in her words.

Liz repeated some of what she had told Bart earlier about Tom Seiler and added a few specifics to emphasize just how formidable a foe Tom Seiler could be. "What I've never told anyone is that the son of a bitch threatened to hurt me. He threatened me in my own office."

"Why didn't you have him arrested?"

"Because it was a 'he said, she said' event." Liz left out the part indicating that arresting Tom Seiler would have ended with her eventual conviction. She finished her wine glass without savoring anything but bitterness. She emptied the half carafe into her glass.

Bart signaled the waitress that he wanted another Johnny Walker Blue. He started to ask another question but was held in check by Liz's raised palm.

She continued, "You're getting me off the subject. What you need to know about Tom Seiler, and I assume it's the same with his brother and sister, is that he follows through on whatever it is he goes after. He knows the law and understands rules of evidence. He's not intimidated by lawyers, judges, or CEOs of oil companies."

Bart swallowed.

She continued without pause. "From my personal experience and what I have been told, he's the best mechanical engineer and expert witness in Texas. But remember what I've already told you." Liz unconsciously lowered her voice again. She waved her finger slowly, deliberately, at Bart before adding, "Tom Seiler is as honest a person as I have ever met. He's not going to be bought off for money. But that honesty has a price. He can fly off the handle and that weakness could get him into trouble. You might just keep record of that in case you need to trip him up. As for me personally, he's a bastard, a sorry bastard." She stopped talking to Bart and started a reflective discussion with herself. She regained her senses and added, "If he senses that something criminal is in the works, he's going after it. He will not stop. Don't be surprised if he's got you on his radar screen already."

Bart swallowed again, but this time the Johnny Walker tasted a little bitter.

Harker's mind pulled her back inside a dark hole. Her situation, to her way of thinking, should never have happened. She should be on her way to being governor of Texas. Instead, she was stuck in New York working as a mid-level executive at

Cornvale & Hickens Global Wealth Management. She detested her job. Tom Seiler had forced her to New York. She wanted complete payback. Bart Miles had to succeed. Bart's success would ruin Tom Seiler and his family while simultaneously providing handsomely for her future. She thought to herself, *Tom Seiler can roast in hell.*

Liz's voice picked up. "What I'm telling you is that you better plan a few steps ahead of the Seilers. Do some 'what if' analysis. Meet with your patent lawyer and make sure everything is on the up and up. If you're wise, you'll have a private investigator checking them all out. In a nutshell, they are all dangerous to you."

Bart tried sounding in control, but the fear was there. "If I have to deal harshly with him, so be it. He's not going to screw us," Bart made it sound like a joint venture with Liz, "out of the oil extraction system." He lifted his glass to his lips.

Liz took notice of two things. First, Bart alluded to the system as rightfully belonging to the two of them; secondly, she remembered that an accomplice of Bart Miles had already killed someone. She could not allow any of the Seilers to be killed.

"Bart." Liz's persona placed her completely in charge of the discussion. "You will not kill any of the Seilers or their family members. Period. I don't care how much you make them suffer, as long as they are not killed." Placing both palms on her side of the table, she leaned well forward, almost to the center of the table, and lifted her face directly in line with his. "I want all of them to experience total defeat and despair for a very long time. I hate them, but they will not be killed. They need to suffer. Are we clear about that?"

Bart understood everything. He looked directly at her, his eyes shielding his thoughts. "Sure, we're clear. We get the system, he and his family suffer, no one's killed, you and

I make a bucket full of money, and we all go our separate ways."

She sat back in her chair and relaxed for the first time since they started talking about the Seilers, satisfied that Bart would not resort to murder.

Bart paid the bill well after three o'clock. The Park Steakhouse's braised short ribs, trio of tuna, profiteroles with cinnamon ice cream, and pecan-crusted cheesecake with eggnog would all have to wait for a victory dinner. Date unknown.

Over two hours were spent in discussion and dining, impeccable service was offered, the cuisine was superb, and Bart Miles was a multi-millionaire. The tip was eight dollars.

Fifty

Wednesday Afternoon,
May 26

Angleton, Texas and Newark, New Jersey

Tom was no more than half-finished with his afternoon testimony when Don remembered: *Damn. I forgot again. Got to call Wendell. Damn.*

Tom's afternoon performance was classic Seiler. He dispensed with the levity and kept it professional. During lunch Don ate a jalapeño burger while Tom and Ed Harvey figured out where the plaintiff's attorney would be headed. Tom and Ed worked well together and their opposing attorney was not the sharpest knife in the drawer. In short, everyone enjoyed the trial, including a new observer–Bartok.

After Tom was dismissed, Don walked as quickly as possible out into the hallway. He limped up to a total stranger and borrowed his cell phone to call Wendell Akers.

Two rings and Wendell answered. "Hey, Mr. Seiler, I'm glad you called me."

"Sorry I took so long. What's up?"

Wendell cut right to the point. "Felix came to the site today and told us that Carlos Aguirre was killed. That's why he hadn't been showing up to the site."

Don was stunned. "What? Carlos? What happened?"

"All I know right now is that he went drinking with some other guys and . . ."

Wendell gave Don a rough paraphrasing of what he had been told. Don processed Wendell's remarks and extrapolated them to the whole situation of the JETS. *Carlos is dead. Juan's dead. The JETS patent is gone. I'm broke. What the hell is happening?*

Don asked Wendell, "Can you get everyone together Friday afternoon? I have to head back to California on Saturday and I need to talk to everyone about this and what we need to do as a group."

"Sure. No problem."

"OK. Make it for two o'clock. I'll see you there."

"We'll be here, Mr. Seiler."

Don added, "Also get a head count of who's attending our get-together Saturday night at the Watermelon Thump. We'll have some drinks and maybe laugh this disaster away." He laughed at something Wendell said and then closed the cover on the phone. He handed the phone back to the stranger. "I really appreciate it."

"My pleasure." The stranger, pleased to be a Good Samaritan, took his phone and walked out of the courthouse.

Tom approached with victory written on his face. "If that doesn't bring a win to our side, nothing will." He saw that Don wasn't smiling. "What's up?"

Don repeated everything Wendell had told him. An unfortunate thing about Don was that he rarely talked softly. He explained everything at one hundred decibels, including his proclamation, "This is murder and it's all about the JETS."

Bartok sat nearby, listening to every loud word out of Don's mouth.

The flight attendant in first class smiled as she bent forward with Bart's pre-flight drink. Dewar's was far removed from the flavor and price of Johnny Walker Blue. But it was scotch, and scotch was the best liquor ever made by man. Bart took the drink without as much as a smile. His mind was elsewhere. In between sips he thought of the future and obstacles in his way. The Seiler family was center stage in his mind. *Don't kill the Seilers. Don't kill the Seilers?* Bart quickly answered his own question with a new rhetorical question and answer. *Who's to tell me what to do? Fuck you and the Seilers.* Bart took a final swallow of his drink and placed the glass on the middle console. He relaxed as instructions were given for the flight. He looked across to New York's skyline. The Twin Towers were gone but it was still an impressive view. A smile finally spread across his face.

Fifty-One

Friday, May 28

Test Site near Luling, Texas

The entire crew sat on the ground with backs against the eastern wall of the maintenance building. The mid-afternoon shade covered their heads, but not their legs. Don and Tom stood in the sun.

"I hoped that this day would never happen." Don's trademark jovial disposition had completely disappeared. He struggled with his thoughts and delivery. He looked down at the ground, the Seabee hat covering his eyes—which was good. It wasn't the sun; instead, it was his emotional state.

Tom stood mute by Don's side. A good fifteen seconds passed before Don spoke again. To Tom it was a slow tick, tick, tick.

Don finally continued. "The truth is that we did lose our patent, at least for the time being. I'm of the opinion that something has gone on that is either criminal or unethical. I'm not going down without a fight. I've put several years and almost every cent I had into the JETS and I don't want to lose everything. But for now I can't do anything unless I get the patent back. I have to close down our operations and concentrate on contesting the patent. Each of you will receive $3,000 in severance pay."

Tom raised his eyebrows and a blank stare spread across his face. He looked at Don as though his younger brother had gone mad. Don and Cindy spent almost everything on the JETS and did not have that kind of money. It was obvious to him that Don didn't care.

Don moved his right leg gently front and back in the dirt. "Once I do get it back." He hesitated, realizing that he had to be honest. "No, I need to be upfront. The words should be, 'If I get the patent back.' If I get the patent back, I will be offering each of you a job." He perked up just a bit, a sliver of strength reaching out toward the men. "With a patent your future and my future would be far different from what they appear to be right now."

Don shifted his weight and almost fell down. Tom reached out and gave him a stabilizing hand. Eduardo, closest to the door, went inside and grabbed a chair. He unfolded it and set it down next to Don. Don didn't hesitate. He sat down.

Leaning forward, Don continued. "Everyone knows Carlos was killed in an accident near Fentress week before last. Two others died with him."

The looks on their faces revealed that they did know of Carlos's death. Not everyone knew of the other two.

Don knew no more than anyone else. He knew Carlos's local address but did not know the whereabouts of his relatives. "I'm going to find out what I can about the circumstances and let you know.

"Oh, and a couple of final items." Don's boyish grin appeared for the first time that afternoon. "First, make sure I have everyone's correct address so I can mail the final checks to the right place. Secondly, don't forget I'm buying the beer for anyone who can make it to Monte's on Saturday night of the Thump. Tom and I will get there sometime around 10:00 p.m."

Tom gave the crew two thumbs-up.

Wendell Akers interjected, "I'll be there."

Eduardo added, "I'll meet you there early."

"Count me in too," Felix added.

Don finished the meeting. "OK. That does it. Here's to each of you. And here's to your families."

The men stood up. Don stood up. Everyone shook hands. Wendell had assumed duties as leader in the absence of Carlos. As Tom and Don made their way to Tom's pickup, Wendell and the crew secured the storage shed and locked the gate.

"Hey, Mr. Seiler. Don't forget the keys."

Don stopped and turned around. He called back to Wendell so that all could hear. "You hang on to them. I'm planning on you needing them some day in the future. When the day comes you'll be the new foreman."

Dust billowed behind the vehicles out of the JETS test site and slowly settled over the landscape. All was deathly quiet.

"Why didn't you tell me you were closing down shop? That's a piss-poor job of keeping me in the loop." Tom, eyes focused on Highway 86, was miffed.

Don stared at the countryside falling away behind the car. *I need to come back to Texas*. Flashes of the story of the JETS, from birth to its being stolen, played in his head.

"Did you even hear me?" Tom said, louder.

"Yeah, I did." Don glanced quickly over at Tom and then returned to the countryside.

Finally, Don spoke. "I just made the decision on the way to the site. It's not fair to the crew. I can't afford to keep paying them. I need to put all of my efforts into getting the patent back. The odds are slim at best. If they're going to get on with their lives, they need to do it now." Don leaned back, his head looking up at the ceiling. "Besides, you're too eager to put more cash into it and I can't have that. I'm not going to do it."

Tom realized that the strain on Don was crushing him. If more money and more effort came to naught, Don would end up paying a price no human could survive.

Tom replied thoughtfully, "Oh, what the hell. I'll stick with you at this point. We can shut down operations for now, but only if you're willing to fight for the patent. If we get the patent back, then I'm going into business with you. No ifs, ands, or buts about it."

Don looked over at his older brother. Then he extended his right hand toward Tom. "It's a deal."

They shook hands and Tom finished the conversation. "Let's get the patent."

Fifty-Two

Friday, June 4

Sugar Land, Texas

Wallis Raymond walked directly into the reception area and stuck his hand out toward Steve.

"Steve, where've you been lately? Don't think I've seen you since the Porter case." Wallis looked over at Katie. "I see you've already met the heartbeat of Raymond Associates." Wallis, a slightly balding man of medium height, displayed far more energy than expected of a man in his late sixties. Gray hair and a solid, jutting chin presented an aura of competence. He walked with just a touch of a strut, enough to appear as though he might be retired military. In fact, Wallis was a retired air force navigator. He followed his air force career with a law degree from William and Mary.

Steve gave Wallis a firm handshake and replied, "Katie's already given me the lowdown on you. She says you're a scary boss."

They chuckled along with Katie. Small in stature, with coal-black hair falling to her neck, the pretty young woman was the operational center of the small law firm. A paralegal herself, Katie had applications in for law school. Wallis abhorred the thought of losing her but he knew she would be an outstanding lawyer. Truth be known, a year earlier he talked her into joining the air force, only to have her return via an asthmatic condition. He had been clear with her that, if the business was still viable and she was willing, she had a new position waiting for her once she had the law degree. She would be his heir apparent.

She invoked additional levity. "And he gets scarier by the day."

The phone rang and Katie returned to her duties.

"Let's talk. Care for some coffee?" Wallis moved toward the conference room.

"Sounds good. I'll make my own. And thanks for seeing me on such short notice. I won't take much of your time."

"No problem. Glad to see you again."

Wallis directed Steve to a small table just outside the conference room. Steve poured a cup of coffee and added sugar and half-and-half. Even with the condiments Steve's cup looked black to him. Wallis poured black coffee—really black coffee.

Wallis noticed Steve looking at his cup. He held the cup in the air and explained. "I navigated C-141s back and forth over the Pacific during Vietnam and drank coffee for the caffeine. Always my last cup of a flight was at least eight to ten hours old. Tasted pretty much like licorice putty. To this day I can't tolerate what others would call good coffee. Sorry if it's too strong."

"No, it's fine. It'll make a man out of me." Steve lied through his teeth; his first sip was his last sip.

The conference room's décor was contemporary lawyer.

After a couple of minutes of casual conversation Wallis

got things rolling. "So, from our phone call, you need some advice on how to go about contesting a patent given to another party."

Steve didn't mince any words. "Wallis, to be honest, this patent appears to be stolen from my uncle, Don Seiler." He scratched absentmindedly at his right arm. "Don, my dad, and several others have worked at finding out what the hell is going on. What we have found out is that our patent for an oil extraction system was denied and a patent for essentially the same device has been awarded to someone else."

Wallis replied, "Seiler. Is your dad Tom Seiler?"

Steve smiled, happy to be listed in company with Tom. "Sure is. Everything I am is owed to him—or should be blamed on him."

Wallis smacked his hand down on the table. "Well, I'll be damned. I never made the connection between the two of you. Give him my best. We worked for the defense on a case some five years ago. He was great on the stand. And what he did in the Alvin case—I've never heard of testimony like his. Unbelievable."

Wallis turned serious, eyeing Steve closely. "Who's the someone else?"

Steve frowned and shook his head. "I'm sure it's Wellington Oil and Exploration. They're based in Houston." He sat up straight and seemed to ponder the question further. "I'll also tell you that the patent lawyer supposedly working with us has been a total roadblock. A friend of ours, an investigator for the Houston Police Department, proved that the lawyer has been lying to us and working with Wellington Oil while they had supposedly been negotiating with Don on the project."

Wallis wrote notes on a legal pad while pondering his next question. Finally, he asked, more to himself than to Don, "Speaking of Wellington Oil, if they had been on the up-and-up with an original design all along, why in the world would they even talk to Don?"

"Bingo. That's what we've been asking." Steve smiled. "They most likely strung Don along while either taking what information Don had given them, or somehow managing to obtain a full copy of the design. My dad thinks they stole our prototype display model."

"Whoo boy. We have ourselves an interesting situation." Wallis tapped his pencil on top of the pad, staring at his notes. He placed the pencil in the writing position and asked, "What's Don's lawyer's name?"

"Fred Barrister."

Wallis asked, "Has an office out on Westheimer?"

"That's the guy."

Wallis took a swallow of his near-tar. "I know him. I've never dealt with him or against him. Only negative I know is that he seems a little too pompous for his own good. He's a status seeker. Gives lawyers a bad name."

Steve replied strongly, "I think he's a crook and is being paid off." He got right to the point. "We'd like to hire you and fire him. Is it a deal?"

Wallis answered immediately, "I'll be glad to work with you." He turned serious. "You do realize that what we are doing is accusing Fred Barrister and possibly the Wellington Oil Company of felony fraud and theft, don't you?"

"Absolutely." Steve was eager to get to the next step.

"All right, we're on. But I'd also recommend that you don't fire Barrister at this time. It's his turn to be strung along." Wallis looked at his watch. "Unfortunately, I have an appointment in Aldine in an hour, and then it's a week with my wife and another couple in Bermuda for our anniversaries." Wallis laughed as he spoke, "Exactly forty-seven years ago we made love all night long. Tonight we'll have a wonderful dinner, enjoy drinks and talking, and be asleep by ten o'clock. Guaranteed." He reached for his calendar, saying, "But let's get back to you and your uncle. We'll need at least two hours to go over my teaching session on patent law, and you can give me a complete rundown as to what you know."

"Right. Here's what I've got so far."

Steve pulled out a stack of letters, sketches, engineering drawings, and bills, many having specific dates of submission, and gave them to Wallis.

"Thanks. I'll study them over the next couple of weeks. More importantly, I'll go online and use the Patent Application Information Retrieval System of the US Patent and Trademark Office to verify what happened to you guys. Wish I could be faster, but I have several time-sensitive cases going on right now and our cruise takes first place."

Wallis called out to Katie and asked for a calendar. He studied it carefully.

"How does early in the morning on June 23 look to you? Say, 8:00 a.m.?"

Steve checked his Blackberry. After a couple of minutes punching buttons, Steve answered affirmatively. They were set.

The men walked toward the front door, only to be confronted by Katie.

"Hold it, Mr. Raymond."

Wallis stopped in his tracks and waited. Katie walked up to him with a deep frown. He stood at attention while she straightened his tie. The whole scene was funny to Steve. Funny with just a touch of loyalty added.

"There. Now you can represent Raymond Associates." She looked at Steve and added, "I'm the associates."

Steve answered, "If he ever fires you, you automatically have a new job."

Wallis laughed with Steve and Katie as he headed out the

door. Steve accompanied Wallis to his car.

"I appreciate your help on this one. My uncle is a great guy who's being ripped off."

Wallis smiled, his chin jutting a little more than normal. "It's been too long since I had a real juicy case. And I get to do it for a friend."

They shook hands.

Frank Milsap, a wide grin covering his face, walked into Bart Miles's office.

"We did it. Bart, I'm telling you, the announcement did it." Frank went on with an almost shrill voice. Rarely had he shown such excitement. "We've got inquiries out the ass for leasing and buying the extractor." Frank sat down in the chair facing Bart. "Phone calls and emails are coming from everywhere." He laughed and spoke again. "T. Boone Pickens can move his butt over, he's no longer the big man on the block." He shook his head in almost disbelief. "Bart, I can't believe it."

Bart's grin almost mirrored Frank's.

Frank continued, "I just need to sit down with our staff to finalize how we're going to break everything out. My best estimate is that we could have half a billion in orders and leasing agreements before the month is over." Frank raised his hands into the air and stretched his legs out to the edge of Bart's desk. "Bart, we officially have the world by the balls!"

Bart stood up and walked to a cherry breakfront directly behind his desk. He pulled two glasses from the shelf along with a bottle of Johnny Walker. While pushing the first glass against the ice cube dispenser, Bart said, "Let's just make sure we don't let anyone get us by the balls. We can't afford any problems, either legally or competitively."

"I just came from a meeting with Morgan Rosewood. He's gone over the legal documents several times and our patent is rock solid. He did have some concern about companies reproducing the extractor on their own."

Bart finished pouring the smooth scotch into the glasses and walked around his desk, extending a glass to his comrade.

They clinked the glasses as Frank continued. "Morgan's real concern is with foreign companies, particularly the fucking Chinese. The bastards will copy anything. Absolutely zero compliance with international law. No question about it, they will be our problem."

Bart sipped gently on his scotch, swished the tart liquid in his mouth, and finally swallowed. Johnny Walker always warmed his throat. It was a pleasant drink and just right for the occasion.

Frank watched Bart walk to the window. Bart looked down at the city for a full minute. He tilted his head back and took another full swallow.

"Frank, no one is going to take this from us. It is ours and no one has any right to infringe upon us. You get Morgan to handle this right."

"I've already told you that we're working on it. It boils down to keeping it in the United States and having full control or going international and developing safeguards for our protection."

The thought that there might be an unscrupulous firm out there was slightly disconcerting.

Just before going to bed Steve made one last check of his emails. The last one had the subject line: Wellington Does Have the Patent. It read:

Steve—went online and did some searching. Wellington has been awarded a patent. The dogfight begins immediately.—Wallis

Fifty-Three

Wednesday, June 23

Sugar Land, Texas

Wallis tilted the cup upward, the last drops of coffee draining into his mouth. He put the cup down. "I did find two things particularly suspicious about the patent. First, the description of the oil device as given in the Wellington patent is almost identical to that from the Donelam Company. The drawings that I saw were not detailed but they appear to be virtually identical to the drawings you gave me. The second thing that struck me as quite the coincidence was that the date of their patent submission was exactly three days earlier than yours."

Steve jotted down a couple of notes on legal paper and studied them. He underlined *three days early*. He replied, "OK, what do we do from here?"

Wallis pulled out a folder and removed several sheets of paper, placing them in front of Steve. "Here's the basic background information that you need." He pointed to the first option. "In a few minutes we'll talk about contesting the patent of Wellington Oil. But first," Wallis said apologetically, "you need a final primer concerning patents. It's important but it's also as much fun as getting sand in your eye." Both Wallis and Steve smiled. Wallis continued, "Patents have been around since the fifteenth century and the first United States patent was in 1790." He put his finger on the first major paragraph. "As you probably know, a patent is nothing more, or less, than a property right granted by the US Government to an inventor. In our case, it's the Jet Extraction Technology System. Once granted, the inventor has the right to exclude anyone else from using, making a replica of, or selling the product to someone else for a certain period of time." He looked at Steve. "How's all this grabbing you?"

Steve replied, "I Googled all that."

"I figured you already knew everything I've said so far. Now I'm going to get into the nitty-gritty. Your invention calls for a utility patent because it addresses a mechanical product that provides a process that is useful; it's a more efficient method of getting oil out of a stripper well. The patent period is twenty years."

Item by item, Wallis traced his finger down the paper and onto succeeding pages. He had a wonderful, un-lawyerly ability to describe patents and associated legal matters in a manner that everyday Americans could understand. A lot like Tom.

Steve realized early on that he really had no need to take notes. Other than a word here and there, he followed the discourse perfectly. He finally interjected, "This is so straightforward that you ought to be disbarred."

Wallis returned a "tip of the hat" gesture and continued. "As for contesting the patent held by Wellington Oil and Exploration, we have a couple of avenues to go down." Wallis sat back in his chair. "Turn to the next page."

Steve responded as directed. He traced his index finger down the page, gathering in information as he speed-read the document.

"I see both avenues involving the concept of 'interference.' From what you have told me about the device and from what I surmised after looking at all of your documentation, Wellington has interfered with your rightful invention of the JETS." Wallis wetted his lips. "It appears that they have done it in one of two ways. First is that they plain stole the device and copied it. In doing so, they solicited the help of an unethical lawyer, in this case, Barrister. That is criminal conspiracy."

Steve looked back at Wallis. "That's certainly what I'd call it. We're trying to put things together, but it's been very complex and we've only been able to grab bits and pieces."

"Well, in order to contest them for criminal conduct you'd better have solid evidence that covers every base. If Wellington is guilty of stealing the JETS, they will have lawyers preparing to defend their patent."

Steve replied, "We're working on it. Sons of bitches."

Wallis added, "A second route we can take is that of 'priority.' Interestingly, the United States is one of only a few nations to decree the patentee must be the first to invent the product. In effect, if we can show that your brother and his partners actually had tested the device before Wellington, then that avenue can be pursued." Wallis's eyebrows lifted slightly. "Another thing for the good guys is that if we can show that your brother and his associates were diligent in taking the invention from concept to practice, and conceived of it before Wellington, they would have a strong case."

"Well, there's no doubt in my mind that the JETS is our invention and we are more than ready for a fight. And you're the boxer in our ring."

Wallis smiled. "Get set for round one."

Steve slid his chair back and stood up. He stretched and rotated his head back and forth, relieving a sore crick in his neck. The meeting had been more than successful. Steve believed there was a chance to overturn what had taken place. Wallis and Steve shook hands again and agreed to meet when Wallis was ready, subject to Steve's full calendar.

"I'll be in Port Aransas over the weekend and on Monday, but should be able to shake a couple of hours free later on next week. Just call me and we can set up a meeting. I'd like you to meet my uncle and see my dad again."

Wallis answered, "It'll be good to see your dad again and I look forward to meeting your uncle. I'll do some research and then all of us can have a meeting here to discuss where we're headed." He was upbeat and added, "Steve, it's difficult, but you're in the game for keeps."

Steve answered as he grasped the doorknob, "Yeah, we are. Many strange things going on. I don't know how much fun this will turn out to be, but it will be interesting to say the least."

"You're right."

Steve walked out into the bright sunlight and headed for his car.

Wallis called out, "Steve, one more thing. Although my first avenue of attack will be interference, let me have a synopsis of whatever criminal evidence you have."

"Will do."

Fifty-Four

Friday, June 25

Port Aransas, Texas

Tom followed the guide's directions and joined the third of four lines moving slowly across the ramp and into position on the Port Aransas Ferry. The temperature inside the car was as comfortable as could be; outside it was hotter than hell. Tom stopped the car as directed, lowered the windows, and turned off the ignition, as required by local authorities. The blast of hot air staggered Susie. The summertime backup of cars stretched behind them for well over a mile on Highway 361. While waiting for the short crossing to Port Aransas to begin, Tom played a quick mind game, calculating that the fifty-three minutes to cover their personal 1.2 mile backup resulted in an average of approximately 1.38 miles an hour. He reached inside the storage console and grabbed his calculator. He punched some buttons.

"Damn. My mind is beginning to fade."

Susie looked over at him, smiled, and asked, "How close were you on this one?" She was referring to the mathematical manifestations of an engineer's brain.

"I estimated 1.38 miles an hour when our average speed was really 1.35849 miles an hour. I'm getting rusty." He smiled back at her.

"Hey, Tom. Tom Seiler."

His car parked directly behind Tom and Susie, John Grant walked up to Tom's window just as the ferry's diesel engines began to whine. A high school friend of Don's, he was part of a small group that never missed joining the Seiler reunion and a chance to go fishing with Don, drink beer, and tell wild stories.

Tom looked up at a beet red face. "Hey, John. Small world. Have you seen your face? You look like the inside of a watermelon."

John laughed. "Linda and I walked the beach for an hour this morning and then we went to Harbor Shrimp in Aransas Pass. I forgot the sunscreen."

"You damn sure did. How're the shrimp?"

"Good as ever. We bought ten pounds for tonight. Hey, Susie."

Susie leaned over and answered, "Hi, John. The shrimp will go perfectly with the barbecue we brought."

"Great. Where'd you get it?"

"At the Gonzales Food Market. It's wonderful."

John answered, "I'll get my share of both." He glanced ahead to the ferry dock looming closer. "See you at the Dunes." John patted Tom's arm and headed back to his car.

The Dunes rises nine stories over the Port Aransas beach. The jetty sits 300 yards to the north; the Horace Caldwell Pier, with concrete piles and floor panels, juts 1200 feet due east and ends in a "T" over the Gulf of Mexico. From Beulah, Allen, and Ike, the pier had its share of hurricane damage and close calls, but this newer version appeared in great shape. Hurricane Ike knocked 1,300-pound floor panels loose, but the pier stood its ground. Unlike many beaches on the East Coast, cars are allowed on the beach, bonfires are seen in a long scattered pattern in the blackness of night, and as many people spend their nights camping in tents as there are relaxing in beach homes and resorts. For the campers the tradeoff is a paucity of bathroom facilities versus the mesmerizing sound of waves rolling onto the sandy beaches. The one real downside comes in the form of layer upon layer of seaweed.

"Welcome to the Dunes." Missy and Emma, two young, pretty, and very friendly receptionists, spoke in unison to the new guests.

Tom and Susie were the last to arrive for the reunion. "Good to be here. We're Tom and Susie Seiler." Tom moved to the reception counter. Through large paneled windows to his right he could see a large boomerang-shaped swimming pool. Sure enough, Paige and Ross were already lounging by the pool as young Grant, Caroline, and Holly frolicked in the water. Next to them, Bill and Renae Newton sunned themselves on heavy plastic lounge chairs.

Missy answered, "Ah yes, the Seiler reunion. The others have checked in. We have you booked in unit 603. Great view of the Gulf and the jetty."

Missy turned around and took a card from a desk. She offered it to Susie. "We thought you'd like a list of everyone's room. We put groups as close together as possible, but we couldn't get you all into a single area; we were, however, able to put you next to your daughter, Paige."

"Suits us fine." Susie looked at the list of names and units.

Tom added, "After four days we'll probably want to be as far from the noise as possible."

They laughed. Tom finished the registration and paid for their stay. Then they headed for their unit. Plenty of baggage carts eliminated tension over moving into individual suites.

In fifteen minutes Tom had brought the suitcases, bags, and barbecue from Gonzales into unit 603. Susie kept up with him bag for bag, including placing beer in the refrigerator, and had them ready to join the party five minutes after Tom's last load arrived. Susie also put the oven on at 200 degrees and placed the barbecue inside. The formal gathering was set for 6:30 p.m. on the second floor deck overlooking the pool.

Time to party.

The late afternoon sun, blazing through the cloudless sky, dropped behind the ninth floor of the Dunes, and a comfortable shadow made its way across the deck. The teenage kids rearranged deck chairs and tables so that the food would be concentrated nearest the building and the socializing would be done with a spectacular view of the water. Ross and Paige brought a large pan of barbecued chicken. Next to it sat a large bowl of boiled shrimp, courtesy of John and Linda Grant. A heavy additive of horseradish rendered the cocktail sauce original and potent. Nancy, with help from her son, two daughters, and five grandkids, arrived with a large pan of corn on the cob, hot and sopping with butter, and a huge pan of buttered noodles. Hot dogs, hamburgers, and chicken tenders would handle the younger kids. Occupying one-half of the table was Tom and Susie's cache of barbecue from the Gonzales Food Market. The aroma of brisket of beef, pork spare ribs, beef spare ribs, sausages, and pulled pork captured every appetite on the deck—and appetites of the uninvited people in the pool below. Three quarts of pinto beans, a gift of the Lopez family, owners of the Gonzales Food Market, and a huge salad rounded out the main meal. Brownies, peach cobbler, and two apple pies completed the menu—except for beverages. John Grant and his shrimp excluded, Don's other buddies, not one of them able to cook a thing, brought in eight cases of Miller Lite, ten bottles of Clos du Bois, and a ton of soft drinks for the kids. It took seven large ice chests to hold the bounty.

Groups of friends and family moved in and out of each other as people made the rounds from one conversation to another. With the exception of Nancy, a devout conservative, when a particular testosterone-laden group would start grousing over the political scene, the women would leave to form their own story session. From time to time Tom glanced around at the kids—it was uplifting to see the teenagers playing around with the younger children. Glow-in-the-dark sticks and bracelets of all colors danced and flew through the air at the whim of the playing youngsters.

The "party" part of the party lasted until eleven o'clock. Don's buddies promised to get up by 4:00 a.m. to take him fishing on the pier. At party's end each one of them was tucked away for a very short night. Finding teenagers to clean was more difficult since they had gone to Nancy's unit to watch television. Some of the women took tired youngsters to bed while the men and remaining women cleaned the area and replaced all chairs and tables to their intended locations. But the night was not over. It was time to play Texas Hold'em.

Paige, Ross, Kelly, Steve, Sally, and Nancy's only son, Tommy Charles, met in Ross and Kelly's unit for the first night's gambling affair. The largest cooler, filled with beer, sat on the floor not an arm's length from Tommy Charles. Nancy and Cindy, having no desire to play, settled down on the balcony porch beneath the outside light. They were content to drink wine while Nancy looked through Cindy's yearly photo album. Tom and Susie invited Bill and Renae to join them in 603.

Local house rules called for a two-dollar maximum bet and a one-dollar raise for each player each round. The intent was to keep the pots tolerable. Even violating the standard rules for doubling the ante each round, a big winner among the Seiler gamblers could walk away with a couple hundred dollars.

Ross was the first dealer. The pot started at a dollar for each player, known as the "compulsory" bet. For what's known as the "pre-flop" round Ross dealt two cards face down to each of the players. Sally looked slowly at her cards and struggled not to smile. The ace of clubs and the ace of spades looked back at her. Paige, to Ross's left, opened the betting with one dollar. No one folded and Sally raised the bet by an additional dollar. First game and the pot was already eighteen dollars. Ross buried the next card in the middle of the deck and then dealt a "flop" of three "community" cards face up in the center of the table. The community cards were to be used by each player to make the strongest hand possible. The initial community cards were the jack of diamonds, seven of hearts, and ace of hearts. Speaking of hearts, Sally's skipped a beat. Her hand held three aces. Paige looked down at a particularly weak hand and folded, as did Steve. Kelly bet a dollar, Sally raised the bet to two dollars, and both Tommy Charles and Ross covered the bets. The pot rose to twenty-six dollars. Another card was burned and the fourth card dealt. The king of diamonds was a good card for Tommy Charles. This time Kelly bet another dollar, Ross folded, Sally raised it to two dollars and Tommy Charles raised it another dollar. The pot hit thirty-five. The final card was the ace of diamonds. Kelly's hand did not improve but she unsuccessfully put on her version of a poker face and bet one dollar. Sally raised it by a dollar. Tommy Charles was stuck. He stared at a pair of aces, a pair of jacks, and a pair of kings. Only the higher two pair could help him. He thought, *Should I pour good money after bad?* The answer was yes, and he covered the bet. Another six dollars brought the evening's first game to forty-one dollars. It was showdown time. Not even close.

Sally proclaimed, "Get used to it, everyone. Tonight's my night." She raked in the stack of money, unable to keep the smirk off of her face.

Sally won six of the first nine hands. The others made the best of a tough situation by drinking most of the beer in the cooler. As they started the tenth hand of the night, Sally was the big winner with $262 and Steve was the big loser, down $98.

Cindy and Nancy enjoyed the waning evening breeze as Nancy made her way through the last of three albums. A picture on the next-to-last page caught Nancy's attention.

Nancy sat back and pointed her finger at the picture. She was baffled. "Where'd you get the picture of Vic Bolton?" She handed the album to Cindy and scooted her chair closer.

Cindy looked at the picture, trying to remember who the person was. "I don't know." She studied the photo. "It's a picture that Don took of a bunch of guys at his office." Then she vaguely remembered his stopping by the house with Don and Elam. "I think Don did some work for him. You may be right on his name. I think it was Vic, or Vince, something like that. But I don't know anything about him."

"That's Vic Bolton. I'm sure of it. I did his taxes."

Cindy was tired and couldn't grasp the significance of what Nancy was talking about.

Nancy, sharpened with a cynical edge and detective's nature, took the album back from Cindy and stared at it. She asked more of herself than of Cindy. "Why would he be at both places? This is unreal. I'm going to check with Don and Tom. Want to go?"

Cindy was too tired. "No, I'll finish the glass and then I'm going to bed. By the way, Don is asleep and is getting up before dawn. Can you check it out with Tom?"

"Yeah, sure." Nancy rose from her chair, tucked the album under her left arm, and, ignoring the bantering going on at the card table, walked out of the door.

"I've never seen him before. I can tell that the picture was taken in Don's office, probably by one of Don's draftsmen." Tom pushed his Broken Wing Ranch baseball cap to the back of his head, shrugged his shoulders, and added, "But, I don't know who he is." He glanced at the clock above Nancy's head. "It's late. I say let's wait until tomorrow morning and we can talk to Don when he gets back from fishing."

Tom looked down at Horace Caldwell Pier and the five men walking toward a white Honda Pilot. One of the men put the wheelchair into the back as the others piled in the passenger doors. The SUV made a U-turn and headed along the sand road toward the Dunes. Tom asked Susie to call the others as he headed for the first floor.

Ten minutes later Susie, Nancy, Ross, Paige, Steve, and Don sat in the living room of unit 603. The picture had been taken from the album and was being passed around. Each person studied the photo carefully before passing it on.

Don spoke first. "His name is Vince Bolduc. I know for sure because I did some simple design work for him. From New York and has a hell of an accent. I mean the guy is right off the block. He seems to be a good guy. After that party on Halloween night he came over to our house with Elam." Don cocked his head. "Yeah, it's Vince Bolduc."

Nancy shook her head sideways, saying, "No, Don, I don't

think so. The chances are that his real name is Vic Bolton. I did his taxes and had his W-2 forms and a couple of schedules. I have a copy of his tax return in my office." She tweaked her head and added, "Of course, everything could be counterfeit."

Tom pieced things together. Already standing, he said as he held the photograph in the air, "This shithead is party to all that's going on with the JETS. Vic Bolton and Vince Bolduc are too close in sound to be a coincidence. Tie that to his meeting both Don and Nancy and you have a con of some sort." He cleared his throat and continued. "I thought about it all night long. For some unknown reason, he's been spying on the family. Whatever the hell is going on with the JETS, he's part of it. And we need to know why."

Nancy looked at Don and added, "I'm calling Betsy Walker in San Antonio. She's my part-time secretary and helps with the simple returns at the high-water mark of tax season. She can pull the file and get his address." Nancy's eyes lit up. "I'm sure he comes from New York. I remember thinking it a little odd that he would give his tax business to me when he lived so far away. It happens, but it's rare. And I thought he had a thick accent too."

Don nodded in agreement. "I'll check him out as well. Given the time, I'll call on our way to the Thump."

"We need to clear the decks for action." Tom surveyed the group. "Let's plan a trip next week to New York for the men. It's time to meet Vinny or Vic."

Steve stood up. "Send me your open dates over the next two weeks and I'll come back with a booking. Nancy, if you can get me an address, I'll find the nearest airport." He sat down.

They vetted the emerging plan for ten minutes. The first order of business would be to obtain the address of Vince or Vic. A confrontation would take place, civil if at all possible, but if hostility were to be required, so be it. The basic questions were who hired him to spy on the Seilers and why. Nancy called Betsy Walker. No answer. Nancy left a message asking Betsy to get the address of Vic Bolton and leave a voicemail.

Enough for the time being. Don headed back to his unit for a nap. The others pursued varied activities prior to heading to Luling and the Annual Watermelon Thump.

Fifty-Five

Saturday, June 26

At the Watermelon Thump, Luling, Texas

Blistering, paint-peeling heat settled over the entire state. Beneath small puffs of scattered cotton clouds the temperature hovered at 103 degrees. But the heat failed to deter anyone from Luling's welcome. Revelers swarmed the town in droves. Most came from Texas, Arkansas, Louisiana, and Mississippi, and others represented many other states and several foreign countries. Tom could get no closer than Laurel Avenue and Austin Street without the certainty that he would get trapped by the record numbers of cars and people entering the middle of town.

"OK, folks," Tom barked. "This is it. Everybody out."

Don, Cindy, Jayme, and Susie clambered out of the car. Each carried a bottle of water. Tom and Don endured an almost out-and-out fight over whether the wheelchair would go as well. Don finally acquiesced to Tom's argument that it would not be fair to everyone else, especially if he wanted to stay late. Another agreement was made that the women, if they wanted, would head back to Port Aransas earlier than the men, catching a ride in Steve and Kelly's SUV with four hyper-fun children.

At Cindy's pleading, Don sat in the wheelchair, straddled its arms with his cane and, pointing upward to Jayme, announced, "OK, Jeeves, take me to the party." Jayme smiled broadly and pushed forward. The festivities were officially underway.

Don held up his hand. "Hold on just a minute." Everyone stopped. Don called his draftsman's cell phone in California. Fortunately, Mark answered and, after a brief conversation, told Don that he would head over to the office on Sunday to get an address for Vince Bolduc.

As for Tom, now several blocks away, he reckoned he hit the jackpot when a car pulled out of a perfect spot on Cottonwood Avenue. The street was home to small modest wooden homes, some with wood siding and some with vinyl. Less than two blocks to the northwest, no homes remained. They were gone, taken by 200-mile-per-hour winds. He braked the 1990 Buick Le Sabre, causing a grey Ford Mustang to slam on its brakes. He felt just a little sheepish as the Mustang gunned its motor in search of another parking place. Tom parked the car, got out, and surveyed his location. Probably close to a mile to the Thump. He put on his BWR cap and walked to the sounds of celebration. Tom looked forward to enjoying the festivities with his family and friends, but he also enjoyed the short respite of solitude offered by the long walk. As he loped along, the crowd morphed from virtually no one on Cottonwood Avenue to a wave of people laughing and joking along Davis Street. Cutoffs, Bermuda shorts, sneakers, baseball caps, Levi's, cowboy hats and boots, and an unending assortment of t-shirts were the dress of the day. I'm as old as I've ever been, Korea has Seoul, and many other printings evoked laughs and snide comments from all over the street. The champion t-shirts, however, were worn by a pregnant couple. Both t-shirts were bright red with white lettering; hers had an arrow pointing down to her ballooning belly with the words *Johnny Did It*– his simply stated in bold letters, *I'm Johnny.* The woman, no longer a spring chicken, seemed very happy with Johnny and her obvious uterine surprise. A unicycle rider, peering down from an eight-foot perch, tipped his hat to Tom as he rode by.

In a way the entire scene was surreal, but it didn't seem to bother the people. With the exception of Monte's and the new watermelon seed-spitting arena, nothing permanent remained along Davis Street from the site where City Market once stood all the way west to Mimosa Avenue. Most of the storm debris had been cleared from the town, a few piles of brick, lumber, and glass yet to be removed. A large tent with a sign reading *Luling Visitors Center* was packed with people buying t-shirts and Luling memorabilia from a pretty Latina woman named Margarita Flores. As for Monte's, it had undergone a facelift. Originally the city council was going to rebuild Davis Street in an orderly manner, including the destruction of Monte's. Terry Keane's impassioned argument that forty-five people had survived the storm using the bar as shelter and that therefore it was a historical landmark carried the day.

With the Watermelon Thump well underway, the area between Davis Street and the tracks serving the Southern Pacific Railroad was packed with people of all varieties. It was an eclectic mass of humanity.

"It'll take Tom a while to get here. Let's check it out." Don pointed to the nearest ticket booth and the ongoing carnival inside the temporary fencing.

Don paid the nominal fare for the group and an ink logo was stamped on the top of each person's hand so that they could exit and enter as they pleased. Inside the carnival area the ground was hard, making it very easy for Jayme to push the wheelchair. Regardless of age, every person felt kid-like.

Two separate pathways, with small booths on each side offering trinkets, games, or food, led to the amusement rides. Funnel cakes, Stromboli, cotton candy, hamburgers, hotdogs, pizza, Cajun delicacies, turkey drumsticks almost as big as an adult's leg, ice cream, sugared pecans, and any of a hundred other tasty tidbits were offered. Pop's jerky–"A Taste of Texas"–was doing an exceptional business, as were the vendors for Texas jewelry, t-shirts, and paintings. Beyond the food and trinket stands were numerous stands with invitations to join some sort of association, whether it be St. John's Catholic Church with the loved Father Jose Alcala and three friendly ladies manning the booth, the Caldwell County Republicans, the Caldwell County Democrats, the Luling Scouts, or the Caldwell County Texas Exes. A jovial man, hosting a full moustache and bushy sides underneath a huge balding head, spun the largest spools of cotton candy ever seen. Over the years, both in Luling and in many other towns throughout Texas, the man had garnered a reputation for giving large portions of the spun sugar and larger portions of optimism. As for the other food booths, the golden rule given to all vendors was clear–there would be no, absolutely no, rip-off-sized servings of any food. Luling was all for the capitalistic system, so long as the souvenirs would be sold at a fair price. Most folks waited until they were about to leave before buying souvenirs. By mid-afternoon, some families with small children were just beginning to start heading for home. The onslaught of buyers had started and some booths were stacked five deep.

"Hey, Thurman," Don yelled from the wheelchair to a man buried among paying customers.

The middle-aged man, in a cowboy shirt with pearl-buttoned pockets and jeans at least ten years old, looked around. Thurman Lairson owned Texas Metal Works, where any design for a wall decoration, almost always with a Texas theme, could be made and shipped. His works, mostly blue metal with powder coating, were well known throughout Texas. Locals and visitors alike besieged Thurman for something Texas.

"Down here." Don struggled and got up from the wheelchair. He pulled his navy Seabee cap off of his head and waved it and his cane over the heads of the crowd. No one minded Don's calling to an old, very busy friend.

Thurman saw Don and gave him a thumbs-up. "Hey, Don. Make sure you stop by later on."

"Will do. Save the Aggie symbol logo over there for me. We'll be back later tonight." Don pointed to a circular logo with the Texas Aggie star on it and *Gig 'em* machine-cut into the metal along the bottom arc. He sat down, licked at the big smile on his lips, and continued his commands: "Time for the auction."

Don's cell phone vibrated and rang. "This is Don Seiler." The noise made it nearly impossible to hear what was being said. Don could tell that his draftsman Mark was on the other end. "Yeah, hey, thanks, Mark. Listen, I can't hear anything because we're at the Thump here in Texas. Speak real loud and let me know if you can hear me." Don squeezed his left hand against his left ear and pushed the cell phone hard against his right ear. "OK, great. I need you to stop by the office and get the address of Vincent Bolduc. We designed a cantilever support system for him last year. He's the guy who came to our Halloween party. Also, get any other personal information that we have on him. Can you hear me?" Don squeezed some more. "What? Oh, OK. Great." He lifted his head and asked, "Who's got a pencil and paper?"

"Just a minute." Susie started browsing through her purse.

Don held his hand up, negating his request for pencil, and then returned to the phone. "Tell you what. Send the information to my brother, Tom. Have you got a pencil?" A split-second pause. "A pencil, have you got a pencil?" It took a few seconds for the discussion to continue.

"OK, Tom's email is t-s-e-i-l-e-r-3-9-8-@-hughes-dot-net." He paused again before answering. "It's 3-9-8." He did his "squeeze the ears" routine again before concluding the conversation. "I appreciate it. Thanks again. I'll drink a cold one or two for you. Yeah, you too. Take care." Don smiled as he closed the cell phone.

The girls and Don arrived at the open-sided, steel-framed building a few minutes before Tom. Large wooden picnic benches lined the sides of the building, and rows of folding metal chairs occupied the middle section facing the temporary stage. Dignitaries of note, meaning that they were the ones with the big money, milled around the first few rows of chairs. Representatives from 86 Oil Company, IBC Bank, Luling Chevrolet, ISI, and Progress Drilling laughed it up as they had done for years. There weren't many individuals who could let go of the amounts of cash that soon would be offered for a watermelon. Behind the stage and a stack of large speakers was a huge American flag. Partially blocking the flag, a banner proclaiming *2010–57th Annual Champion Melon Auction, Luling, Texas* hung from the ceiling. They found a bench no more than fifty feet from the stage with about five other people waiting for the auction. The crowd buildup was far larger than ever seen at the auction. The whole country seemed to be in Luling for the day. Don's wheelchair obstructed the passageway between benches and chairs a bit, but not enough to either cause a bottleneck or to warrant a command by an official staff member to move it. Susie, Cindy, and Jayme spread out as they sat down to make enough room for Tom.

"Look at that." Don pointed up to a huge, octagonal-bladed fan blowing cool air onto the crowd. Each blade must have been at least eight feet in length. The ladies looked up and saw a big fan; they just could not appreciate the mechanical genius that Don saw.

Tom arrived as the auctioneer was checking out the microphone. "Good seats. I could use a sit." Without fanfare, he placed five ice-cold beers, purchased at the nearest beer stand, on the bench.

Jayme, still holding half a bottle of water, was not a beer drinker. Rather than keep it in the family, she offered it to a man at the bench. "Would you like a cold beer? It would just be wasted on me."

"Yeah, sure. Why thank you, young lady." The man, probably in his late fifties, pulled the tab on the can and raised it toward Jayme. "Here's to you, ma'am."

The small gang of five bantered back and forth with all the people at their bench. A young Mexican couple, owners of a home destroyed on Hackberry Avenue, had expressed that they were just glad to be alive. They were living with relatives on the south side of the town. Another couple, having already helped with the cleanup of tiny Ogelsby, came from Weatherford, Texas to enjoy the Watermelon Thump and support Luling's rebirth. A young man, A. J., came down from Little Rock, Arkansas, hell-bent to get into the seed-spitting contest. This was his sixth trip to the Watermelon Thump and he had yet to hit the lottery to become a contestant.

"All right, ladies and gentlemen, let's get started with this year's champion melon auction." A white cowboy hat sat atop the auctioneer's head, and a plaid dark blue long-sleeve shirt, Levi's, and well-worn cowboy boots completed his ensemble. His thick leather belt with a silver emblem of Texas signified that he was as Texas as you could get. He continued to address the audience, the speakers booming through the huge crowd. "But first, let me just say to all of you who have come from all over the country," he turned a little teary-eyed but held his composure, "that we really appreciate what you have done for our town. From all we can tell, the attendance at the Thump is more'n double–that's right folks–double our previous high attendance." He pumped his fist into the air and the crowd roared. "I reckon this town will be as good as ever because of everyone's determination. We're a pretty friendly bunch, so consider yourselves family and make sure you come back whenever you can." He boomed, "Welcome to Luling, Texas!"

The place erupted again with hand clapping, whistling, and patting each other on the back.

Not all clapped, cheered, or smiled. A tall man leaned against a steel column about thirty feet away, studying the people at the bench. Behind him, standing on top of a concrete footing and holding onto a wide-flanged steel column, a second man surveyed the scene as well.

The auctioneer announced, "All right ladies and gentlemen, our first watermelon is this year's grand champion," and the auction began.

Halfway through the auction Don looked at his watch and quickly signaled to the others. "Time to make tracks. If we don't get there soon, we won't have a place to sit." Without waiting for the others, Don started wheeling his way toward the side of the open building. He stopped and yelled back to A. J. "A. J., join us. We're going to bring each other some luck."

A. J. gave Don two thumbs-up and joined them for the short walk to the official Watermelon Spitway.

Don made a wise decision. The crowd, still an hour away from the contest, was building rapidly. Hardly worth it in the long run, Don's MS temporarily made him somewhat of a celebrity, and other hopeful contestants moved him toward the entrance with his entourage. The spitway had been rebuilt in 2008 only to be destroyed in the tornado. Once nestled safely between two brick buildings, all that remained was the spitway itself. A temporary chain-link fence replaced the original wrought iron fence and the tan brick entranceway. It extended around what had once been the sides of the buildings. The fabric canopy used in years past replaced the destroyed roof. Many of the contest veterans did miss the murals of watermelons that had once adorned the building sides. As for the spitway, it had been mechanically buffed and repainted in white. Its slick surface and a possible strong tailwind might make a new world record possible. Possible, yes, but even with an aiding wind a spit in excess of 68 feet, 9 inches–the official Guinness world record–would be difficult to achieve. Optimism ran rampant.

"Hey, you back again, huh?" A tall, middle-aged man with a Fu Manchu moustache and a t-shirt reading *Does Not Play Well with Others* patted A. J. on the back.

A. J. smiled back at him. "Yeah, if I can only win the lottery to get into the damn contest."

"The reason you can't get in is because you're wearing a cowboy hat with those dumb-looking shoes." Mr. T-shirt pointed at a pair of black, lace-'em-up shoes.

A. J. scratched at his small goatee while searching for an answer. "Hey, my cowboy boots got stolen back in Arkansas. Besides, these shoes have magic power. Just watch me take everyone apart today. Shoes and all." Not a bad retort for someone wearing god-awful black shoes.

Past champions were automatically in the hunt. Everyone else had to sign a roster and roster numbers were picked at random. Some people hit the lottery year after year–others missed the lottery year after year. Skip and Joanie came from

Lake Charles, Louisiana, on motorcycle. In fifteen previous tries he had managed a third place in 2006. Don and the others laughed when Skip confessed that Joanie had taken a second place in her only competition. Justin, a local for all his life, won the contest in 2006 and was automatically in.

Tom said to the women, "OK, here's what we're going to do. Everyone has to sign up. It gives us more chances to enter the contest."

"No way. I'm not going to get out there and spit all over the place." Susie held her hands in front of her face, shaking her head back and forth.

"Aw, come on, Aunt Susie. We can do it." Jayme was having a great time and felt a refreshing surge of freedom sweep over her. "Tell you what. If your name gets picked and mine doesn't, I'll tell them I'm you."

"OK," Susie reluctantly responded with her authentic Dickinson accent. "But I'm not going up there. No way."

"Hey Tom, Susie, you sign up and we'll save some seats in the bleachers," Bill Newton, with Renae by his side, bellowed over the crowd.

Just then the call was made for would-be contestants to start signing up. Once a person had signed the roster, he or she would find a seat in the bleachers. Don was the first one to sign. He found a place next to the spitting line and wheeled next to the first row. The others filed in next to him. Including newfound friends, the Seiler party had grown to twenty people. Everyone liked Don and his family.

Justin, the former champion, explained, "You just curl your tongue around the seed and cut off all air around it. Keep your lips sealed. Then, when you're ready to fire away, use your body and slam it forward as you spit. Like this." He reached into his pants pocket and pulled out several watermelon seeds. He put one in his mouth. His lips puckered tightly. He reared back and then rapidly forward, exploding his breath—and the practice seed—toward the center of the spitway.

"Holy shit," Don exclaimed, "that seed went thirty feet at least." He shook his head.

Justin took another seed and offered it to the girls. "OK, your turn."

Timidly, all three declined. Deep down, they all hoped their names would not be called. Not so with the Seiler brothers. A contest is a challenge. A challenge is an opportunity.

Cindy, sitting next to Don on the second row of seats, shook Tom's shoulder and pointed. Sure enough, the Seilers were competitors. "Look over there. Nancy is over there signing up for the contest."

Nancy and Sally were at the official contestant table signing their names. Erin and Cristen Jane could be seen shaking their heads and laughing at their mother and grandmother. Bill Newton couldn't stand the thought of being a wimp; he got up and sauntered to the registration table.

"Nancy. Sally. Girls. We're over here," Susie called over the crowd.

In the noise of the crowd, Nancy could not hear them, so Tom sauntered over and grabbed them.

It was a very good day for the cohort of new friends. Don, Jayme, and A. J. were picked as contestants. Justin was already in.

Burt Kingston, the large-girthed master of ceremonies, took center stage. He did not specifically mention the tornado, but gave a sincere welcome to all who came to be part of Luling's future. He next introduced the pretty young Paige Weller, the Watermelon Thump Queen. Paige, in the spirit of the day, gave her best shot at seed spitting. Her effort was far better than those of previous queens. Had she been an official contestant, Paige would have been solidly in the middle of the pack. The crowd cheered lustily and she returned the greeting. Everyone was on "rock and roll."

As it turned out, Don was not the only contestant with a disability. At first he thought he was given some favoritism because of his MS. Not the case. The lottery had been fair and square. A young man with cerebral palsy joined in with the other forty-plus contenders. But the first man up was Don Seiler.

No way would Don compete from his wheelchair. He got up, tipped his Seabee hat to the crowd and, with help from his cane, walked to the starting line. The crowd gave him a standing ovation. At the spitting line, sitting on a table, was a watermelon. Don grabbed two seeds and moved to the head judge.

"Ladies and gentlemen, our first contestant is . . ." Burt held the microphone to Don's mouth.

"Don Seiler."

"Where's home, Don?"

"Ventura, California. But I'm a Texan."

The crowd cheered again.

"I see a military cap on your head. Are you a veteran?"

"I sure am, and I'm proud of it."

The crowd was made up of a lot of patriotic Americans. No small number had seen their share of hell–either in war or in the storm. Again they cheered and stamped their feet on the floorboards of the stands.

"All right, Don. You get two attempts. Are you ready?"

"Let's do it."

On Don's first attempt, he reared back and, as best he could, roared forward, expelling the seed into a high arc. He also lost his balance and stumbled over the line. He scratched.

"Folks. What do you say about giving Don another shot at it? We'll give him a Mulligan."

The crowd agreed vociferously. Don didn't.

"No, sir. Can't do that. I'm a contestant just like everybody else. That's it."

The crowd quieted some and the judge added, "OK, Don, no special treatment. I got it. Good luck on this try."

Don took the seed and placed it in his mouth. Lips tight and puckered. Head back. Thrust forward. Spit.

The seed left his mouth in a perfect arc. It sailed upward, forward, and eventually downward. Everyone watched it in slow motion. Upon impact, the seed took a friendly bounce and continued forward. A second bounce took it over a small joint line in the concrete and on to its final resting place. One judge held the end of an extended non-metallic tape measure to the spit line while another judge took the far end to the watermelon seed. He measured the distance.

"Thirty-eight feet, six inches."

The crowd went wild. First time ever and Don was in the running.

As for A. J., he had the most unorthodox form in the contest—feet pigeon-toed, arms outstretched like gangly wings, and ballooning cheeks—but his spit was fantastic. His spit was the longest of the day until the next-to-last spitter. The gods gave that contender a fortunate bounce that ended exactly one inch beyond A. J.'s mark. Life is not always fair.

When the dust settled it had been a very good day for the home team. A. J. won $150 for his second place finish. Don ended up fourth, barely out of the money but good enough for some serious bragging rights. Jayme had a spit of thirty-three feet. It turned out to be the best among women, but in this contest gender was not a factor. Still, all three had done very well. As for the young man with cerebral palsy, he spit the seed thirty feet, well ahead of most contestants. The throng of people, many patting Don on the shoulder, made its way out of the spitway and onto Davis Street and the carnival.

A winsome breeze, impeded only by trees, assorted debris piles, and people walking in all directions, danced along with the small caravan as it made its way to Luling Bar-B-Q. The temperature maxed out at 104 degrees and had finally begun its descent. Other family members already occupied three of the picnic benches lining a concrete block wall. Luling Bar-B-Q had been rebuilt a few years earlier after being torched by some idiot. The walls still appeared freshly painted in white. In addition to the picnic benches, booths with red padded seats lined the opposite wall. Small pictures were hung in a haphazard manner. A sign on the wall still remained from an earlier Thump proclaiming one of their former workers, young Amanda Collins, as the Watermelon Queen. This wasn't the first time the gang had eaten at Luling-Bar-B-Q and everyone knew the rules for popular hours. Grab a bench.

"Yo, ho. There they are. Over here." Ross got up from the nearest bench.

Paige kept her side of the bench lest the mob of patrons take it over. At the next bench sat Steve, Kelly, and to their pleasant surprise, Bill and Renae Newton. Seven youngsters, crawling all over the third bench, laughed at some funny thing that one of them was doing. Best of all, there was enough brisket of beef, sausage, ribs, potato salad, bread, and onions to feed a regiment of soldiers. A finicky eater could feast on either a succulent grilled steak or a thick cheeseburger. Finishing the layout were several cans of soft drinks and beer.

Everyone squeezed in and began the bad-mannered ritual of talking and eating at the same time. The food was too good not to devour and everyone wanted to talk to other family members. The Seiler family did deserve its own Guinness record for not bitching and moaning at relatives. Don grabbed Erin's hand and wheeled his way down to the kids' table. She squeezed in at the near end of the bench as three youngsters scooted nearer the wall.

Don leaned forward, eyeing the kids. "Hey, little people. What's so funny down here?"

The kids were giggling and pointing at Grant. Being the oldest male grandchild did not make him the most mature. He had a dab of mustard on his nose and a french-fried potato sticking out of each ear. All of a sudden the kids howled—along with most of the patrons in the restaurant.

"Don't corrupt our grandkids," Tom yelled at Don's back as everyone turned his attention to his younger brother.

Don turned around and, with his shoulders hunched up and palms of his hands facing the ceiling, looked quizzically at Tom. "You got a problem?" French fries stuck out of his nose.

The meal was as good as advertised. Don returned to the adults, leaving the kids to their harmless mischief. The topics of discussion centered on the watermelon auction and the watermelon seed-spitting contest.

"Damn, damn, damn. I missed winning $100 by inches. Little bitty tiny inches!" Don shook his head, then added, "but our A. J. won $150 for second place. That guy knows how to spit.

"But my little daughter was the top woman finisher," Don said, and he stretched from his wheelchair and put his arm around Jayme. He rocked her back and forth and continued, "A little luck and she'd be buying us dinner."

Jayme lowered her head in an attempt to not be the center of attention.

Cindy wanted to take attention away from Jayme, so she changed the subject. "Speaking of money, can you believe the amount they paid for watermelons? When they passed the $10,000 mark I thought I'd flip out."

"Not only that, most of the money goes to the person who grew it," Tom added. "Hell, I raised my kids and each one cost me a fortune."

Paige countered, "Face it, Dad, we're the best deal you ever had."

The conversation continued for a few more minutes until Tom, always on the clock, announced, "We need to give up these benches. Too many people waiting for a seat." He rose from the bench and called to the kids. "OK, monsters, everyone clean up your mess and make a trip to the bathroom."

Next on the youth activity list was a visit to the carnival midway.

"Paw-paw, Gram-maw, look up here." Little hands waved from fifty feet in the air.

The Ferris wheel seats belonged to the youngsters. Most of the children were still living in Fantasy Land. With the kids happily airborne and the grown-ups standing safely on the ground, life was indeed good. The descending sun painted the sky with orange in the west and bluebonnets in the east. Beautiful nights were common in Texas, but this particular night had virtually no comparison.

Next came rides on the merry-go-round. Multi-colored horses, bedecked with painted saddles and glittering reins, galloped up and down in repeating circles. Old-time melodies wafted from the organ, and mirrors surrounded with soft yellow light bulbs reflected happiness back to the riders. Three times was just right for the kids, and then it was off to the next amusement park challenge. The younger kids rode on small cars, boats, and a dragon-themed roller coaster. The older kids thrilled themselves on the Kamikaze with its two baskets moving in opposite directions at the end of long-armed counterweights, a spinning "zero-gravity" ride, and the haunted house with *Ghost Party* painted on the front.

To their credit, the youngest children hung tough until a little before ten o'clock. Then the wall caved in on them. Three-year-old Ellis started melting down when told that she had to use the Porta-Potty. The Porta-Potty had the same effect on sisters Sully and Graeme. Noland, barely a year old, called it a night on Kelly's shoulder an hour earlier.

Kelly announced that the evening was coming to an end. "This family has had its day. Time to go home. Does anyone need a ride?"

Similar announcements were made by others having children to take care of. The last ones standing were Tom, Don, Bill Newton, Susie, Cindy, and Jayme.

Tom offered an earlier escape to the women. "You ladies climb in with Steve and Kelly. Don, Bill, and I are off to Monte's. It'll be a while and it's a long drive home."

Susie felt a little reluctant but the same wall that hit the kids had taken a bead on her.

Cindy solved the problem. "Let's take the offer, Susie. Once Don starts telling stories with his crew there'll be no telling what time he'll leave. My guess is that he'll close the place down."

Susie, a little worry showing on her face, acquiesced with a caveat. "OK. But you've got to promise me that you will find a motel and spend the night if you get tired. Promise?"

"It's a promise."

At that moment Bill Newton added, "I'll be staying as well. I'll guarantee that we'll stop for the night if it's too late."

Susie trusted Bill and knew that he would come through for her. Her worries faded.

Everyone did their hugging and kissing good-byes.

Don suddenly remembered something. He asked Susie, "Susie, could you stop by the Texas Metal Works booth and pick up my Texas A&M logo from Thurman? I'll pay you back."

The thing about Susie is that she would walk over hot coals for a stranger. "Sure, Don. I'm headed there now."

Susie and her car group headed back to the merchandise area. Others headed for either their cars or, for the remaining men, Monte's Bar.

Fifty-Six

Saturday night,
June 26

Monte's Bar,
Luling, Texas

With the Ferris wheel spinning out giant circles in the sky, Tom, Don, and Bill crossed Davis Street through a throng of tired yet very happy people. Most were families headed to their cars with children hoisted on shoulders or held with their heads tucked in the crooks of parents' necks. Others were making their way toward the Watermelon Thump Main Stage, hoping to get there before Josh Abbott and his band cranked up the crowd with "She's Like Texas." Don got out of the wheelchair, making it clear that he wanted to walk, not ride, into his old stomping grounds. Bill closed the wheelchair like an accordion and carried it inside. The tornado had taken the original entrance and now a neon sign with *Monte's* scripted in red hung above the door. Tom entered first; music and smoke spilled out into the street. Monte's was packed three-deep at the bar. The old jukebox and Waylon Jennings tried their best to compete with the noise. Sweaty, body-to-body couples were packed on top of each other on the tiny dance floor. No such thing as the Texas Two-Step tonight. Maybe not even a Texas One-Step. Of course, no one cared; it was party time. The normal clientele intermingled with visitors from all over.

Just to the right of the entrance door, Felix stood up from a circular table tucked beneath a picture of a scantily clad blond smiling at the patrons. Beneath the perfect breasts encased in a white top, delightful buns outlined by Levi cutoffs, and a face as pretty as can be, was the logo *Perfectly Cut*. Truer words were never spoken—or written.

"Mr. Seiler, we're over here."

Don turned to his right and gave Felix a wave. Felix, Eduardo, and Wendell Akers had been sitting at the table for over an hour. They had invited two couples to join them until their boss arrived. One couple would forever remain anonymous; the other couple would remain half-anonymous. The female half looked like Maria Sharapova. Long blond hair, piercing eyes, perfect nose, and lips that called to every man's testosterone made her appear almost sculptured. The upper third of her left arm was adorned with a tattoo of Texas. She was the ultimate piece of work.

"Hi, boys," she smiled and waved seductively to the new arrivals. "Bye, boys." She rubbed her hands over Felix's head, gave an open-hand wave, and sauntered off to the dance floor.

Bill put the wheelchair against the paneled wall between their table and that of three couples playing a dangerous game of darts and with whom Felix, Eduardo, Wendell, and the two temporary couples shared many laughs since the early part of the night.

Alan, a bespectacled, lanky, friendly native of Luling, smoked like a chimney while enjoying his beer and laughing at the lack of quality of the other dart throwers. Pat, a blond with a Monte's T-shirt on, had just lofted her dart almost a foot above the dartboard. Their friends Eddie, Kristi, Tom, and

Penny howled at her lack of skill. Given the lack of accuracy and the massive crowd, Debbie Keane came over from the bar and gently persuaded Pat to relinquish the darts lest there be a fatality in the making. Wise decision. As for the knockout leaving their table, Don pointed toward her and asked, "How can you let something like that walk out on us?"

Wendell Akers answered, "'cause we're out of our minds. But we still got little Sally Mae." He pointed to the poster above his head with Miss Blond Bombshell on it.

"Eduardo, put this over there if you would." Don gave his cane to Eduardo.

Up popped the waitress.

"These must be the ones we're expecting. Welcome to Monte's. A round of Miller Lites on the way." Annabeth, much smaller but in her own way just as pretty as Maria, grabbed some empty bottles and headed down the row of tables to the bar. She was back in a flash.

Don looked around the packed insides of Monte's. He asked Annabeth, "Where's the dentist?"

"In the back getting more beer out of the freezer. I'll tell him you're here." She was gone in a flash.

Wendell asked, "Why do you call him 'the dentist'?"

"Shee-it." Don had been an eyewitness to the whole thing. "A couple of years ago we were in here drinking beer and shooting the bull. While telling wild stories, Terry told one about his extracting a molar from his own mother. I can't even imagine doing that to my mother. Damn." Don knew he had the table's attention and continued. "The next day, and I was there, a crew was working on the railroad tracks across the street. The crew chief had been in Monte's when Terry told his story so he brings this poor guy in with the side of his jaw looking like a grapefruit. Terry took it in stride and took the guy into the bathroom. With a small towel, a glass of whiskey to swish away the blood and pain, and a pair of pliers, Terry pulled the tooth. Blood everywhere." Don visualized the incident and started laughing. "About five hours later the worker comes in and looks terrific. He says to Terry, 'Damn if you ain't the best dentist in the whole world. Give me your business card.'" Everyone at the table laughed and guffawed. The story was the perfect catalyst to loosen inhibitions. It was followed by the story of Terry cutting off another patron's finger that had been ripped to shreds in a lathe.

Over the next hour everyone got to know each other, and the table discussion was relaxed and often funny. Don, a couple of beers beyond his ration, broke silence on an unasked question. There had to be a story behind it. He leaned toward the center of the table and took aim at Wendell Akers.

"Wendell. Now don't take this the wrong way, but the time has come to satisfy my wild curiosity." He sort of pointed his beer bottle in Wendell's direction.

Wendell leaned forward as well and cocked his head so he could hear over the din of the crowd.

Don continued, the boyish grin not much different than it had been a half century before, "Why in the hell do you dress the way you do?"

The others looked at the Hawaiian shirt that was six thousand miles out of place in Monte's. Everyone laughed wildly. The moment of truth was upon them. Would Wendell take it in stride or slug the man with MS?

He false-chuckled and, same as the others, leaned toward the table center. "Well, I'll be damned. Someone finally had the gonads to ask me." He gazed around the table, adding, "And you wusses have wondered that since I first walked on site."

Wendell was more than happy to address the subject of his attire. "Damn right, there's a story behind what I wear. First of all, I can wear anything I damn well please. Not a soul's gonna tell me what to wear, except maybe my ma." Wendell pointed toward the bar where Terry Keane was doing double duty as a bartender. "Look at him. He's wearing a shirt that none of you would ever wear. That's 'cause he likes the damn shirt and he has the balls to wear anything he wants. He's a man."

Sure enough, Terry was easy to spot in his mottled black-and-white shirt. If Waldo of *Where's Waldo?* fame had a similar shirt, he would have been very easy to find.

Everyone nodded in agreement.

Wendell continued, "I was born and raised on a ranch outside of Idabel, Oklahoma. All my life I was a cowboy. I mean, a real cowboy. I worked my ass off. Didn't play sports in high school because I was working every minute on my father's ranch. At eighteen I competed in my first rodeo. I wore nothing but cowboy shirts, Levi's, cowboy boots, a cowboy belt, and a big fucking cowboy hat. I could throw a rope and take a dally as well as any man in Oklahoma or Texas. None better. It was cowboy, cowboy, cowboy. But I didn't want to be a cowboy. I wanted to make millions. So far that hasn't happened, but it will." He grinned and leaned back. "And, once I do, I'll still wear whatever I want to."

Wendell put the trimmings on his story, telling of the unexpected pregnancy of his girlfriend, how much her father hated him, and the fact that they and their black Lab named Happy would do just fine in the long run. "Yep, she was born into big money and I'll be damned if I'm going to ask for one penny from her nasty old son-of-a-bitch father."

Bill Newton interjected, "You're a helluva man, Wendell. Here's to you."

Bill raised his beer. The others hoisted bottles in proud allegiance to the only man in Texas who wore Hawaiian shirts and sneakers to an oilrig. But there still remained a final unspoken question—a question none of them, not even Don, had the courage to ask: *Why do you wear those Wrangler jeans so high that your pecker and balls stick out?*

"Listen to that." Wendell held his finger up to his ear as he rotated in the direction of the jukebox.

Don asked, "Listen to what?" Hearing anything was almost impossible given the raucous behavior of most of the people in Monte's.

"That. It's Waylon Jennings and Willie Nelson singing 'Mammas Don't Let Your Babies Grow Up to Be Cowboys'. See, even them guys are telling me not to be a cowboy. They're two smart hombres and I ain't going to be a cowboy."

Throughout the night, Don's mental state switched back and forth between the hell-raising going on with his brother, whom he respected above all other men, a very good friend who had risked his career to solve a deadly mystery involving Tom, and three loyal, damn hard-working roustabouts, and the burdening sensation that his life was folding in on top of him. Don could have been very comfortable with his engineering firm. But he chose to take a risk that, if successful, would make life much better for him, Cindy, and Jayme, and at the same time make life better for every stripper well owner in this country or around the world. His eyes seemed to focus in on speaker after speaker as his tablemates laughed at off-the-wall stories, but all the revelry going on around him couldn't diminish the thought of the hell he had put his family and brother through, and what the future held for the other three men at the table. He spied the petite waitress.

"Annabeth. Fill 'em up again."

Annabeth came up to the table and held a small canvas bag in front of her. "You guys need to fill this up."

All the empty bottles were gone in a couple of seconds and replaced two minutes later with the new round of beer. The activity helped Don to switch back to a happier mood. He decided not to talk at all about the loss of the patent. Now was the time to party.

The jukebox did its duty as best it could but Saturday night at the Luling Watermelon Thump was coming to an end. One couple remained entangled on the dance floor and a couple of newcomers came in for a last beer. Terry and Debbie Keane stopped by a few minutes earlier and gave the table a round of beer on the house. The laughter had been raucous but the group behaved well all night long.

Tom asked how many patrons Terry had to throw out of Monte's. Terry answered matter-of-factly, "The body count came to an even dozen."

Tom responded, "Given the numbers, sounds like all went well." He glanced first at his watch and then at Don and the others. "Guys, it's been great but we have a long trip ahead of us and it's time to bring this year's Thump to a close."

No one objected.

Tom added, "Bill, you get to ride shotgun."

Bill Newton nodded, "I'll take you up on it. And if you get tired, I'll be glad to drive."

"Agreed."

Tom, Don, and Bill split the tab. Once each ponied up a 25-percent tip, Tom gave the money to Annabeth. No one noticed that he added a nice crisp hundred-dollar bill on top. Annabeth eyed Ben Franklin looking pleasantly in her direction and broke into a huge grin.

"You have made my day. My feet aren't nearly as tired as they were ten seconds ago. I really appreciate it."

"Annabeth, you worked yourself to the bone making sure we were happy and well stocked. So I appreciate you as well.

We'll see you in the future."

"You're welcome anytime. Have a great night." With a skip in her step, Annabeth headed off toward the table of new arrivals.

Outside of Monte's the group shook hands firmly and moved in opposite directions. Felix, Eduardo, and Wendell headed west down Davis Street as a group. Tom, Don, and Bill headed east.

One by one, the carnival lights were put to sleep for the night. Most of the vendors had closed up shop in hopes of getting a decent night's sleep before Sunday's finale. A diminishing glare came over the men's shoulders as they walked east on Davis Street. Tom, pushing Don in the wheelchair, guided them past the darkened Luling Bar-B-Q and the Stanley Antique Store. He took a left on Oak Avenue and then a right on Fannin Street. Most of the Thump celebrants went south on Oak to find their cars. At each subsequent turn, the number of fellow travelers dwindled. At Elm Avenue it was a trickle; crossing Beech Street they were, with the exception of a couple of men walking separately almost a block behind them, alone.

"What'd you do, go for the last space in Luling?" Don's comment was meant in jest but it accentuated the fact that Tom had parked a long, long way from the midway.

"Next street should be Cottonwood." Tom was dead tired and dreaded the ride home. "If I had a lick of sense, I would have walked to the car on my own and come back to get you. That's the price for being tired."

Homes along Cottonwood Avenue and down Cummings Street and Armstrong Avenue were barely discernable in the inky blackness. One light, powered by a gasoline generator, was visible at the beginning of Cottonwood Avenue. The streetlights were physically in place but power restoration for the entire northern grid was two weeks away. Except for the sounds of a few pebbles caught beneath the wheelchair and the muffled sounds of sneakers on asphalt, it was as quiet as it was dark.

"There she is."

Sure enough, the reliable Buick and one other car were all that remained on Cottonwood Avenue.

Don spoke. "Stop at the trunk and I'll get out there." He reached down to pull up the footrests.

"Tom, I'll take it." Bill offered to put the wheelchair in the trunk.

Don stood up and, with the help of his cane, walked shakily to the door and climbed into the back seat. He closed the door, addicted to thoughts of stretching out and sleeping for the next ten hours. Tom went to the driver's side of the car in search of the trunk release just below the seat. He pulled the release and got into the car, closing the door and extinguishing the overhead light.

Bill, holding the wheelchair easily in his grasp, bent over and started to place it into the trunk. It was pitch black and Bill didn't see a thing. Suddenly he felt cold steel pressing against the back of his neck.

"Don't say a word." A deep but nearly gentle voice from a man equally as large as Bill gave instructions. "Put it in the trunk gently. Then step around to the side of the car and don't say a word."

Bill did exactly as instructed.

The man spoke quietly, in total control. "Now lie down and put your hands in your back pockets. Move them and I will kill you."

Tom and Don were tired and did not notice anything at all. Bill did as ordered.

Tom was inserting the keys into the ignition system when

the man opened the passenger door and put a Glock 34 9mm pistol, with an attached AAC Evolution suppressor, directly into Tom's face. Tom was frozen in place.

"Don't move one fucking inch." The man took a small ball-peen hammer from his shirt pocket and smashed the overhead lights. What little light there had been was now extinguished. Total darkness engulfed the car. "I want you to get out of the car, come around to this side, and lie down next to your friend. If you even think of running, I'll kill Mister Wheelchair." The man turned to the backseat and pointed the gun in Don's face, speaking again. "You in the back. If you move I'll kill your friend up here. Once he's on the ground you will get out and lie down next to your friends."

Don was the only one who had a clear enough view to see that the intruder had a silencer attached to the pistol. Don thought, *Not a street thug; he's professional.* He had no means of fighting him off. Don had precious little time to thwart what was happening but his mind started searching for solutions. He answered meekly, "OK, just know that it's difficult for me to move."

"If you do anything other than what I tell you, I will kill all three of you." He spoke again to Tom. "Driver, get out now."

Tom took the keys out of the ignition, hoping somehow that they might serve as a weapon, and slowly walked around the front of the car. He wanted to charge the man but, with the gun squarely in Don's face, did as he was told and assumed the prone position next to Bill.

"Both of you, take your wallet out of your back pocket, place it arm's length in front of your head, then put your hands in your back pockets." Bartok waited while Tom and Bill did exactly as told.

Tom and Bill were side by side, hands in back pockets.

Neither had any option except to hope it was a simple armed robbery. Both Tom and Bill were relieved that the man wanted their wallets. They might make it out alive after all.

Don knew different.

A dog started barking a few houses away on Armstrong Avenue.

The man opened the back door. "OK, cripple. Get out and lie down."

Even in the situation Don didn't appreciate the title "cripple." He struggled to get up. Once his upper torso was vertical he moved toward the edge of the seat using his cane to gain stability. He started to stand up.

Suddenly Don lunged forward, swinging the cane at the man and screaming, "Run!"

A perfect strike. The cane hit the man in the throat. But the man was large and agile.

Pop. Pop. Two shots rang out. The first bullet hit Don in the left shoulder, taking out muscle and a small shard of his clavicle. The second bullet hit Bill Newton in the back. Bartok easily rolled the pistol toward Tom.

Another shot rang out. This time the sound was different. The bullet slammed into Bartok, piercing his side and entering his chest cavity. Staggered, he instinctively turned and tried to roll away. He saw the flash of a second bullet. The new bullet hit him in the leg, but it did not keep him from firing at the flash. The figure in the dark dropped like a rock to the ground and curled up into the fetal position. Don, working solely on adrenaline, didn't feel any pain at all. He staggered to the wounded assailant. The man was trying to get up, still having the pistol in his grasp. Tom looked up and, for the second time in his life, knew he had to charge into the line of fire. Bill Newton didn't move. Don stepped on something and fell down, almost face-to-face with the killer. Feeling around on the ground he realized that the something was his cane. He grabbed it by the tip end and made a powerful swing. The reel portion slammed into the killer's face, breaking his nose and splitting his left cheek. Blood poured from his nose. *Thwap!* The killer recoiled in a series of jerks. *Thwap!* Then again: *Thwap!*

Someone grabbed Don. He tried to turn his cane on the new assailant.

"Don. Stop! Stop! You'll kill him." Tom let go of Don's arm and moved past him. He kicked the pistol out of the man's hand.

"Get out of my way. The son of a bitch was going to kill us." Don had another clear shot at the man's head and hit him again. The man was motionless.

Don almost fought Tom off for another hit.

Tom pushed his own brother down. "Damn it, Don, the man's down. So is Bill."

Don awoke from a nightmare. He looked in the direction of Bill Newton. Another nightmare.

From fenced yards or inside homes, dogs barked up and down the street. They wanted in on the action. A couple of generator-powered house lights went on. Two men from adjacent homes crept outside to see what was happening. One had a pistol and the other had a hammer.

The unknown man rolled over on his back and looked silently into the night sky, his breathing labored. Unknown to Tom and Don, the second bullet to hit their assailant had severed his femoral artery.

Tom picked up the gun and gave it to Don. "If he does anything, either hit him or shoot. I've got to get to Bill."

"What's going on over there?" A large man called from his yard, his pistol at the ready.

Tom yelled at him, "Call the police. We've been attacked.

Call 911. We've been shot."

Both men rushed back into their homes. A few lights flicked on from the south side of the railroad tracks where the power grid was intact. Little did Tom know that the word "we've" was correct. Don, grasping for breath, felt an increasing throb in his right shoulder. He tried moving it up and down, only to be hit by a withering stab of pain.

Tom knelt down next to Bill Newton's head. "How you doing, Bill?"

"I'm hurt, Tom. Can't move my legs. I'm hurt bad."

With the lights coming on all over, Tom was able to see blood all over Bill's shirt. He pulled Bill's shirt away and saw a hole just right of center at the lower end of Bill's spine. Then he noticed blood beginning to pool beneath Bill's body.

Tom knew he shouldn't move Bill, but he didn't want him to bleed to death. He ran to his car and grabbed a face towel from behind the front seat. He wadded it into a sausage roll. As gently as possible, Tom moved the rolled towel underneath Bill's lower abdomen. He hoped the pressure would slow the bleeding. He looked at his friend. *Where's the ambulance?*

He yelled, "Please people, get an ambulance. My friend has been shot."

Tom looked around to see if anyone was coming to help. He was astonished by what he saw. Ten feet away a man lay moaning next to a Ford Mustang. *Who is he?* Tom got off his knees and made his way to the unidentified third party. The man remained in the fetal position, obviously in intense pain.

Tom kneeled and asked, "Can you hear me?"

The man moaned again, then grasped Tom's hand. "Mr. Seiler, I'm Carlos. Talk to my sister. Angelina Esco . . . The man killed my friends. . . and now he killed me. I saw him follow you . . ." Carlos struggled to talk, his words spaced by time. He tilted his head toward Tom. "He . . . follow to kill you and Mr.

Seiler. I'm sorry." His speech was hard to understand. Blood spewed from his mouth, weaving into small rivulets through his beard, and spilled on the ground. "I want to go home." He looked up at Tom. His eyes didn't close. He was dead.

Tom was confused. He placed his other hand over Carlos's hand and looked into the dead face. Then he put it down gently, got up, and walked over to Don, Bill, and the assailant.

Bartok rolled his eyes in Tom's direction. A small grin, unseen in the darkness, crossed his face. "Had a good time. Miles . . ." For the second time in less than two minutes, a man's eyes glazed over in death.

Sirens wailed in the distance.

Fifty-Seven

Sunday Early Morning, June 27

Luling, Texas

The Bell 430 sounded like Emeril chopping celery on a cutting board. It dropped out of the sky onto the small helicopter pad adjacent to the emergency room of the Edgar B. Davis Hospital. While a physician's assistant and two nurses prepped Don for surgery, a frenzy of activity took place in the adjacent room. Bill Newton's injuries were critical and his situation called for the bulk of the medical resources. The bullet struck his lumbar-5 vertebra, severing the spinal cord. It continued through his lower intestine and exited through his right pelvis. While waiting on the San Antonio AirLIFE helicopter, a single trauma doctor, another physician's assistant, and four nurses frantically worked to stabilize Bill. Both entrance and exit wounds had been opened and cleaned as best as could be done in the time allotted. Nothing had been done to remove bone fragments and the degree of damage to his lower intestine was unknown. The surgeon made the call that it was better to get him on the helicopter immediately rather than to open Bill up. Bill lay unconscious and intubated on the gurney. A split second after touching down, the EMS crew, working with Old Guard precision, transferred Bill to the helicopter stretcher and began hooking him up to a vast network of life support apparatus. A minute later the whine of the helicopter blades increased and the air ambulance rose into the hot, clear night sky. The helicopter, at its maximum cruise speed of 139 knots, delivered Bill to University Hospital in San Antonio in less than thirty minutes. Every second was critical.

Tom watched the departing helicopter for a short while. He was gravely concerned about Bill's condition, yet his observation of the helicopter was more his natural curiosity of flying machines than the person inside the machine. Then it dawned on him—his brother was injured. He ran back to the small hospital.

Don was conscious, though lightly sedated, and talking to the ceiling as the medical team hovered over him.

"That no-good son of a bitch. If my brother hadn't stopped me, I'd 'a killed him myself. Sorry son of a bitch. Ooooh, damn, that hurts." He wasn't quite with it, but he had enough sensation to know when something was stuck into his shoulder. "Do that again and I'll take my cane to you. Just kidding." A little bravado didn't hurt.

Tom accompanied Don for the short trip to the operating room.

Don looked up at Tom and exclaimed. "We got that son of a bitch, didn't we?"

Tom nodded. "We got him. Good luck. I'll see you soon."

Tom returned to the emergency room and started making calls. He called Susie first.

Susie, still groggy, expected a call in which Tom would tell her that Tom, Don, and Bill were staying in the Luling area.

"Hi honey. Where're you staying?"

"Susie, you need to wake up. We have a problem." He waited a few seconds to allow her to comprehend what he was about to say. His urgent voice tore Susie from her sleep.

"What happened?" Susie was wide awake. "Where are you?"

Tom answered slowly, quietly, his words measured. "First, everyone is alive and being taken care of, but we were attacked tonight after the Thump. Both Don and Bill have been shot. I'm at the Luling Hospital with Don. Bill Newton was flown to San Antonio. I don't know his condition, but he is in bad shape. Don was awake and talking to the doctors. He's in surgery for a wound to his left shoulder."

"Oh my God. My God." Susie's head was spinning. Something inside her felt safer with Tom on the other end of the discussion.

"Susie, I think it would be best for you not to wake anyone except Renae and Cindy right now. I'm going to call Nancy when I hang up. Renae's in 706. I don't have enough information and you're the only one who can do anything right now." He paused. "Once she's awake, the two of you can call me. You can drive her to San Antonio in her own car. I'll meet both of you at the University Health System Trauma Center. I'll ask Nancy to stop in your unit and give her house keys to Renae. While you and Renae head to San Antonio, Nancy can take Cindy to Luling. After we link up and everything is stabilized in San Antonio you and I can head to Luling to see Don, Cindy, and Nancy. Got a pencil?"

Susie found a ballpoint pen and a guest notepad. "Got it. I'm ready."

"The address is 4502 Medical Drive in San Antonio. You'll have to use the car's GPS. If I remember correctly, the hospital is off of Wurzbach Road."

"I will," she said as she wrote down the address of the trauma center. "I'm going down to Renae's in five minutes. We'll call you."

They hung up.

Tom tried his best to make sense of all that had happened. It broke down into two themes. His immediate attention needed to focus on the injuries of Don and Bill. Later he could dig into why the shooting had taken place. However, his sketchy memory of the original shooting and of Carlos's final words demanded that he spend a few minutes jotting down notes describing all that had happened. He sat down and pulled out his small notepad. But he couldn't remember everything. *Damn, I can't remember Carlos's sister's name.*

Tom called Nancy three minutes later.

"I understand. I'm going to Renae's unit first to give her the house keys. Then I'll wake Cindy and get ready for the trip to Luling." Nancy understood what needed to be done; she was calm—dead serious, but calm.

"Good. I need to hang up for now so Renae can call me." Tom was urgent to hear from Renae.

"Give me a call later on. We'll be on the road in thirty minutes. Good luck, Tom." Nancy hung up.

Tom sat down on a small plastic chair, racking his brain over the name of Carlos's sister. No luck. Ten minutes later his cell phone rang. "This is Tom."

Renae spoke quietly. She had taken enough time to gain some control of her emotions. Still, her speech was halting. "Hi, Tom."

Tom got right to the point. "Bill is alive but he's been hurt. He was shot last night in what may have been a robbery attempt."

Renae did not reply for a moment. Finally she said, "Tom, if he's not dead, I can handle it. Please tell me everything."

Tom answered quickly. "I don't know the extent of his injuries, but I do know he was shot in the back. Don was also shot, but his wounds are not as severe.

"Susie will drive you to San Antonio in your car. Nancy will be down to your room in a couple of minutes to give you her house keys and San Antonio address. You'll be staying with her while Bill gets stabilized."

"Tom, there's no need to have Susie drive me. I am fine. I have the GPS and can make it there with no trouble."

"Please, let Susie take you. I need to have her here anyway and it will save us an extra car ride to Port Aransas."

"OK, Tom, I'll see you in San Antonio. Will you be at this phone number?"

"Yes. It's my cell phone."

"OK. Thank you, Tom. Bye."

"Bye." Tom looked down at the phone and visualized the woman he had been speaking to. Then he thought of the man who had held them up. Then he thought of his own brother. *If only Don hadn't jumped the guy. Let him take the damn wallets and go. Don jumped him . . .*

Renae closed her cell phone and cried.

Don spent two hours in surgery as the medical personnel worked at removing tiny bone shards that had scattered like birdshot throughout his shoulder region. Don's clavicle did not suffer a complete break. The surgeon went over the surgery, noting that Don would hurt for a while but that he was remarkably tough given his medical history. Don, deep in sleep, was wheeled into a small recovery room next to the operating room at exactly 7:00 a.m. Tom had to leave in order to get to San Antonio within the next hour. He wrote a note:

Don,

Hope you enjoyed your nap. I'm off to San Antonio to see
Bill Newton. I'll see you this afternoon. Nancy's bringing
Cindy. I'll give you an update. Hang tough–

Tom

He gave the note to a nurse who promised she would have the note passed on to Don when he woke up. Tom walked out of the hospital and went directly to the police station. He spoke briefly with the on-duty officer and wrote a statement. The officer, Willie Pedersen, with approval from the chief of police, allowed Tom to leave for San Antonio to see his critically wounded friend. Tom agreed to return on Monday morning. Outside the police station, the risen sun greeted Tom and the daily baking started. Tom sat down in the driver's seat and leaned back. He had never been so tired. He closed his eyes and fell asleep.

The billowing heat woke Tom with a start. "Oh, damn." He looked down at his watch. He had been asleep almost forty-five minutes. He shook his head, yawned widely, and started the car. He was on I-10 in five minutes.

En route to San Antonio Tom violated both of his cardinal rules of the road. He drove almost ten miles an hour over the speed limit and he talked on his cell phone without it being harnessed. Nancy called and told him she and Cindy were going through Sinton on the way to Luling. Susie called from Pleasanton; she and Renae were about an hour away. He pulled into the Trauma Center parking lot minutes before the women and went directly to the reception counter. He obtained a visitor's pass and information for directions to the trauma facilities.

"Tom!" Susie called as they approached the counter.

Renae grabbed on to Tom and cried. "Thank you, thank you." Tom held her firmly as she sobbed into his dirty shirt.

Unfortunately, Tom knew nothing of Bill's condition. "Here, let me get passes for both of you." He led Susie and Renae to the receptionist who made the process as painless as possible.

They hurried toward the B elevator suite as Tom passed on the little information he did have. "Bill is on the second floor in the trauma surgery area. That's all I know."

The elevator was much too slow for Renae, even for a ride to the second floor. She held both Tom's and Susie's hands and stared at the digital number changing ever so slowly from a *1* to a *2*. The doors opened and they walked quickly to the nurses' station.

The nurse on duty was as polite as could be. "He's been stabilized and is still in surgery. His wound is very severe and he will be in surgery for probably another two to three hours. His surgeon is Dr. Deshmukh. I'll let him know you are here. Once the operation is complete he will let you know what to expect." She smiled gently at Renae. "He is a superb neurosurgeon. There is a phone in the waiting room and a surgical nurse will call once or twice to give you an update. They already know you are here."

The nurse gave directions to the cafeteria and the waiting room. No one felt like eating but a hot cup of coffee seemed to fit the bill. Tom demanded that he get the coffee so that the women could head to the waiting room. They all wanted to make sure that someone was available to speak with Dr. Deshmukh whenever he might stop by.

Don's eyes fluttered. He strained to open them, then gave up and fell back asleep. Nancy and Cindy sat in small chairs brought in by a nurse's assistant. They waited.

Dr. Vijay Deshmukh entered the waiting room. A muscular man, probably in his late thirties, of medium height with dark skin, coal-black eyes, and black hair with the first vestiges of grey gave a reassuring, youthful smile toward Susie and Renae. For a surgeon who had just finished a sixteen-hour day his energy seemed remarkable.

"Mrs. Newton?" He wasn't quite sure which of the women was Bill's wife, although his intuition pointed toward Renae. "I'm Vijay Deshmukh." No formal title.

Renae responded as the three visitors rose from their seats, "I'm Renae Newton. Thank you so much."

Dr. Deshmukh, gesturing for them to sit down again, spoke. "Please have a seat. It will take me a few minutes to describe what his injuries are and the prognosis for his recovery. Most importantly though, his chances of survival are quite good."

His "survival" comment was all Renae needed to know. She could handle anything else. Her whole body relaxed–but only momentarily. She sat back up and grabbed the hands of her close friends.

Dr. Vijay Deshmukh, still in his surgical scrubs, pulled up a chair and sat down facing the three of them. His eyes, intense beneath the furrowed forehead and downward-turning eyebrows, gave a preview of what he was about to say.

"Your husband has a very serious gunshot wound. It was a single high-velocity bullet that entered at the lumbar-5 vertebra, destroying it and severing his spinal cord." Dr. Deshmukh's voice trailed off just a bit. "He won't have use of his legs. I'm sorry."

Renae squeezed her friends' hands with superhuman strength.

Dr. Deshmukh resumed his comments. "The bullet exited through the pelvis. Fortunately," Dr. Deshmukh turned to Tom, "his loss of blood was tempered at the shooting site with a makeshift compress. Did you do that?"

Susie and Renae looked at Tom. He answered matter-of-factly, "I did what I could."

Dr. Deshmukh remarked, "You saved his life." He continued his description of the surgery. "We were able to stabilize him enough to have X-rays and a CT scan performed. He was given blood. The vertebra was shattered and we needed to remove small bone fragments. As terrible a wound as it is, we were able to repair a couple of injuries to his intestines and the lower wall of his abdomen. At this point he is stabilized. He'll be unconscious or very groggy for most of the day but you will be able to see him tonight. He will be intubated so you will have to do all the talking. Do you have a place to go for a few hours?"

Renae answered, "I do, but I'm going to stay here. I'll catch a nap in a chair. I appreciate your help so much."

Everyone stood up. Dr. Deshmukh shook hands with Tom and Susie and reached over and gave Renae a genuine hug. His bedside manner was wonderful. He looked Renae in the eyes and said, "Your husband will have to undergo some surgeries in the future, but he has the support he needs." He squeezed her shoulder and walked out of the waiting room. Before the three could sit down again, Dr. Deshmukh peered through the open door. "Oh, I did want you to know that later on when you are with your husband, I'll teach you all you need to know about the spine and the spinal cord." He nodded, waved his hand, and disappeared.

No sooner had Dr. Deshmukh departed than one of the staff walked in and offered a friendly hand. She briefed them as to the logistics of Bill's stay at the hospital. She explained Bill was given methylprednisolone in the hope that it would immediately reduce inflammation of the nerves surrounding the wound. The possible side effects were virtually astronomical, ranging from eye protrusion to inflammation of the pancreas. Still, given his condition, it was worth the risk and he would be monitored very carefully. Bill would be taken to the Surgical Trauma Intensive Care Unit–STICU–later in the day, where he would have continual nursing care. Since rest was a major concern, visiting hours were limited and followed very strictly. On rare occasions the head nurse would allow a spouse to visit during non-visiting hours. Using the D elevators, visitors could use the large waiting area on the eighth floor. There was a courtesy phone that provided communication with the STICU nursing staff during non-visiting hours.

Bill Newton, once shot through the leg in Vietnam, was in for the roughest ride of his life. Few people were as tough as Bill–he would survive his second shooting.

Fifty-Eight

Monday Morning,
June 28

Luling, Texas

Police officers Horace Smalling and Bert Rivera sat with Tom in Smalling's office. Each sipped on coffee.

"I thought it was an out-and-out robbery. This surprises me." Tom looked at both other men, hoping there would be an explanation. "A silencer. I don't get it."

Tom traced out the events again, this time stumbling over previous thoughts. *If only Don hadn't jumped the guy. Take the damn wallets and go. Don jumped him.* Tom realized Don had seen the silencer and jumped the hitman to save their lives. *Don knew.*

Bert Rivera seemed skeptical, not knowing what to think of it all. "Do you know of anyone who would want to kill you?"

Tom didn't know how to respond. The final words of Carlos Aguirre haunted him. Another recollection, this one from a dying Carlos—*He killed my friends.* It was too confusing at the moment. Loose ends everywhere. "No. I've done a lot of testifying in court and I'm sure some people may have been upset at the result of a trial. But no, I can't think of anyone specific." He took a sip of coffee. He had barely slept a total of six hours since Saturday morning. He was dead tired. But at least he wasn't dead.

Horace was satisfied that Tom was telling him everything he knew. But, just like Tom, he suspected that it was not a random shooting at all. Tom, Don, and Bill were targeted by a dead, unknown assailant.

Tom asked, "Has this guy been identified?"

Horace answered, "No. Not yet. The car was stolen and he had no identification on him at all. Tracing the pistol will be hard. We're running DNA now and his picture will be forwarded around the state. We will find out who he is in the next couple of days, I'm sure."

Bert, had there been a need, would have been the bad cop in a good cop/bad cop environment. By nature, he was always looking for some angle that would eventually stick out to let him solve the problem. The events and the players were so separate and yet intertwined that Bert saw this as one of those rare "crimes of the century."

He said, "Tom, you mentioned that you knew Carlos Aguirre. Do you know why he was even there Saturday night?"

Tom shifted in his chair. "I barely knew him at all. My brother Don was his boss. Best I can tell, Carlos worked hard and was in charge of the crew. About six weeks ago, according to the crew, he was killed in an accident in Fentress. He and two others went into the San Marcos River. His body was never found. It's obvious now that he didn't die in the river. But as to why he was there Saturday night, I just don't know." Tom wasn't quite sure and did not want to add confusion to the Luling police. What he did know, however, was that a scrambled ball of string was winding tighter around the JETS.

Horace asked, "How is your brother doing? We'd like to talk to him and your other friend as soon as possible."

"Let me tell you what I know right now about our friend, Bill Newton." Tom paused, veering slightly off path. "First of all, and I apologize if I hadn't mentioned this before, he's a Houston police detective and a very close friend." Tom saw minor surprise in Horace's expression but none in Bert's. Tom continued. "He has critical spinal-cord wounds. He's at University Hospital in San Antonio. Right now the only person who has been allowed to see him is his wife. What I have been told is that he will be there for several days and then transferred to Ben Taub in Houston. My brother is doing well and is full of piss and vinegar. The guy's got MS, was just shot for the second time in his life, is covered with a casts and tubes, and wants to get out of the hospital right now."

Horace and Bert looked at each other. Whether on an investigation or not they wanted to meet this guy.

Before either could say anything, Tom added, "He'll be in the hospital for a few days, then we'll take him back to my place northwest of Houston. As for you, he is chomping at the bit to talk with you."

"Great." Horace ended the conversation. "We'll head to the hospital right away."

Frank Milsap and Bart Miles engaged in a private discussion. Lying at the center of the coffee table, page A-10 of the Houston Chronicle gave full coverage of a shooting at the Luling Watermelon Thump. Don Seiler and Bill Newton were identified; the two deceased men were not.

"Don't you understand? It's got to be Bartok." Frank paced back and forth, his eyes darting down to a placid Bart Miles. Frank stopped and leaned down into Bart's personal space. Frank wanted to scream. "Once they identify him, all kinds of shit will break loose. And who the hell is the other dead one?" He lifted his palms into the air in frustration. "We're looking at a murder investigation. I never agreed to have people murdered. I want this shit to stop."

Bart looked up at Frank with an almost fatherly gaze. "Don't be such a pussy. Relax. This might be good. Good for two reasons." Bart leaned back and lifted his coffee cup. He took a generous drink and returned the cup to its saucer. He stood up and walked to the window. A magnificent view. He spoke, almost wistfully, into the window. "First, we would have eventually had to do something about Bartok. That's been taken care of." He turned around with his god-awful smile. "Secondly, if Don Seiler has significant wounds he may be out of the picture, in which case all this shit will dry up and go away. We've got the patent, Seiler's not a threat to us legally, and all we need to do is tie up a few loose ends with Barrister and French. By that I mean that we will pay them handsomely and, at the same time, threaten them with their lives if they do anything. Frank, you and I are now very wealthy. Very wealthy indeed. Instead of crying like a baby, why don't you think of things to do and places to go?"

Fifty-Nine

Friday, July 9

Broken Wing Ranch

"You make the reservations?" Tom looked across the table at his son. He was proud that, after Tom Jr.'s death, Steve really stepped up to the plate. Steve was rock-solid. Smart lawyer, yes; hell-raiser, yes; family man, yes; honest, yes; horse's ass, no.

"We fly out on Monday on US Airways flight 1407 at 7:05 in the morning." Steve hesitated and shrugged his shoulders. "It has an intermediate stop in Charlotte and gets to Newark about 1:30 p.m." Before either Tom or Ross could whine, Steve added, "But it also saves us over $1,500. Non-stop Continental flights are booked solid." He continued, "We're registered at the Newark Airport Marriott and have a car rental with Budget."

Tom asked, "When do we get back?"

"We leave on Wednesday at 3:55 p.m. and arrive in Houston at 10:25 p.m. How's that for a good memory?"

Don, shirtless with his right arm still in a sling and a cast covering the entire shoulder, offered, "I still ought to be in on this one. I'd knock the shit out of Bolduc, or whoever the hell he is."

"Not an option. You'll get your chance at him one of these days, but first I'll have to take your lethal weapon away."

Don lifted the fishing rod cane and looked at it. "This baby brought one worthless son of a bitch down. I could do it again." He was frustrated that he would not have the first shot at a man who spied on him, but he knew he would burden the efforts of the other three. Don placed the fishing cane on the floor and reached for his Diet Coke.

"Here. Take these. They came from Don's office at Point Hueneme and Nancy's assistant in San Antonio." Tom gave a sheet of paper to each of the other men. On them were the addresses of Don's client, Mr. Vince Bolduc, and Nancy's client, Mr. Vic Bolton. Both had the same P.O. Box number in Hastings-On-Hudson, New York. Additionally, Nancy had a home address also in Hastings-On-Hudson.

He returned to the discussion. "I suggest that once we get there, we get settled at the Marriott, have a bite to eat, and then move out to check on the two addresses we have for what's-his-name."

"Should we rent a second car and split up for a day to recon?" Ross was wired. He married into the family without ever imagining what a journey it would be.

"No, I don't think so. With these maps," Tom said, referring to the maps of New Jersey and the Lower Hudson Valley spread across the dining room table, "and with the GPS we shouldn't have any problem at all.

"Now, here's what we're faced with and what I propose we do."

Cindy drove, Don hung on to the seat, and Susie sat in the back of the golf cart for their quick trip to the pond. Stratus clouds, flat as a table but not yet pregnant with rain, moved slowly overhead, shading the landscape. Susie and Cindy, both fair-skinned, saw the rare event as a chance to get outside without contracting cancer. Tom and Steve stayed in the house discussing strategy. For Don it was another chance to fish. Of course, given his condition, the fishing would be done by Susie, the other real fisherman—or fisherwoman—in the family. Don contented himself with simply being next to a body of water. Cindy enjoyed being outside in non-stifling temperatures. Susie caught two large catfish in five minutes. She put both in the fish box and only needed one more to provide for a fried catfish dinner.

Don's cell phone rang. While Susie cast into the pond again Cindy took the phone from his waist and answered.

"This is Cindy, Don's wife."

It was quiet. Then a frail voice sounded, "Could I speak with Mr. Seiler?"

"Sure. Hang on a minute." Cindy looked quizzically at the phone, then handed it over to Don.

Susie hooked into the biggest catfish of the day.

"Hello, this is Don Seiler."

"Mr. Seiler, my name is Angelina Escobar. Carlos Aguirre is my brother. I don't know where he is and I need to speak with you. It's very important."

Hair stood up on Don's neck. He knew immediately that she did not know that Carlos was dead. They wanted to track her down but Tom couldn't remember her name.

Don tried to stand but lost his balance and had to sit down again.

The fish fought for all he was worth but Susie proved a better fighter.

Cindy stared at her husband. She knew it was a serious matter.

"Angelina, I am out in the woods right now. Could you call me back in fifteen minutes so that I can get your address and phone number?"

Susie, unaware of the phone call, landed the catfish.

"Yes. And thank you, Mr. Seiler."

"Sure. Talk to you in a few minutes." Don closed the lid on the phone. He used his cane to stand up. "We have to go. That was Carlos Aguirre's sister. She wants to talk to me."

The third catfish went into the fish box.

Cindy helped Don to the golf cart while Susie lugged the fish box up the pond embankment to the roadway for the short trip back across the field.

Fifteen minutes later Angelina Escobar called again. Sitting at the patio table were Tom, Don, Susie, Cindy, and Steve. Don picked up the phone and put it on speaker mode.

"Hi Angelina, thanks for calling me back." Don had an opportunity to think it through. He knew that she was very fragile and that it would be better not to tell her about Carlos until he met with her in person.

She was terrified and could barely get the words out. "Carlos told me some things. Some of it is very bad. He is scared and I am so scared. He wants to apologize to you and make everything right. But he needs you to help him." She took a deep breath and pleaded into the phone, "But I think he is gone someplace. He is afraid he will be killed. I need to talk to you, to someone."

"Angelina, just let me know where you live and I will come there."

"I live about two miles south of Smiley, on the left side of Route 108."

Don knew Smiley, a small town some twenty-plus miles

southwest of Gonzales. It was a long haul and he needed to talk to Tom first.

"Angelina. Can we meet early Sunday afternoon?" Don looked around the table, raising his shoulders as best he could in a questioning manner. Tom and Steve nodded positively. "I have multiple sclerosis and it would be very difficult to make it tonight."

"Yes, Mr. Seiler. I can meet you at one o'clock. I will go to the eleven o'clock mass."

"One o'clock on Sunday. My brother Tom will come with me. Maybe my sister Nancy and nephew Steve."

"That is good. The address is . . ."

For Bill, the die had been cast; he would never walk again. Still, his outlook on the future was not that bleak. Some color had returned to his face, the many tubes were gone, and he managed a pretty solid smile. After eight days in the STICU in San Antonio, Bill was transferred to a step-down unit at the Ben Taub Hospital Trauma Center in Houston. Physical, speech, and occupational therapists swarmed over him for almost a week. His next stop would be in-patient rehab. His current nurses enjoyed him as a patient and he was grateful for what they had done. He lay in a single-bed room, not huge but big enough for several people to visit at the same time. Diffused sunlight, soft pastel blue walls, and paintings of sailing vessels brightened Bill's temporary home.

He looked up at Tom. "OK, you guys are off to New York to solve this whole mess and I get to watch television and fill out retirement papers. Wish I could be there to offer my personal perspective to Mr. What's-his-name."

Tom answered, "We wish the same, Bill. Tell you what.

We'll give you a blow-by-blow account of our trip. If it gets real juicy we'll call you midstream for laughs and, if needed, for advice."

"That's what I wanted to hear. Private investigators come in all flavors. Not all are out there packing .44 Magnums." Pointing to Tom and Don, Bill continued, "If this guy is like both of you he might even work with you. But remember, he's been paid by someone else so he's not your ally at this point."

During their conversation, Bill's hands and arms were full of animation. His legs did not move. Tom described what they planned to do.

"We're going to visit with Carlos's sister tomorrow. Nancy will join us." Tom bit at his lip. "Angelina doesn't know right now that Carlos is dead. We've got to tell her. It won't be easy."

Bill shook his head, saying, "I've been there, done that. It's not pleasant."

Don answered, "Yeah, we know. Still, she obviously has some information that might shine some light on all that is going on. Everything is so damn complex."

"I'd like to know why I was shot." Bill shook his head and grimaced slightly. Then he asked, "So, after speaking with her, what then?" Bill wanted to know some specific details. "What're you going to do up north?"

Tom described the plan of attack. Bill thought their plan simple and potentially productive. He was relieved to hear that Tom, Don, and Steve were organizing all of the evidence for turnover to the appropriate police. Through his harrowing experience in Alvin Tom understood the danger associated with going it alone.

"Anything we can do for you before we hit the trail?"

Bill thought for just a moment and then smiled. "Actually, there is. Teach me how to have a bowel movement without feeling anything."

Tom and Don chuckled slightly, not feeling comfortable with any response. Both touched Bill's arm and walked out of the room. Renae's eyes filled.

Sixty

Sunday, July 11

Smiley, Texas

Tom and Don linked up with Nancy at Nellie's Café in Nixon, ten miles from Angelina Escobar's small home outside of Smiley. Steve was locked in the middle of a case and remained in Houston working on an upcoming deposition. Tom and Don ate voraciously bacon and eggs, orange juice, and toast with peanut butter. Nancy had scrambled eggs and ate one piece of toast. From Nellie's they drove along US 87 to Angelina's home. Two black dogs—they could have been cousins of Bear and Catfish—barked, jumped around, and finally came close enough to sniff the three Seiler siblings. Angelina came to the door before Tom had a chance to knock.

She was small of stature, with jet-black hair and piercing near-black eyes. Angelina appeared to be no more than twenty years old. She smiled at them.

"Please come in. Thank you so much. I am so worried."

Once inside the house, Tom, Don, and Nancy took seats in the small living room while Angelina disappeared into the kitchen to get some drinks. Tea sounded good to everyone. Each visitor, in his or her own way, surveyed the quaint house; the home was modest and clean as a whistle. A small window-unit air conditioner hummed away in another room. The house was warm but not uncomfortable. The living room appeared small, almost dwarfed with a large tan couch, coffee table, light tables at each end of the couch, and two matching upholstered chairs. A third chair had been brought in from the kitchen. A crucifix was tacked above the front door and picture frames, most of them housing photos of three generations of family, hung from the walls. Against the side wall next to a small curtained window was an upright piano. A worn music book rested at eye level, a sign that the piano would always be a centerpiece of the Escobar family.

Angelina returned with the drinks. "I hope you like it. My husband makes the tea. It is sweet and very refreshing."

The tea was more than sweet. It made one's mouth contort to drink it.

Angelina sat down and the hard part began.

Before Angelina could say anything, Tom took over. "Angelina. We thank you very much for calling us. Many things have happened over the last several months. Most of them were not good. There is no easy way to say that recent events have also been bad."

She looked at Tom and instantly sensed what was coming. A wave of remorse swept over her face.

Tom barely opened his mouth, "Angelina, Carlos was ki–"

She held her hand up to her mouth. "Oh, *mi Dios*. Oh, God. No. No. No." Angelina's head fell and she started sobbing. "Oh, no. He wasn't a bad man. Oh, my Carlos. My brother."

Nancy moved to the couch and sat next to Angelina. She put her arm around her. Tom and Don felt awkward beyond belief. Angelina continued crying, trying to turn the clock back.

It wouldn't turn. Clocks don't go back. They never go back.

Several minutes later, with Nancy still at her side, Angelina looked up and around at the strangers in her house. She didn't blame them but she wished Carlos had never met Don Seiler.

"*No es posible.*" She wiped her eyes again and placed both hands in her lap. "Carlos was so smart. I don't understand how . . ." Her head dropped again. Looking up, her eyes like polished coal, Angelina almost pleaded, "Or why. I don't know why he did things. I will never know."

Don shifted toward her as best he could. He still hurt, his arm nesting helplessly in a sling below his cast. "Angelina, Carlos worked very hard for our company. He was the leader and all the men respected him. He made mistakes, but he also did some good things. Do you know that he saved Tom's life and mine? He died protecting us and a friend of ours." Don sucked in a deep breath. "His last act was heroic."

"Where is he now? I need to see him." Angelina wanted to see her brother right away.

Tom answered gently, "We knew who he was and Don called the Luling Police Department. They called the Bexar County Morgue and identified him. The Medical Examiner's Office in San Antonio now knows that you are next of kin. We can call them in a few minutes."

She looked up and stared at Don. Her eyes trained solidly on Don's. "Thank you." She looked at Nancy and Tom. "Thank you. I know he changed very much since working at your company." As she talked, Angelina gathered some composure. She wiped her eyes a couple of times as she started to tell a story about Carlos's behavior over the previous seven months.

"Carlos was a, how to say, a cocky man. He always wanted to do big things and he wanted to make money. Then early this year he started working for your company." She nodded her head in Don's direction. "He would stop by and . . ."

The front door opened and Hector Escobar walked in. Dressed in Levi's, straw cowboy hat, boots, and a white, slightly dirty, long-sleeved shirt, Hector was a typical native of south central Texas. He worked for the Texas Department of Transportation and earned every penny he made.

Hector shifted a large paper bag to his left side and reached out to shake hands with the visitors. "I'm Hector. Glad to meet you." He shook hands with each and then turned to Angelina. He could see it in her eyes.

"Carlos is dead." Angelina's eyes locked on Hector, tiny bloodshot strands glowing beneath a covering of tears. "He's in the Bexar County Morgue."

Hector placed the paper sack on a side table and walked to Angelina. She stood up and reached out to him. They embraced for a moment, her body trembling with sobs.

Hector released his wife, saying, "I will be right back." He held Angelina's hand as she lowered herself to the couch. He took the sack into the kitchen, placed some items in the refrigerator, and left the others on the counter. He poured himself a glass of tea and returned to sit next to his wife.

Angelina patted Hector's knee and continued her story. "I was talking about Carlos working for Mr. Seiler."

"Please call me Don."

"He would stop by and talk about your oil machine. He also said he liked working for you." Angelina opened her hand toward Don.

Don swallowed hard.

"Carlos said you were very honest, a funny man, keeping everybody happy. But he also talked about working for someone else who was going to buy your machine and make him rich."

Tom and Don each wanted to ask who but thought better of it at that moment; the question could be asked later.

Hector knew much of Carlos's story, but not to the level of detail that Angelina was going through this day. Angelina spoke sweetly at times and forlornly at times as she described Carlos's behavior throughout the period he worked for Don. Then she told the story of a rainy Sunday morning in May and of Carlos's actions during the following weeks. The others, Hector included, sat mute as Angelina described the stark terror in Carlos's eyes, his confession of what he had done, and his hope to cleanse his soul.

Don's emotions went binary again, shifting back and forth between anger and sadness at the strange mosaic of human strength painted across a massive backdrop of human weakness. Carlos had been the one who killed Juan Delgado.

Angelina spoke of Carlos growing a beard and refusing to go outside. She ended with her story of Carlos deciding to go to the Watermelon Thump in Luling.

"I don't know why he had to go that night. Each day for about two weeks before the Thump Carlos would talk about going. But he never left the house until the Thump. Carlos left here around noon." Angelina choked up, holding her hands to her mouth. "He never came back."

Angelina's story seared each person in the room. No one could say a word. Whether true or not, Angelina gained solace from Carlos's telling her that he had not intended to kill Juan Delgado.

Tom's mind searched for a way to tie what Angelina was saying to the bits and pieces of circumstantial evidence he had collected. Some of the pieces were beginning to attach with others, but he knew they were a long way from convicting those who stole the JETS.

A few seconds elapsed before Angelina stood up. "I have something."

Angelina walked to her bedroom and returned a minute later with a cardboard box. She gave it to Don.

"Inside is a recorded message from Carlos. You can have the recorder. Also inside is a statement that Carlos wrote. He signed it. I made the recording the morning after he was almost killed. He signed the statement."

Don looked down at the box. Tom and Nancy looked at Don and then at Angelina.

Don, almost dumbfounded by this enormous stroke of luck, asked, "May I play the tape?"

It was the mother lode.

Steve and Ross arrived at the ranch in Steve's car early Sunday evening. They would stay overnight and fly out with Tom in the morning. Tom and Don returned just after eight o'clock. As appropriate, Miller Lites, water, or soft drinks were given out and each took his or her seat at the table. Pound cake and peanuts occupied the far end of the table. Tom took out the recorder and multiple copies of the written statement from Carlos. He put Carlos's original signed statement back in a plastic briefcase with other important evidence.

"You can read the statements on your own. They pretty much state the same thing that you'll hear on the recorder. Carlos is dead and I'm not up to date on whether or not this can be used as evidence."

Steve broke in. "Absolutely. It's Rule 804 in the Federal Rules of Evidence. It's a death declaration. If the declarant, and that's Carlos, is deceased, the evidence is admissible. Both written and spoken. We need to verify that the signature and voice came from Carlos."

Don added, "Hell's bells. We've got his signature on his

Donelam application."

"Good. The voice evidence may be contested, but I have access to voice recognition experts and technology. Angelina has ample movie film in which Carlos does a lot of speaking. Assuming the evidence is just what you've said about it, we might have enough here to convene a grand jury."

Sixty-One

Monday, July 12

En Route: Newark, New Jersey, and Hastings-on-Hudson, New York

They spent the first leg from Houston to Charlotte on board an Embraer 190. Ross and Steve took aisle seats and Tom took a window. Comfort was not a consideration on the two-by-two seated aircraft; wherever you sat was tight. For the second leg ending at Newark Tom had a window seat while Steve and Ross suffered the "middle seat" syndrome. But, as Confucius said, "He who books late sits in the middle seat." Tom sipped on a Sprite and gazed out of the window. The "dog days of August" were a month early in the Northeast and haze shrouded the passing countryside below him. He enjoyed flying of any type but piloting was far superior to being a passenger. He could not help but process what had happened in the past, including the Alvin incident, and what the future held once they landed. He hoped that the meeting with Vince or Vic would bring order out of the chaos of the last seven months.

The flight time passed quickly; Tom was surprised when the Airbus 320 decelerated and lowered its nose. Tom predicted the landing: *Probably thirty-seven minutes out.* Thirty-six minutes later the wheels touched the pavement at Liberty International Airport, Newark, New Jersey. Tom looked toward Manhattan and focused on the woman who welcomed the huddled masses to our shores. No matter that haze and film on the window obscured her stark beauty, the Statue of Liberty pulled from his gut the realization that the United States was the greatest country in human history. She also pulled from the gut his fear that the country was involved in unnecessary political mudslinging and decades-long governmental mismanagement from both sides of the aisle.

With no checked baggage the three men immediately boarded the monorail to Budget Car Rental. Steve used his credit card for the full-sized Ford Taurus. They made a quick stop at the Budget restroom and proceeded to the car. Steve walked the car for dents and scratches, checked the operating system, and started the ignition. A few minutes later they were following the horde of traffic around the concrete maze while hunting for the turnoff to the Marriott. After missing it the first time Steve pulled into the self-parking lot. Check-in was quick and they were in their rooms, all on the fifth floor, within minutes. Tom banged on Steve's door, and they in turn banged on Ross's door. Tom carried a briefcase with maps and all the information they had on Vince Bolduc or Vic Bolton.

They ordered sandwiches and iced tea at Chatfield's English Pub in the hotel and went over their plan while waiting for the food. The first order of business was to find Vic or Vince's home and the post office in Hastings-on-Hudson, New York. The first sign of bad news was the GPS. Steve tried punching in the address to no avail; Peliteer Street was not in the database.

Tom made a quick decision. "Forget his home for now. Just plug in 'City Center' and when we get close I'll do a search for the post office."

Steve threaded his way to the Garden State Parkway and eventually caught the New York Thruway headed toward New York.

"Can you believe that?" Ross pointed to the traffic on the opposite side of the Tappan Zee Bridge. It was stacked bumper to bumper as far as the eye could see. Ross thought he was looking at ten million cars. "Who could put up with that every working day of his life? No way."

Steve's eyes were glued on his own traffic. Tom looked over and shook his head.

"Give me Texas any day." He grinned and added, "Just don't make it Houston at the same time of the day." He shifted his gaze to the Hudson River passing beneath the car. Sailboats and powerboats romped freely over the water. A rusted T-3 freighter plowed its way through the water, headed to Albany.

Once across the Tappan Zee they drove to exit 9 and took US 9 north. The landscape switched from urban sprawl to pretty woodland settings. Many of the towns were quaint, with homes and buildings dating back to the eighteenth century. Hastings-on-Hudson was one of the prettiest towns of them all. Tom punched "points of interest—post office" into the GPS. No problem.

From the city sign proclaiming *Welcome to Hastings-on-Hudson,* it was three minutes to Warburton Avenue and the United States Post Office, zip code 10706. Steve pulled to a stop in the parking lot. "OK, troops, we have landed."

Tom began the plan. "First thing. Take another look at the photograph from Don's office in California."

Each man had a separate copy of Vince or Vic. He had a big smile and a big gut.

After a minute's time Tom said, "Let's go in one at a time and just get a feel for it. We need to know exactly which box is 22212. Browse around and get the lay of the land. I'll go first."

Tom got out of the car and walked slowly into the building. Quite a few people were conducting business at the counter while others were checking their personal boxes for mail. Tom walked to the far end of the post office. Mailboxes arrayed in military order of rows and columns covered the entire wall facing the parking lot. He glanced at the numbers and quickly learned how the numbering system worked. He found box 22212 waist-high and three columns from the end. No problem, just a matter of time. Tom fixed the location in his mind and nonchalantly walked out of the building.

Ross went second and Steve third. Each went into the building a second time to make sure they knew exactly which was the correct box.

Back in the car, the men came up with a schedule and refined their plan.

"Fifteen minutes each. I'll go first. Whoever sees this guy follows him out. Get as close to him as possible, and if it appears to be the same guy as in the photograph, rub the top of your head. Whoever is in the passenger seat will take a picture of him and his car. Get the license plate if possible. If, and this is important, whichever of us is following him can't make it back to the car, just stay at the post office and the driver will follow this guy's car. We can keep in touch via cell phones."

All nodded in agreement.

Tom's turn inside the post office was uneventful.

Ross walked into the building and the waiting continued. It was a short wait. Five minutes after entering the post office Ross walked out rubbing the top of his head. The man in front of him walked slowly to the small parking lot. Just under six feet in height, a full head of brown hair with wisps of gray, and a waistline too large for his age and profession, the man sorted through a small stack of mail, unaware of those around him. He stopped at his car and Ross kept walking.

Ross got in the back of the Taurus, speaking into his small recorder. "ENV 4077, New York. Toyota Camry. Beige."

"Got the pictures. Take a look." Tom showed the other two the pictures he had taken. They were clear enough to know that the person in the new photograph was the same as the visitor to Don's Halloween party over eight months before. Tom and Ross agreed with the identification of Vince, Vic, or whoever he was.

Their target backed up his Camry in a large arc. He glanced over and made eye contact with Steve. Steve couldn't tell if the man knew something was up. It unsettled him. When the man turned his head back toward the front Tom took one last picture of the car. The car turned right on Warburton Avenue and accelerated. Steve had to wait for three cars to pass before entering the street. Tom from the passenger seat and Ross from the back seat strained to see the target vehicle. A mile down the road the target vehicle turned right again before turning left into a parking lot next to a three-story commercial building. Steve kept going.

"I'll circle the block and park across the street." Steve signaled a right turn.

"Good idea. We can scout the building out."

Steve, concerned with the eye-to-eye contact, said, "I think I ought to stay in the car. He looked at me at the post office. I don't know if there's anything to it but we ought to be prudent."

Tom and Ross agreed.

The building was vintage turn-of-the-century. Burnt-orange brick with beige facing, the building appeared to have been renovated in the recent past. Lush bushes covered the entire front of the building, and two Japanese Maples, each on opposite sides of the entrance walkway, stood majestically on the front lawn. Tom and Ross walked in.

The marble floor and flat walls were impressive and amplified sounds. Large, heavy, dark-stained doors with company logos lined the hallway. Several potted plants were placed at strategic locations.

"Here we go." Tom pointed to a glass-protected company directory.

They looked at the names of the different companies, a couple of them familiar and most of them not. Few of the signs told the actual purpose of the companies behind the doors. The legal and accounting firms, with their special identification letters to the right of the company name, were obvious, but not the others.

"Let's take a walk up and down the hallways. I'll be right back." Tom walked out of the door to let Steve know that it may be a while.

When Tom returned, he and Ross walked by each office door. Those that were identifiable as not belonging to a private investigator were eliminated. The others were tagged with the name of the company and the room number.

"Piper and Associates, 224." Tom stated the room number and name while Ross added the information to the tablet. They looked at every office.

Tom and Ross finished their cataloging a little after 6:00 p.m. A couple of exiting employees looked at them quizzically, but for the most part, the stereotype of the hurried, uninvolved New Yorker held true. Most didn't even know that Tom and Ross existed. On the way down, Ross counted the unidentified companies.

"Fifteen unknown offices, all spread throughout the building. Damn." Ross bit at the end of his mechanical pencil, studying the names.

"I've got an idea that should work well. I'll explain it to you and Steve in the car."

Tom, Ross, and Steve ate burgers and drank a couple of beers at the sports bar in the Marriott. The burgers were strictly plain vanilla and too dry for any of their tastes. Baseball games filled most of the screens.

"It's pretty simple," said Tom. "We'll break down the names on our list, five to each of us. Do a Google with the company name, the words 'private investigator,' and 'Hastings-on-Hudson.'" Tom smiled. "I'll bet it won't take half an hour. My room after eating."

They met in Tom's room, the other two carrying their briefcases and laptops. Ten minutes later Steve stood up. "Got it. There he is." He pointed down at the screen.

Tom and Ross got up and looked at Steve's computer. A very professional webpage stared back at them. A photograph of the New York skyline rising majestically above the Hudson River was superimposed over the lettering:

Pi Associates
Private Investigations
Licensed & Insured
Civil–Criminal–Domestic–Child Custody–
Commercial–Industrial

The remainder of the website discussed the company's being in business for twenty years, its professionalism, and its promise that "all information is kept strictly confidential appropriate to Federal and New York State statutes." At the bottom was an address and phone number.

Ross spoke to no one in particular, "That's got to be the guy. I thought that 'Pi' referred to an engineering firm. It's probably P-I for Private Investigator. Duh."

"Yep, that's him. Tomorrow will be a very interesting day." Tom sat down and started taking notes from the screen. He finished and announced, "It's getting late. Let's call it a night. How about breakfast at 7:30 a.m. followed by a phone call and appointment with Pi Associates?"

They went to their rooms. In his room, Tom called Don with an idea.

Everyone gorged on the breakfast buffet. In half an hour all three had gone from healthy men to cardiac risks. At 9:00 a.m. Ross called Pi Associates from Tom's room.

"Good morning, Pi Associates, this is Micheleen. How may I direct your call?"

"Hi. My name is Ross Royster. I'd like to set up an appointment today with one of your investigators. It's a confidential matter." He cleared his throat.

"Just a moment, please."

Micheleen looked at the calendar, made a couple of notes, and returned to the phone. "Mr. Bolen is out all day. Would tomorrow afternoon at 3:00 p.m. be all right?"

"Just a minute." Ross looked at Tom and Steve.

Tom scratched out a quick note.

Ross answered, "Unfortunately, I have a flight out tomorrow afternoon. Could we meet in the morning around 10:00 a.m.?"

Another pause. "That would be fine. Ten in the morning. Is there anything else I can do?"

Ross paused. "Oh, thanks, I do have a couple of things. First, I just wanted you to know that two friends of mine will be with me, but I'm the guy who needs the help. Also, what's the first name of our investigator?"

"His name is Vincent but he goes by Vince. I'll make sure he knows there will be three of you. Have a wonderful day."

"You too." Ross hung the phone up.

With a day to kill, the three men returned to Hastings-on-Hudson and drove around in an effort to become familiar with the town. They ate lunch in town and made plans to see *Chicago* at the Ambassador Theatre. May as well enjoy a trip to the Big Apple. As for the play, Steve and Ross loved it; Tom fell asleep.

Micheleen, Vince's secretary, greeted the trio very politely, offering them water or coffee. They refused, having eaten too much breakfast for the second straight day. The men looked around at the well-decorated office. The office was not out of a Sam Spade novel. No dark, dusty corners, no debris-stacked, worn-out desk, no secretary pounding away at a broken typewriter—and certainly no wisecracking private dick named Sam Spade. Dashiell Hammett's novel *The Maltese Falcon* was almost eighty years old, but stereotypes die slowly.

Tom looked down at his watch. Ten fifteen. He leaned forward, rubbing his hands together. He wanted to get the show on the road. Ross and Steve grabbed magazines and were unconcerned. A couple of minutes later a heavy-set, somewhat-disheveled man walked out of his office door and down the hall to the waiting men.

"Sorry about the delay. I had to reschedule my calendar somewhat and a phone client went on too long. I'm Vince, Vince Bolen." It was the same guy that Ross followed out of the post office. He seemed friendly and, after shaking hands, escorted the three men to his office. He was the spitting image of the man in the photograph: gentlemen, meet Vince Bolduc, Vic Bolton, or Vince Bolen—take your pick.

Inside, his office was clean and unremarkable. Vince Bolen's desk was a faux-mahogany masterpiece covered with a glass top, and except for a file folder, it had only a phone and lamp to take away from its large surface. He directed the men to two armchairs and a folding chair that Micheleen had added.

After no more than a couple of minutes Vince got into the topic at hand.

"So, what is it that I can specifically do for you?"

"Excuse me. I apologize, but an important call just came in." Tom got up and walked out of the room.

Once in the hallway, Tom called Don. For his part, Ross occupied the time with a very inaccurate biography of his life and an introduction to his fake predicament.

Don, from 1,200 miles away, asked, "We ready to crank it up?"

"OK. It's starting. I'm in the middle."

"Right. Here we go."

They hung up and Tom returned to the office.

"I'm sorry, but it was very important."

Ross, on cue, continued his part of the charade. "It's a major problem. There are some people I know who I believe are involved in serious criminal behavior. If I'm right, we're in the middle of a very dangerous situation. If I'm wrong then it's just a matter of middle-aged paranoia. Here, let me show you these." He reached for his briefcase and started sorting out some documents.

Vince looked over his desk at Ross. Just then his cell phone rang. He looked down at the dial and saw the caller's name. He ignored it.

Ross put a couple of pictures on the table. They were photographs of friends of his, one with his wife boating on Lake Conroe. The photos had nothing to do with what was taking place.

"These two men and the woman may be involved with drug smuggling into the New York area."

Vince's cell phone rang again. He looked down.

Clearly unhappy, Vince stated, "Excuse me for just a second." He put the phone to his ear. "This is Vince. I don't mean to cut you off, but I'm in a conference."

Don answered. "Hey, Vince, this is Don Seiler. I did some work for you out here in California. Could I speak with my brother?"

Vince was confused. "With who? What do you want?" He was unnerved.

Don continued, "My brother, Tom Seiler, he's sitting in the middle chair. Dark, thinning hair. All around great guy."

Micheleen knocked on the door, opened it, and peered in. "Mr. Bolen, a Nancy Gardner is on the phone. She says it's an emergency."

Vince Bolen, alias Vic Bolton or Vince Bolduc, held up his hand. Without speaking, he closed the cell phone cover and then answered Micheleen. "Tell Mrs. Gardner that I'm talking to her brother."

Confused as could be, Micheleen gently shut the door.

Tom had enjoyed the game for a minute or so. He wasn't happy for long.

"First of all, what is your name? Is it Bolduc, Bolen, or Bolton? And I mean your real name."

Vince Bolen sighed, leaned back in his chair, interlocked his fingers, and stared at Tom. He wasn't actually afraid, but he was concerned as to where this meeting was headed.

"Vince Bolen."

Tom took over, Ross and Steve sitting passively in their chairs.

"Why have you been spying on my brother and my sister?" He added, "Before you answer, know that my brother has been shot and I'm really not in the mood for bullshit."

Vince studied Tom's face. He wasn't a young man, but Tom Seiler looked strong and healthy. Vince next glanced over at Steve and Ross. Something in his mind told him that he had seen Steve before.

Vince measured his words. "I wish I could tell you, but I can't. By federal and state laws I have confidentiality requirements and I can't divulge any information."

Tom answered quickly. "Yeah, we saw your website. Actually, in a criminal event you can divulge information, either voluntarily or with a pickaxe stuck up your ass. And that's what we have here. Deception on your part."

He put both hands on Vince's glass desktop and stared directly into his eyes. "Seven people are dead. Fucking stone-cold dead. Five of the seven were out-and-out murdered. My brother is just out of the hospital with a gunshot wound and a close friend is paralyzed from a gunshot to the back. And you, you sorry bastard, are dead center in the middle of this whole mess."

Vince's bravado cracked.

Now he looked scared. He was playing defense and trying to save his own ass. "Now, wait a minute. I had a client who asked me to investigate your brother and sister. I was also asked for information on any other members of the family, but your brother and sister came first."

Steve and Ross looked at each other.

"That's all I did." Vince raised his hands, palms out. "I didn't do anything illegal."

"That's not the way I see it. You, you sorry sack of shit, are the key to everything that has happened. Who hired you?" No sooner were the words out of his mouth than Tom knew the answer to his own question.

"Privileged information."

"And I'll bet that privileged information is tall and good-looking, with long dark hair and smart as a whip."

Vince said nothing. A slight, unconscious nod of the head answered Tom's question.

Tom, as confused as he was angry, asked, "So, what did you find on my brother that's so important?"

Vince answered, "The only thing of interest at all was his invention for some sort of oil field device. I just passed the information on to my client. Other than that I found nothing." He cleared his throat before continuing. "I was hoping to find something that he was doing illegally or immorally. I found neither."

Tom asked, "What about our sister? What'd you find on her?"

"Nothing. Nothing at all. I investigated her business and thought she might be a tax cheat. But she's not. She's just the best tax accountant I've run into." He tried to add some levity to the discussion. "I'd let her do my taxes anytime."

Tom got up. He bit his lip in an attempt to control his anger. Then he spoke. "Mr. Bolen, you will hear from us again and I am certain you will hear from the law. You better damn well have a good lawyer."

They walked out the door.

"Thanks, Micheleen. You have some boss there." The tone of Tom's remarks was difficult to read.

Micheleen looked up, smiled, and wanted to respond. The three men were gone.

Elizabeth Harker's cell phone rang. She grabbed it from the small side compartment of her purse, checked to see who was calling—and then put it back. She went back to the meeting in her office. She hadn't talked to Vince Bolen in a while and something about this call didn't sit right with her. Distracted by the call and bored with the topic of discussion, she allowed the meeting another five minutes and called it prematurely to a close.

"That's enough for now. We'll sort everything out tomorrow morning."

A young woman, probably at step two of the ladder of success, whined, "But I need a decision now so I can call Prokop. They need to have an answer today."

Harker, now a group director, looked her in the eye and slowly answered, "Get out of my office." End of discussion.

The small group, each member bewildered by the vicious exchange and abrupt ending of the meeting, left her office. There would be plenty of fodder for water cooler conversation.

Liz Harker stood up and walked over to the window overlooking Forty-Ninth Street. She stared down at the minions going about insignificant tasks. She had only contempt for everyone on that street. But at the same time, she realized that she was but one of them, a minion herself. She had gone from a life of power to one of insignificance. She had settled for her meaningless position with Cornvale & Hickens. *I'm a nobody.*

She used the redial function to call Vince Bolen back. The call bypassed Micheleen.

"Bolen."

"It's Elizabeth Harker. What do you want?"

Though no need existed, Vince spoke quietly into the phone. "I was just visited by a Tom Seiler, his son, and his son-in-law. They know that I have investigated both his brother and sister."

Liz Harker exploded. "What? How in the hell did you let that happen?" She wanted to throw her cell phone through the window. Rage ran rampant through her veins. No composure— just rage. "You stupid imbecile. You're supposed to be a professional and they know all about you." She gathered herself just enough to forge ahead. "What did they tell you and what do they know?"

Vince answered, his sweating face and armpits unseen by Liz Harker. "All he knows is that I have met both Don Seiler and Nancy Gardner." He paused briefly, unconsciously looking down at his watch. "I know you want to know, so the answer is no, he doesn't know who hired me. What bothers me is that Tom Seiler mentioned that there have been some murders going on around him. I never signed on to be part of murder. I don't know what you've gotten–"

"Shut up. Just shut up." Liz was confused and angry . . . and confused and angry mix like oil and water. She spoke again. "Are you certain that they don't know who contacted you?"

"If they do know, it's not because I told them anything." Vince relaxed slightly. "I really think Seiler is on a hunting expedition. But he got nothing from me. He did try to threaten me but I haven't done anything illegal." The more Vince talked, the more he wanted to distance himself from what was happening. "Look, I don't know what you've done with my information, but I don't want any part of illegal operations."

For the first time since leaving Houston, Liz Harker's overarching emotion was fear, not anger. She sucked in a deep breath and looked down again on the street below. *Minions.* From the minions, Liz Harker started thinking seriously about Tom and Don Seiler. *They're after me.*

"All right. You keep my name out of it. And you let me know everything that happens about this."

"I'll do that."

Liz Harker hung up. She looked again at the street. *Minions.* Vince Bolen looked at his closed cell phone. *Bitch.*

On the plane ride back to Houston, Steve and Ross managed aisle seats and Tom took his standard window seat, all in row 25. Their short trip to New Jersey and New York had been more than fruitful as events played out at lightning speed. Steve slept, Ross read a hilarious Dave Barry book, and Tom dissected situations, posed questions, and jotted down notes. Tom's first order of business would be to call Bill Newton and relay what had happened. Then he would go for the kill.

Sixty-Two

Friday, July 16

Houston Police Department, Houston, Texas

Eight men sat around a conference room table in the Houston Police Department office building in downtown Houston. Two detectives and two policemen sat side by side down the long axis of the table; Steve and Ross sat at the ends of the table; Tom and Don occupied the other long side of the table. The police officers were Horace Smalling and Bert Rivera from Luling. Detectives Mike Carney and Ben Rubalcava represented the Houston Police Department Criminal Investigations Command. Tom felt relief that he wasn't waiting until the last minute to turn over evidence to the proper authorities. He also knew that Susie was beyond relief. As for jurisdictions, Tom wasn't sure who would take over since events played out at differing locations in Texas, and possibly criminal activity occurred in both California and New York.

Tom opened his briefcase. "This is what we have at this point." He pulled out several manila folders, each labeled neatly, a CD labeled *Testimony—Mr. Carlos Aguirre, May–June*

2010, a small voice recorder, and some photographs. Each was placed in specific order along the center of the conference table.

"What I have here are pieces of evidence that we gathered over the past several months. I've arranged them in order to tell a story. We would have turned this over to you earlier," he eyed the men sitting opposite him, "but we didn't even know what we had until last Sunday." Tom started at his right, the items upside down to his view but readable to the officers and detectives. Everything he placed on the table was replicated and stored at the ranch. "The CD is a voice confession by Carlos Aguirre. He lays everything out. I mean, he really spilled the beans." Tom looked up to see the intense features on every face in the room. "And before I get into the folders, I don't want to forget to let you know that Elam Duquette's Cadillac is out at my ranch. It'd probably be wise to check out the damage against that normally found from an encounter with an F-5 tornado. Now for the folders." He touched the first folder with his index finger. "The first folder concerns our Jet Extraction Technology System and all the correspondence related to our efforts to obtain a patent." He touched the far left folder and pushed it slightly toward Mike Carney. The folder was almost an inch thick.

Carney peeled through the papers, measuring its importance by its volume rather than by reading anything. He passed it on to Benjamin Rubalcava, who mimicked Carney and, in turn, passed it on to the Luling detectives.

Tom continued, "The second folder is written testimony by Mr. Herman Soboda, a patent attorney who was threatened with severe harm if he did not retire immediately from his business. At the time he was the patent lawyer for Don and Elam Duquette." The second folder went hand-to-hand down the conveyor belt.

The third folder held all the correspondence related to the work of Fred Barrister and the eventual loss of the patent to Wellington Oil and Exploration Company.

The final folder contained the legal investigation conducted by Wallis Raymond. Not only did he do his homework, Wallis verified the counterfeit nature of the Wellington patent and tied everything together with a timeline showing collusion between Fred Barrister and someone at Wellington Oil. The linkage between the Wallis Raymond investigation and the statements of Carlos Aguirre left the CEO of Wellington Oil and Exploration, Mr. Bart Miles, hanging in the air as a criminal of the first order.

Tom held the last folder momentarily in the air. "In addition to all of the associations that Mr. Raymond described, take note of this particular point in the timeline." He turned to a paperclip near the end of the papers. "This section verifies that the final Donelam design was used in an actual demonstration to Caprock well before Wellington submitted its design." He had a hard time suppressing a smile. "Not only that, but the same demonstration was given to Wellington after the Caprock show. A former vice president by the name of James Bitters has written a statement verifying the date of the Wellington demonstration. He also states that there was no discussion as to an in-house design of a similar device at Wellington. They hadn't done zip."

Ben jumped on the statement. "What you're saying is that if Wellington already had a design, why would they be out there looking to use somebody else's design?"

"That's the whole point." Tom released the folder for inspection.

After the documentation had made its way around the table Mike Carney blew out a small breath of air. "I've got to give it to you. Eighteen years in the job and this is the most complete package of information I've ever seen."

Don leaned forward while answering, "Yeah, and this is only what we've found so far. There must be a thousand bits of evidence we haven't even touched. For crooks, Wellington has some really stupid people." He eyed the Houston detectives and, making a gesture toward the Luling detectives, stated, "Horace and Bert have additional information on the shooter at the Watermelon Thump."

"Yeah, right." Bert reached into his briefcase and pulled out another folder. In it were pictures of the shooting scene, including the pistol with silencer, the bodies of Carlos Aguirre and the dead shooter, and a fax from the Criminal Justice Information Services, CJIS, up in West Virginia. "They have a biometric database of more than fifty million criminal fingerprints." He pulled out the sheet. "We hit it lucky. This guy was on the file. He only had one police incident, an assault on three men in a bar in Washington, DC. Not another thing on him. His name is John Bartocci. At this point we have no other information on him, but we're working on it."

Ben took a small toothpick out of his mouth, gently rolling it back and forth in his fingers. "Based on what I've heard so far, we are dealing with intellectual property theft, corporate fraud, multiple murders-for-hire, and conspiracy that has spilled across state lines." He added matter-of-factly, "We need to bring the FBI into this one." Both he and Mike Carney could be considered anomalies as detectives. They had worked with and gotten along well with the FBI.

Horace Smalling and Bert Rivera had never worked with the FBI—there had never been such a need in Luling. No question about it, the case had exploded. Neither said a word.

Carney answered, "Look. It's almost noon. How about getting lunch somewhere and we can get the FBI down here to continue this later today? I'll call you when I firm up the time.

In the meantime, Ben and I will read what you've brought us in more detail."

"Sounds fair." Don turned to Horace and Bert. "Care to join us?"

"We're with you." Horace asked Mike and Ben, "Where's a good place to eat?"

Mike smiled and his eyes lit up, even though he wouldn't be able to go. "Try Otto's Bar-B-Que and Hamburgers over on Dallas Street. It's just over a mile and I'd suggest you just walk it. Parking is a problem at this time of the day and you'll find the burgers well worth the walk." He looked at Don and reworded things. "Sorry, on the other hand you might want to take a taxi."

Don looked up at Mike Carney. "No sweat. We'll make it, even with me. By the way, the recording will blow you away." The boyish grin broke across his face as he tapped his finger next to the small red recorder.

Ben stuck the toothpick back in his mouth and picked up the recorder. "I'm sure it will."

The men shook hands with the Houston detectives and left.

The others walked to Otto's while Tom and Don traveled by cab. Don's cell phone rang one minute into the ride.

"Don Seiler."

"Don, this is Ben Rubalcava. The FBI will send two agents down to meet us at three o'clock. Can you be here a half hour early so we can go over the details again?"

"We'll be there."

"Is the FBI going to throw a wrench into the investigation? I don't want to see this thing go on and on." Don grabbed his chili cheeseburger by both hands and bit into it.

Steve answered, "No. Actually, they'll speed things up. They'll conduct investigations that cover any geographical place that all this shit leads them. What they do as the investigative arm of the US Department of Justice is sort out all the details and provide in-depth analysis of the evidence. From there decisions are made as to whom the bad guys are and what to do about them. All of this helps in tying an investigation down tightly."

Don, not quite finished with his current mouthful, asked, "OK. But how soon can we expect them to make arrests?" He dabbed his mouth with a napkin and reached for a fat french fry.

Steve, pointing his finger first at Horace and then at Bert, answered, "Actually, you get the honor. The FBI investigates violations of federal law, but the agents only have limited arresting authority. In most cases they are invited as a courtesy to participate in an arrest. You'll do the arresting of anyone in the Luling area, and Mike, Ben, and whoever else will make arrests in Houston. As to the deaths in Fentress, we'll just cross that bridge when we get to it." Steve added with a shake of the head, "No pun intended. Depending on where this leads us, I'm sure arrests will be made in other states."

The conversation, interspersed with huge gulps of juicy, plump burgers and fries, drifted away from the topic of the day and toward life in Luling.

The conference room was dwarfed by the size of the crowd. Joining the original eight men were two FBI agents. Wearing dark blue jackets, tan cotton-twill trousers, and light blue open-collar shirts, the men seemed to have shopped at the same TJ

Maxx. Both appeared strong, with muscular, broad shoulders, premature gray at the temples, and crowfeet wrinkles at the corners of the eyes. Not to be mistaken for brothers, their physical attributes could not have been more dissimilar. The blue-eyed Charles Ritchie, Chuck to his friends, stood six feet nine and had played basketball for Syracuse. The brown-eyed and balding Dave Bertelli stood five feet ten and sported a razor-thin scar from the right corner of his mouth to the front of his ear.

Tom repeated most of what he had told Mike and Ben earlier that day. Dave Bertelli and Chuck Ritchie listened intently, giving full attention to the orderly sequence of events. The evidence, while mostly circumstantial, was detailed and arranged in a manner that could be tied to physical evidence in other parts of the state. Just as he had done a thousand times, Tom could tell a complex tale in ordinary terms.

Tom finished and sat down in a small folding chair brought in from a storage closet.

Chuck spoke for the FBI. "What you've given us is pretty remarkable. The recording is astounding." Sitting down, Chuck still towered over the other men in the room. "There have to be twenty different directions we can go in, so Dave and I will follow our standard protocol. We'll investigate those things that are closest to home and then reach out in order of importance."

"Where do you start?" Don wanted to get the show on the road.

"We'll start with the patent attorney without alerting him. I'll call Mr. Raymond before leaving today. He can do an audit trail related to patents handled by Barrister. Concurrently we'll link what we learn there with what we have learned about Wellington Oil. Certainly we plan to do a Dun and Bradstreet on Wellington. If we do make a move on Barrister and Wellington we'll find any correspondence between them.

We'll also do a check on the private investigator up in New York. Dave, what else?"

Dave Bertelli tapped a drum roll with his pencil eraser while pondering the question for a few seconds. He answered with, "We'll also take a hard look at the physical events beginning with the patent attorney who was threatened, including the money he received. If we can find some DNA that matches that of Carlos Aguirre then we have a direct linkage with Aguirre, Soboda, and Miles. That should segue into the other deaths and timelines you described. We'll start with the assumption that the first guy who worked for you, Delgado," Dave glanced over to Don, "was killed by Aguirre, whether accidental or not, who had been hired to either threaten or kill him." He reached down and opened the manila folder with the information on John Bartocci, studying the photograph of the dead killer. "As for Mr. John Bartocci, we do have access to resources that can help us track down his alias and where he lived." Dave looked at Horace and Bert and asked, "If you could, keep pursuing his Texas domicile and background on your own."

Horace and Bert nodded confidently.

Dave looked back at Chuck. "What do you think about a timeline for doing things?"

"Given the thoroughness of the evidence, probably two weeks and we can be ready for search warrants and arrests. We don't want to alert anyone until we make our sweep."

Almost as an afterthought, Tom added. "One other thing. I don't know for sure if there is anything to it and I don't have any evidence, but I'd recommend that the FBI take a look at the activities of Elizabeth Harker. In particular, it's my belief that she's the one who hired the private investigator to find dirt on Don and our sister, Nancy. I wrote down notes from our meeting with him." Tom pulled out another folder. "The notes are in here. The sole purpose was to screw them. Instead, he found Don's invention. I'd sure be interested to know if she ever had an association with the CEO of Wellington."

"Elizabeth Harker? The former Houston DA?"

Tom answered, a grim look dominating his face, "That's her. A real sweetheart." Tom unconsciously shook his head. "The former, and one-time formidable, Houston district attorney. I think she hates me probably more than I hate her . . . but the relative difference is insignificant. I think she's part and parcel of everything that's happened. Don't know how, but she probably got the whole thing started."

Chuck stood up, his huge frame actually casting a shadow across half of the table. He glanced briefly at the calendar component of his watch.

"Today's the sixteenth. I'll toss out Tuesday, August 3, as our sweep day. We'll break down tasks here today. We can hit each target at the same time, say 10:00 a.m. New York time, 9:00 a.m. local. Everything we do must be kept clandestine until then. Since our jurisdiction is national, Dave and I will be glad to serve as the focal point. It's your choice on how we do it."

Everyone looked at each other, mumbled a few words, and nodded in agreement.

Mike Carney spoke for both Ben and himself. "It's a plan. I think our only addition to what's been said is that we ought to meet or have a conference call on the thirtieth to finalize evidence and verify who we're picking up and how."

Horace Smalling asked, "What's the plan if something gets compromised?"

Chuck answered, "If we can stovepipe the problem, we'll hit the compromised target immediately and keep the others on schedule. If that breaks down each target will be hit as soon as possible. I'll set up the conference call."

Nods of approval all around.

Sixty-Three

Tuesday Morning,
August 3

Various Locations

Law enforcement teams made surgical strikes in Texas, Louisiana, and New York with MQ-1 Predator drone accuracy. In each case a subpoena was issued and offices were quarantined. The first strike took place in Houston on Westheimer Road.

Three detectives, with Mike Carney in the lead, approached Fred Barrister in his office parking lot.

"Mr. Barrister?" Mike didn't need to make it a question. He knew his target well.

Fred Barrister looked at the men and immediately turned slate grey. "Yes. Yes, who are you?"

"Detective Mike Carney. Houston Police Department. You need to accompany us downtown."

"Why? I haven't done anything." Fred Barrister's eyes

darted from man to man; his body flinched spasmodically.

"Mr. Barrister, you can either come voluntarily or I can arrest you. Take your pick."

One minute later Fred Barrister was sitting in the back seat of Mike Carney's assigned car. Not one word was spoken between his office and downtown Houston.

Bart Miles leaned back on the office couch, his feet stretched atop the coffee table. Between sips of hot coffee, he reread the Houston Chronicle article on page A-8:

> *Texas Railroad Commission Endorses Wellington Oil Invention*
>
> *August 2nd*–Today the Texas Railroad Commission, manager of domestic oil and gas in the state, approved the demonstration request of Wellington Oil & Exploration, Inc., of Houston. The request will allow the company to demonstrate . . . .

He lifted his arms up in the air and folded them back behind his head, hands joined at his neck. A sensual feeling of power and personal satisfaction warmed his body. The feeling, and it was truly sensual and warm, lasted another sixteen seconds.

Ben Rubalcava, accompanied by Chuck Ritchie and a young detective on his first major arrest, entered the office suite of Wellington Oil Exploration at nine o'clock. There would be no choice in this case; they had an arrest warrant in hand.

"May I help you?" Macy Buckles, as professional as she was pretty, smiled at the entourage.

Ben pulled out his wallet and showed his identification. "Houston police. We need to see Mr. Miles immediately."

Macy suddenly felt cold; she was not surprised, just cold. "I'll let him know you are here."

She called Bart Miles on his intercom.

"Yes."

"Mr. Miles, some men from the Houston Police Department are here and asked to speak with you."

Stark terror. *What's going on?* Small beads of sweat popped up all over his face. He got up from his desk, walked to his coffee table, and returned wringing his hands. He knew it was the JETS. He sat back down and answered, "Have them come in."

Bart expected an opportunity to talk his way out of any controversy. For their part, Ben, Chuck, and the new detective had no intention of a discussion. They were arresting Bart Miles.

"Mr. Miles, I am Detective Benjamin Rubalcava, Houston Police Department." He pulled out an arrest warrant. "You are under arrest for criminal activities including patent fraud, extortion, and capital murder." Then he pulled out a search warrant. "Your offices are now officially quarantined."

"This is preposterous. You're insane." Bart Miles blurted out his protestations to an unsympathetic audience.

The detectives placed Bart's hands behind his back and cuffed them. They walked him into the reception area and stopped. Ben pulled out a card and began reading. "You have the right to remain silent. Anything you say can and will be used against you in a court of law. You have the right to an attorney present during questioning. If you cannot afford an attorney, one will be appointed for you. Do you understand these rights?"

Bart answered curtly, "Yeah." He turned to Macy. "Call Mr. Fremont. Tell him to meet me at the Houston Police Department on Travis Street."

Macy, clearly shaken, answered, "Yes, sir."

Ben addressed the new detective. "Keep the entire suite closed down until the forensic team arrives. They should be here any minute."

Macy watched in horror as Ben and Chuck led the CEO of Wellington Oil and Exploration out of the office. She picked up the phone and started dialing.

All eyes focused on Bart Miles's arrest. No one noticed Frank Milsap walk calmly to the elevator and, within a minute, into the parking lot. He walked by the forensic team as they headed into the skyscraper, disappearing into the heavy Houston traffic in his silver GS 460 Lexus. Five minutes later every computer at Wellington Oil and Exploration was shut down. All employees, save Macy Buckles, were told to leave for the day. She would be called to come back and close up the office.

Vince Bolen was neither surprised nor frightened when local detectives, accompanied by an FBI agent, entered his office in Hastings-on-Hudson. *I've done nothing wrong.*

Jason French was brought to Lake Charles, Louisiana, for questioning. The FBI wanted to know his activities related to the design of an oil extraction device for Wellington Oil and Exploration. He was not about to protect Bart Miles.

Phone calls were made to Angelina Escobar, Herman Soboda, and Wallis Raymond, asking them to come talk with law personnel from both Luling and Houston. All gladly accepted.

As for Elizabeth Harker, no warrant had been issued—the presiding judge ruled there was not sufficient evidence to bring her in.

Sixty-Four

Tuesday Late Morning, August 3

Houston Police Department

Interrogation Room 3 houses a three-by-five-foot tan, wood-grained table, three comfortable leather chairs, all with arm rests, three overhead lights, a camera mounted at the juncture of the back wall and ceiling and directed over the backs of police detectives to the front of the interviewee, two microphones, and a blank glass window that Fred Barrister knew served as an observation station. The dark walls were covered with acoustical squares, with alternating vertical and horizontal ridges of pseudo-carpeting. The walls mimicked a giant checkerboard. Both Fred Barrister and his lawyer, Lamont Bird, were wedged along the same side of the conference table; they faced the observation window and, obviously, the camera. Fred could only imagine who was peering through the glass at him; he was scared, the lawyer unable to calm his nerves. Fred's coat hung over the back of his chair with his tie stuffed in the inside pocket. He looked disheveled and nauseous. The interrogation was taped, beginning with the Miranda rights.

Mike Carney did not play the bad cop role. His demeanor was always the same—straightforward, professional, and, except on rare occasions, respectful. He placed a Diet Coke each in front of Fred Barrister and his lawyer.

Mike made standard comments identifying the who, what, when, why, and where of the interview. Then he addressed the patent lawyer. "Mr. Barrister, here's what we have at this point. Which ones you are directly related to will be determined over the next few days. But there are many parts of our investigation that you appear to be connected to." He looked down at a bullet list of items on a sheet of paper. He shifted his eyes back and forth between the paper and Fred Barrister's contorted face. "Assault, five counts of murder, extortion, patent fraud, conspiracy. Additional evidence for what we have keeps coming in." He reached into a large manila envelope. "Let's start with these."

Mike pulled out numerous photographs. In a slow, deliberate manner he laid down the most grotesque photos, in order, of Elam Duquette, Sarah Bettner, Manuel Rodriguez, Emilio Garcia, and Carlos Aguirre. "In addition to these, two others have been shot, with one paralyzed for life. Two other men are dead, but you don't appear to have a link to either of them."

The photographs horrified Fred Barrister. His expression was one of stark terror. He blurted out, "I swear to God, I had nothing to do with all of this. I had no idea what was going on."

Lamont Bird leaned sideways and whispered into Fred's ear. Fred nodded his head. Lamont looked back at Mike Carney and asked. "Could we have a few minutes alone, without any recording? Attorney–client privilege."

Mike spoke into the microphone. "Eleven eighteen. Mr. Barrister and Mr. Bird will engage in private conversation." He turned off the recording system and got up, saying, "Just signal at the window when you want me to return." He walked out, quietly closed the door, and left them in silence.

Even with the sound system turned off, Lamont and Fred whispered to each other as they searched for a way out of the dire situation that was strangling Fred. After ten minutes Lamont raised his hand, beckoning Mike Carney to return to the room.

Mike returned, sat down, and turned the sound system back on. He spoke into the microphone. "Eleven twenty-nine. Mr. Barrister and Mr. Bird have concluded a private conversation.

"Having had the opportunity to converse with each other, is there anything you wish to say before we proceed?" Mike sensed what was coming.

Lamont Bird looked at Mike and then at the window. Finally, he spoke very matter-of-factly into the microphone.

"We would like full immunity in exchange for Mr. Barrister's testimony as to everything he knows about all events and circumstances related to this investigation."

Jackpot.

The physical components in Interrogation Room 5 were identical to Interrogation Room 3. There were no similarities in the human interactions.

Ben Rubalcava sat across from Bart Miles and Gary Fremont. Stathos Papadopoulos, a tall, slender, second-generation Greek American, sat on a metal chair nearest the door. From behind the window Horace Smalling and Bert Rivera were fixated on a man who allegedly was the root cause of seven deaths in and around Luling, Texas. Ben was relaxed as, for the second time, he administered the Miranda rights to Bart Miles. Bart seemed ready to explode.

"I want to get the hell out of here. You have no right to bring me here." Bart pushed his chair back and stood up.

Ben stood up as well. "Sit down, Mr. Miles, or I will have you chained to the chair." He pointed at Bart's chair. "Sit down right now."

Bart looked at his attorney. No help there. He sat down.

Ben sat back down and continued the discourse. He spoke into the recorder with the preamble to the interrogation—names, subject of interrogation, date, participants, and so on.

"Mr. Miles. We are investigating your possible involvement in a criminal enterprise which has resulted in multiple murders, patent fraud . . ." Ben followed the exact same protocol as Mike Carney using a duplicate set of evidence.

Gary Fremont, ever stoic, answered Ben. "Mr. Miles will have nothing to say to you. We will be asking for disclosure of everything you have concerning this accusation."

Ben never was a man of diplomatic proclivities. "Fine. Then we're finished here. Mr. Miles will be arraigned early this afternoon. I'll notify you of the time. Do you have a phone number?"

Gary Fremont pulled a business card from inside his immaculate silk coat pocket. "Use the cell phone number."

Ben answered, "Stathos, please escort Mr. Miles to the holding cell."

Mr. Fremont intervened. "I would like to have Mr. Miles released until his arraignment. I will take him back to my office where we can have some privacy."

"No. If you want to talk to him, you may accompany him to his cell. Take all the time you want." Ben walked out of Room 5.

Stathos had Bart stand. He placed the handcuffs back on and escorted both men to a holding cell.

Ben Rubalcava was finishing a homemade ham and turkey sandwich when Mike Carney knocked on the side of his cubicle. Ben looked up into a huge grin covering his partner's entire face. "Let me guess. You're Ed McMahon incarnate and I've just won a million dollars." He swiveled around in his chair and waited for a response.

"Well, I shouldn't smile, but if you wanted to bet, I'm willing to wager that Bart Miles is going to cash in all his chips at Huntsville. They found Bartocci's home out near Onalaska. They searched the place from top to bottom and came up with enough evidence to fry his fat ass."

"I give up. What'd they get?"

"A digital recording and a schedule of phone calls between Bartocci and Miles. In the recording he lays out every piece of information tying Miles to hiring him to execute people. Not only on this case, but on two other unsolved ones. He must have been one sadistic son of a bitch because he described each killing in rich detail, so they told me." Mike shifted his weight, placing his arm vertical on the cubicle divider. "They're bringing it in now. Looks like Mr. Bartocci didn't trust Miles for the long run. The calls were recorded and can be traced to Bart Miles. He may be a CEO but he's got to be the dumbest son of a bitch around." Mike made an addendum, "And if that wasn't enough, Bartocci has evidence concerning another nine executions, including who was killed and who the bad guys were. The bad guys included two women who didn't much care for their husbands. It's crazy."

Ben rolled his chair as far back as he could. "I know they initially identified Bartocci through the FBI, but how'd they find out where he lived?"

"You're gonna love this," Mike beamed, and he pointed at Ben. "Remember your idea to show photos all around and how it got poo-pooed?"

"Yeah, that sure pissed me off."

"Well, taking all the credit for it, the DA's office finally placed a picture of Bartocci on local television and asked the people to call in with information. They got a phone call five minutes after it hit the screens. I think they tried to keep that information away from us." Mike laughed out loud and then whispered down at Ben, "Don't tell anyone, but they've got self-esteem problems. But back to my story. A neighbor recognized him and had noted that his mail had not been picked up for weeks. The neighbor turned over a huge stack of mail. Unbelievably simple."

Sixty-Five

Tuesday Evening,
August 3

Across the Country

News travels fast. CNN broke the story first with the 10:00 p.m. airing of Anderson Cooper. Details were sketchy but the arrest of an oil company CEO and a cohort of other suspects on conspiracy and murder charges was delicious to the American public. Give 'em a juicy murder case and place it on top of anti-oil company sentiment, and Mr. John Q. Public will feed for weeks. The other networks scrambled to find out anything available about the case. The snowball rolled down the hill.

"Oh, really?" Susie listened intently. "No, I don't think he does. Wait a minute." Susie called to Tom. "Tom. It's Paige. Come out here and look at CNN. Come here quick."

Susie, still clinging to the phone, heard some muffled sounds as she walked toward the television. Tom appeared in the doorway naked as a Jaybird and brushing his teeth.

"It's Paige on the phone. Everything is on the news."

Tom returned to the bedroom and reappeared without the toothbrush but with pajama bottoms. He joined Susie, Anderson Cooper, and via the phone, Paige.

"Arrests were made in several states and the scope of this story is still unfolding." Backdropping Anderson was a photo of Bart Miles, exiting a police car handcuffed and under guard. "The Houston Assistant District Attorney had no further information but stated that a press briefing would be held at ten o'clock tomorrow morning. We'll bring you updates as more is learned."

Paige, now on the speaker system, asked, "Dad, did you know anything about this?"

"I wasn't certain but I knew they were hot on the trail. I was hoping for today and here we have it." Tom scrolled through the other news channels but nothing appeared on the screen related to the arrests. "I don't see anything on the other channels but I'm sure it's about to hit the fan. You call Steve and Bill Newton and we'll call Don. Get set for interesting times."

Hit the fan it did. Elizabeth Harker, still in her neatly tailored suit, studied Anderson speaking directly to her. She walked to the liquor cabinet but not to have her evening glass of wine. Her right hand shook uncontrollably as she twisted the cap on a bottle of Grey Goose. The bottle, full the night before, emptied before filling her glass. She turned it upside-down and tapped the bottom for the few last drops. With glass in hand, she walked back to her couch and grabbed the remote. She channel-surfed and on the third troll caught breaking news of the events on MSNBC and ABC. At Fox News the banner scrolling right to left along the bottom of the screen read:

Houston oil executive and others arrested in murder conspiracy.

She stared at the screen. Here it was again. It would be just a matter of time before they came after her. Liz Harker's psyche frayed. She was turning psychotic. Delusions had become her reality. Time was precious but the television kept calling to her. She thought of the Seilers. *Assholes.* She thought of Bart Miles. *He's going to bring me into this. He's cracking and will turn on me. Vince Bolen has probably already given them my name. They're coming after me as well.* Her thoughts turned again to Tom Seiler. *Once Seiler hears my name he will expose me for my part in the Alvin murders.* For the second time Tom Seiler had ruined her life. She was the victim. Enraged, she stood and violently hurled the glass at the sliding patio door. The wine glass shattered into hundreds of shards. Liz pulled the patio door open and walked to the railing. Below her, the street and sidewalks were jammed with vehicles and people. *I can end this misery.* For a second or two she contemplated, and came precariously close to, jumping over the railing and onto the backs of the nobodies on the street. But beyond the white-hot emotions of hate, fear, rage, and depression was a need. She wanted to survive—at any cost. In response to all that had happened in the Alvin situation Liz had done some long-range planning even before leaving Houston for New York. From out of nowhere came a thought—a thought perfectly normal for a narcissistic sociopath. She took in a large breath, exhaled slowly into the steamy New York night, and walked directly to her bedroom.

She began taking her clothes off, well aware that it could be a long time before she had the opportunity to dress in a manner she deserved. She changed to sweatpants and sneakers. Casual clothes, her makeup bag, and a pair of jeans fit snugly into two small suitcases.

At eye-level in her closet was a safe—not large, not small. She punched in the required numbers and listened. A slight grinding sound preceded a small click. Liz turned the handle and opened the door. Inside, a thick manila envelope rested on the bottom. She took the envelope and, without looking at it, placed it in her large shoulder handbag. She called for a taxi. Liz made a final look around the apartment living room. It was a charming, even elegant, place to live. Few people could enjoy a better view in all of New York City. But this home, and everything else in her life, was being taken from her. She walked out of the door.

Tom picked up the phone and looked at his watch. *Who'd call at this hour?*

"Tom Seiler."

"Mr. Seiler. My name is Megyn Kelly from Fox News. I apologize for calling at this hour, but . . ."

Sixty-Six

Wednesday Morning,
August 4

Houston, Texas

The national news media honed in on the sensational murder
case involving Tom Seiler. Once again Tom had won a
dubious and very unlucky lottery. His picture flashed across
screens, along with those of Don, Elam, Sarah, Bart Miles,
and John Bartocci. Tom, Don Seiler, and Elam Duquette were
being hailed as heroes while the press excoriated Bart Miles.
Newsgathering efforts spread like a virus across the networks.
After Fox News and *The O'Reilly Factor*, NBC's *Dateline* called
at seven in the morning, followed by *20/20* and *Primetime*.
The staff of *The O'Reilly Factor* worked feverishly to book Tom
and Don for a prime-time interview with Bill O'Reilly. All
the networks cast Elam as something of a homespun national
hero: a hardworking guy whose shot at the American Dream
was destroyed by a greedy, scum-of-the-earth oilman. It was
the perfect footnote to the tale of corporate greed. CNN
broadcasters amplified the original story and ABC, NBC,
and CBS each gave a variation of a common theme: the little

guy against vile capitalists. The public, atheist to evangelist, relished the new biblical tale of David and Goliath. As grisly as it was, the story served as a respite from Cap and Trade, National Healthcare, Afghanistan, and in-your-face partisan politics. The downside of it all was that neither Tom nor Don would agree to appear on a show.

Liz Harker's prediction came true. During that first fitful night Bart weighed his options. The stack of evidence given to Gary Fremont overwhelmed his senses. He had been bagged and the top of the bag tied securely around his neck. Bart possessed a frantic notion that by pulling Liz into the crime he would somehow absolve his guilt. He did everything possible to tie Liz directly to every facet of the terrible story. Over the protestations of Gary Fremont, Bart vetted his frustrations.

"She's the one who started the whole fucking mess," Bart fumed at the investigators. "She hated Tom Seiler because he knew she was involved in those murders in Alvin a couple of years back. She went after the Seilers and planned to make a fortune from me. She found out about the JETS and knew that, in the right hands, it would be worth hundreds of millions, even billions. She was going to destroy them and, in the process, make money. If it weren't for her, nothing would have ever happened. Go get her. She's the real bastard in this. And not just on this. She's done more shit than you can imagine."

Ben wrote a note to himself: *Discuss later—other criminal activity.* He remembered Tom's statement to check her out. *Need a warrant immediately.*

Once he started to crack, Bart went beyond accusations of Elizabeth Harker. Everyone was a target. Ignoring his attorney completely, Bart tried to foster the idea that Frank Milsap was the real catalyst for all that took place within Wellington Oil. Fred Barrister supposedly came first to Frank Milsap with the idea to steal the patent. Bart gave an explanation that his only sin was not taking an active role in preventing the crime. And certainly he had not ordered anyone to be killed. Carlos Aguirre murdered Juan, Elam, and Sarah on his own, with no complicity on Bart's part.

The only levity to the whole sordid mess was when Bart Miles explained away his contracts with John Bartocci.

"They really were land contracts. I own properties all over Texas."

He tried to suppress it, but Ben laughed, as much at Gary Fremont's expression at Bart's statement. He answered as professionally as possible. Rather than saying *Right, and I'm the tooth fairy,* he opted for, "We'll let the jury decide."

Ben offered nothing in return for Bart's information, but Bart sang for another hour like a canary. A pissant canary at that. And Elizabeth Harker was the main subject of the song.

As Bart Miles hobbled down the hall toward his cell Gary Fremont turned to Ben and stated, "I'd like to address a plea bargain with the district attorney."

Ben looked him in the eye. "The office is in Suite 600. I don't make those calls, which is good for you because my vote is capital one with max punishment. It's your job to defend him but I wouldn't plan on being his attorney for very long." Ben walked away.

Ben returned to his cubicle and called Patricia Lykos's office. Twenty minutes later he walked into Suite 600 just as Gary Fremont was leaving. He gave a slight nod of the head but said nothing. His meeting with the district attorney lasted fifteen minutes. With her full approval, Ben called the New York Police Department. Within three hours, an arrest warrant was issued for Ms. Elizabeth T. Harker and NYPD detectives, accompanied by two FBI agents, were on their way to Cornvale & Hickens.

"Hey, let's go get a beer," said Mike Carney, appearing out of nowhere. "It's been a good week."

Before Ben could answer, his phone rang. He picked it up. "Detective Rubalcava." He quickly responded, "Sure, fire away." He stared into blank space as the person on the other end of the phone spoke. Ben's facial expressions showed intense interest in the conversation. He finally responded, "It doesn't matter about the timing. If you want to bring it down here right now why don't you meet Mike and me at the Front Porch Pub?" A quick pause preceded his final comment. "Great. We'll see you there in an hour." Ben hung up the phone and looked up at his partner with a humongous smile plastered all over his face.

"I give up again. What's the good news?"

"It was Tom Seiler. He wants to share a wealth of circumstantial evidence against our former DA Elizabeth Harker. It's all related to the murder case out of Alvin, when the attorney Barry Colter committed suicide. Seems as though Harker is probably a criminal of the first degree. Tom will join us for a beer and blow open the whole justice system. I love it."

Mike answered, "All the more reason to celebrate. Let's make tracks."

Ben stacked some folders in the middle of his desk, tossed an empty cardboard coffee cup into the trashcan, and stood up. "Justice is about to be served."

They walked out into the boiling streets of Houston, their spirits higher than the temperature.

Shortly before the end of the business day FBI agents and New York City detectives arrived at the corporate headquarters of Cornvale & Hickens Global Wealth Management in search of Elizabeth Harker.

The receptionist responded by turning pale and going into a serious panic attack. "I, I don't remember seeing her today." She called Liz's phone but no one answered. "She doesn't seem to be in her office. You might talk to one of our other executives."

"Thank you. We are in a hurry."

In half a minute, a tall man in his late fifties and sporting a thousand-dollar suit approached the investigators. "I'm Henry Fulton. What can I do for you?"

In the short discussion, Henry told them that neither he nor any of the other employees had seen Elizabeth Harker that day.

"We need her address right away."

The receptionist fumbled at the computer before printing out an address on Forty-Ninth Street. The lead agent gave four business cards to Henry Fulton and the receptionist. "If you see or hear from her, contact me immediately. This is a criminal investigation."

On the way out of the door FBI agent Sam Waters punched at his cell phone. "This is Sam. She hasn't been here all day. We're about twenty-five minutes away. If you have anyone near Forty-Ninth and Broadway send them there immediately and seal the apartment off. The apartment is at . . ."

Two policemen met the agents at the entrance to the apartment complex. No sign of Elizabeth Harker. The agents used the superintendent's master key to gain access to her apartment.

In her bedroom they found a business suit on her bed and a significant assortment of dresses, pants, sweaters, blouses, and shoes still neatly hanging or stacked inside her walk-in closet. The only thing clearly out of place was shattered glass near the patio door. Neither she nor her suitcases were found. Where she had gone, nobody knew.

Sixty-Seven

Thursday, February 10

Houston, Texas

All rise. The 295th Judicial District Court, South District of Texas, Houston Division, is now in session, the Honorable Richard Prosser presiding." Everyone in the courtroom stood at the bailiff's command. Only six months from his initial arrest, Bart Miles was on trial for his life. Relative to other states, Texas capital justice does not get mired down in red tape. A national audience followed the trial.

Walter Vitter presented a chronological conveyor belt of witnesses and evidence, each piece tightening the metaphorical noose around Bart Miles's neck. Vince Bolen testified first, stating that Ms. Elizabeth Harker hired him to find some dirt, any dirt, on the Seiler family. His testimony concerning Don Seiler and the JETS established the link between Liz Harker and Don's invention. Jason French admitted on the stand that he made new plans from the prototype stolen the night of the tornado in Luling. Herman Soboda's tale of the threats he received, the ruthless killing of his dog, and the envelope full of money was riveting. His testimony tied in perfectly with the evidence from Carlos Aguirre, including Carlos's DNA on the money. Carlos's letter of confession and the tape recording were admitted into evidence over the protestations of the defense. Bill Newton, wheeled into the courtroom by an assistant district attorney, made the link between Fred Barrister and Wellington Oil. In exchange for his testimony, Fred Barrister plea-bargained for a three-year sentence. He had kept detailed records and the timeline of phone calls and visits with Wellington Oil matched events on the ground quite well. If there was anyone to feel sorry for during the trial, Gary Fremont, the defense attorney for Bart Miles, was high on the list. Painting Bart Miles as an innocent victim of circumstance was not just difficult, it was impossible.

Three witnesses were taken out of order and saved until last: Tom Seiler, a forensic pathology expert, and Don Seiler.

Tom was called to the stand on Monday, February 14. It felt strange not being called as an expert witness, but rather as a witness to parts of an astounding series of criminal actions.

As he walked through the door toward the witness stand, Tom felt a cold sweat spring from his body. *The same courtroom,* he thought. It was, indeed, the same courtroom in which he testified concerning an 18-wheeler accident that killed four family members. He was grilled at length by then-District Attorney Elizabeth Harker. Tom glanced to his left and saw the two rows of jury members sitting in comfortable, dark leather chairs. Next he looked at Judge Prosser, the Texas flag at the judge's left rear, and the United States flag to his right. The circular seal of the state of Texas formed an almost perfect halo above the judge's head. Tom stopped a few feet from the witness stand and was sworn in.

"Do you solemnly swear that the testimony you are about to give will be the truth, the whole truth, and nothing but the truth, so help you God?"

"I do." Tom had given the same answer at hundreds of times before. He proceeded to the enclosed wooden witness box and sat down in another comfortable chair. He surveyed the courtroom. At the back of the room sat a packed gathering of family, friends, and reporters. The walls were painted beige with magnificent cherry wood paneling. Next to the rear doors were thin vertical windows through which police officers peered; in addition to two marshals in the courtroom, the officers were ready to suppress any trouble that might occur. Probably fifteen feet to Tom's left front were the mahogany tables hosting the defense lawyers and Bart Miles. Approximately ten feet to the right was the table for the prosecution. Two young attorneys sat at the table; Assistant District Attorney Walter Vitter, a handsome man in his late-thirties, stood in front of Tom. Vitter, nephew of Senator David Vitter of Louisiana, would lead the prosecution. Tom had the occasion to work with Walter Vitter on a few occasions during the past ten years. Walter Vitter was competent in Tom's eyes.

A quick overview of his personal history was given—no professional fanfare recognizing him as the best expert witness in this part of Texas.

"Do you recognize these photographs?" Walter Vitter gave a sizable stack of photos to Tom.

Tom looked closely at several of the photographs and then glanced quickly at the others. When finished, he calmly aligned the photos back into a neat stack. "Yes, sir. I took the photos at the Breuner Funeral Home in Luling, Texas."

"Your Honor, I would like to enter these photographs as exhibits . . ." The photos were placed into evidence. Walter Vitter continued.

"Why did you even consider taking these pictures?"

"Well sir, I have always been an inquisitive person." Tom sat up straight in the chair. "And I'm also a tornado buff. I've seen hundreds of hours of tornado videos, damaged towns and cities, and injured and dead people. My wife even bought me a six-day tour with Extreme Chase Tours."

"Objection. Irrelevant." Gary Fremont needed to get in a blow or two of his own.

Judge Prosser asked Walter Vitter, "Are you going someplace with this questioning?"

"Yes, your Honor. There is a direct link between Mr. Seiler's background and the photographs."

"Overruled. You may continue." The judge nodded at Tom.

Tom continued, "As I said, I have seen the results of tornadoes on the bodies of victims. In addition to catastrophic injuries, people who have ridden through a tornado tend to be covered with cuts and scratches from sand, rocks, twigs, and other airborne debris. The markings that I have seen are everywhere on the persons." He paused just enough to allow his comments to sink in with the jury. He wasn't testifying as an expert witness but he was every bit the expert witness. "When I looked at Mr. Duquette and Ms. Bettner I was sure that they did not have those kinds of injuries. Once the mud had been cleaned off of their faces, I knew something was wrong."

"Objection. Mr. Seiler is not an expert witness."

Vitter was quick to react. "Your Honor, I am not asking for an expert witness. I am only asking Mr. Seiler why he took the pictures. The photographs will speak for themselves."

"Overruled."

Tom's testimony continued in the same vein for the next two hours. The flow of the questions and answers chronologically covered Tom's analysis of the strange injury to Juan Delgado, the photographs of Elam and Sarah, suspicions concerning Fred Barrister, what Don had told him of his meetings with Wellington Oil and Exploration, the attempted murder of Don, Bill, and himself, and the confrontation with Vince Bolen in New York. Walter Vitter had done his homework.

Gary Fremont made a strategic decision to get Tom off of the stand as quickly as possible. Tom was far too experienced in forensic engineering and he was still well known for his good-guy-finishes-first encounter with prosecutors in the Alvin murder case.

"I have no questions."

As Tom exited the courtroom, Walter Vitter called his next witness. "The prosecution wishes to call Doctor James Marcuson to the stand." Doctor Marcuson was an expert in traumatic injuries and had operated on scores of tornado victims throughout the state of Texas. He verified that Tom's suspicions of the injuries to Elam and Sarah were correct. He was off the stand in twenty minutes without being cross-examined.

"Nope. Not going to do it. I want no sympathy, I want them to hang the son of a bitch strictly on facts."

Walter Vitter acquiesced. "I got it. It's your call. Let's get after it." He turned and walked through the courtroom door. Don followed.

Don, dressed in nice tan trousers and an upscale, plaid long-sleeved shirt but no tie, tried walking erect and strong down the center of the courtroom, but it just didn't work.

Without his cane he had little stability. He wove back and forth until reaching the witness stand; while the bailiff conducted the swearing-in ritual, sweat dripped from Don's forehead. He refused help to the witness stand and willed himself into the cushioned chair. Two minutes had passed, no questions asked, and Don was already exhausted.

"Mr. Seiler, would you please state your full name, your occupation, place of residence, and . . . ."

Don's journey to this courtroom was starkly different than that of his older brother. He kept his historical background succinct but riveting.

"Yes, sir. My name is Donald Hudson Seiler. I grew up in San Antonio, Texas, and attended MacArthur High School until my own immaturity got me expelled." Out came a sheepish grin. "Like most teenage boys in my predicament, I enlisted in the navy. I served two tours in the Vietnam War, one on the USS John Hancock and the second one in-country at Cam Ranh Bay. I wasn't any kind of hero, I just did my duty for four years." Dan paused and looked around the courtroom.

Walter Vitter prodded Don. "What happened after the navy?"

Don made a stoic facial expression as he reflected upon the question. He arched his back, trying to relieve a spasm, and then answered, "I wish I could say the navy made me grow up, but it didn't. I had a few minor scrapes with the police here in Houston. Once I began to get it, I used the GI Bill to get an education, first at San Jac—er, that's San Jacinto—Junior College and then at Texas A&M."

Fremont, realizing that Don was a poster child for the sympathetic witness, had to interrupt.

"Objection, your honor. We don't need a full biography of Mr. Seiler. I'll stipulate that he turned himself around and is a good guy."

Vitter expected the objection sooner. "Your honor, we are almost finished with Mr. Seiler's personal background and I assure you that it is all relevant to my follow-up questions."

"Make sure it is. Overruled."

Vitter glanced at Fremont; a wisp of a smile rose from the corner of his mouth. He continued, "As succinctly as possible, Mr. Seiler, give us an overview of your life since entering Texas A&M as it relates to your profession."

"Yes, sir. I graduated with a degree in civil engineering," Don continued without realizing that he was talking to himself, "and that confirms the existence of God."

The courtroom burst into laughter simultaneously with Fremont's objection. It was sustained along with Judge Prosser's order to separate church and state.

Don wrapped things up with, "My degree emphasized structures, and since I had always loved the Gulf of Mexico, I signed on with Poole Offshore. I stayed with Poole for twenty years in Louisiana, California, and Alaska until multiple sclerosis told me to stay the hell off of high places."

Giggles all around the courtroom.

Vitter walked closer to the jury but turned his head partly toward the courtroom spectators. He asked, "Did you retire or go on worker's compensation?"

"Objection, your honor. Irrelevant."

"Sustained."

Walter Vitter altered the question. "Mr. Seiler, what did you do after discovering you had MS?"

"Sir, that was over twenty years ago and I was still pretty mobile and had good eyesight. I decided to start my own engineering firm specializing in structural design for offshore platforms. Seiler Engineering." He sighed, his cheeks like deflating balloons. "For a former loser, I was pretty successful before sinking most of my life savings into the JETS."

Gary Fremont's objection only served to ally Don to the jury. They had heard vast testimony pointing to greed, corruption, and murder. Now they were looking into the face of the one living man most affected by the whole sordid sequence of events. Three of the six male jurors had passed through similar turbulence; in fact, one of them, only twenty-six years old, sensed a cathartic reaction to Don's testimony.

Don testified for almost two hours, interrupted only by lunch. Walter proved remarkable in emphasizing the full metanoia of Don's life: hard working, strong husband and father, member of several civic groups, and, though not religious, an active volunteer for numerous community church projects in Ventura, California. The timing was fortunate; Vitter wrapped up the most significant testimony following lunch.

"All rise . . ." The bailiff did his duty.

"Do you know a Mr. Elam Duquette?"

Don replied with a twist of anger. "I did until he was murdered." Don looked directly at Bart Miles. His stare was not lost on the jury—or the judge.

Gary Fremont virtually leaped out of his chair. "Objection! His statement is preposterous and coached by Mr. Vitter. Your honor, I ask for a mistrial."

Judge Prosser was pleased with neither Don nor Walter Vitter. "Sidebar in my chambers. We'll recess for twenty minutes."

In his chambers, Judge Prosser mauled Walter Vitter while Gary Fremont stood by and gloated. "I'll give you one minute to get your witness straightened out. One more shot like that and you'll both be held in contempt."

Once the courtroom settled down and Don's statement was stricken from the record, Don was led into telling the story of Elam and the JETS. He met Elam while working with Poole Offshore in Alaska. Elam was assigned to the Sam

Magee platform and Don was a structural engineer tasked to design and plan the retrofit of some damaged lateral bracing members. Don described Elam succinctly and accurately. "Elam Duquette was one crusty guy, but he was loyal to a fault. With all his time in the oil business, both on land and at sea, he knew all there is about getting oil out of the ground." Led by Walter Vitter's questions, Don outlined how their friendship kept them in touch with each other and Elam's approaching Don to start a joint venture for a simple system to extract oil from stripper wells.

"And that was it. He had the original idea; I came up with an original design; eventually my brother Tom, who testified earlier, took my design and improved upon it. I believe the system we now have is the best existing anywhere in the world."

The discourse flowed more melodically than a Beethoven symphony. Vitter asked the questions and Don told the story. A friend's idea, given life through blood, sweat, and a life's savings, had come to fruition—all except obtaining a patent.

Like Bolero, Vitter slowly brought Don's testimony toward a climax.

"Mr. Seiler, you stated that Mr. Miles asserted that they were close to finishing their own design. What was your response?"

Don answered without histrionics. "I just told Mr. Miles the truth; if they were so close then the meeting never would have taken place."

Not just the jury; all in attendance had enough common sense to see the validity of Don's statement.

"Was anything else said between you and any of the executives from Wellington?"

Again, Don remained stoic. "Yes, we did agree to a demonstration. Matter of fact, that was right after I expressed my aversion to dealing with arrogant assholes." He did not want to manipulate the jury; Don just spoke his mind. That some of the jurors either smiled at or nudged their neighbors uplifted Walter Vitter to the same degree that it crushed the defense team.

Walter returned to an earlier statement. "Mr. Seiler, let's go back to what you said a few minutes ago."

The jurors had heard overwhelming evidence against Bart Miles and his co-conspirators. They sat riveted to their chairs.

Walter Vitter asked, "You said words to the effect, 'The system we now have'. Do you actually 'have' the system? Does the JETS belong to you?"

Don looked again at Bart Miles, the jury following his lead. "Well, sir, we do have our design sitting dormant at our work site. But if you mean, 'do we have the patent so that we can do with it as we please?' then the answer is no." Without waiting for a question, Don added, his emotions clearly uncontrolled, "But Wellington Oil does have a patent. And sir," Don leaned to his side toward Judge Prosser, "if I didn't have MS I'd hammer the shit out of that sorry son of a bitch over there." He pointed at Bart Miles.

The courtroom exploded.

So did Judge Prosser. "Hold it right there, Mr. Seiler."

"Your Honor . . ." Gary Fremont stood up, hoping to gain the advantage.

"Be quiet, Mr. Fremont, and sit down." He held an outstretched hand in the defense attorney's direction. "This courtroom will come to order. Everyone be quiet or you will be expelled."

"That's it. Mr. Vitter and Mr. Seiler, you are in contempt of court and are fined $1,000 each. This is the last time. Do you understand, the last time? One more comment like that and both of you will spend the weekend in the Harris County jail. Am I making myself clear?"

Two voices echoed in tandem, "Yes, your Honor."

The proceedings finally settled down, allowing Walter Vitter to bring the testimony to a close. His final topic of the day secured the link between Fred Barrister's turning state's evidence and Herman Soboda's terrifying testimony.

"Mr. Seiler, why do you personally know that Mr. Miles hired Mr. Barrister to slow down your patenting efforts?" Walter placed his hands in his pockets and stepped back away from the witness stand.

"Two reasons. First, after my nephew and Detective Newton talked to Mr. Soboda, I talked to him. He told me he never talked to Mr. Barrister about taking over his caseload. Second, Mr. Duquette personally told me that Mr. Barrister called him and stated that Mr. Soboda was having medical problems and asked him to take our case because it was, in Mr. Barrister's words, 'Mr. Soboda's most important case.'"

"Thank you, Mr. Seiler. Your honor, the prosecution has no further witnesses."

It took three hours for the jury of the 295th District Court of Harris County, Texas, to render its verdict. "We the jury find the defendant, Mr. Bartholomew Harman Miles, guilty of capital murder as charged in the indictment." Most juries display physical signs of nervousness; this jury did not. They believed in their verdict; they despised the defendant.

Three men sat side by side in the filled courtroom. Josh's face muscles tightened like a vice. *He'll never pay enough.* He glanced quickly to his left and right. To his left, Josh saw the smile spread across Don's face; to his right, Tom sat mute as a statue.

The jury remained the focus of the trial. "What say you all to this verdict . . ."

To each charge the jury found Bart Miles guilty as charged. Josh watched the reply of the jury; Tom and Don looked at the pallid face of Bart Miles. Tears welled up and traced down Bart's puffy cheeks. As an uncontrollable quiver ravaged his body, the once arrogant and powerful CEO of Wellington Oil and Exploration slumped into his chair. He was a beaten man. He knew he would die sometime in the not too distant future. Premeditated murder carries a life sentence in some states; in Texas the predator will be executed–guaranteed. Bart leaned forward and sobbed with agonizing indignity.

Sixty-Eight

Sunday, March 20

Broken Wing Ranch

Seven and a half months following the initial arrests, Don received all patent rights to the JETS. Without the bulldog efforts of Wallis Raymond it would have been years. Frank Milsap was apprehended in Vincennes, Indiana, in October. Preparation for his trial moved much swifter than the others. Elizabeth Harker disappeared without a trace. Law enforcement, helped by *America's Most Wanted,* placed her on the Ten Most Wanted list. Life settled down and celebration time finally arrived. In typical Seiler fashion another party broke out at the Broken Wing Ranch. The weather was unseasonably warm and the skies dusted with feathered cirrus clouds. Exactly one year had passed since the night of the Luling tornado. It was a beautiful day in Texas, and Bear and Catfish had agreed to serve once again as honorary hosts. Barking, wagging their tails, and licking everyone possible, the two canines set the tone for the day. Everyone who had any part in the successful case against Wellington Oil and Exploration joined in the mix.

Other close friends—Jo and James, Randy and Jeanie, Frank and Arcellia from across FM 1486, even Serial Killer—made for a festive gathering. Ada Pittinger, owner of the Ainsworth House, Terry and Debbie Keane from Monte's bar, and Mary Otter came from Luling. Hector and Angelina drove in from Smiley. The prosecutors from the trial, really good guys, partied with the best of them. All the detectives and FBI agents came to the party. One of the first invitations, gladly accepted, was to Delana, the taxi driver. Josh Bettner arrived the day before, spending the night in the unfinished room in the attic. The final icing on the cake came with Jim Bitters, one-time executive with Wellington Oil and Exploration. It was an enormous celebration. Unfortunately, Bill Newton was fighting the good fight to recovery and just couldn't make it. The one major departure from tradition could be seen in the absence of children. They had always been the staple of Seiler parties, but on this occasion common sense excluded them. Multiple coolers of beer, all of it Miller Lite, wine, and soft drinks were in a military "dress it right and cover down" formation at the far end of the patio. To the front of the patio, two long tables housed a Texas smorgasbord of beef brisket, sirloin steaks hot off the grill, pulled pork from the roasted pig, barbecue chicken, hamburgers, hot dogs, potato and tossed salads, green beans, chips and salsa, and fresh rolls. Country music from XM Radio Channel 17 played out in the background. Tom and Susie took turns giving tours of the caboose.

As the day rolled on, small groups gathered in conversation. Unlike basketball coaches who talk of little except the game, everyone mixed it up in grand fashion. "Tell me about Luling and that Watermelon Thump." "What's the latest from UT with your daughter?" "Did you hear about the renovations over on Lake Conroe?" "What's the economy look like to you?" "A little Cajun boy comes to his Poppa and says . . ." The topics ran the gauntlet from family history to political malfeasance, with a good deal spent on all that had happened in the last year.

"Did you ever think about giving up on the patent? I mean, they had it in their hands." Randy Rouse, thin and wiry, another Aggie and a retired lieutenant general whose ranch spread across a neighboring five-hundred-acre piece of land, asked the critical question.

Don, beer in one hand, cane in the other, walked slowly toward the caboose as he answered, "No, I really didn't. I made some overtures to just getting out of the business altogether. But I knew that things weren't right and that I had to find out what was wrong. To be honest, it was Tom and his never-ending attention to detail that kept me going. When we walked out of the funeral home after the tornado he knew that Elam and Sarah had been murdered. That always stuck in my mind even as seemingly unrelated things came our way."

Randy didn't drink alcohol. He sipped on a Mountain Dew as they made their way toward the caboose with the Santa Fe logo. "So, what's up with your invention now?"

Don stopped and pointed back toward the flagpole. "See those people at the flag? Check out the one with the glasses and red shirt."

Randy nodded in the affirmative. "Right. I see him."

"Well, he's probably the best patent attorney around. Great guy. Retired blue suiter. From the minute he joined forces with us, he just ran with the ball. Without him, we'd still be mired in the mud. It doesn't matter that it was obvious I had been screwed out of the patent, it would have taken forever to re-establish my claim to it."

They both stared at the laughing Wallis Raymond, obviously engaged in the telling of a war story of some sort. Wallis's wife Gracie, a stunning Virginia native possessing a youthful smile and a soft accent defining her southern heritage, raised her eyebrows in mock disbelief of an off-color punch line.

Don continued, "He went on a crusade to bring us back the patent." Don smiled broadly. "We waited until the patent belonged to us to have this party. Now I get to reap some benefits from an enterprise that cost us so dearly."

Josh appeared out of nowhere. "Hey, Mr. Seiler. Don't know if anyone can throw a party like the Seilers." He held up another can of soda.

Don reached toward Josh and spoke to Randy. "Randy, this is Josh Bettner. His mother is Sarah. He's the one I spoke about." Then he turned to Josh. "And Josh, this is Randy Rouse, a former Aggie and a retired three-star general. I'd be willing to bet he served in the 82nd Airborne Division."

Randy gave his condolences to Josh over his great loss.

"Thank you, sir. She was the nicest person I've ever known. I know she's my mother but I really do mean that. Others will say the same thing."

"I'm sure you do and I'm sure she was." Randy changed the subject. "By the way, Don was right. I did serve with the 82nd, both at Fort Bragg and in Vietnam. I commanded a rifle company in the 508th Infantry, the Red Devils. Tell me a little about your great-grandfather." Soon the retired officer and the young man were engaged in a deep discussion of the army and the expectations of what might be in store for a new soldier in basic training. Tom drifted off to another gathering of storytellers. By evening's end Josh put the final stamp on his decision to enlist in the army with the intention of serving in the All-American division of his great-grandfather. Within a year, Josh would be serving his country in Afghanistan.

Don hobbled over to the flagpole and started talking to James and Jo. As soon as Jo meandered over to a group of women, Serial Killer walked up from out of nowhere, not so much to talk as to just listen.

James patted Don on the shoulder and asked, "So, are you off to buy a Mercedes or a Porsche?"

Don put things into perspective. "Naw, I'm going to grab Cindy, Tom, and Susie and haul them down to Tiki Island to do some fishing."

It never really was about the money. It was about doing something meaningful.

From the steps of the caboose Tom looked over at a laughing Don seemingly oblivious to the ravages of MS. *I don't know how he does it.* Tom's thoughts ran through his own life episodes: keeping Don out of trouble on more occasions than one could count; going through high school with his now deceased brother, Jack; and raising his three children. He thought of Tom Jr., an airline pilot killed in a boating accident, and the younger two, both quite successful and happily married–Paige, the engineer and part-time colleague, and Steve, the lawyer. He looked beyond his brother and saw Susie laughing with a mixed crowd of men and women, young and old. *I really do love that woman. She is the tonic keeping me going.* His next thought was of his mother. Janie Seiler would have been ninety-five. He thought gently of her. *What a woman. What a spectacular woman.* He smiled at the thought of the means by which she garnered the title of Profanity Jane. It was the wrong crowd now, but later on in the evening, when only the close friends and family remained, he would start another round of Janie Seiler stories. Tom also longed to tell stories of his many friends over the years, particularly the irreplaceable Travis White, killed in the maelstrom of the Alvin incident. Too many of Tom's friends and family had died. However measured, Tom sat far off at the wrong end of the bell-shaped curve for tragedy.

Tom's mood changed to a darker tone. The noisy laughter, happy faces, and the genuine good mood faded away, disappearing into thin air. He fought with his own demons as he searched for an answer to his question of human behavior. *Why is there so much evil? From what human sewer do people like Bart Miles rise?* He thought of himself and of the people who had surrounded his life. *I have to stop thinking of the evil and believe in the good. I am destroying myself.* Another story—of Carlos Aguirre, a genuinely evil person who might have been on the road to redemption—would not go away. *Is there always some hope for even the worst?*

Tom needed release. No one really noticed as he walked away from the party and toward the small hangar. Five minutes later the throng of people were drawn to the sight and sound of the yellow Piper Cub moving to the end of the runway. Tom waved to the party from the cockpit, turned 180 degrees, gave full throttle and soared from the runway. Tom normally buzzed the ranch but this time he continued due east and disappeared into the sky. Turning to the south, Tom caught up with FM 1486 and followed it past Dacus and Dobbin, surveying the growing countryside. Houston's tentacles reached into Grimes County.

Cool, dense air rushed by his open cockpit and the clear spring skies lifted his spirits—but only for a few short moments. The thoughts kept slipping out of the box lid of his mind. The memory of his meeting with Angelina Escobar and hearing her story of Sarah and Elam's murders made Tom sick to the stomach. The horizon, the demarcation between land and sky, lay directly before him but he could not see it; nor could he enjoy the pine trees and homes passing beneath him. Angelina's tale held his thoughts in bondage. To the constant, gentle vibration of the engine Tom saw visions: Elam, Sarah,

Juan Delgado, a shooting in Luling, Bill Newton paralyzed on the ground, and the sorry son of a bitch Bart Miles. Then an apparition appeared before him, somewhere in front of the plane. The vision above them all was the one person who could have averted everything–Elizabeth Harker.

Forty-five minutes, enough time to worry Susie, passed before he returned. Though his heart wasn't in it, Tom buzzed the party from the southwest one time. The wings swayed up and down in salute to his friends and family. A wide turn south and then a vector due west brought the Cub into alignment with the runway. He touched down, slowed, and moved directly into the hangar. The demons were still there, but his mechanical friend made them smaller. Tom got out of the plane and grabbed his first beer of the day. It would not be the last.

The party ended around midnight. Most had gone home or to motels down in Conroe. Before leaving, Ada Pittinger, Terry and Debbie Keane, and Mary Otter each asked on separate occasions that Tom, Don, Nancy, and the rest of the family join them for the upcoming Watermelon Thump.

When Ada asked the question, Don's answer blew her away.

"Ada, Cindy and I are going one step further."

Cindy heard him and walked up next to him. She put her arms around his waist.

Don continued, "Maybe the best way to say it is, 'Hi, neighbor.' We bought the small grey house on East Houston. It's been renovated and is just what we need."

"You what?" Ada drew her hands to her face, her eyes as big as saucers and her mouth wide open. "Oh, my goodness. That's wonderful, just wonderful!"

She threw her arms around both Don and Cindy. "We'll make sure you get the red carpet treatment."

"We've thought about it quite a bit. Texas, here we come."

Everyone clapped, hooted, and hollered. Don, without question, and Cindy, with some reservation, were moving to Luling, Texas.

Ada was wise. She cornered Cindy just enough to give her the lowdown on life in small-town Texas. Peaceful, friendly, historical with charming architecture, local events galore, and access to Austin and San Antonio were among the best features. Ada, not wanting to intimidate Cindy, backed off with a simple statement of fact—their town straddling the Southern Pacific Railroad was one of the best-kept secrets in Texas. She added a small disclaimer: "Matter of fact, the only real downsides to it all are that some places do smell like crude oil and that, on a personal note, we sold the Ainsworth House. My cooking proved so good that I've decided to dedicate my time to the best family restaurant and catering business in Texas."

Don rubbed his hands together and answered with a question. "What's the name and where is it?"

"We're calling it 'Ada Lou's Two Chicks Cooking' and it's located next to the Watermelon Shop."

Another piece of the Texas landscape was passing into history while another was being born.

The out-of-town guests left, escorted dutifully by Bear and Catfish. The whole family, accompanied by James and Jo and Frank and Arcellia, stayed long enough to clean up the mess. They filled plastic construction bags with paper plates, plastic knives, and forks; empty beer cans were placed in separate bags and placed next to the side of the garage. Tom always put them there so that Raymer Johnson, a poor black handyman living in Dacus, could take them to a nearby recycling center. Tom paid him more than fairly for work he would do around the house. For his part, Raymer never slacked off on a job. They were friends who, in spite of a huge economic chasm between them, respected each other. Tom invited him to the party but Raymer declined. Leftovers were given to Steve and Kelly, Ross and Paige, and a few of the "late-party animals." James and Jo, food in hand, were the last to leave. It was past two o'clock in the morning.

Nancy, Tom, Susie, Don, and Cindy sat at the patio table. Josh was upstairs dead asleep, totally exhausted by the Seiler family. Small sparkles of diamonds lit the heavens. At one point a meteorite slashed through the night sky. The family was, like Josh, dead tired but relaxed and pleased with the gathering. The party did bring some closure to all that had taken place. At least, it was a good start.

Cindy inhaled deeply on her last cigarette of the night. She mused on life. "Isn't it amazing how life unfolds and how people affect others? Everything is so connected."

Nancy, her head resting on the back of the wrought iron chair, answered. "It really is. I wonder what would have happened had the photograph of Vince Bolen not been taken?"

No one answered either question, each with individual silent thoughts.

Nancy continued, "Do you ever think about what went through the mind of the CEO, Miles? I mean, how could a person we never knew wield such power over our lives?"

Don's thoughts turned to her question. "As rotten as he was, Miles was more stupid than anything else. If he had a lick of sense he would have noticed that problems were bubbling up all over the place. He's the face of insatiable greed. He made more money in a year than most people ever have and the son of a bitch just couldn't be satisfied. You'd sorta think that once Carlos killed the kid, Juan, Miles would have realized that things had already gone too far. At every step of the way Miles had the opportunity to stop the madness; instead, he sucked more people into his circle, and the final outcome was virtually predictable. Still, the addiction to wealth drove everything he did." Don lifted the bill of his Seabee cap until it comfortably covered the bald spot on the back of his head. "Sadly, he's a microcosm of some of the crap that's been going on in our country. For God's sake, how much is enough?" He brought his beer can to his mouth and tilted back.

Nancy rolled her head toward Don and offered, "That's a great question, little brother, and add to that the question, how many people in the world are like him?"

Don always spoke his mind. "A whole shitpot full. Matter of fact . . ."

While the others waited for him to continue, images appeared in his mind. For reasons unknown, his faces of evil–Madoff, Hitler, Stalin, Mao, John Wayne Gacy, Hugo Chavez, and others with recognizable faces but unknown names–tended to be smiling.

Nancy finally prodded him. "Matter of fact, what?"

Don was unaware of the others. All of his attention focused on a final face–a young Don Seiler. No one else would have given it a thought, but Don understood how easily he could have ended up as another Bart Miles. He answered, "Matter of fact–me.

"I could have been another Bart Miles, my butt in a death row cell at Huntsville. You guys, except maybe you, Tom, didn't know it, but I was a thug . . . a true died-in-the-wool shithead." He looked at his beer can, rotated it in his hands, and then gently set it on the table. "I drank too much, took pleasure in beating the shit out of guys who did nothing to me, was a petty thief, and did everything I could to be the meanest hombre in the valley. Worst of all, I chose the wrong friends in high school. None of us had a moral compass. Just immature, dumb kids." Don stopped.

No one replied.

Finally, Tom had his say. "Give yourself a break. You got your act together, received an education, and married the right woman. Sounds like a pretty solid turnaround to me."

Again, everyone waited for a response.

A definite quiver in his voice, Don looked at Tom. Their eyes met briefly and then they turned away.

"You saved my ass from the law more than you should have and I don't think I ever really appreciated it. I'd say thanks and all that, then go out and do something else stupid. I was too close to you and couldn't hear what you were saying. Jeez, was I a loser." Don leaned forward and grabbed the edge of the table; he surveyed his family. "Tom, if it weren't for you and a judge who reamed me one day in court I would not be here. I'd be dead. Jack died serving the country and Tom Jr. died in a tragic accident. I would have died running from a cop." His words were now coming out in broken syllables. He tried to lighten up. "Tom, as the guy said in the TV ad, 'I love you man.' But I mean it. And I apologize."

Neither being the hugging type, both men reached over and shook hands.

Tom brought closure to Don's uneasiness. "Apology accepted." Then, quite unexpectedly, he turned his focus on the whole group. "I may be the most non-religious man in Texas, but I absolutely believe that Jesus did have it right when he spoke of redemption for those who really are sorry for past transgressions. I don't really know about an afterlife, but if there is one, we'll all be surprised by who ends up in heaven and who ends up in hell."

That Tom would speak of heaven or hell left everyone dumbfounded—and mute.

Tom stretched out and crossed his legs, then added his take on the subject. "I'm a pure capitalist. Always will be. And I want the government to keep their damn hands out of my business. But at the same time, corporate America is overrun with greedy sons of bitches—CEOs, senior executives, boards of directors, and everyone else whose pay involves bonuses and back-dated options. They suck. 'I'll give you millions and you give me millions. Fuck the little guys.' Yeah, it's Enron, Adelphia, AIG, Merrill Lynch, Lehman Brothers, and all the others. Take Merrill Lynch. How in the hell can a CEO bankrupt a company and walk with more than $160 million? It's insane." Tom stared down at a small lizard making its way up the stone column. "Don't tell me that it's a case of a few bad apples. Too much of Corporate America, at least at the very top, has rigged the deck. We probably don't need a lot more in the way of regulations but we do need to enforce the ones that are on the books. Obey and enforce the damn law. Throw the crooks in the slammer."

Don turned to his oldest brother. Sixty years had passed in a flash. "And Congress, as a whole, only wants to buy votes. Like you said, Tom, you, Nancy, and I are too old to be affected. But I look at the grandkids and I just want to hit someone. Power, money, votes—what the hell is going on in our country? Screw 'em all. Left or right, Republican or Democrat, liberal or conservative. We don't need promises, we need honesty."

Don leaned forward and placed his hands on the metal arms of the chair. "And that, my friends, is my final comment. I've had a great day, and I'm going to bed."

"Me too."

"And me."

One by one, each stood up. Except Tom and Susie.

"You guys go ahead and hit the sack. We're going to perform last rites on the beer."

Sixty-Nine

Monday Early Morning, March 21

Broken Wing Ranch

How about that one last beer?" Tom stood up as he spoke to Susie.

"No thanks, honey. I'm set." Susie patted Tom on his hip as he walked by her toward the patio door. She sat in silence, enjoying the quiet.

Tom returned a minute later, turning off the patio lights before coming out. It was pitch dark save the stars above and a hint of light from the southeast and Houston. He dropped a light jacket on her lap and rubbed the top of her head. He pulled up an empty chair and turned it so that it faced both Susie and him. Tom sat down and placed his legs on one side of the vacant chair. "Care to share a footrest with me?" Unseen to her, he smiled at his wife.

Susie put her feet on the chair, edging her right foot next to his left foot.

Tom looked over at Susie. She twisted her head and answered his unasked question.

"Yes, you have. You've made my life more than interesting."

Both of them smiled. Tom reached over with his left hand and placed it on top of her right hand. He tapped out a quick drum cadence on her hand and gently stroked her hand back and forth.

"So, my handsome prince. Where to from here?"

Tom considered her very difficult question. *Where do we go from here? How's our life going to change?*

"Well, the first thing is that Don and Cindy are in good shape. They will finally reap a just reward. He, Steve, and Wallis Raymond are working out a contract with Caprock that will make him very wealthy. Don approached Jim Bitters today about joining Donelam and I think Jim will accept. That will allow Don to slow down some. Back to Caprock, those folks were my choice from day one. I'm glad Don agreed." Tom paused for just a second and then added, "I wish nothing had happened to Elam, but God knows he would have been an obstacle in working with Caprock."

Susie waited a few more seconds. "I know, but you're not answering my question."

Silence dominated the patio for a few seconds. Tom finally answered, "I think you and I ought to try our best to live our lives with no big changes. Given the economy, tort reform in Texas, and my growing older, business has slacked off just right. We're still busy enough but now we can do some of the traveling that we always wanted to do."

Susie smiled. "You're on. I'll start checking out cruises and a safari or two today."

He squeezed her hand. "I really mean it. We've worked hard. I don't think it would be wise to simply retire, but I am prepared to work more on our clock than on everyone else's clock." He took a final swallow of his Miller Lite. "What say we go to bed?"

They picked up a couple of empty beer cans, Cindy's ashtray, and a glass. At the door Tom looked down at a loyal sidekick: Bear slept in a recess next to the door. Tom extended his foot and rubbed it back and forth across Bear's side. Bear looked up at Tom, rolled over on his back, and moaned in pure canine pleasure.

In bed, Tom and Susie kissed. One of those sweet kisses that once led to other physical activities. Tonight it was a sign that all was well between them. They turned on their left sides and Tom placed his arm around her. He moved his hand to her face and stroked it gently. Susie felt secure and happy. She was asleep in one minute.

Tom tried but couldn't fall sleep. Something gnawed at him. Unfinished business. The visions returned to torment him. Juxtaposed with his recollections of the past year were memories of the murders in Alvin. He could not escape the evil that had surrounded him for much too long.

Tom gently got out of bed. He quietly opened the bedroom door, exited, and closed it without making a sound. He put on an old Tulane University sweatshirt and his jogging shorts and headed for the patio door. He took one more beer from the refrigerator. A dog barked somewhere across FM 1486. Tom stretched out again and looked out into the night sky. Comprehending evil is tough; for those having a strong sense of ethics, reconciling the relativism of behavior of those who use people with those who serve people is virtually impossible. Tom thought of Angelina Escobar. As honest and caring a person as ever lived, she was the sister, raised by the same parents, of Carlos Aguirre. *How could they be so different?* For all the detective work done by Tom, Don, Steve, Ross, and everyone else, it was Angelina Escobar who tied everything together into a very neat package. Without her convincing Carlos to put everything down a good lawyer might have been successful with placing reasonable doubt into the minds of jurors. He would never tell her, but Tom had doubts that Bart Miles would be executed without her evidence. She didn't want anyone killed; Tom did.

Tom remembered the story she told him that day they met her at her home in Smiley. In his mind he returned to her living room:

The loud, frantic knocking at the door startled Angelina. She retreated to the back of the house as the screams became louder. She wanted to call 911 but her phone was in the living room. After a few seconds, the terrifying sounds began to seem familiar. She slowly walked to the door, still unsure of her safety. She looked through the window to the man pounding on her door— her brother. It was Carlos. She released the deadbolt and opened the door. Carlos staggered in and made his way to the couch. He looked completely disheveled, with mud and strange bits of small debris covering his body, and shook with fear and cold.

"Oh, my God! What happened?" She stood above her brother, leaning forward and wanting, but too afraid, to touch his shoulder.

Carlos held his head in trembling hands and mumbled something. It was unclear what he said.

"Carlos, I can't understand. What did you say?"

He looked up, still shivering. "They're going to kill me." He started sobbing.

Carlos was terrified. He was known throughout his life for his macho bravado. Not now. He was a scared, crying little boy.

Angelina put her hand on his shoulder. He didn't notice. She felt his whole body shaking.

*Carlos spoke again. "They killed Emilio and Manuel.
I was lucky. I was lucky. Got loose and was washed
against a big tree. Took hours to get back to Luling to get
my car. I have to hide. They're after me."*

Tom tried to shake the scene from his mind. It was impossible. In vivid detail he saw Angelina's story changing— changing from Carlos's fear of being killed to that of a confessional.

*"I did some terrible things. I've killed people."
Angelina grabbed at her chest, not wanting to believe
the words being spoken. Carlos, gathering some composure,
spoke of his deeds.*

Tom remembered her story. He remembered Angelina telling Don and him that, as her conversation with Carlos got deeper and deeper into evil, she asked if she could record what he was saying.

*"I think you should tell me everything that happened.
Everything from the very beginning. Please let me make
a recording."*

She had been smart, real smart. Carlos agreed and began all over again.

*"I did some terrible things. I killed people. I killed a man
so that I could take his place on the work crew for a new
stripper well system. But, and I swear to God, I did not
mean to kill him. I was just going to scare him. But it
went wrong when I hit him. Wellington Oil is who had
me do it. The owner is Mr. Miles. He's a terrible man.*

But he's no more bad than me. I wish I could go back and change it."

Carlos never looked up. He just talked directly to the recorder. "We were told to steal the display of the oil system. It was the night of the tornado. We got caught by one of the owners, Mr. Duquette. He hit me hard and knocked me down. I picked up a tool, a crowbar, and hit him. He died." Carlos finally looked up, tears streaming from his face. Blood drained from him, leaving a pallid, living corpse. "There was a woman in his car. She would have been telling everyone what happened. I didn't want to kill Mr. Duquette. I didn't want to kill the woman."

Angelina had to sit down. Carlos kept talking, both to Angelina and to the small cassette recorder. The tape rolled slowly off of one spool and on to the other, catching every word of Carlos's confession.

"I thought I was going to make millions of dollars. I was stupid and greedy. Mr. Miles never would have given me real money. He always gave me some, but just to make me believe I would make a fortune. I think he planned to kill me the first day. I don't know how much, but Mr. Milsap also knows all about what the plan was."

Tom took a swallow of beer and then began his habit of rotating the can in his hands. He remembered Carlos saying that he could not recall a great deal of Frank Milsap; only that Milsap was in on some of the discussions between Bart Miles and himself. He remembered Carlos's story of the night he was almost killed by an assassin.

"The man was tall. We played pool and he was much larger than any of us. He was the best pool player I

ever saw. We shot a couple of games and then he played Manuel for money. The man was a hustler. As soon as money was on the table he never lost. Manuel was good but not as good as him. The man took Manuel's money and bought some drinks. I don't know anything else until I was drowning in the truck. I remember being on a tree. I was cold. I was so cold. But I was scared that the man would come back."

There was a pause. After a moment, Angelina asked, "Can you describe the man?"

"He was more than tall. He was very strong, with plenty of muscle. Not heavy, just tall and strong. His beard was dark and he wore glasses. But I think . . ." Carlos stopped long enough to focus on that night. "I think he took his glasses off when he played Manuel."

Carlos averted Angelina's eyes. He focused on small pieces of twigs and leaves that had fallen from his clothes to the floor.

Finally, he looked up at her. "I am so sorry. I want to start all over again. What can I do?"

A tiny smile appeared on Tom's face. He remembered exactly what Angelina told Carlos.

"First, you need to go to confession and Mass. Then come back home and write it down as well. Then you need to sign it."

Had it not been for her, no one would ever know why Carlos went to the Watermelon Thump the night of the shootout.

"What is that? What are you doing?" Angelina was hysterical.

Buttoning his long-sleeved denim shirt, Carlos looked at her through cautious eyes. She didn't even know who this man was anymore.

"You don't need a gun, Carlos. Please give me the gun."

He ignored her. He looked into the living room mirror to make sure his beard covered most of his facial features. He pulled a dark brown baseball cap over his eyes.

Angelina stood in front of the door trying to block his way. "Don't go, Carlos. Don't go."

He pushed her aside with incredible strength. "I have to go. Mr. Seiler and the crew are going to be there. I need to see them. I am worried about them."

He opened the front door and walked to his car.

That was the last time she saw him.

Tom pictured his last conversation with Carlos.

"He . . . follow to kill you and Mr. Seiler. I'm sorry."

He thought about Carlos's last actions on that night. Carlos was bad news—a bully. Yet his last living act was extraordinarily heroic. Tom whispered his thought, "Maybe there is redemption." Then he looked up into the black sky and, in the recesses of his mind, pondered another question: *Is there more to this universe than random molecules?*

Tom sat in the chair for another two hours thinking. No beer, no Coke, just thinking. Many episodes of his life played out in his head. Finally, he stood up. Just inside the door he grabbed his jogging shoes and socks; he sat at the edge of the patio and put them on. He got up and stretched. This time Bear, aware of the stretching routine, got up with him. Catfish joined them as they neared the grass airstrip. Three beings, friends all, walked from one end of the airstrip to the other. Bear and Catfish were glad to own such a nice human. Tom was glad to have their company. Behind Tom the sky still slumbered in darkness; to the east the first signs of a new day were sneaking above the horizon. Tom was buoyed with thoughts of a better future. At the end of the runway Tom started a slow jog. His stride lengthened and his lungs inhaled deep pockets of air. It would be an exhilarating run and he felt free of life's burdens. The two dogs joined in until they reached the breach in the fence. Smart dogs, they knew Tom was going for the long haul. Both peeled off, Catfish for a swim in the pond and Bear to wait by the pond for Tom's return. Almost an hour later, with the sun just peeking through the trees, their human returned. They jumped up and joined Tom on the runway.

"C'mon, guys. I'll give you an early bone."

Tom and his sidekicks headed back toward the ranch.

Seventy

Wednesday, April 13

Lubbock, Texas

That makes it official." Don lifted the pen from the signature line of the contract. Nine pages of legal wording, most of which he could understand, provided the full provisions of an agreement between Donelam Oil Systems and Caprock Industries.

The gathering, including the full contingent from Caprock along with Don, Tom, Steve, Ross, and, as a special member of the party, Josh Bettner, clapped and shook hands. Somewhat against protocol, Heather Brace was the first to give Don a huge bear hug. Bob Ames followed suit by shaking Tom's hand and then making his way to everyone else.

The contract's wording, usually subjugated by the requisite standards of law, was tempered by Heather's ability to keep things simple. Wallis Raymond prepared the legal work for Don's side of the ledger.

In effect, the presented contract called for a lump sum payment paid up front and a system through which residual monies would be transferred to Donelam Oil Systems. Donelam would receive eight million dollars immediately, 7 percent of all sales of the JETS for a period of ten years, 7 percent of leasing receipts for ten years, and 4 percent of the price per barrel of oil owned and extracted by Caprock for the remainder of Don's or Cindy's life, whomever lived longer. Cindy would be secure for her full life. The bottom line was that, after almost eight years of hard work and struggle, Don Hudson Seiler was a multi-millionaire. In turn, the only change Don made was that the Donelam monies would be distributed in the ratio of the percentage ownership of his new partners in the company resulting in 70 percent for him, 20 percent for Tom, and, because Elam had no relatives, 10 percent for Josh Bettner. The residual monies would last for the lifetimes of each partner and spouse, not just Don and Cindy's. Steve and Ross had declined any compensation except for one hell of a party back at the ranch. Josh Bettner had no idea at all that he would be receiving 10 percent of what would be no small fortune.

"Sir, I didn't do anything to deserve this. I don't think you—"

Don held his hand up signaling all to be quiet. "Josh, if you want to take the money and burn it, you can. But you do deserve it, and if my knowledge of people is half as good as I think it is, you will put your money to far better use than any of us." He smiled and closed the discussion. "You'll have to sue me to give the money back."

Champagne, hors d'oeuvres, and conversation consumed the next hour. Clearly, each member of Caprock wanted a chance to congratulate Tom and Don. Until the shock waves hit the media, none of them had any idea of the tragedies that had befallen the Seiler brothers over the previous year. All they initially knew was that something was very fishy about the JETS patent.

"So what's your plan from here on out? You certainly don't need to work any more." Bob Ames asked the question with Ken Farmer standing next to him.

Don had asked himself the same questions many times before. He sipped his champagne, a drink he detested, and answered truthfully. "I don't know. The only thing I do know is that there are some men down in Luling who have worked their butts off making this thing work. I can't hang them out to dry. I'll start by paying off the company bills and then give each crewmember $40,000." He looked seriously at Bob, pausing just a moment. "Given my condition, I need to go fishing more and I need to take the pressure off of my wife, Cindy. We're coming back to Texas by summer. So I will retire from the oil business, but not before I take care of one last item for my crew. So, here's my question to you. Do you plan to work the stripper wells in South Texas?"

"Matter of fact, we do. And to answer your question, if you mean what you said about them, we'll hire every one. They can stay in the area."

Don smiled and reached out to shake hands. It was the final wrapping on the package. He took another sip. He looked around the room, fully aware that he had picked the right company to negotiate with. Heather and Josh talked quietly at the middle of the conference table and a larger group chatted away next to the large window. It struck him that these were the type of people with whom he could have probably sealed the deal with only a handshake. Of course, those days were gone forever.

Ed Bishop and Sam Shelton joined Tom, Steve, and Ross at the window. A quick glance of the landscape revealed that the quiet, warm weather was undergoing a change. Along the ground a phalanx of tumbleweeds rolled inside clouds of dust from the north. Above the turbulent ground was a sky so clear and dark blue that it would catch one's breath. Tom had seen northers in San Antonio that he thought were awesome, but nothing compared to what was taking place outside. He tried to focus on the discussion.

"We've read and seen about everything in the news and on television," said Sam Shelton. "Never wanted to get in your way so that's why we stayed away from everything until the trials were over." He wanted to explain the relative distance Caprock had kept during the trial.

Tom answered honestly, "We really did appreciate that. It was not a good time and so much was going on. Glad you didn't give up on us."

Sam replied, "To be honest, we were concerned about the patent. We never thought you weren't who you said you were, but at the same time we also know how legal inertia can be impossible to change."

"Yeah, I know." Tom pointed his thumb, sticking out and away from his closed fist, toward his son and son-in-law. "But if we didn't have these guys taking some serious, dangerous risks, none of us would be here celebrating. I mean that. They never stopped hammering away at all the dirty obstacles that were thrown at us."

Steve and Ross felt uncomfortable at the accolades. They said nothing.

"Looks like you picked the right family."

"Sure did."

Heather purposely directed Josh toward the food. Young men are always hungry.

"So, what does your future look like now?" She loved the thought that, after the horrible murder of his mother, Josh had come across some good fortune in his life.

Josh quickly chewed a couple of times before answering. "I had no idea that Mr. Seiler was going to give me what he did. Now I know why he invited me to come to Lubbock."

Heather smiled enthusiastically. "I know. Mr. Seiler did not want you to know until today."

Josh replied, "Back to your question. Nothing's going to change for now. First thing I'll do is sit down with my sisters. Each of us will get one-fifth of the income. My enlistment into the army won't change. I take my oath of allegiance on May 16. I'm looking forward to jumping out of airplanes. College will follow, and I'll join ROTC." Josh smiled broadly, "Given what has happened with Mr. Seiler providing for my sisters and me, I don't think I will get much in the way of financial aid, but I'll still check into the GI Bill."

Heather laughed along with the young man. She thought to herself, *maybe this country is in good hands after all.*

It was a joyous occasion for everyone. Tom, Don, and the others were offered, and accepted, return trips to Lubbock and site visits to any oil well using the new Jet Extraction Technology System owned by Caprock Industries.

Outside, the winds howled and the temperature had dropped at least thirty degrees. To the men from South Texas, it was the mother of all blue northers. They huddled in their jackets and shuffled headlong into the wind. Opening the doors to the car was no small feat.

"Geez. Give me Houston any day." As the others settled in their seats, Tom started the ignition and turned on the headlights.

They all had doubts about any flights leaving Lubbock that day. Few did. Wanting to get home, the group waited standby and caught the 8:46 p.m. flight to Hobby.

Tom, Don, and Josh slipped in the door nearest the porte-cochere at a quarter past two in the morning. The double beeps from the alarm system and the welcome barks of the dogs woke the women up.

Josh headed straight up to the attic. Not wanting to wake Cindy, Don walked into the "Jack and Jill" bathroom from the other guest bedroom. He brushed his teeth quietly and turned off the bathroom light. Having MS in darkness made it tough on Don. He struggled to make it to the near side of the bed.

"It's right here." Cindy reached out and touched his hand as he groped at the bed. She pulled down the covers and let him settle into a comfortable position. Then she placed the covers over him. "Welcome home, sailor. How did it turn out?"

"Cindy. How many years has it been?" Don looked up at the darkness.

Cindy watched the fan blades spinning above their heads. Don's eyesight was not good and he saw nothing. It didn't really matter.

"About a hundred."

"I think we've made it. Everything went well today. This is a very good day." He smiled into the night. "And tomorrow will be better. We have an appointment in Tiki Island at noon. The house on Makatea is up for sale." Don spoke of a small shared-ownership waterfront home offering charm, comfort, and great fishing off of the back deck. "We'll headquarter in Luling and spend five weeks a year fishing and doing whatever it is that we want to do. Life has changed for us. It's a new world, pardner."

Cindy rolled over, straddling his chest. She kissed him. "You can be a real pain in the ass, but above all, you are a good man. Who knows, I may end up being a real Texan someday. Here's to tomorrow."

She rolled over and went back to sleep. Don smiled at the darkness. *Yep, here's to tomorrow.*

Tom's ritual was similar. A quick trip to the bathroom and then to bed.

"Hi, hon. Welcome home. Did Don sign the contract?"

Tom slipped under the covers, raised himself up on his right elbow, and turned to kiss Susie. "He did. It couldn't have been any better." He leaned down and found Susie's lips in the dark. They kissed. "Wallis handled the contract from our side. Caprock is an honest company and Don's going to make out very well. He certainly won't have to work again. With his eyesight and lack of mobility he made it in the nick of time. He's getting a bundle up front and has a lifelong revenue stream coming in. Josh and I, including you, are also lifelong winners."

Tom rolled over on his back. Both Tom and Susie looked up at their fan tracing out circles in the sky.

Tom couldn't see her face. Tears fell down both cheeks to her pillow. *Finally*, she thought, *I can cry and be happy at the same time.*

Shortly after seven o'clock in the morning Susie opened her eyes. She rolled over, glancing at the fan. Then she looked to her side. Tom wasn't there. She got out of bed, put on her night robe, and walked into the kitchen. Tom hadn't even turned on the coffee. It didn't seem quite right to her. *Maybe he's on the porch.* Susie walked outside to the patio. She was worried.

Then she heard it. Off in the distance was a sound—a familiar one at that. Looking directly south, Susie saw a speck in the sky coming directly at her. It grew in size until she saw the unmistakable yellow wings. The small plane raced toward her as fast as it would go. Suddenly it rose into the air, leveled off, and plunged toward the ranch. No more that forty feet above ground, the pilot rotated the wings in salute and, as the plane passed overhead, surged back into the air. Tom gave a thumbs-up and Susie could actually see the smile on his face.

Susie waved back into the sky with both hands. She was so happy. Susie cupped her face in her hands and wept again. A whole new life lay before them.

Epilogue

The woman shifted her position in a sculptured plastic chair and turned her attention to the nearly empty paper cup of dark, rich, Brazilian coffee. The coffee was delicious but its strength made her all the more restless. She looked at her wristwatch; mercifully, the minute hand passed ever so slowly past the "12" and announced the time had reached nine in the morning. Passing through security was not a problem in Sao Paulo; it would be a bigger deal with Miami customs. She unconsciously bit at the inside of her mouth, unaware of the droves of people walking through Guarulhos International Airport. The opening shops signaled another busy day for the burgeoning Brazilian travel industry. Passengers in the boarding area of Wing B were more subdued, many of them nodding off under the effects of boredom. As for Maria Aragon, she was well rested from a full night at the Marriott Airport Hotel. Her flight from Rio the night before had been uneventful, notwithstanding the irritable sight of flags, posters, and lapel buttons, and the never-ending television commentary of Rio's triumph over Chicago, Madrid, and Tokyo in the bid for the 2016 Summer Olympics.

A few months ago Maria's lips were thinner, her nose slightly broader, and her fine, silky hair longer. The TSA customs agent in Miami had smiled, wished her well, and made no pause at the photograph of Elizabeth T. Harker. The agent for her return trip did take a second look at the photograph of Maria Aragon. Maria's blood pressure rose but the likeness was enough for her to pass through with no major problem. Liz Harker no longer existed.

TAM is Brazil's major airline. Maria thought it best not to fly an American carrier. Flight 8092 would touch down at 3:40 p.m. in Miami. Then she would take US Airways flight 2061 to Charlotte, North Carolina. Once in Charlotte, Maria Aragon would also cease to exist.

The gate agent announced the initial boarding instructions for the Miami flight and people began assembling. Maria knew she had plenty of time. She swallowed a final mouthful of coffee and pulled a piece of paper from her purse. On it was a list of names. She studied the list carefully even though there was no need for the list at all; Maria had committed all the names to memory. She wadded up the paper and threw it in the trash receptacle along with her coffee cup. Then she walked toward the gate.

The piece of paper, stained with drops of coffee, unfolded slightly. Had anyone cared to notice, he or she would have seen that one of the names on the list was circled.

Susie Seiler.

About the Author

With a voracious appetite for studying and writing about human behavior, Jack Grubbs continues to develop stories about the best and worst of the human condition. His technical degrees from West Point, Princeton University, and Rensselaer Polytechnic Institute provide a reservoir of engineering principles as a backdrop for his novels. His first novel of the Tom Seiler trilogy, *Bad Intentions*, opened to outstanding reviews, and he is deep into writing the climax novel to be published in 2012. He and his wife, Judy, split time between the friendly confines of Charlotte, North Carolina, and the sandy beaches of South Florida.